THE PLAYROOM

Also by John Connor

Phoenix

THE PLAYROOM

JOHN CONNOR

ORION

First published in Great Britain in 2004 by Orion,
an imprint of the Orion Publishing Group Ltd.

A CIP catalogue record for this book is available from the British Library.

ISBNS: 0 75285 776 2 (hardback); 0 75285 777 0 (trade paperback)

Typeset by Deltatype Ltd, Birkenhead, Merseyside

Printed in Great Britain by Clays Ltd, St Ives plc

All the characters in this book are fictitious, and any
resemblance to actual persons living or dead is purely coincidental.

The Orion Publishing Group Ltd
Orion House
5 Upper Saint Martin's Lane
London, WC2H 9EA

www.orionbooks.co.uk

For Anna Ollila

With thanks again to DC John Markham and
Chief Superintendent Max Mclean.
Special thanks also to Rachel Leyshon.

1987

PROLOGUE

She was with her mummy again. She was sitting on the table in their dining room and her mother was leaning towards her, laughing. She could hear the laughter, hear its lightness and warmth. Her mother had on her head a light shade, which she had taken from the bulb above the table. She had put it on her head to be funny, pulling faces at her, speaking in a strange voice. It was a wide, flat sixties design that looked like a Chinese peasant hat and her mother was making her eyes into slits, pretending to be oriental.

She felt like nobody in the world could hurt her. She was laughing the way only two-year-olds can laugh, without any memory of pain. Around them the house was hot and comfortable. There were no men, no father figures, no one to hit her or make her do things to them she didn't want to do.

The image ran through her mind. There was no aching now, no pounding in her head, no parched mouth or stabbing pains in her gut. All that had gone. The image was protecting her. She felt as if she were floating. She had never remembered the memory before. Before she had been brought here her first memory had always been the same. She was five or six years old and her mother was brushing her hair. Her mother hated her hair, told her it was frizzy and ugly. She had tried to get rid of it, cutting it off or pulling it back into pigtails. She had stood there crying as her mum dragged it back from her scalp, forcing it into an elastic band, to 'keep it out of her eyes', pulling it so hard it had come out at the roots . . .

The memory made her panic. Immediately, she remembered other things that weren't so good. Only a year ago her mum had stopped her seeing a boy from the other end of the street. He had been nice to her, told her she was pretty, bought her sweets from the corner shop. But her mother had read her diary and found out what she had felt for the boy. When she caught her mum reading her private thoughts she had hit her. Not hard, just lashing out with frustration, slapping her arm through tears of rage and betrayal.

Things had been bad between them since then. Too bad to want to think about. Sometimes she had thought there was something wrong with her mum.

Her mother had handed her over to the man who had put her here, in this hole in the ground. She had seen the look in her eyes as she leaned towards her and told her to behave for him. Eyes shifting from her. Had she known it was going to happen? Before it had become impossible to cry she had screamed for her mum so much her throat had closed up, silencing her.

She could not cry any more, could not even open her eyes. Her body was dried up, vanishing. She was only vaguely aware of it now. Everything that was happening was going on inside her head, behind her eyelids. She couldn't move. There had been two others down there with her. Two little girls. Before the pain had crippled them all, before they had become too weak, they had tried desperately to get out of the place, digging and clawing at the damp, earthen walls with their bare fingers until the nails were stripped away and her hands felt like enormous balloons of searing pain.

It had been no use. They had hit stones and rocks immediately. The darkness was so total it wasn't even possible to work out where they should have been digging. Then they had started to get really thirsty. The ache had swollen inside her head so that all she could do was lie on the dirt floor of the trench in a huddle, trying to keep the chill out, trying to console the other two. They had been worse than her, more frightened.

She was still hanging onto them now. She had forgotten their names, knew only that they were twelve, a year younger than her, that once they had been warm and had kept her warm. She had tried to help them, told them repeatedly that they would get out of this, that they should just go to sleep and wait.

Now their bodies, pushed up against her to either side, were cold and stiff. They didn't move anymore, didn't speak, didn't even breathe. She could not remember how long they had been like that, but she knew what it meant. Before the numbness had come over her she had been able to smell them.

It meant she was alone. Alone in the darkness and sinking slowly towards them. Soon she would be there with them.

She tried to go back to the memory of the Chinese hat, to her mother laughing. She didn't want to panic. She still believed this would be over, that she would come out of it. Her mother would open the trapdoor above her and be standing there, laughing. She would reach down into the pit and lift her out, hugging her, running her hand through her hair, whispering that she loved her, that she was safe, that it had all been a joke.

She lay there, crushed between two dead bodies in a six-foot hole beneath the cellar of a house. The look on her face was peaceful, her cracked lips bleeding as she moved her muscles into the best smile she could manage.

WEST YORKSHIRE
1997

ONE

The yellow school bus dropped Sophie Kenyon at the bottom of The Grove, as usual. But instead of going straight home she walked slowly past the entrance to her street and took Wells Road up towards the moor, holding her satchel by its straps at arm's length, so that it was almost dragging along the ground beside her. She kept her eyes down and as she got higher up the hill she began to cry.

A middle-aged woman with a wide hat and a brown Spaniel on a leash passed her without looking. The dog paused momentarily to sniff her leg, but Sophie didn't notice it. She was too lost in herself.

For the same reason she didn't see the van coming up behind her, from The Grove. When it was close, however, she heard the engine slowing and she looked up. A man was leaning through the open window of the driver's door, speaking to her. Through the tears she couldn't see his face well, but he was asking her if she was OK. Though his voice sounded kind and concerned, she didn't know him, so she turned away without answering and walked on, hurrying a little. It was only as she opened the gate onto the moor that something clicked in her memory and she realized she had seen the van before.

She stopped, turned round and looked back down the road, drying her eyes so that she could see properly. The van had gone.

She looked around her. She was on the edge of Ilkley, about to step onto the moor. The area was wealthy, full of large, detached houses built at the turn of the century. Below and to both sides were high walls enclosing large gardens backing onto the moor. Some of the houses belonged to school friends or people her father knew. The whole area was familiar to her, safe. She looked back up towards the high horizon, jagged with pine trees. It was a bright summer day, too warm for either a coat or a jumper, 23 June 1997, her birthday and the start of her teenage years. Something she should have been celebrating.

She stepped onto the dirt track up to 'the tarn', as it was known locally. The mud under her shiny, black school shoes was baked solid by a week of high temperatures and no rain. She was wearing her navy school tunic, short white socks and a loose white shirt, open at the neck – she had removed her tie that afternoon during art class. She still had smudges of paint on her hands and fingers.

As she walked she remembered she had seen the van as she was getting off the bus last week. She had noticed because she had seen it two nights in a row, turning onto Eaton Road after her. It was a white van with a faded blue stripe along the side, as if it had once been a police van, but the stripe had been painted over. The realization triggered a tiny trace of confusion, somewhere in the back of her mind, but not enough to make her change her plans.

When she reached 'the tarn' she saw with dull pleasure that she had it to herself. She could see no one else in any direction. Being alone was what she preferred these days. She sat down on a bench.

She had been coming here nearly all her life, first with her mother, then with her nanny, then by herself. The place was a duck pond, surrounded by small trees and bushes, hidden from view by the folds of the moor. She liked many things about it – particularly the memories it brought: her mum standing at the water's edge and throwing scraps of bread onto the water; the feel of her mum's long fingers interlaced through her own; the scramble of the ducks all rushing to get the same piece of bread. She could see it all happening now as if her mum had never been taken from her. It brought a lump to her throat. She tried to ignore it and concentrate on other details. There were other reasons she liked being here. She liked sitting in silence beside the water watching the birds, dreaming she was somewhere else.

The lump got the better of her and she started to cry again. Everything about the day was miserable. They were organizing a party for her back at the house. She knew they would be wondering where she was. It was meant to be a surprise party, but she knew all about it because she had overheard them planning it one night in their bed. That wasn't all she heard from their bed. There were louder, stranger noises too, things Trisha Merrington had told her about in science classes.

She hated her father's new wife, more than she had ever hated anything in her life. The woman was too young, too stupid, too pretty. She didn't even speak English properly. She knew why he was with her, knew what was going on and thought it was pathetic. Because of her, because he was with her and because he was continually taking her side, she was beginning to hate her dad as well.

She felt sick thinking about what she would have to go back to. There would be bunting and balloons, party games, musical chairs and ducking apples – as if she were eight years old. To make things worse they had secretly invited all her friends. The whole thing would be embarrassing, juvenile. She looked at her watch. Ten to five. They would be beginning to worry about her already. She stood up with a sigh.

He was standing right in front of her. She hadn't noticed him approach because she had been too lost in her own thoughts.

'Sophie?' he asked.

She recognized the voice at once. He was the driver of the van.

'I work for your dad.'

She frowned. 'What do you mean?' He was standing too close to her, boxing her in. She looked quickly to either side. The paths were deserted still. 'My dad doesn't have anybody working for him,' she said. She was about to add, '*He's a judge,*' but quickly thought better of it. What if this man was someone her father had sent to prison, someone dangerous?

'I look after him,' the man said. 'I actually work for the police.'

She looked up at him, relaxing a little, but still worried. 'Look after him?'

'I work with something called Special Branch. Your dad has to deal with a lot of evil people at work. You must know that already. I watch over him. It's my job to protect him from them.'

She frowned again. Her father had never mentioned this. She took a step back. 'What do you want? Have you got ID?'

He stepped forwards, towards her, at the same time digging in his pocket and flashing a pass at her, a laminated piece of card with his photograph on it. She had time to register the face – his – and the West Yorkshire Police logo, then it was gone. She noticed he was wearing a dark grey suit. 'Something bad has happened,' he said. Your dad is in Bradford, in a safe place. You can't go back to your house. I've been sent to bring you out to him.'

Her heart began to beat faster. 'What has happened?'

He smiled at her. 'We are in a hurry, Sophie,' he said. 'Follow me back to the van and I'll tell you on the way.' He began to walk away from her.

She followed, feeling suddenly panicky, frightened. 'What has happened?'

'Nothing to worry about.' He was two steps ahead of her, walking swiftly. 'We just can't go back to your house. Not right now.'

'Why?'

'Some men are there. They are trying to kill your dad.'

She gasped in shock, stopping.

He stopped as well and leaned towards her, putting an arm around her shoulder. 'I shouldn't have told you,' he said. His voice was gentle. 'What you need to know is that your father is safe and we are dealing with it. I'll take you to him and you can have the party later, when all this is over.'

She looked down at his hand, where it was resting against her upper arm. The nails on his fingers were bitten back, cracked, the tips of the fingers stained yellow. She felt a ripple of disgust run through her.

'Let's go,' he said, still holding onto her.

She had to walk quickly to keep up with him. The way he had his arm around her meant she would actually fall over if she didn't hurry. She tried to control the panic she was feeling about her dad until they got back to Wells Road. Once there she saw the van parked up by the gate to the moor.

He stepped over to the passenger door, taking his arm from her, then paused.

'Best if you travel in the back,' he said. 'We don't want them spotting you.'

She nodded and followed him to the back of the van. As he was opening the doors, she said, her voice trembling, 'Are you sure my daddy is OK?'

He opened the door and smiled at her. He had a nice smile, reassuring. 'He's safe,' he said, pointing into the van, indicating that she should step in. She saw that the back of it was empty except for a mattress lying on the floor. It looked dirty. There were no windows. 'And you will be too,' he said to her. 'Once we get you out of here.'

The mattress puzzled her and she hesitated. But only for a second.

She climbed inside, then turned round to look at him, but already the door was slamming shut.

TWO

DC Karen Sharpe looked at the woman called Pamela Mathews. They were in one of the interview rooms used by the CPT – the Child Protection and Domestic Violence Team – at Eccleshill Police Station. In front of Karen, on the table between them, were nine sheets of A4 covered with her own dense, nearly illegible handwriting.

Following the usual legal declaration on the first page there was a preamble Karen used every time she took a statement, giving the witness's name and a small amount of background history – their home circumstances, marital position etc. Pamela had given her age as twenty-three and an address in Otley. After the preamble the story began.

Detectives took statements in one of three ways. You either wrote down what was said, as it was said – in which case it usually came out a jumbled-up mess – or you gave the witness the paper and told them to do it themselves unaided (it came out worse), or you got them to sit with you and tell the whole thing as it came to them, from start to finish, taking notes and asking clarifying questions as you went along, then going back over it all again when they were finished and writing the statement for them.

Karen always picked the latter option. She listened carefully, got a sense of what was going on, went back over unclear parts and got things straight, then she took the victim through it all again, directing their focus where she needed it and writing as she went. Lastly she read it back to them and got them to sign it as accurate. She began to read Pamela what she had written:

I can recall clearly that the man told me that my mum and dad were in danger. And that was why I got into the van with him. He was a young man – not as old as my dad – but apart from this I can remember little about him. He spoke well, not like someone without an education. Once I was in the van he continued to talk to me as he was closing the doors. This was in the back of the van. I noticed he was getting into the back of the van with me and started to ask him about this. As he turned towards me he hit me with something. He struck me in the face. I don't know what he used. I fell down and I was bleeding from the head and crying.

After that I could feel him doing something to my arm, then I was falling asleep or passing out. As I started to lose consciousness I could hear him talking softly to me – as if he cared about me – he was stroking my hair and I couldn't move. I was paralysed by the thing he had given me, the drug he had injected into my arm. He told me that I shouldn't be frightened; he said he was taking me somewhere safe. That was all I can remember him saying.

I was thirteen years old and I was terrified. I can remember how terrified I was, even now. It was so frightening because I didn't know what was going on. I was shouting for my mummy but he had something in my mouth. He was pushing it into my mouth so that I was beginning to choke and couldn't breathe. Then everything went black.

I woke up somewhere dark with my head hurting. When I could see I realized I was tied up on some kind of bed and couldn't really move. I started shouting out, crying and begging for help. I had no clothes on and I was cold. I can remember I could touch one of the walls with the fingers of my hand – it was rough and damp, more like a cave than the wall of a house. I don't know how long I was like that, but no one heard me and no one came. I was shivering and frightened and I wet myself, but still no one came.

I don't know how long I was kept there by myself. I drifted in and out of sleep, I think. Most of the time I was awake I was either crying to myself or shouting for my mum. Sometimes I just lay there listening and trembling.

The first time he came back I must have been asleep because I woke up with the lights really bright in my eyes and he was injecting something into my arm again. I know now that was what he was doing, at the time I could just feel a sharp pain and then the effects, afterwards. I started to struggle, to try to fight him, but I was tied down very tightly. I don't know what he gave me but it didn't knock me out, instead I went limp. My heart was racing and I could see and hear everything, but I had no energy, no ability to move or shout or even speak.

When I was like that, dumb and paralysed, he untied me and sat me up and began to feed me from a baby bottle. I had to suck on it to get some kind of liquid into my throat. But I could hardly even suck. It took all my concentration to move my mouth. I don't know what it was he was feeding me. I couldn't taste anything, but I was so thirsty I tried to suck in as much as I could. He was talking to me as he did all this, but I can't remember now what he was saying. I was terrified of him. When I had drunk enough of the liquid he rolled me over onto my tummy, still on the bed I had been tied to. He took my new dress off me. It was a dress my mother had given me for my birthday. He tore it. Then I could feel him doing something to my bottom, from behind. But everything was numb and I couldn't move. I could feel him on top of me. He was so heavy I had difficulty breathing, but I didn't know what he was doing. I could hear him panting and shouting things, but I didn't know why. I still – to this day – do not know what he did to me. Because of the drugs, I think, it didn't hurt me.

At some point I was moved. He drugged me again to move me, I think, because I can recall little of the journey. It might only have been a move from one part of the house to another. I don't know. I can remember lying in a kind of stupor. I wasn't tied up or anything. I just felt so sluggish I couldn't really move. I think that by this point I must have been feeling numb, I think the fear must have gone from me, because I can recall lying on a big bed somewhere, with sheets and warmth and light. And I remember feeling very happy. I think they must have shot me up with heroin or coke or some kind of narcotic drug. I can't recall them cleaning me up but they must have because I smelled different, even to myself. Maybe they sprayed perfume on me. I don't know. They had dressed me as well – in clothes which weren't mine. A dress, tights, a bra, knickers. I had never worn a bra before.

I lay on that bed and it was like I was floating in some kind of dream. Through the floor I could hear feet moving and music. It was like they were having a party somewhere else in the building. At some point a woman came in and she started brushing my hair as I lay there. She gave me something to drink and smiled at me. I *just looked at her and smiled back. I had forgotten everything that was happening.*

Later on they came down in a group. I don't know who they were. They came into the room and they were laughing. There were at least three of them. As they were coming through the door I heard one of them say, 'This is the playroom, the room where little girls play.' Then they all laughed, as if it were a joke.

They did things to me and I just lay there. I couldn't react, I couldn't feel pain. I just lay there like a pillow or a bag of rags. They moved me around and did what they wanted to me.

Some time after they were gone I was able to move. Not so much that I could walk around, but so that I could look at where I was. The noise from downstairs was still continuing. I saw that I wasn't alone in the room. There were two other girls in there with me. I don't know their names or how old they were. They were both lying on beds. There were four beds in the room, but only three had mattresses. The room had wallpaper and pictures of fish jumping through a sea. There were childish mobiles hanging from the ceiling and, in one corner, a doll's house and some toys. All around the walls, from the door to the window, they had painted a huge, twisting, Chinese dragon, with a gaping mouth and flames – not frightening, but childish. It looked like a child had painted it. I didn't realize it at the time, but I think now that this must have really been a playroom, a room belonging to some children.

I don't remember speaking to the other two girls. They were dressed up as I was, in fancy dresses and underwear. I remember one of the girls kept saying that her tummy was hurting and she was bleeding. I could see the blood on the sheets around her. She was sobbing and holding a blanket to her mouth. I don't know how old she was.

At some point they came again, but there were more of them this time and this time I could feel things and I knew what was happening. It lasted a long time. They tore the clothes off me and hit me. I started to cry and struggle, but they pinned my arms back. Two of them pinned my arms back and held my legs while he did it to me. I can remember him now. He was fat and sweating and he didn't look at me. At one point he collapsed on top of me and they threw some cold water on him. I think he was drunk and drugged. I think he was actually passing out. He was hurting me, inside me. I was shouting at him. I was shouting and screaming so loudly that they pushed something in my mouth and he kept going. I saw his face very clearly. All the lights were on. It was the man I saw on TV last week. I have no doubt about it. He was younger then, but still fat. His eyes were the same. His name is Geoff Reed.

He raped me and didn't care. When he was finished another one took over and they turned me over and I could feel that they were doing it from behind me, to my bottom. I had my face pressed sideways and I could see the one called Geoff Reed sitting in a chair watching, his trousers around his ankles. He was wearing a flower – a red rosette – in the lapel of his jacket and he had a champagne glass in his hand. He was celebrating something. I am sure of it. From the way they were talking to him I thought the party was his, or for him.

Karen stopped and slid the last few sheets across the table to Pamela and pointed to where she should sign them. Pamela took the pen from her with difficulty. She was a nervous wreck, shaking uncontrollably, hands covering and uncovering her face in quick, compulsive gestures, clearly terrified of something that Karen could only guess at – because as far as her present circumstances were concerned, she had refused to give Karen a single detail.

The present circumstances looked unpleasant. Karen had mentally ticked off and noted them as she walked the woman to the interview room. Beneath her hands Pamela's face was a mess. Both eyes were blackened, the right so badly it had closed up. Her lips were split in several places, her nose swollen and showing signs of deviation. From the way she spoke she wasn't getting any air through it. There was dried blood around her mouth from where the nose was still haemorrhaging. The blood was running in a steady trickle across her top lip, into the mouth and out again, making her occasionally sputter as she spoke. When she had first opened her mouth, Karen had caught a glimpse of a bloody coagulation in her lower jaw, where several teeth had been knocked out. She had also observed three areas to the rear of the woman's head where clumps of hair were missing.

Beneath it all Karen guessed she might be attractive. She would be about five feet six inches, in her bare feet. She had shoulder-length black, frizzy hair, which even in her present condition she had applied some kind of product to, in a vain attempt to unravel the frizz and turn it into a tight curl. Karen could smell the perfume in the product, though the odour was vying with the stronger smell of stale alcohol coming from her breath. Her face was difficult to judge, bruised as it was, but the one eye Karen could see was a good, clear blue and there was a dense pattern of freckles across the skin, from her forehead to her toes. She was so skinny that Karen guessed she would have been anorexic in her teens, maybe still was.

The face and head wasn't the only problem. Both arms were bruised, showing characteristic green and yellow patterns typical of gripping injuries about two, maybe three, days old. She held one of her fingers so delicately that Karen felt sure it was fractured. She limped. When she stood up it was apparent that she suffered sharp pains in the chest that made her pause and hold her breath; broken ribs perhaps. Beneath the knee-length denim skirt she wore, there was extensive bruising to both calves and thighs. On the upper surface of her right foot – visible through the straps of the sandals she was probably wearing so as not to irritate it – there was an ugly, infected burn at the centre of which was a small, circular, weeping sore roughly the dimensions of a cigarette end.

But none of this had anything to do with the story she was telling.

Karen leaned towards her across the table and asked again the same questions she had already asked three times: 'You are sure about this, Pamela? What you have told me, what we have written into this statement – it all happened ten years ago?'

'Yes.'

Karen sighed. 'So when will that have been?'

'Nineteen eighty-seven. The summer of nineteen eighty-seven.'

'And you have only just recently remembered it all?'

Pamela nodded.

'When? Exactly when did you remember it?'

'Two weeks ago. On Wednesday.'

Karen looked at the wall calendar, a picture of the South Pennines in deep snow, a West Yorkshire Police helicopter hovering over a flock of startled sheep. She traced the days back from Tuesday, 24 June 1997.

'The eleventh?' she asked. 'The eleventh of June 1997?'

'That's it. It was a programme on TV. They were interviewing him, speaking to him. I saw his face and remembered him. I didn't want to. I didn't want to remember any of this . . .'

'And you didn't even know it had happened before you saw the TV programme?'

'No. I mean ... no ... not clearly ...'

'Not clearly? Or not at all?'

The woman stared at her hands, the muscles in her face working. 'Not at all,' she said finally. 'Not like that – like a memory. But I've always known that something was wrong ...'

Karen waited for her to sign the pages, then took the sheets back off her. It was a recovered memory case. She had two in her tray already. Without some kind of corroborative evidence they went nowhere, weren't even charged. Getting corroboration from ten years ago was usually a non-starter.

But this one was different. She studied the statement in front of her, then looked up at Pamela Mathews and experienced a tiny thrill of pleasure – the feeling she got when she was about to start on something dangerous. Geoff Reed, the man Pamela said she had recognized on TV, was the longest serving MP in Bradford. The statement in front of Karen ought to have been burning a hole through the table.

THREE

John Munro sat on the largest sofa in the room and waited, looking around him at the balloons, bunting and streamers. There was a large painted banner above the door – 'HAPPY THIRTEENTH BIRTHDAY, SOPHIE.' Maybe they were still hoping she would walk through the door and they could pick up where they had left off, as if nothing had happened.

The judge was keeping them waiting. Though they said it happened frequently in his courts, Munro thought it inappropriate in the present circumstances. He had arranged – with a woman he assumed was a housekeeper – to meet His Honour Judge Kenyon at 2 p.m. Both Ricky Spencer and he had arrived, independently, with ten minutes to spare. It was now fifteen minutes past. Spencer was still on his feet, pacing around the room, looking at the pictures and decorations.

'Sit down, Ricky. You're making me nervous.'

Spencer was staring at a huge oil painting hanging over the main mantelpiece, depicting some kind of hunting scene in the rain. 'It's all very standard,' he said, without looking back at Munro. 'What you'd expect of a judge.'

Munro frowned at his back. Spencer had made no move to sit down; he was used to giving orders, not taking them. A young, good-looking detective inspector, he had obviously done something to displease the Command Team. Just over six months ago they had given him the Child Protection and Domestic Violence Team based at Eccleshill Police Station – known as the 'shopping squad' because of the amount of women in the unit. It wasn't a good career posting.

Being placed as the senior investigating officer's deputy on a major enquiry would normally signal the start of his rehabilitation, but things were more dubious on this enquiry – and the SIO was John

21

Munro. Munro was still trying to work out when his own rehabilitation would begin.

'We're waiting five minutes more,' Spencer said, as if it was his enquiry, 'then we're off.'

At that moment the door opened and a woman walked in. She was young, much younger than Munro would have expected, and obviously oriental in origin. Munro guessed Thai. He had heard the rumours about Kenyon's new wife, but had never actually seen her.

'Hello, Officer.' Her voice was heavily accented. She walked towards him like something from a Geisha bar, long silk floral skirt down to her ankles, small steps, no taller than five foot, petite and extremely attractive. Munro guessed her to be no older than twenty-five. The rumour was that the judge had 'bought' his new wife through some kind of dating agency. Munro stood to greet her.

'Hello. I'm John Munro. I'm the senior investigating officer looking into Sophie's disappearance.'

She looked at him as if she hadn't understood a word. Spencer came over and stood beside Munro.

'This is Richard Spencer. He's my deputy.'

She shook hands, smiling. 'My husband is . . .' She stopped. 'He will be with you soon. He is very unwell.'

'It must be a very stressful time,' Munro volunteered.

'Yes,' she said. 'You want a tea or a coffee?'

They both declined politely.

'Maybe we can take this opportunity – before your husband appears,' Munro said, 'to speak to *you* about Sophie?'

She looked confused.

'It's just routine,' Spencer chipped in.

'Of course,' she said. 'What you want to know?'

Munro took out his notebook. She was still standing there in front of him.

'Shall we sit down?' he asked.

She sat, drawing her legs together, smoothing the skirt over them. He sat down beside her, then moved a foot back. Spencer remained standing, which irritated Munro again.

'So you know Sophie well?' he asked.

'Of course. She is my daughter.'

'Your daughter?'

'Not my *normal* daughter—'

'*Natural* daughter,' Spencer corrected.

Munro looked up at him, communicating 'shut up and let me do it'.

'Yes. Thank you.' She blushed slightly. 'Not my *natural* daughter. But she is *like a daughter* to me.'

'I'm sure.' Munro smiled at her. 'How long have you been married to Judge Kenyon?'

'More than two years.'

'And how has Sophie taken that?'

'She has not run away, if that's what you mean. She is far—'

The door opened again, stopping her mid-sentence. A noticeably older man stepped into the room. Munro reckoned him to be in his mid-fifties. He was about five seven and dressed in a white bathrobe. His hair was bone white, but surprisingly long and full, hanging lankly back over the collar of the robe. It looked greasy and un-washed. He stood in the doorway staring at them. His eyes were rimmed with blackness, so dark as to be like bruising, the skin beneath them waxen, fleshy. He wore no shoes and where his arm was extended and still gripping the door handle it was trembling.

Munro stood. 'Judge Kenyon?' Munro didn't recognize him. There were only eleven resident judges covering Bradford and Leeds. Munro had thought he knew them all.

'Who are you?' Kenyon's voice was barely audible, shaky.

'John Munro, SIO. This is—'

Mrs Kenyon stood suddenly and ran to her husband with quick, short steps. Standing beside him and holding his arm – as if to support him – she looked like a child. She came up to his chest.

'My husband is unwell—' she began.

Kenyon cut her off. 'Be quiet, Lan. I must deal with this.'

'He has not slept since—'

'Leave us.' The voice raised slightly, Munro could detect the plummy public school accent.

His wife looked hurt. Munro wanted her to stay. He had questions for her too. He needed to assess the family situation. She started to back out through the door.

'Actually,' Munro said, 'it would be useful if your wife—'

'No. She is not the child's mother.'

'I realize that, but—'

'No.'

He turned his back on Munro and closed the door on her. Munro frowned.

'Sit down, Officer,' Kenyon said, shuffling towards him. 'I have some questions for you.'

Munro thought about putting him right, but there was time enough for everything. Judge Kenyon was a parent missing his child. He clearly hadn't slept or washed since she had vanished and probably hadn't eaten. If Munro was to get what he needed he would have to understand the situation and take it into account. He sat down.

'*We* have some quite urgent questions for *you*, Judge,' Spencer said.

'That's all right, Ricky.' Munro tried to keep the annoyance from his voice. 'All in good time.' He turned from him. 'My deputy,' he said. 'DI Spencer.'

Kenyon ignored Spencer and sat down on an armchair opposite the sofa and some distance from it across the polished wood floor. 'I've heard of you, Munro,' he said, panting slightly. Munro wondered in what way he was ill. 'You were the SIO for that case where the officer was shot, last year.'

'That's right,' Munro said, face set.

Had Mark Harrison, the assistant chief constable, told him? Division would normally have dealt with a disappearance at this stage, but Kenyon had pulled strings. In the early hours of the morning he had called Mark Harrison and demanded a 'proper' enquiry.

'You were taken off the case. Why?'

Munro shook his head. 'I'm sorry, Judge. I can't discuss that sort of operational detail with you—'

'Rubbish. Are you embarrassed?'

'Of course not. It just wouldn't be correct.'

'Was it because you blew it? Did they remove you from it because you were no good?'

Munro took a breath and counted to five.

'I'm not getting at you, Munro. I need to know who you are though. I need to know.'

'I am—' Munro began.

Kenyon sat forward suddenly, interrupting him. 'My daughter's life depends upon you.'

Munro glanced up at Spencer who looked back at him, a smile playing around the corners of his eyes. Spencer had made his thoughts clear earlier in the day. Keighley Division alone – which covered Ilkley – pulled an average of five missing persons every night. In the last year not one had turned out to be suspicious. Spencer was sure Sophie Kenyon would be no different. She would be at a relative's or friend's house.

'Do you know Mark Harrison?' Kenyon asked Munro.

Munro stared at him. 'Of course I do. You spoke to him? You must—'

Kenyon stood immediately. '*How* do you know him?'

'How?'

He paced quickly towards Munro. His hands were balled into fists at his side. He looked angry. Munro couldn't understand it. He sat still, waiting.

'Yes. How? Are you a friend of his?' He was almost shouting the words, his face reddening, the muscles in his jaw working.

'I think you should calm down, Judge,' Spencer said.

Kenyon didn't even look at him. 'Do you like the man, Munro? Do you *like* Mark Harrison?'

Munro felt stumped. Something was going on, but he couldn't work it out. 'ACC Harrison is my commanding officer,' he said calmly.

'Is he a friend?'

'I have known him a long time.' He was determined not to answer. Harrison wasn't a friend. The truth was he hated Harrison. Most people under him did. But that was none of Kenyon's business.

'In what way have you known him?'

'As a commanding officer.' It was time to assert himself. He stood up, towering above Kenyon, stepping towards him.

'I'm here to try to find Sophie,' he said. He kept his voice measured. 'There are things we need to know quickly. We're wasting time here.'

Kenyon glared at him. Then something else registered behind his eyes and he nodded quickly. The movement was like a flinch, as if Munro had raised his hand to hit him. He took two paces back, collapsed into the chair, put his head in his hands and began to sob.

FOUR

Karen took her own battered Volvo and drove up through the Aire Valley to Keighley. 'Brontë Country' the brown tourist sign proclaimed as she hit the trunk road up the valley. They were in the middle of what the papers were calling a heatwave and the day was bright and hot. She travelled with the windows wound fully down. Summers were usually wet and grey in West Yorkshire, barely distinguishable from any other season; you had to make the most of freak conditions.

In London it had been different. She had come to West Yorkshire nearly eight years ago and almost every summer since had been filled with drizzle. She put her shades on and let her eyes follow the lines of the hills rising to either side – to her left topped with woods and hedgerows, shimmering with iridescence in the heat, to the right rising steeply towards the darker slopes of Rombauld's Moor. Above the horizon the sky was already bleached, the profound morning blue scorched out of it and washed white by the sunlight. Even with shades, it was too bright to look at. She watched a flock of rooks circling crazily above the tree line and remembered that the weather was about all she missed of London.

She checked registration numbers in her mirrors as she drove, watching casually for patterns, similarities. Over the last year the security checks had become routine, but they were still something from her past she had hoped to leave behind. In London they had taught her to read mirror image, reverse number sequences so fast she could still do it without trying. Until a year ago she hadn't needed the skill. But getting rid of the past was never as simple as forgetting it.

She checked her car so regularly now she was becoming relaxed about it. Too relaxed. Sometimes she did it sloppily, sometimes she didn't do it at all. Before leaving Eccleshill fifteen minutes ago she had skipped using the angled mirror device she kept in the boot to check the underside for devices. And checking was only half the task. If she was doing it properly she should take a random detour on each routine journey, checking behind her as she went. In the world she had tried to leave behind, routines killed people.

She swiped her card at the entrance to New Devonshire House – the ugly seventies annexe to the main station – and walked up to the command corridor. The superintendent (Crime) – Gary Miller – was an ex Drugs Squad boss who knew and liked her. She had been transferred out of the Drugs Squad into the Child Protection Team only eleven months before and Miller had moved at around the same time, though for very different reasons; in his case promotion, in hers – though nobody would say it – under a burden of failure and disgrace. When she had been in the Drugs Squad Karen too had thought of the CPT as a dumping ground for problematic women.

A secretary told her Miller was in the CID office with DI Ryan and she took the back staircase to a virtually deserted crime desk at the back of which was the small, partitioned room that served as the DI's office. The door was wide open and she could see that Miller and Ryan were discussing something, Ryan sitting at his desk, Miller leaning over him. She stood at the open door and waited for them to notice her. After a while Miller glanced towards her, looked away then did a quick double take, recognizing her.

'Karen. What brings you here?'

She smiled at him, but he didn't return it. He looked hassled.

'An enquiry, sir.'

'Do you need me or Ian?' He looked down at Ryan who was staring at her now. 'Have you met Ian Ryan? This is DC Sharpe, the best Drugs Squad detective I ever worked with, no matter what anyone else says.'

'We haven't met,' Ryan said, face stony. 'But I know who she is. Can I help you?'

She stepped in. His response didn't surprise her. 'I'm looking for old MISPER reports. I might need to root around in the station stores. I thought I'd check with you first.'

'Be my guest,' Miller said. 'Is it to do with Operation Shade?'

'Shade?'

'We've got a MISPER gone awry.' Miller explained. 'They're setting up an Operations Room on the fifth floor, calling it Shade.

John Munro is the SIO. I thought they might have put you onto it. They've taken half my detectives – that's why it's so quiet out there – I was told they were going to strip the CPT as well. You're CPT now, right?'

'I am. But I've not heard anything about it.'

'So if you're not on Shade what are you looking for?' Ryan interrupted, the tone making clear that, despite Miller's rank, she would need his clearance as well.

'I have a woman saying she's recently remembered a kidnap and sexual assault from ten years before. I'm just trying to get a feel for it, see if there's any corrob, see if anything came in—'

'An old Keighley case?' Ryan asked.

'It would be – if there's any truth to it. The childhood address is given as Oxenhope.'

'A recovered memory job?' It was Miller who asked the question.

'That's right,' she said. She watched the scepticism cloud his features. He looked away, uninterested.

'Anything I need to know about it now?' Ryan asked.

He didn't trust her and he was asking the right questions. She shook her head. She wasn't going to give him the right answers, not just yet. 'It's all standard,' she said. 'Dig out a few dead ends. Send it to the CPS for advice.'

'So they can knock it?' Miller asked again, still looking away from her, a trace of bitterness in his voice.

She shrugged.

'OK. Let me know what you find then,' Ryan said.

She nodded. '*If* I find anything. Do you know where I should look?'

'Ask the storeman. Basement in the main building.'

Miller spoke as she was turning to leave: 'Any progress, Karen?'

He didn't have to explain what he was talking about. She knew. The whole Force knew.

'They don't tell me,' she said. She looked at Miller, but could see Ryan's eyes on her. 'I'm a witness, remember?'

Miller nodded. 'I heard they were going to drop the whole thing,' he said. 'The fucking Crown Prosecution Service.'

She shrugged again. 'Like I said, they tell me nothing.' She tried to work out whether there was some grudging reference to her present 'partner' involved. The man she was living with – Neil Gayle – was a prosecuter in Leeds. How would Miller know that, though?

'If they bin it, it will be a travesty,' Miller said. 'Phil Leech was a good detective.'

She nodded sympathetically. She always did when they made these comments. Then she turned and pulled the door closed behind her. She walked three paces and paused. She could hear Ryan saying something. She stepped back, listening.

'I used to rate her,' she heard Miller say. 'I wouldn't trust her as far as I could throw her now.'

She took a breath.

'Do you know what it was?' Ryan asked. 'What it was about?'

'Nobody knows. That's why London took it. So we wouldn't find out. It got Phil Leech killed though.'

'How old is she?'

'No idea. Her file says mid-thirties, if you want to believe that. But who knows anything about her now? They say the kid is hers. That's the rumour.'

'She looks younger. And fit. Not like she had a kid. You like them tall like that?'

She heard them laugh, crude male complicity.

Then Ryan spoke again. 'I can see what Phil Leech was attracted to. She'd definitely get it.'

'Fit as a butcher's dog,' Miller said. 'But Phil Leech wouldn't have touched her.'

'Why not?'

'Too fucking complicated.'

She thought only briefly about pushing the door open and letting them see she had heard. Only fourteen months ago Miller had liked her, professionally. She had never thought him above the sexist crap – none of them were – but she had thought him above the rumours, or at least above believing them. But he had pretended to her just now, pretended to be normal, pretended that nothing had happened fourteen months ago. At the end of the day the whole of the Force was the same – everyone thought she had killed Phil Leech.

FIVE

She crouched down on the dusty floor of the furthest recess of the storeroom cage and began to hunt through the filing boxes for 1987. She tried to concentrate, but Miller's comments rankled. She didn't feel bad for Phil Leech, didn't care what they might think about *her*; that wasn't the part that bit at her. It was the way it all came out, bouncing around on the jungle drums. Soon it would get back to Mairead.

Mairead was a child, nine years old, innocent of everything. Karen had tried to keep her out of it, to set up a screen around her – even lying to her to protect her. But fourteen months later they were still talking about Leech's death, still guessing at the connections to the child she was now looking after. *They say the kid is hers.*

Her hands shook as she pulled the files from 1987. What would she do if Mairead found out?

Concentrate on other things, she thought. She paused, closed her eyes, focused on her breathing. She waited five minutes, breathing carefully, concentrating on nothing else, exactly as they had taught her in London. Then she brought Pamela Mathews's battered face before her, looked at it and listened again to her story. That was what she was doing now, that was why she was here. She opened her eyes and began to look through the folders.

The panic had gone.

There were nearly 300 missing person reports from 1987, with no index and no way of knowing even what month they had been processed without reading them. A quick sift did not produce the name Mathews, so she had to order and look through them all.

By three-thirty she had got up to the last week in July and had found nothing even vaguely resembling the tale Pamela had given her. Pamela had dated her abduction by reference to a new dress she had been given for her thirteenth birthday, on 1 June 1987. She had remembered the dress being torn from her body. She had told Karen she remembered that the dress was only 'weeks old'. To be safe Karen continued until she had looked at everything up to the end of August.

She was working on the assumption that, unless Pamela's parents had been involved in her 'abduction' – and nothing Pamela had said pointed that way – then they would have reported it. If they had the MISPER log would be here. So unless Pamela had forgotten her own name, something was amiss.

She filled out a property form at the gate to the cage and pushed the forms into her briefcase. The next most logical source of corroboration would be with doctors' surgeries in Oxenhope. Pamela didn't recall whether she had been treated by a doctor, didn't even recall how she had come to escape her captivity and be released. But clearly – if there was any truth to her story – she had somehow got away and, once again, on that assumption, her parents should have taken her to a doctor or a hospital. But since Pamela couldn't recall who her childhood doctor had been (and since her parents had both died within months of each other, she said, five years ago) that enquiry would be time-consuming. It was already coming up to 4 p.m., so it would have to wait.

On the way back to Bradford she tuned to Radio Leeds and listened to harmless middle-of-the-road pop music until the drive-time news came up. Operation Shade was the headline story. A judge's daughter was missing from Ilkley, last seen tea-time the day before. There was an interview with the judge – Michael Kenyon (the name rang vague bells) – and then a quote from the SIO they had appointed. She recognized the soft Scottish accent as soon as he started speaking, before they even introduced him.

Detective Chief Superintendent John Munro had been out of the limelight for a long time – fourteen months, in fact. His involvement as SIO explained why she hadn't even been told about Shade that morning. Munro might recruit the entire CPT onto his manhunt team, but he would never take her. Not again. Munro had been the original SIO on Phoenix – the enquiry into Phil Leech's shooting. He had brought Karen onto the team before London realized what was really going on and took it off him. Her activities between those two points hadn't pleased him. He had learned his lesson.

She smiled as she listened. Munro was playing politics with the resources. Asked how large his team was he replied, 'Not large enough at the moment. But the Command Team have promised me a significant increase should that prove necessary. We will find little Sophie Kenyon.' She waited for him to add the words 'dead or alive'. 'I am confident of that,' he said.

Munro was good at using the press. The words transmitted the hidden message clearly: 'I haven't got enough men to find her. If she dies the Command Team is to blame.' He would get his extra men.

She parked up in the Bradford Crown Court car park and walked over to the offices of the local rag – the *Telegraph & Argos*. Checking news copy was the quickest way she could think of to find out what Geoffrey Reed had been up to in 1987. In reception she asked for Phil Patterson, a crime reporter she had met at court in the past and had once stupidly conceded a post-trial drink to. He had called her four times after that, asking for a 'follow-up,' but obviously interested in something else. He wasn't unattractive, but she didn't trust him. She didn't trust anyone who wanted to ask her questions.

'Karen. What can I do for you?' Patterson's tone was suspicious. She stood in front of him, smiling, a good six inches taller than him. Another reason she hadn't been interested.

'I'm on an enquiry,' she said. 'I need help.'

'Have you a production order?'

She reached over and touched his arm. She saw it register. He shifted stance, stepping back. He was nervous of her.

'There'll be no need for legal stuff, Phil. I just want your help. When you hear what I have to say you'll want to help. It could be interesting for you.'

He looked hard at her, frowning, trying to work out her motives. 'I mean it,' she said.

Finally he nodded, but he looked reluctant.

She followed him to a busy, open-plan office full of computer terminals and sat down on a chair alongside what was presumably his little bit of desk space. Patterson was one of two journalists covering crime for the *T&A*, the junior one. The actual crime correspondent was a skinny youth called Kevin Down with an irritating Essex accent. 'Kev' probably had his own office; Phil didn't. Behind her there were at least two others in earshot.

She shook her head. 'We need somewhere private,' she said. 'This is just for you and it's sensitive.'

She watched the light switch on behind his eyes. He stood up and led her to an empty glass-partitioned office at the edge of the room.

'I need information from nineteen eighty-seven,' she said, when he had taken the seat behind the cheap Formica desk. 'Do you have records going back to then?'

'Of course. Information about what?'

'This has to go no further than me and you. If it does you get nothing from me about this or anything else, ever.'

'I've never gotten anything off you before, Karen. Why would that worry me?'

'You'll get nothing more about this. That would bother you.'

'Tell me more.'

'Tell me it goes no further.'

'It goes no further.' He smiled. He was lying, but she didn't really care.

'I need information about Geoff Reed. Anything and everything about him from the summer of nineteen eighty-seven.'

She watched his tongue dart across his upper lip. 'Geoff Reed the MP?'

'That's him.'

'Why?'

'Can't tell you that now. If something comes from it I'll give you it first though.'

'Are you investigating him?'

'Do we have a deal?'

He nodded.

'So I'll tell you first if anything goes down. Not now. That's the deal.'

'OK. I'll check for you first thing tomorrow. It might take a while. Between what dates do you want me to search?'

'Between, say, May and August.'

'Looking for anything in particular?'

'Yes. See if he took part in any elections or such-like around then.' She was thinking of the rosette Pamela had described. 'Or any post-election celebrations. Or fund-raising parties. I need everything. But those things would be the priority.'

'Is this to do with his funding?'

'I can't give you *anything* now.'

'You know there was a general election in June of that year?'

She raised her eyebrows, embarrassed. 'No. I didn't. I suppose I was busy with other things at the time. When was it?'

'Eleventh of June. Thatcher's third term. That was when Reed was first elected up here.'

'Sounds good,' she said. Pamela had said it was the eleventh of June two weeks ago that she had seen Reed on TV. Maybe they had been interviewing him because of the anniversary. She thought for a moment. 'You couldn't just go and pull me all the copy for that date now, could you? I can wait for the rest.'

He stood. 'I'll try. You'll have to wait back outside though.'

'You can leave me in here.'

'I can't. It's against the rules.'

'Don't you trust me, Phil?'

'Not after last time.'

She followed him out and sat down to consider what he had meant. 'Last time' as far as she could recall, nothing had happened at all. She went for a drink with him, he got ideas. That was it.

He took half an hour before returning, by which time her mobile had gone off three times. The number coming up was her home number, so she ignored it. On the third try the caller left a message and she listened to it. It was Neil, worrying about her, wondering where she was. She checked the time. It wasn't even six and he was ringing to track her down.

When Patterson returned she gave him her card and took the bundle of photocopies off him.

'He was at a lot of parties,' the reporter said. 'One at the constituency offices, then off on the circuit – all the people he owed, I guess. That's what they do. Once the polls have closed they have a fifteen-hour wait. You're lucky. There was a reporter from a national 'shadowing' him. The bright young face of Labour – as he was then. He was radical back in eighty-seven. He's decidedly old school now. We picked up the copy from the national a few days later. There are even a few photos.'

She looked quickly through the material, stopping at a photo of Reed, arms aloft, triumphant, red rosette prominent at his lapel.

SIX

Munro looked at his watch, the fifth time he had done so in as many minutes. Beside him he saw Spencer notice the movement. They were in the conference room at Keighley Police Station, a room hardly large enough to contain a normal divisional enquiry, let alone something major. But then this wasn't, in anything but name, a major enquiry. This was an exercise in cynicism. Mark Harrison had so far given him only twelve bodies, seven of those the women Ricky Spencer had brought with him from the CPT. The rest had been pulled straight from Keighley Division – a move which suggested Harrison expected them to be back there before long. Munro was still waiting to see whether his words to the press earlier that day would have the desired effect.

It was five-eighteen. He had called the de-brief for five o'clock sharp. Around the large oval conference table there were only ten people so far, himself and Spencer included. Four of the seven CPT detectives were late. Sitting to his right Spencer looked unconcerned. He was chewing gum.

'Do they have pagers?' Munro asked his deputy, without looking at him. He had already been told that the missing women were not answering their mobiles.

'Yes. You want me to page them?' Spencer asked.

'Yes.' *You should have done it already*, he thought.

Spencer left the room. So far they hadn't got round to putting phone lines into the place. He watched the eight detectives chatting amongst themselves, laughing, joking. Not a care in the world. It seemed he was alone with his fears for Sophie Kenyon. Everyone he spoke to thought she was alive and well and hiding out. They thought that without knowing the first thing about her or her family. Because that was what usually happened.

He looked at his watch again. He was the only one concerned about the clock.

'You know the scene,' he said, quietly, as if he was talking to himself. He heard the murmurs fade away as they tried to listen. 'Everyone thinks this is bullshit, that Sophie is sitting pretty with an aunt or a friend. Well, I don't. Not because I know any better, but because if I have any other attitude I won't do my job. And if we don't do the job properly and she is not with an aunt or a friend then she's in trouble. Big trouble. There's only us to get her away from that. No one else.' He looked up at them. 'So if you think she's safe and well you should get up now. Get up and get out. I'll get others to help.' He was aware he sounded nervous, angry. They looked back at him, meeting his eyes, frowning, not quite able to work him out.

The door opened and Spencer came back into the room, followed closely by three of the four missing detectives. They sat down without apologizing. Spencer told him the fourth – DC Westerman – had run into childcare problems and wouldn't be making it. Munro just nodded. He would deal with the crap later, including the three who were late without excuse.

'Good. Let's get started. Who had her friends?'

One of the three who were late raised a hand. 'I did, sir. I've just finished with the last on the list. That's why I was late, sorry.'

He nodded, looking only at her. It was still no excuse. 'What's your name, Officer? I've forgotten.'

She was pretty, he thought. But a little too young for him.

She coloured. 'DC Cooper. Sara Cooper.'

'So tell us, Sara.'

She cleared her throat, looked at the sheaf of papers in front of her. 'Nothing,' she said. 'Ali, Beth and I,' she pointed to the women sitting to her right, the other two who were late, 'did this together. We worked a list of six close friends and a wider list of fifteen possibles. We've spoken to each and every one, personally. They haven't seen her. She's not with a friend.'

Munro let her words hang for a while. A nice, short, report, he thought. Straight to the point. 'OK,' he said. 'We'll come back to follow-ups and detail in a moment. Who has the relatives?'

A detective called Malcolm Dickson, who Munro knew from previous murder enquiries, spoke up. 'Jack, Eric, Pete and I chased the relatives,' he said. Munro knew they were all Keighley detectives.

'We've got one distant cousin left – lives in London – and that's it. Most contact by phone, but it all sounded straight up. Doubtful she's with the one outstanding. She hardly knew him. I would say she's not with a relative.'

Munro glanced at Spencer. He was writing it all into his policy log. He looked back at the group. 'Not with a relative. Not with a friend. So where is she?'

No one answered. He settled his eyes on each face in turn. Some met his gaze, others looked away. He stood up.

'I'll tell you where she is,' he said. 'She's dead. Some sadistic pervert has taken her from under her parents' noses, raped and brutalized her, then dumped her body somewhere that will keep us looking for months whilst the evidence dissipates. That's what's happened.'

He paused by the whiteboard at the far end of the room and looked back at them. Shock was written across their faces. Even Spencer had stopped writing and was staring at him.

'Any of you got kids?' he asked them.

Most of the women nodded. Only Bains looked away. Bains had a nasty history as far as kids went. Munro remembered it.

'I have too,' he said. 'Imagine it's your kid that died like that. In pain, frightened, lonely, shouting for her mummy.' Spencer started to say something, probably some kind of objection. Munro held his hand up. 'That's the reality of it. That's what we're dealing with. Let's have it out on the table in front of us. Have any of you been on a MISPER enquiry before?'

Blank faces. He began to pace around the table, holding their attention.

'I have. I remember it well. We sat around for three days laughing and joking and running down the obvious clues. We came in late for briefings. We had childcare problems. Whatever. We didn't give a shit because we were sure she was alive. About day three or four all the obvious clues ran out. Six months later we pulled her from the canal. Nine years old. So decomposed she was falling to bits. Hands bound behind her back. Probably while we were all sitting on our arses laughing about it – during the first few days.' He stopped behind Spencer. 'That isn't going to happen here. This is my enquiry and you lot are going to do it as if it was your daughter out there. Got it?'

The response was murmured, suppressed. He could see them computing the images, thinking about their own kids, flinching.

'The first twenty-four hours are crucial,' he said. 'We know as a fact that most kidnapped children are murdered within that period, if they are going to be murdered at all. So we are going to assume she's dead already. Our twenty-four hours is up. This is a murder enquiry.'

He took out his mobile phone and pulled Harrison's number from the memory. Around the table they watched him without speaking. It rang three times before Harrison answered.

'John?' Harrison obviously had caller ID on.

'Yes, sir.'

'Have you found her?'

'No, sir. We've checked all the obvious places and some besides. She's not at a relatives' and not with friends. She's missing. I would assume kidnapped. I would assume dead. But we need to ramp this thing up just in case she's not, in case there's still time. We need more men. We need serious resources.'

There was a long silence. Munro waited. He waited so long he thought the connection had cut. 'Are you still—' he started.

'I'm here, John. I'm thinking.'

'Yes, sir.'

Another gap. Munro filled it again. 'I have a press interview in half an hour, sir. I need to be able to—'

'Not yet.'

'I'm sorry?'

'Not yet. Keep going as you are. If you have nothing by this time tomorrow then I'll go with your request.'

Munro looked at his team. The nearer ones could probably hear what Harrison was saying. He repeated it aloud anyway: 'That's your decision, sir? That we keep going as now and if we haven't found her by this time tomorrow you will raise the category?'

'That's right, John. And if you throw any more tricks at the press conferences I'll take you off the thing. Do you understand?'

Munro bit his tongue. He was used to authority, but not to being spoken to like that.

Harrison didn't wait for an answer. 'Get on with it, then.' He cut the line.

Munro took a breath, looked up at them. 'Well, until this time tomorrow it's just us,' he said. He stepped over to the whiteboard. 'Some of you have already been on murder enquiries. Tomorrow, when our ACC wakes up and reads his newspaper, we'll get another forty men, HOLMES and the full works. A bigger incident room as well. For now we do it all on paper from this cupboard. They might not be taking it seriously higher up, but in here we have to. We have to keep it moving right through the night. This is the worst kind of murder enquiry you can have. No body. No scene. Nothing obvious to work at, no obvious place to start. But we're still going to work it and I hope you weren't expecting to get home tonight.' He began to write headings on the board.

'This is what we do. Six possible lines, off the top of my head. When I'm done, chip in with any you think I've missed.

'Number one: Daddy killed her and has been abusing her for years. Alternatively a close relative, an uncle or such like, or close friend of the family. In six out of ten child abductions the abductor is the person who calls it in, usually a parent. We'll need to get specialists from the yard onto it, get profiles and trace similarities across the country. Number two: someone the judge put away has done it. Simple enough. Time consuming to check for possibles, but we have to do it. Number three: her boyfriend did it. So far we think she hasn't got one. If no boyfriend then a male friend, or friend of a friend, someone connected to her who came into contact with her and therefore left us with a trail. Number four: a stranger, a genuine paedophile abduction. That would be my first guess. But even strangers have to plan and the planning leaves a trail. We can find him. Five: it's an accident and she's down a railway cutting, at the side of a road or the bottom of a river. Discount that for now. I won't even write it up. If it's an accident there's no hurry and we'll get to it last. When we get proper resources we can start scouring the moor. Six: she's run away. We've almost bottomed that one already. That's how I see it. Anyone else got any theories?'

He stepped back and waited. A few shook their heads, most were still writing down what he had put on the board, taken aback by his speed.

'OK. Here's how we cut it up. DC Cooper and myself will deal with the profiling. We need to get London up here tonight. Or go down there. DC Cooper can also double up as office manager and statement reader, for now. Ricky will take three of you and do the judge and his wife. You'll need a warrant for the house, in case he says no, though try with cooperation first. Do it top to bottom, assume he's the man, go for it. Don't worry about him being a judge.

Dickson, Conroy and Henshaw will do the sex offenders' register. Pull out and knock up anyone within a three-mile radius. If you draw a blank, widen the circle and keep going. Don't worry about human rights. Knock them up, get in, check she's not there. Check with Intelligence and the local LIO too. Anything that looks good. You too,' he pointed to two women whose names he didn't know or recall, 'what're your names?'

'DC King.'

'DC James.'

'King and James, you need to work on the revenge plot. The judge bins someone who comes out and comes back for his daughter. Do you know how to do it?'

They looked blankly at him.

'No?'

They shook heads.

'See me later,' Spencer said, from the far end of the table. 'I'll tell you.'

'What does that cover?' Munro asked himself the question and turned back to the board. He had five headings on the board and four sub-headings corresponding to the tasks he had just assigned: 'Profiling', 'Sex Offenders', 'Parents/relatives' and 'Ex-Cons'. He added a fifth – 'Boyfriend' – then pointed to one of the Keighley detectives. 'You dig into that. Assume she had a boyfriend and find out who he was. If she didn't then find out if she ever had one, find out her sexual history, find out if anyone was interested in her. Liaise with Sara and Malcolm, but since they've drawn blanks I'm assuming that if one existed she kept him secret. That leaves . . .' He thought for a moment.

Spencer spoke up from the back. 'Door to doors?'

'Correct. Thanks, Ricky. Who is left?' He looked behind him.

'I'll take Pete Bains and Jeff Black for the warrant and the judge,' Spencer said. 'I'll only need two. I think that leaves Hall and Westerman for door to doors. Westerman kicked it off anyway today.'

'Good. You'll need to get onto Westerman and get her back here—'

'I've already seen to it.'

Munro smiled at him, surprised. 'Good. Pull all the CCTV stuff in as well. That can be part of the door to door assignment. Now, does anyone else have anything from their personal lives that they need to sort out before we bottom the detail from today?'

He looked round. They were intent now, focused. No one said anything.

'Excellent,' he said. He turned back to Sara Cooper. 'Over to you again, Sara. Give us the detail.'

SEVEN

Almost as soon as Karen got through the doors to the CPT, her partner – George Wright – greeted her with the news that Ricky Spencer, their DI, had been made Deputy SIO on Shade and had left her 'in charge'. As she walked over to her desk she surveyed the empty, open-plan office. Wright remained by the doors, jacket on, obviously about to leave regardless.

'How many have they taken?' she asked him.

'Almost everyone except us,' he said.

When he was gone she set to work catching up. Running down possible corroboration for Pamela Mathews had taken up most of the day. She had two cases up for Plea and Directions Hearings within the next two weeks. In both the judge had set the CPS a fourteen-day deadline to disclose unused material. The deadline expired in the morning. So she either got the work done that night or the cases ran the risk of being kicked out. She could feel her mobile vibrating in her pocket as she scanned the documents she had to consider. She ignored it.

It was nearing nine-thirty and there were another five unanswered messages on the mobile by the time she was done. She drove slowly up the Aire Valley trunk road, her mind restless and irritated. Her house was in the countryside beyond Skipton, off the road to Settle, on the edge of the south-western dales. It was about a mile from the nearest road and stood by itself in a stand of sycamores. The closest dwelling was the farmhouse another mile up the lane. There was a pub – her local – about a mile and a half to the west, but no shops. She had lived there for almost seven years now. She had picked the place deliberately for its isolation, because there would be nobody to stare through her windows, because it gave her space.

She stopped the Volvo at the end of the land leading from the main road and let the minutes pass over her, doing nothing, trying not to think that it was *her* house up there in the distance, occupied by strangers, taken over. She realised with shame that those were the exact words that ran through her brain – '*occupied by strangers*'.

It was still light. This far north, mid-summer, the day would be waning for another hour or so. If Neil or Mairead was bothering to watch from her windows they would see her sitting here, waiting. She wondered what kind of reaction that would provoke. She wondered if that was what she wanted – to provoke something.

She sighed and sat in the evening silence, the light fading around her. She watched long tongues of blood-red and pink seep into the deepening blue above her. She watched a breeze moving through the topmost branches of the trees alongside the road. She tried to keep her mind empty, but it was difficult.

Finally she took the mobile out and listened to the messages. They were all from Neil. The first two were functional. Could she ring to let him know what time she would be back? Could she say whether she wanted to eat with them? But as the evening wore on he began to sound worried for her. There was no recrimination, no reproach, just the simple concern of someone who cared. He knew something of her story and her past, knew the danger that could come out of it. It was that simple, that hard to accept.

She rested her forehead on the steering wheel and listened to the evening silence. How had she ended up here? How had she come to this? She believed in nothing, in neither God nor religion. She had no morals or moral code she could speak of. But her heart felt strained within her, weighed down with a burden of guilt and evil. She was worse than the child abusers and rapists she spent her waking hours chasing. They, at least, believed in *something* – if only themselves. But she was travelling through life on autopilot, filling the hours. She was living for nothing.

She had no reason to be here, sitting here, doing this, no reason not to. And a mile away there were people who cared about her, loved her, waited for her, *needed* her. She looked up towards the house and saw the lights coming on. She tried to think of what she felt for Neil. But nothing came to her. And it wasn't just him.

If she wanted to she could get rid of Neil Gayle, get him out of there. But Mairead was her daughter, her own flesh and blood. There had to be something broken inside her if she could look at the house and think it occupied by strangers.

Over eight years ago she had thought she would never see Mairead again. The facts were stark, the actions those of someone she no longer recognized, operating in different times, in crueller circumstances. She had walked out on the child before she had even been old enough to recognize her as her mother. But the past had not been so easy to bury and like so much else from it, Mairead had returned. For just over a year Karen had been trying to live with that. Mairead had been thrust back into her life because her father was right now on remand in the high security wing of Durham jail. Mairead still didn't know that Karen was her mother. That fact left Karen trembling with guilt, tears starting to well up in her eyes. Why could she not face up to it? Why could she not tell Mairead?

Karen knew what mothers looked like – real mothers – how they reacted to their children. She had studied them. She could copy them, go through the motions, control herself, pretend. Any kind of lying came easy to her. She could even pretend to Mairead. But not so that it wouldn't damage her. Children sucked in the truth at a level below consciousness. Karen felt love for Mairead, but love wasn't enough. She was meant to be her mother. She was meant to *feel* the things that mothers felt, not just do them. Sooner or later Mairead was going to find that out. What had been happening in her life when Mairead was born was so traumatic Karen was still living with the consequences. Vast chunks of her memory had dropped clean out of existence to prevent her thinking about it. She couldn't even remember Mairead's birth. How could a child grow up undamaged when her mother couldn't recall her birth?

She would never get away from it. It had been with her for nine years, corrupting everything, destroying one relationship after another. She had told Neil some of it. But there were things that she had done that would make normal people look at her as if she were a monster. She couldn't let him go there, couldn't let him see those things. She didn't want to see the disgust in his eyes.

It was better Mairead didn't know who she was. It would have been even better if Mairead had not known her at all.

She started the engine. She couldn't go back there yet. It wasn't her home. Not any longer. She needed a drink. She would go to the pub, call in late, make her excuses, hope that by the time she got in they had given up and gone to bed. That way she wouldn't have to face them.

EIGHT

Wednesday morning found her alone in the spare bedroom listening to the sounds of Neil and Mairead getting ready for the day. The alarm/radio was tuned to Radio Leeds and woke her just before nine with a traffic report about a lorry shedding its load on the M62. She was about to roll over and hit the snooze button when John Munro's soft Scottish lilt began to tell the world yet again about Operation Shade and Sophie Kenyon. She sighed. It was nothing to do with her. Without taking in the words, she rolled her feet onto the floor and switched him off.

Downstairs she was greeted by a stony silence. They were both seated at the table as she entered, and had been talking happily – she could hear them as she walked down the stairs – but as soon as she stepped into view they shut up. Neither looked at her.

She walked over to the kettle, filled it with water and plugged it in. Then she turned to look at them, leaning back against the sink. Mairead's eyes flicked up at her and averted immediately, a slight smile crinkling the corners of her mouth, as if it were a game, a conspiracy between Neil and her. To encourage something like that would be unlike Neil, but there was a first time for everything. Karen stopped herself from asking him what was going on. If he had said something to Mairead, she thought, it would be the first and last time.

Neil was reading *The Times*, an empty cereal bowl in front of him, legs crossed to the side. They were both already dressed. Neil was in a dark pinstripe suit, immaculately pressed white cotton shirt and crimson tie, shoes buffed so efficiently Karen fancied she would be able to see her reflection in them. His hair was still wet from the shower, his cheeks glistening, smooth, freshly shaved. He smelled vaguely of cologne. Mairead was in her summer school uniform, short tunic and light-blue shirt, smelling of the orange-scented soap

45

Neil had bought for her. He had plaited her long dark hair into a braided ponytail, something Karen would never have been able to do as competently, and certainly not in the morning while rushing to get to work. She took a breath and watched them for a moment, as they studiously tried to ignore her.

What had she seen in Neil Gayle? She had been with him nearly a year and the question still dogged her. He was attractive enough, tall enough (a few inches shorter than her, but then, at just over six foot two, she wasn't short), physically well built and fit. He worked out three times a week at a gym in Leeds – if he wasn't looking after Mairead – and ate moderately. He hardly ever drank so much that he got drunk. He looked trim, neat, controlled. He had a full head of dark brown, curly hair, intelligent green eyes. She had heard he was good at his job too. He was almost exactly her age. But none of that would have made her invite him into her life.

It was only a year since they had first met, yet she found it difficult to recall now why she was with him. He was pleasant, friendly, concerned, gentle, caring. He was loving with both Mairead and her, interesting to talk to about virtually anything. In his spare time he was trying to write a book about a case he had prosecuted almost ten years ago – a fictionalized account, a legal thriller (if there was such a thing). Since moving in he didn't get much spare time and it wasn't going well. Nevertheless, when he spoke about it he became interesting to her, animated, lit up with something she had perhaps seen within him the very first time they had met. He had never wanted to be a lawyer. She liked that. There weren't many lawyers she would give the time of day to. But even with his non-legal aspirations he was little more than a nice standard guy. And she didn't go for that.

She glanced over at the end of the table. She had left a note there last night, apologizing for her late return, saying she had been forced to work late. It was still there.

'Did you read my note?' she asked him quietly.

He turned a page of the paper, taking his time, then answered without looking at her. 'Yes. We read it this morning.' His voice was emotionless, as if her presence was something optional.

She resisted the urge to respond. Not in front of Mairead. Was he beginning to doubt her? Normally he could be relied upon to question nothing she told him. She stepped up behind Mairead and placed her hand on her hair, ruffling it slightly, wanting to feel something more than the pain she felt every time she looked into the child's eyes.

'Don't I get a kiss?' she asked.

Mairead looked up at her and grinned. Karen felt her heart flutter. She bent down and kissed her on the cheek. Her daughter kissed her back, bringing her arms up and hugging her tightly.

'We waited for you last night,' Mairead whispered into her ear, before she let go. 'Neil cooked lasagne.'

'I couldn't get back,' Karen said. 'I'm sorry. I'll be early tonight.' She crouched down beside her and whispered the words, the bond between them back. 'The braid looks good.'

'Neil did it.'

Still he didn't look at her. 'He's good to you,' Karen said. 'Did he do it this morning?'

Mairead nodded.

Neil folded the paper and glanced at the clock on the wall, then looked Karen directly in the eyes. 'Are you definitely back tonight?'

'Yes,' she said. 'Definitely.' She looked away.

'Because we need to talk,' he said.

She nodded. Mairead rolled her eyes.

'You finished?' he asked Mairead, voice softening. The bowl in front of her still contained a mush of soggy Weetabix.

'You should eat that—' Karen started.

'You've had enough,' Neil said, interrupting. 'You can leave the rest if you want.' He stood up. Karen bit her tongue. 'Go and get your satchel, Mairead,' he added. 'We're in a rush now.'

When she had disappeared upstairs, Karen straightened up and looked at him. 'What's the matter?' she asked.

'You know,' he said.

'I don't. Is this because I was late in?'

'No. It's because you slept in the spare room. Because you've slept in the spare room for the last eight days. Maybe *you* should be telling *me* what's the matter?'

'I didn't want to wake you, that's all.'

'Yeah. I thought so.' He squeezed past her and walked into the lounge. 'We'll talk tonight,' he said, over his shoulder. 'I've got to get her to school now.'

She watched as he fussed over her child, placing a packed lunch he

47

had made the night before in her satchel, straightening her hair, kissing her on the forehead. He acted in every way as if he were her father and Mairead responded accordingly. On the surface it looked as if he was closer to the child than Karen was. But though Mairead thought Karen was her aunt, not her mother, the way she responded to her was intimate, immediately complicit. Despite the lie, the bond was there every time Karen touched her, as if it were something natural, something that couldn't be hidden. The way Mairead reacted to Neil was different.

Karen watched them leave, waving to Mairead from the window. It was hard to avoid the conclusion that she was with Neil Gayle for just (and only) this reason – because he was good with her daughter. Maybe that was also why he was with her. Maybe what he wanted really was a child, not a partner.

Karen had met him less than eight weeks after Mairead had returned to her life, at a point where the implications of looking after an eight-year-old child were beginning to overwhelm her. Weeks before Mairead had seen her father arrested and handcuffed and had not seen him since. The loss had produced difficult behaviour and Karen had no idea how to cope with it. That Mairead was relatively happy now was largely due to Neil. Karen frowned. If she had to ask him to leave it would probably be harder on Mairead than her.

When she had a mug of coffee in her hands she rang Geoff Reed's constituency office. She needed to find out whether he was in the area and what he was doing. She needed to get her mind off problems she couldn't solve then and there. The office obliged with information that Reid was holding a 'mini-surgery' that morning. Mini-surgeries were held at the party offices instead of the town hall and you had to have an appointment to get in. She told them she was a policewoman and her business was urgent and personal. It did the trick.

Outside she could tell it was going to be another hot, clear day. She wore a tight, white T-shirt, a light suede jacket and black jeans. Her hair was getting too long for the heat – almost down to between her shoulder blades now. She pulled it back into a ponytail, dug out her shades and pulled the door shut behind her just after eleven. It took another three minutes to run the mirror along the bottom of the car, checking for wires, packages, leaks, batteries or anything different. As she set off she promised herself she would do what she had said – she would get home early.

NINE

In a decaying, semi-detached Victorian mansion somewhere near Dudley Hill she sat down in a waiting room that wasn't unlike a doctor's surgery and joined the queue of believers waiting for a cure.

She considered what she wanted out of this meeting while she waited for her ticket number to be called. There was nothing she could take from it evidentially, not like this, not without announcing it and doing it by the book – so why was she bothering? She unfolded Pamela's statement and read through it again. The truth was she had so far spent a day on this and she already had enough dead ends to know it was going nowhere. She was here to let Geoff Reed put the finishing touches to that, to give him his chance to seem normal, to come across as the kind of person who wouldn't rape a thirteen-year-old girl.

About half an hour after the time they had given her Karen looked up from the statement and saw a young woman standing in front of her. She had a stud in her left nostril and her hair tied back in long dreads. The young face of new Labour – bright, trendy, cocky – finally triumphant after eighteen years in the wilderness. The girl was white and would be conventionally pretty, beneath the disguise, which said: '*I want to be black, I wish I had grown up on a South London Estate.*' But her accent, when she spoke, was straight Oxbridge.

'Karen Sharpe?'

'That's me.'

'I'm Geoff's assistant.' Disdain in her voice. 'Geoff will see you now.'

The first thing she noted about Geoff Reed was that he was fatter than he looked on TV.

The room she was shown into was what would have been the

sitting room, when the place had been a residence. At one end of it, in front of a wide bay window, Reed had placed a large hardwood desk, but he wasn't behind it as Karen entered. Instead, in the rest of the room there was an arrangement of sofas, easy chairs and armchairs forming a loose half-circle around a small sofa on which Reed was sitting. Beside him was a clipboard and a sheaf of papers. As Karen entered he was using a large silver fountain pen, writing up the notes from the last supplicant, presumably. He didn't look up at her.

She sat down on the armchair nearest to him and watched him.

'Give me a moment, please,' he said, still without looking at her. He had a slight Yorkshire accent, nothing too loud.

She put him at well over eighteen stone and guessed he would stand at five nine or ten. He was wearing slacks and a cotton shirt with a button-down collar, no tie. He would have looked good in 'smart-casual', but the way his belly was straining against the shirt buttons and hanging over his groin spoiled the effect. There was a thick wooden walking stick leaning against the arm of the sofa.

The folds of flab around his chin and jaw were clean shaven and glistening slightly with sweat. She guessed that at that weight even writing had to quicken your heart rate. He had a pair of half-rimmed reading glasses, which might have succeeded in giving him a studious air, were it not for the flab. As it was Karen thought that all he lacked to fit the standard paedophile image was a raincoat, stains down his trousers and dirty shoes. But then, as she knew all too well, real-life paedophiles didn't fit the image, they looked normal.

Finished observing him, she studied his room. No posters advertising Labour's success, no leaflets or pamphlets. The floor was polished wood with a massive oriental rug spread out under the chairs. The walls were panelled and mainly occupied with bookshelves. She didn't have time to check the titles. The place was unlike the waiting room though. More like the chambers of an Oxford don.

There were three paintings, all looking original, oils of local scenic spots. While she was looking at them she noticed in her peripheral vision that he had stopped writing and was peering over the half-rims in her direction. He shifted in the sagging sofa.

'How can I help you, Karen?' he asked, after a while. A quiet, gentle voice, lulling you to vote.

'Mr Reed. Thanks for agreeing to see me—'

'Geoffrey. Please.' He smiled. He had a full set of perfectly white teeth. She guessed they were his own. The press clippings said that he was fifty-two.

'Geoffrey. I'm not really sure I should be here.' She paused and frowned, looking slightly afraid. He kept his eyes on her. 'Did they tell you I was a police officer?'

He nodded, looking down at his notes. 'Yes. Detective Constable Karen Sharpe. But you're not a constituent of mine, are you?'

She wondered whether he had run some kind of check on her. 'No. Not in terms of where I live. But I'm a Bradford officer. I work out of Eccleshill. I think that's your constituency, isn't it?'

He ignored the question. 'Eccleshill Police Station? You work for Eccleshill Division?'

'No. For the Child Protection Team. That's what I'm here about really.'

He put the pen down and shifted again in the sofa, into a more upright, attentive position. He had known already, she thought, that the CPT worked out of Eccleshill.

'I feel a bit embarrassed,' she said. 'I've never done anything like this before – complained to an MP . . .'

'You want to complain about something?'

'Yes. About a case. I'm not sure that . . .'

'Have you spoken to your supervisors, to your own people?'

'No. That's what I mean. I don't even think I'm meant to be here. I feel like a bit of a whistle-blower . . .' She let her words trail off. He was a politician, he would take the bait.

'Well, we are the government now, of course,' he said, unable to get the pride wholly out of his voice. 'That means we shouldn't really condone things like whistle-blowing. There should be robust internal complaint systems and we are working to achieve that. You know about the Freedom of Information Bill?'

'That won't help me,' she said. 'I think an injustice has been done and I think police officers have colluded in it. I want to tell somebody and I want to tell them now, before it's too late to do anything about it.'

He frowned, but she could see the little glimmer in the back of his eyes. Even if it wasn't worth publicity, dirt was dirt. It would always be useful.

'You can tell me,' he said eventually, 'though I'm not sure I'll be able to do anything.'

'If you listen first,' she said, 'that will be a start.'

He nodded, looked down at the clipboard and made to write something.

'No notes, please,' she said. 'What we say is between us unless I say so. Do you agree to that? No one must know I was here.'

He looked at her again, thinking about that, chewing slightly on his lower lip. 'Of course,' he said finally. 'You have my absolute guarantee of confidentiality.'

She sighed, as if relieved, then stood up. The movement startled him. 'I can't sit,' she said, impatiently. 'Not while I'm telling you this. It affects me too much.'

She paced over to his desk and leaned on it, eyes moving quickly over the papers spread across it, reading what she could. Behind her she could hear him waiting. She knew what she was going to say. She had constructed the lie on the way over.

'Five months ago,' she started, turning to face him, 'a woman came to see me—'

'At the Child Protection Team?'

'Yes. She claimed she had been raped ten years ago.' She saw him look down then up, calculating the year.

'That would be nineteen eighty-seven,' he said.

She nodded. He adjusted the glasses on the bridge of his nose. No other reaction.

'The woman told me a terrifying tale,' she continued. 'She said she had been thirteen years old at the time. Somebody kidnapped her, drugged her and used her for sex.' She paused, as if expecting a reaction from him.

He looked back at her, face expressionless. 'Go on,' he said. She thought that perhaps his facial colour had changed fractionally – a little paler, maybe. But it was hardly noticeable.

'They drugged her to control her. They took her to some kind of party and a man was brought in and raped her. That's her account of it.'

He was frowning again. She let the silence grow between them, waiting for him to get uncomfortable with it.

'Just one man?' he asked.

'Yes. Does it matter?'

He shook his head. 'I'm just trying to understand the detail.' He cleared his throat, shifted again in the chair. He wasn't looking at her now. 'Why has she only reported this now?' he asked.

'She only just remembered it happened.'

He placed the pen down on the sofa beside him then took the glasses off. She watched him extract a cleaning rag from his trouser pocket and proceed to clean the glasses deliberately and methodically before replacing them on the bridge of his nose.

'A recovered memory case,' he said, at the end of it all. His voice was calm, unexcited. It had taken him nearly a minute to clean the glasses, nearly a minute, she thought, to control it – assuming Pamela was right, that he was guilty. 'I've heard of such cases, obviously,' he continued. 'But why tell *me* about it?'

'She named a police officer as the rapist.'

Once again, she waited for a suitable reaction to the lie. Relief would have worked – relief that he wasn't in the frame (assuming Pamela wasn't lying). Or, if Pamela was wrong, shock that it was a policeman. Instead, he continued to look at the paperwork on his lap, no movement at all in his features. The blankness wasn't what she was used to. It was unimpeachable, of course, controlled, effective. But it wasn't what she was used to.

'You don't seem surprised,' she said.

'Should I be? Police officers are as capable of crimes as anyone else.' He looked at his watch – not a quick movement, but deliberate, intended to convey something to her. It wasn't that his interest was gone. He wanted her out. He was handling it, but he was uncomfortable.

'That officer has not been prosecuted,' she said.

He nodded again, as if expecting this. 'I'm not a lawyer, he said, slowly, 'but I imagine it's quite hard to find evidence from that long ago.'

'We had her account. She could have told that to a jury.'

'Did you send the case to the CPS?'

'No. My superiors decided it wasn't worth it.'

'And that's your complaint?'

'Yes. I think that because he was a police officer – a high-ranking police officer – because he was in a position of considerable power and public trust, because it would look bad for the Force, because he was one of their own – for all these reasons they decided to bury it.'

'You're sure it wasn't because the case was hopeless? One person's word against another – ten years between. Who could prepare a defence after ten years? It wouldn't be fair to prosecute, don't you think? We will have the European Convention on Human Rights enacted into our domestic legislation before long. It's a manifesto promise—'

'What about Nazis? Would you say the same about Nazi war criminals?'

He stopped speaking and for the first time she saw him colour slightly, tiny pinpricks of blood appearing high up on his cheeks. Not because of the question about Nazis, she assumed, but because he had allowed himself momentarily to run on, giving too much away, defending a possible rapist. He looked at his watch again. She recknoned she had been in the room less than five minutes.

'These appointments are meant to be very short,' he started. His tone was just starting to turn hostile.

She stepped quickly across the floor space towards him. 'I came to you because I thought you would see the problem. But you'd rather the policeman remained in office and got away with it—'

'I'm not saying that,' he interrupted her. 'I'm trying to have a reasonable reaction to your problem. How old was this officer when this happened?'

The question surprised her. She thought about it, thought about what he wanted from it. To minimize the culpability, she guessed. She decided to help him.

'Does that matter? He was sixteen at the time,' she said.

A slight smile appeared on his face. 'Sixteen? He was himself a child, then. He probably hardly remembers the incident. Are we even the same people now as we were that long ago? How much of your childhood do you recall, Officer? Enough to be able to go to trial and defend yourself against something someone said happened twenty years ago?'

'Ten years ago.'

'Ten. Twenty. Whatever. I think your problem is an evidential one, something to take up with your supervisors. That would be my advice to you.'

She shook her head. She had intended to act it, but *felt* unease now. The differences were subtle, but they were there. He had not reacted normally since she had walked into the room. He had reacted *carefully*.

'You don't want that advice, I see—'

'No. On the contrary, I think it's very . . .' she pretended to consider her words, 'very *reasonable*. You have, as you say, reacted *reasonably* to what I've told you.'

She watched a thin line of sweat break free from his hair and trickle across his temple.

'It's hot in here,' she remarked.

'Yes.' He looked away from her. 'What was this officer's name?' he asked.

She shook her head. 'No names.'

He shrugged. 'As you wish. I would have made enquiries if you were prepared to tell me.' He looked at his watch again. 'Was there anything else?'

She shook her head, still staring at him.

'Well, I'm very busy,' he said. He couldn't meet her eyes. 'We could discuss this at greater length, but you should write to me about it first. That's the way it's normally done.'

She decided she'd had enough and moved towards the door, but he stopped her as she was opening it.

'DC Sharpe!'

She turned back to him.

'Have you been a detective long? Forgive me for saying so, but you seem to be taking things personally.'

'It should be just a job, right?'

'Not just a job. But experience gives a different perspective on things sometimes. I don't mean to be rude . . .' he paused momentarily, 'but I believe I remember your name. Weren't you the officer involved in those shootings last year?'

She had no doubt that he remembered nothing. Someone had checked her for him.

'I've been a detective for eight years,' she said. 'I've been in the job for fifteen. I'm sure you are aware of that already. Maybe you know about my past. But I certainly know about yours.'

She watched the colour leave his cheeks. Before he could say anything she stepped towards him. He moved back slightly in the chair, as if she were on the point of hitting him. She took a West Yorkshire Police pen from her pocket. It was a cheap little blue biro, stencilled with the Force logo and motto 'In the Public Service'.

'Let me give you one of our pens,' she said to him. She held it towards him. He took it automatically, not thinking. 'It's got the switchboard number on it,' she said. 'In case you need to call us. We're here to serve. It says that on the pen.'

TEN

Pete Bains stood at the patio doors leading into his garden. He had a glass of iced coffee in his right hand, the left in the pocket of a pair of faded blue jeans. The patio doors were open and the mid-morning sun was bright on his clean, white T-shirt. His hair was still wet from his morning shower, his feet were bare. It was hot and he looked relaxed.

He wasn't. He had gotten away from the Keighley incident room only five hours before. It had taken him half an hour to drive back to his home in Heaton, and he had been unable to sleep for another two. He didn't look tired, but he was. Even the brief two hours he had managed had been fitful, disturbed. Shade was bringing back to him things he had hoped to forget.

He was staring at the sunlight reflecting off the cracked blue paintwork along the tiles of his drained swimming pool. The kidney-shaped pool was at the bottom of his rear garden, almost completely surrounded by overgrown vegetation, some of which had trailed into the pool itself. Once upon a time the whole area had been landscaped. What now looked like a jungle had been carefully tended garden plants, bushes and creepers. They had paid a company to do it, though looking at it now that was hard to believe. Nature had moved on quickly. For Bains it hadn't been so easy.

The land sloped sharply down from the back of the house to the terraced area where the pool had been built. From where he was standing he could see almost to the bottom of it. There was no shallow end – the depth was the same from one end to the other – 1.5 metres. When there had been water in it the level had come to below his waist.

His parents had put it in – paid for it, designed it, stood looking proudly at it, organized barbecues alongside it for their friends. A status symbol. They had done everything but swim in it, in fact. No one had swam in it. When it had been filled Bains had got into it once and once only, but on that occasion there hadn't been a need to swim.

That had been 30 July 1989. A Sunday. The pool had been completed towards the end of May of that year and though there had been at least one barbecue that he could remember during June, no one had been brave enough to take their clothes off and swim in the thing, despite the heat. No one would ever swim in it now.

There was no chance of him ever forgetting the 30 July. That wasn't what Shade had brought back. The 30 July was a headache that would always be with him. It hadn't started as a headache. It had started as a grief so intense he had been unable to see, talk, walk, think. It had been like something physical, suffocating him, weighing him down. At first it had been so total there hadn't been room for guilt. Just loss. The crushing consciousness of loss each and every minute, each hour, each day.

Then the guilt had come. What had been 'like' something physical turned slowly into the real thing – a devastating pain behind his eyes, so intense he couldn't function, couldn't even get out of bed. Almost every year since it had happened he had been forced to take time off work to get past it, to calm it, to reduce it to normal proportions. Or sufficiently 'normal' so that people wouldn't be able to tell what was happening inside him. There hadn't been any real sense to the word 'normal' since that day. And the headache had never gone away, not completely.

But there were other details from 1989 that he had discarded, details from around the time, from the delayed consequences. Judge Michael Kenyon was one of those details.

He stepped out through the door and onto the first flags of the patio, now trailed with weeds and moss. His hand reached out and closed around the patio door handle, gripping it tightly, then letting go and running his fingers along the metal in a more careful way, looking down at it, thinking, taking himself back. The door handle was long – an effective lever for a latch mechanism that was otherwise very stiff – and made of some kind of alloy, plated with silver or nickel. He had touched it so much in the last eight years it had worn down to the cheap base metal beneath, all remnants of where her actual fingers had touched it obliterated by the movement of his own. It had taken him nearly the whole eight years to come to terms with the fact that so much could turn on the design of a door handle. It was a lesson good enough to give perspective on virtually any problem life could throw up. Including the present one.

He looked away from it and pictured Kenyon's face. He had not seen Kenyon yesterday, when they had searched his premises. The judge had decided not to stay. And, perhaps surprisingly, he had not come across the man in court even once since 1989. So his memories were of a Michael Kenyon eight years younger, in a wig and gown.

Kenyon's hair had been totally white, whiter than the horsehair in the wig he wore. Bains thought he had the hair of a corpse. He knew this because, as he had delivered his judgement upon him, Kenyon had first emptied the court and then removed his wig. So Bains had got a good look at his face, from the raised platform of the witness box, not seven yards from where Kenyon was sitting above him, looking down on him, judging him.

But details were difficult to recall from back then. He could remember the white hair, the hooked nose, but little else. Nothing about the eyes, for instance, nothing about the expression on his face – whether it had been contemptuous, disgusted, impassive. He hadn't a clue.

But he did remember the words. '*I have heard that you are under considerable personal pressure,*' Kenyon had said, the tone aloof, yet matter of fact. '*I have been told the reasons why. I'm not interested. Nothing can excuse your barbarity. It is clear to me that you have acted like an ape, an animal. You were trusted to be professional and you chose to be the precise opposite. Your actions have destroyed this case.*'

Bains didn't care about the case, didn't care that they had lost it – not now, maybe not ever. Without his 'actions' – alleged actions (he had never been prosecuted for them, let alone convicted) – there would have been no case at all. And that had to be true even on Kenyon's specious reasoning. Kenyon had binned the job because the defence had produced photos to back up the defendant's claim that Bains had beat a confession out of him. Without the confession, the judge had decided, there was insufficient evidence to leave the case to the jury.

Bains didn't even care that Kenyon had been told his story – the intense, private, personal details of the 30 July and the months that had followed, culminating in the brutality he was said to have inflicted on the prisoner. Bains had listened without movement or words as DS Bill Edwards had spoken of him as if he were a psychiatric patient. Kenyon had failed to find even a shred of understanding for the blackness he had been functioning within, but that hadn't bothered him either. That a judge should fail to respond as a normal human being didn't surprise him.

What Bains had cared about were the words Kenyon had used. He had spent his whole life shrugging off such malice, moving on despite it. But on this one occasion the hook had caught. Kenyon's voice might have been measured, controlled and calm, but the choice of words gave him away. The undertones were obvious – the comparison to animals, specifically to apes – the suggestion that Bains was somehow inhuman, that what he had done was *barbaric*. And behind it all the upper-class accent, the assumption of superiority, hearing the pathetic tale of domestic loss and responding only with the dismissive languor of the English public school: '*I'm not interested. You were an ape.*'

For that – at the time – Bains had hated Kenyon in a way that was beyond rationality. Everything that had been going on inside him had, on that day, suddenly become attached to this stupid white judge, who dismissed his case and smeared his character with uncalled-for excess.

There had been no enquiry at that point. The defendant was another middle-class bastion of local society, a part of the secret class club Kenyon belonged to – an estate agent called Eric Pardoe, accused by a thirteen-year-old of rape. No one knew at that point whether he had fabricated his injuries on the night of his release and concocted the torture scene the defence had set out in court in order to walk free. But Kenyon had heard enough to make his mind up without an enquiry.

It had been enough for D&C as well. Bains had been suspended at once. An enquiry lasting thirteen months had followed. After which a report had gone up the line to the CPS recommending no further action. The CPS had concurred. There had been no record of Pardoe's injuries in the custody record. He had walked out of the station on his own two feet. That he had apparently collapsed on his way home and been admitted to a hospital with internal injuries made no difference. People other than DC Bains could have been responsible for that. There was only Pardoe to say they weren't.

Bains frowned, looking down again at the door handle. It was unlike him to hold a grudge. That was something done by those who lacked perspective, who cared about the little things because they had never been deprived of the big things. Bains knew better. And if he had borne a grudge all these years he had done so without realizing it.

But Shade had brought back to him that he did have a grudge, that the hatred for Judge Michael Kenyon was still there.

ELEVEN

It didn't take her long to work out that Pamela had given her a duff address in Otley. Karen had guessed as much anyway. At the beginning of their interview the day before, Pamela had refused to give any address at all. Karen had pushed her on it enough to realize that the reluctance was down to fear – fear that either Karen or another police officer (in uniform, in her worst-case scenario) would at some point turn up at her door and the man she probably lived with, the man who no doubt had delivered the beating she was still suffering from, would put two and two together and get five, assuming she had reported the assault.

In fact, throughout her time with Karen, Pamela had steadfastly refused to say anything about the assault, refused even to acknowledge that she *had* been assaulted. She would not let Karen get her medical attention, would not even acknowledge that she was injured.

When Karen had returned to the address question at the end of the interview – this time insisting on a contact point before the allegation would be even registered as a complaint – Pamela had grudgingly given the address of the decaying council semi on the Western Estate in Otley that Karen was now parked outside. Pamela had begged Karen to promise she would never use the address, never pay her a visit. Karen had promised. It was just after one-twenty and she had already been up and knocked on the door to number eight, Priestley Road. A woman in her late sixties had answered, denied all knowledge of 'Pamela Mathews' and allowed her in to check. The address was duff.

She used her mobile to call the ACR and got an electoral roll check against Pamela Mathews. There were eleven in the Bradford area, but none in Otley. If it came to it she would have to contact all eleven. Or take the gift she was being handed and forget about it. But Geoff Reed had gotten under her skin now. She didn't want to leave it.

She decided to give it half an hour. Pamela had lied about the address, but she guessed that the lie would have been fairly close to the truth. Suspicious, Karen had asked her to describe the location of the street and she had been able to do so without problems. So she probably lived in this street or one of the two identical streets either side. That she wasn't on the electoral roll meant little – maybe she simply hadn't registered, or hadn't been at the address long. Karen pulled the car out onto the main road, parked where she could see the exit to Priestley Road and waited.

For once she struck lucky. Within minutes a blue Nissan Sunny was turning into the street. She recognized Pamela as the front seat passenger. The driver was a male she didn't know. She watched as the car reversed into a space outside what she calculated was number twenty-three or twenty-five, about fifty yards further up on the opposite side to number eight. The man got out first, then walked round to open the door for Pamela. A gentleman, Karen thought, and waited for the real reason to emerge.

She mentally chalked up his description: five eleven to six foot, thin but wiry looking, dressed casually in khaki chinos, a blue check shirt and black sports jacket, black shoes that might have been boots, she couldn't be sure from the distance. Boots were good for kicking, of course – she remembered the bruises on Pamela's legs.

He had short dark-brown hair, possibly waxed on top, a dark neat moustache. He looked normal enough, wouldn't stand out in a crowd. Some people had their class and occupation written all over them – police were the worst for it – this guy didn't. She wouldn't have a clue what he did just by looking at him. He walked confidently, shoulders back, attention focused on the door he was opening, not even a quick glance around him to check for company. He looked to be in his late thirties.

At the open door he had some kind of argument with Pamela, who didn't immediately get out of the vehicle. Karen couldn't get the words from fifty yards away, but the male wasn't shouting. After half a minute or so he leaned into the vehicle, took hold of Pamela with both hands and dragged her out onto the road. The ease with which he completed the movement betrayed a strength behind the skinniness. Pamela stumbled as she brought her feet through the door and fell to one knee. He stepped back then and looked around himself. From his stance Karen thought he was thinking about hitting her. She watched as his glance passed across her car, unsure whether he had clocked her or not. Probably not, she decided, as his next action was to take hold of Pamela's thick, black frizz and wrench her to her feet.

She watched them both walk into one of the houses then. Pamela was shouting things at him, but she walked without assistance and didn't seem particularly afraid of him, from the surface gestures, at least. Whatever she was shouting Karen had a feeling she was drunk; the words were muffled and barely coherent. A typical domestic scene, she thought. None of the neighbours in any of the nearby houses showed any signs of reacting.

She checked her watch and thought about her options. She didn't want to get Pamela another beating. On the other hand, she did want to explain the hopelessness of the situation to her and see what she came up with. But now she had Pamela's true address it would be relatively easy to get the phone number to the place. She could then call and spin some story either to get Pamela to the phone or the partner out of the place. She was on the point of starting up and driving off when the front door opened and the male emerged alone. He was opening the driver's door to the car, keys in hand, when Karen decided. She got out quickly and ran towards him.

He saw her coming before he was in the vehicle, paused, glanced back towards the house, then got in and closed the driver's door just as Karen reached it. She saw him fitting the key into the ignition. She rapped on the window and watched as he looked up at her, raised his eyebrows questioningly, but made no move to open either the door or the window. The expression on his face was untroubled, calm. She took out her warrant card and pressed it against the glass.

'Can you get out of the car, please?' she asked, loud enough for him to hear.

She stepped back; he opened the door and stepped out.

'Yeah, what?' he asked.

She added a note to the mental picture of him – he had dealt with the police before, probably he had a record. You could tell it immediately by the first comment. Only citizens who knew their rights responded to a badge by saying, 'Yeah, what?'

'DC Sharpe,' she said, stepping closer to him. 'This your car, sir?'

'Obviously.' He looked at his watch. 'I'm late. What do you want?'

Karen stepped away from him and pulled her pocket book from her jacket. She looked down the side of the car. 'We'll start with your name,' she said, stepping over to the front of the vehicle.

He didn't respond. She bent down by the fender and put her finger on a sizeable and rusting dent. She guessed he had run it into a wall – the metal was gashed open from the end of the dent to the beginning of the fender in a line about six inches long. The end of the fender was twisted away, a sharp edge pointing outwards. It was nothing and it didn't interest her in the slightest.

'You realize this is a construction and use offence,' she told him. She stood up to find him frowning at her. She smiled at him. 'That's a dangerous condition ticket,' she said. 'If you were to come into contact with a child while driving that—'

'What did you say your name was?' he interrupted her.

'Did you miss it?' she asked, stepping forward until she was about two feet in front of him. Her proximity didn't seem to make him uncomfortable.

'Did you say you were a *detective*?' he asked, stressing her role, putting two and two together now, working out that she wasn't interested in the condition of his car.

'I did,' she said. 'DC Sharpe. Now what's your name? I won't ask a third time.'

'Before what?'

'Before I arrest you.'

He shrugged. 'For what?'

'For not giving me your name and address.'

'Is that an offence?'

'No. But it gives me a power of arrest for common assault.'

He nodded, seeing it coming now. 'Common assault?'

'Yes.' She pointed back to her own car. 'I was sitting over there just now. I watched you assault the woman who walked into that house.' She pointed to the house, noting that it was number twenty-seven.

'Give me a break. You haven't even spoken to her. If you did you would realize she was drunk and I was only—'

'Give me your name.'

He sighed, gritted his teeth, weighed it up. She had asked him three times, she realized. But the last thing she wanted was to arrest him.

'Simon Devereux,' he said finally. He spelled out the surname for her without being asked.

She wrote it down in the pocket book. 'Devereux' sounded foreign, but she had come across it before in Yorkshire. Certainly he had no recognizable foreign accent. No accent at all, in fact, not even a Yorkshire one.

'Date of birth?' she asked.

Another sigh. 'Twentieth of April nineteen fifty-eight.'

That made him thirty-nine. Pamela had said her birthday was 1 June 1974, making her twenty-three and putting a sixteen-year age difference between them. She looked up at him and kept the detail on hold. For now she didn't even know the exact nature of the relationship between them.

'Who was the woman?' she asked.

'Ask her yourself,' he said. 'See if you can get anywhere with her.'

She nodded. 'Maybe I will. Do you live at those premises, Mr Devereux?'

He shook his head. 'No. She's a friend. That's all. She got drunk and I was helping her out.'

'That right? Have you also been drinking then?' She couldn't smell it on him.

'No. I picked her up from the pub. She called me.'

Karen recalled that Pamela had denied having a mobile phone. Possibly another lie.

'Where do you live then?' she asked him.

'Why?'

She stared at him.

'Dean Lane,' he said after a pause. She didn't know it.

'Where's that? Bradford?'

He paused momentarily, something flickering in his eyes. 'No. Shipley.'

She held his eyes, waiting for him to look away. He didn't.

'House number?'

'Thirty-eight.'

She wrote it all down. She could check it all later, if there was any point.

'What do you do for a living, Mr Devereux?'

'I'm a builder.'

She looked with scepticism at his clothing, then his hands, which were rough enough, the ring and index finger of his right hand stained yellow from holding cigarettes cupped under his palm. The nails looked dirty and cracked enough to be builder's nails. Only the clothing looked out of place, a touch too neat.

'Where are you going now?' she asked.

'To work, if you'll let me. Is there any point to any of this?'

She ignored the question. 'Where do you work?'

'The Wimpey site in Shipley.'

'You're lucky I'm busy with something else,' she said, looking pointedly at her watch. 'Next time you think to drag someone out of a car by the hair remember that it's assault. This time I'm giving you a warning only. If I see it happen again I'll do something about it. We've had complaints from this neighbourhood.'

'Yeah, right.' He looked bored now, realizing she was going anyway, that nothing was going to happen. His expression said 'bullshit, fuck you'. She looked into his eyes, pausing a moment to read the thoughts. He had eyes so dark it looked like there was no iris. She tried to find the colour of the iris, but couldn't. She held the gaze for a moment longer than was comfortable, and felt a ripple of disturbance in her spine.

She folded her book, nodded to dismiss him and began to walk back to her car. She heard him start the engine and pull off before she had got to it. She got in and waited five minutes, to be sure he hadn't changed his mind, then drove up to number twenty-seven and parked in the space he had just vacated.

When Pamela finally opened the door, the bleary, drunken look began to change to one of outright fear.

'It's all right, Pamela,' Karen said, silencing her. She stepped through the opening before Pamela could shut it in her face. 'He's not here. I know. I checked. I need to speak to you—'

'But I told you never—'

'It's important.' Karen spoke loudly, communicating the message 'shut up and listen'. Pamela shrank back inside herself immediately, making Karen regret her tone. Pamela responded well to commands.

Karen quickly took in her physical state. She was still dressed, but looked crumpled, like she had collapsed onto a bed or a sofa as soon as she had got in. The bruises were still livid and fresh. There was a smell of stale wine on her breath. She clearly hadn't witnessed the exchange with Devereux.

'Get your stuff,' Karen said. 'I'll take you to Weetwood nick. We'll be safe enough there—'

'I can't . . . I can't do anything like that . . . he made me . . .'

'I don't care. Get your stuff. I've just spoken to him outside . . .' She saw the panic leaping into her eyes. 'I pretended I was interested in his car, Pamela. He doesn't know, so don't worry. But I've seen him is what I'm saying. You've no need to be frightened of him. Besides, he told me he doesn't even live here.'

'He lied. He lives here.'

'He said he lived someplace called Dean Lane.'

'Dean Lane?' She frowned. 'Maybe he knows someone there. He doesn't live there. He lives in fantasy land. You're more likely to find him punting smack from his flat on the Thorpe Edge.'

'Smack? He told me he had work. On the Wimpey site in Shipley?'

Pamela shrugged. 'He doesn't work. He lied to you. He's a good liar.' There was a depth of sadness and despair to her voice that Karen hadn't noticed before.

'Look, Pamela. If he did this to you,' she pointed to the bruises on her face, then you don't need to just put up with it—'

'He did not do it. He hasn't touched me.'

'I saw him drag you from the car.'

'I was drunk. He was helping me.'

Karen paused, took a breath. It wasn't worth it. No matter what she felt about it, it wasn't worth it. 'OK. Whatever. That's not what I'm here about. Are you coming with me or not?'

She waited while Pamela tried to think it through and compute the consequences. She watched the expression of fear give way to something far less obvious.

'My car's outside,' she said after a while. 'We going or not?'

Pamela nodded.

TWELVE

'This is where we're at, Pamela. I want you to be clear about it. That's why I brought you in here.'

They were in one of the interview rooms at Weetwood Police Station. Just being there reminded Karen that, if she wanted, she had another legitimate reason to hand off Pamela's complaint. Though Pamela had made an allegation of a crime that had taken place on Keighley Division – her childhood address being in Oxenhope – she now lived in Otley, on Weetwood Division, just over the boundary from Western Area CPT. If she wanted to she could get Leeds CPT to deal with it.

'There's one of me,' she said. 'Just one. That's all there's ever going to be looking into your story. We haven't the manpower to do it any other way. Now, as it happens, I believe you.' She paused to let that sink in. Across the table from her, Pamela looked truculent, irritable. 'But for your account to get anywhere – for us to be able to do anything with it – I need corroboration. In a case like this that is difficult. Usually next to impossible.'

'What do you need?'

'Well, I'll tell you what I've looked for so far. So far I've been looking for reports of missing children from ten years ago in the Keighley and Oxenhope area. I've found nothing.'

Pamela looked down at the table, silent. Karen made a mental note that, control eroded by the alcohol, her voice was acquiring just a tinge of an inflexion other than her normal mild West Yorkshire accent. Karen guessed Liverpool.

'I assume,' she continued, 'that if you had been kidnapped from your parents they would have reported your loss. We keep all those reports. You told me that you thought you had been kidnapped from a country lane in Oxenhope. You told me your parents lived there.

That means they would have gone to Keighley nick. I've spent three hours looking through all the reports of lost children from nineteen eighty-seven held at Keighley. There's no report for Pamela Mathews.' She waited for Pamela to look up at her, then asked the question: 'Why is that?'

Pamela began to cry immediately. Karen watched her face and demeanour change within seconds. Eyes cast down, shoulders slumped, bottom lip stuck out, she looked guilty, threatened, like a little child caught stealing. The tears ran silently down her cheeks. Karen waited, but after a few minutes it became clear she wasn't going to answer.

'I asked you about whether you went to the doctor, Pamela, after you were rescued. Do you remember that?'

Pamela nodded without looking at her, or stopping the tears. She hadn't said she had been 'rescued', in fact. She had been unable to remember anything about how she had got away from her captors.

'*Were* you rescued? Do you remember that now?'

She shook her head again, a slight blubbing sound coming from her lips. She mouthed the words, '*I don't know. I don't know.*'

'I asked about the doctor because your parents would have taken you there. Tomorrow morning I'm going to go round all the surgeries in Oxenhope to try to find medical records for the Mathews family. Will I find any, or will that be a waste of my time?'

More tears, louder now.

'You've been lying to me, haven't you?'

She started to sob uncontrollably. Karen looked around for a box of tissues, but there was nothing in the room apart from the table, two chairs and themselves. She reached across the table and placed her hand on Pamela's arm, gently. When there was no response she squeezed it slightly. She was surprised when Pamela's other hand moved away from her face and closed over her own. She looked at the fingers curling around her palm, gripping her like a baby. They were long and slender. In some other world they would have been elegant. The hand was trembling.

'You don't have to worry if you have lied,' she said. 'You just have to tell me what was a lie and why. So I can save myself doing things I needn't do. You're not going to get into trouble.' She tried to keep her voice soft. The fingers tightened around her hand, the tears continued. 'Pamela.' She squeezed the arm again. 'Pamela. Are you listening to me?'

It took a few minutes for things to change. Gradually, the sobbing began to stop. Finally, she took her hand away from Karen's, wiped her eyes and looked at her.

'I lied,' she said. 'I'm sorry. I lied.' Her voice was shaky, still full of guilt and fear.

Karen nodded, moving her hand away from her arm. 'I know,' she said. 'Don't worry about it. *Did* you live in Oxenhope?'

Pamela shook her head.

'You lived in Liverpool, right?'

'Yes.'

'Were you kidnapped from there?'

'I think so.' She whispered the words.

'Do you remember?'

'Not really. I remember it happening, but I don't know where . . .'

She looked lost again, forlorn, the absence of the memory apparently genuine and a source of distress to her.

'But you lived in Liverpool,' Karen said. 'Where, exactly?'

Pamela looked back at her across the table, meeting her eyes. 'Crosby.'

'OK. Do you have an address?'

'Why?'

'Because I will check the doctors' surgeries there. You were kept for days, you said. Your parents will have taken you to the doctor when—'

'No.'

Karen frowned. 'No? No what?'

'No. They wouldn't. And it wasn't "them". It was just my mum. I never knew my dad.'

'You told me yesterday that your mum and dad died about five years ago, within a very short—'

'I lied. I never knew my dad. It was my mum. And she won't have taken me to the doctor.'

Karen sat back, perplexed. 'Why not, Pamela?'

Pamela began to cry again, shaking her head, biting her left hand. 'I can't tell you,' she said, words barely clear. 'I can't tell you. She didn't take me to a doctor. I don't know why . . .'

'Was she involved in your kidnapping?'

Furious head shaking. 'No. No. No. Not my mum. No.'

'OK. Let's take it from another direction then. Why have you told me these lies, Pamela?'

'Because I wanted you to investigate it. You wouldn't have taken it if I'd told you it had happened in Liverpool. You'd have told me to go to the Liverpool police ...' She brought the words out between huge racking sobs that made her wince with chest pain. Karen had guessed the day before that her ribs were at least bruised. She had no doubt that Pamela had still not sought medical attention.

'It's all right, Pamela,' she said, noticing that she was speaking to her the same way she spoke to Mairead when she was distressed. 'Just slow down,' she continued. 'Calm down, take your time.'

'I wanted you to investigate this,' Pamela said. '*You*. I didn't want to go to Liverpool. I wanted *you*.'

'Me? Why? Why me?'

'Because Helen told me you were good. Helen said to come to you. She said you would get him, she said you would do it.'

'Who is Helen?'

'Helen Mawson. A friend.'

Karen shook her head, frowning again. 'Do I know her?'

'She came to you four years ago. Her boyfriend was beating her up. He broke her jaw. You got him to court and he served eighteen months.'

The name meant nothing to Karen. But that wasn't surprising. The case details didn't sound particularly memorable. She had dealt with perhaps a hundred such cases in the last four years.

'So why lie about your parents dying?' she asked. 'Did they die?'

'I don't know. I never knew my dad. I don't know where my mother is. She might be dead. I don't know. I'm sorry. I just don't know. I told you that because I was ashamed ...'

'Ashamed? Of what?'

'I don't know. I don't know ...'

Karen leaned forward. There was something – perhaps a lot of things – that Pamela wasn't telling her, but right now it didn't matter. 'OK, Pamela,' she said, her voice firm. 'Listen to me. Are you listening?' She waited for the crying to stop, waited until Pamela was looking at her. 'These are the facts. You have made an allegation of something called historic child abuse – that is, it happened a while back. The courts don't like that. They like people to complain as soon as it happens—'

'But that's not—'

Karen held a hand up. 'Wait. Just listen. I don't make the rules up. I don't make the laws. I'm just telling you how it is, like it or not. What you said happened to you, happened ten years ago. Juries don't like that. Worse than that, though, is something called "recovered memory syndrome". The courts, the lawyers, the judges, the juries, *really* don't like that. That's what you have. You have a recovered memory – one you've only just remembered, long after the event – of historic abuse. To do anything with that, to get the lawyers even to think of running it, I need more than just your story. They will not let you go to court and put Geoffrey Reed MP in the dock on the strength of *just* your story, on *just* what you have told me happened. Do you understand what I'm telling you?'

'Yes. You want more than I've told you.'

'Not more. More from *someone* else, or *somewhere* else. Something that backs it up and doesn't come from you.'

'But it happened. And I've told you when. *You* should be able to find out where it happened.'

'What good would that do? Even if I could do it, which I doubt I can on the detail you've given me, knowing *where* it happened won't help after ten years.'

'OK, I'll tell you more.'

Karen sat back in her seat. She let a silence settle between them. She didn't want to encourage Pamela to make things up just to keep the thing going.

'Like what?' she asked, eventually. 'What are you going to tell me? Whatever you tell me, I can't see it making this into—'

'I've remembered more.'

Karen raised an eyebrow, sceptical.

'I remember more all the time. Little details. But that's not what I mean. I remember worse. Something big.'

Pamela's eyes were dry now, the edge to her voice betraying something else, an anger, a suppressed rage. Her mood was changing.

'I could take another statement off you,' Karen said. 'But I'm not sure that it would make any—'

'This would,' Pamela said quickly. 'This will make a difference.'

Karen sighed, then nodded at her. 'OK. Tell me.'

73

'I wasn't alone. I wasn't alone in there. That's what I haven't told you.'

Karen sat motionless, staring fixedly into Pamela's damaged face. The bruises made it difficult to judge her expression, to guess accurately whether she was lying. Karen had not suspected the previous lies at all. She slotted that fact away as a little warning marker – that Pamela could lie like an actress.

'Who were you with?' she asked.

Pamela paused, her eyes flickering with cold strength for a brief moment, then she looked away and was quiet. Karen said nothing. A tiny, strangled sob escaped from Pamela's throat. When she looked back towards Karen her eyes were brimming with tears again.

'There were two little girls in there with me,' she said, voice cracking.

'Two little girls. I even remember their names. Anna and Kirsty.'

She stopped again. Her legs began to shake violently under the table. She moved the chair back and leaned over them, hunched up as if she had a sudden, severe stomach cramp.

'Are you OK, Pamela?'

She nodded, still hunched over her legs.

'Are you in pain?'

'No. No pain. I'm remembering.' Her voice was breathless, the words rushed.

'What do you remember? Where was this? Where was it that they were with you?'

'In both places. In the playroom and in that ... other place ... They were in that ...' she faltered, unable to say it, 'in that *hole* with me. That trench in the ground ...'

Karen held her breath. 'What do you remember about them?'

There was a long silence. Pamela began to rock slightly from side to side, then wrapped her arms around her legs and pulled them close to her chest, hugging herself. There was a faint moaning coming from her mouth. Suddenly she sat bolt upright in the chair, looking directly at Karen with blank, dry eyes.

'They died,' she said, voice perfectly steady. 'They starved to death in that hole. They died. I was there with them when it happened.'

THIRTEEN

Munro watched the door to the lecture theatre opening and closing. They were coming in streams now, one or two every minute. Mark Harrison had given in at lunchtime, upgrading Operation Shade to Category A and assigning forty detectives, culled from across the area, plus all the technical back-up he needed. Already there were nearly 200 uniforms out on Ilkley Moor, searching. Munro had fixed the 'first' briefing for 3.30 p.m. It was 3.15 now and he was watching the seats fill.

From the large wall clock behind him he could hear the second hand ticking off the seconds, relentlessly. He felt something like satisfaction, vindication, but also fear. Was it all too late? Time was against them now. He watched the detectives shambling in at a leisurely pace and suppressed an urge to shout at them. Somewhere out there – if they were lucky – a little girl was relying on them.

Restless, he stood up and began to fiddle with a marker pen for the whiteboards lined up to one side of the stage. The enquiry was in a different room, a different station. No room at Keighley to run a Cat A, so they were down in The Tyrls now, Bradford Central, with an annexe at Ilkley for the local work. Next door to the theatre he was now in, in the large conference room, Mark Harrison was finishing a press conference to which he, Munro, had pointedly not been invited. The papers, the radio, the TV – everyone was there except the enquiry SIO. Harrison had given in to him, but not without chalking it up against him.

Munro was calm about that. Since Phoenix they had kept him off the big stuff. He had spent a year working three multi-handed armed robbery operations. It was good work, but it wasn't senior SIO work. This was the first job worthy of the rank and though they hadn't intended it like this, hadn't even intended to give it to him, they couldn't take it off him now.

He read the three words he had doodled in big red letters on one of the whiteboards: *TIME. SPEED. RUN!!!!*

No one seemed to have noticed.

At 3.35, with the seats in the hall almost filled and Ricky Spencer standing beside him and ready to kick off, Harrison walked through the doors and beckoned to Munro. He sighed and told Spencer to start without him if he wasn't back in five minutes, cover the admin and domestics, and, if necessary, get onto the teams. He would pick up with the pep talk, the motivation, the lines. Spencer looked phased for a moment. He had been nowhere near addressing rooms of forty detectives.

'It's the same lines as yesterday,' Munro said. 'Just bigger teams. You'll be OK with it. Yeah?'

Spencer nodded, uncertainty in his eyes.

Harrison took Munro through to the now empty conference room where he had just held the press briefing. There were some technician types in there, dismantling spotlights and reflectors they had in for the TV cameras. Harrison asked them to leave and closed the door on them. They sat down, Harrison one side of the big conference table, Munro the other. The room still smelled of body heat and sweat. All the windows were open and the day was hot.

Mark Harrison, the ACC for the Western side of the Force, was a tall man – though not quite reaching to Munro's six four – with sallow, leathery skin, prominent cheekbones and breath that always stank. When he smiled his teeth showed as yellowing and crooked. He rarely made decisions that commanded respect with operational officers. Those who could recall him from his time as DS or DI remembered a man who was good at delegation, unless there was some kind of political capital to be made from a case, in which case he was straight in there, fingers in the pie, handcuffs out for the press and TV reporters. Always an eye to the publicity. Yet, when he spoke at public meetings or gave interviews, he was drab and uninspiring, a damp squib.

How had he managed to get this far? It was the sort of career story that depressed Munro. Catching criminals would appear very low on Harrison's list of priorities and it would have been that way throughout his career. If he cared at all.

For Sophie Kenyon his involvement might have been fatal. Michael Kenyon had pulled strings on the night of his daughter's disappearance, calling Harrison personally some time before midnight. Harrison had the choice then to turn the report into a major enquiry and allocate a Senior Investigating Officer and proper resources, or leave it to Division. He had left it with the plods until midday Tuesday. Then he had gone for window dressing – an SIO, an operational name – (Shade) and a handful of detectives. Enough, he would have hoped, to keep the judge happy and the press off his back.

But after Munro's press conference to Radio Leeds – hinting that he didn't have enough resources – Kenyon had called Harrison again, shotgunning him into the changes by threatening to go to the press himself and complain. Munro knew this because Harrison had called and told him that morning, the anger plain in his voice.

Munro didn't care. It was Wednesday, 25 June 1997, forty-eight hours since Sophie had last been seen alive, and Harrison had left it too late to make the changes to his resources.

As usual there was a thin sheen of sweat on Harrison's face. Not just on his forehead, but all over. Like he was sweating grease, even now, at three-thirty in the afternoon. Munro wondered whether he was an alcoholic, whether it was the poisons working their way out of him. Every time he had met the ACC he had noticed the same effect. Harrison was impeccably kitted out in the full dress uniform, no doubt specially wheeled out for the press conference, but Munro hoped he had kept the tunic closed for the cameras. As he sat to speak to Munro he loosened the buttons and Munro saw the same spreading patches of dampness beneath his armpits.

'We've been a bit slow on this,' Munro said, not giving Harrison the chance to start.

'Be careful, John,' Harrison said, voice tetchy. 'Be careful what you say to anyone outside these walls. Just in case. It's easy to be wise with hindsight. What would you have done if the man had come to you?'

'A judge? I'd have played it safe, Mark.'

He left it hanging. They were on first-name terms but they hated each other and they both knew it. He watched Harrison staring at him, eyes narrowing, angry that he wasn't falling into line. Harrison wanted Munro to agree with him, respect the authority structure, look for ways to minimize the damage.

'I'm satisfied with my decision,' Harrison said, closing his doubt and Munro's effect on it.

Munro smiled at him. 'As long as *you're* happy, sir,' He was, he realized, bordering on the insubordinate.

Harrison waved a hand dismissively, no longer interested in his views. 'It's your problem now, John.'

'Yes. I know that. And the clock is ticking against me. I'm about to start the first briefing—'

'I won't keep you long. I just wanted to make clear to you what is at stake.'

Harrison paused as his pager went off. He unhooked it, read the message then placed it on the table in front of him.

'The BBC,' he said. 'In London. They want an interview for the national news. See what you've done, John?'

'What *I've* done?'

'Getting the press involved.'

'I had to. I needed witnesses. I needed to fix people on the time and place of her disappearance. I needed all that quickly and—'

'Yes. Yes. Yes. But you didn't need to wind it up into something it wasn't. You did that for *you*, John, not for Sophie Kenyon. For your career.'

Munro frowned and started to speak, anger rising quickly within him. Harrison held up a hand to stop him. He ignored it.

'I resent that. I resent that you—'

'Shut up and listen, John.'

'—are suggesting that I would—'

'*I said shut up.*'

Harrison raised his voice only slightly. Munro stopped. Harrison waited in silence, staring at him. When Munro broke eye contact, Harrison started speaking again.

'That was a silly thing to do, John,' he said. 'I didn't appreciate it. I think this girl is probably still somewhere harmless. I could be wrong. But even if I'm not, I'm still your boss. You need to remember that. You may have got what you want for now – a major enquiry – but when this is over I'm going to come back to this. Your actions were not *corporate* yesterday. They surprised me.'

Munro bit his tongue. It was a ticking-off session, as he had suspected it would be. He would put up with it, move on, get on with his job. Harrison didn't know what made him tick. *He* was satisfied with his motivations. Harrison was wrong.

'What you've achieved,' Harrison continued, 'is to put yourself under the spotlight. It's a harsh place to be if you get it wrong. You more than most should know that.' He paused. Munro kept his mouth shut. 'You're about to discover what happens to a major enquiry when the national media gets hold of an abducted child. It will be instructive for you. I predict that by this time tomorrow you will be drowning in actions. I hope you're up to dealing with it.' He stood up, apparently finished.

'Is that all, sir?' Munro asked, looking at his watch.

'Not quite.' Harrison was buttoning up the tunic again. 'Karen Sharpe. I believe you know her.'

Munro frowned, surprised. 'I've worked with her. Why?'

'Is she on your enquiry?'

'No.'

'Why not? She works from the CPT. I thought you were taking everyone from there?'

'Not everyone. We had to leave some to keep it ticking over.'

'You sure there're not more personal reasons?'

Munro paused, risking a glance at Harrison's face. What exactly did he know about Karen Sharpe and himself? His expression said nothing. 'No,' he said, carefully. 'No personal reasons. But I wouldn't want to work with her again. For professional reasons.'

'You don't trust her? Or something else?'

Munro stood up. Spencer would be starting the briefing now. He needed to get on with it. He couldn't see what Harrison was getting at. 'Where is this going, sir?' he asked. 'What has Karen Sharpe to do with anything?'

Harrison shrugged and began to pull on his black leather gloves, holding the dress cap in the crook of his arm as he did so. 'Does Geoffrey Reed come up anywhere in your enquiries so far?' he asked.

Munro was even more taken aback. 'The MP?'

'Yes.'

'No. Not that I know of.'

Harrison nodded. 'Good. Sharpe has been pestering him about some child abuse allegation. I just wondered if it was because she was on your team, working for you.'

'No. It will be her CPT stuff. I know nothing about it.'

79

'You don't think she would be better under your nose?'

'Under my nose?'

'Where you could keep an eye on her.'

'She's not my problem, not my responsibility. Why would I wish to do that?'

Harrison seemed to think about this for a moment, then fitted the cap on his head, gave a short nod and started for the door. 'I'll have to have a word with her, then,' he said. He left without looking back at Munro.

Munro waited for the door to close then walked after him, puzzled by the questions. It was a long time since Karen Sharpe had been thrown into his field of vision. He felt a slight bitter taste in his mouth. Sharpe's activities on Phoenix were largely responsible for him being cast into the investigative wilderness. He certainly didn't want her anywhere near his squad.

As he walked the short distance to the lecture theatre he reflected that 'having a word' with Karen Sharpe would be a complete waste of time. But Harrison could find that out for himself.

FOURTEEN

Driving once more along the Aire Valley trunk road, Karen reflected that, so far, she hadn't even 'crimed' Pamela Mathews's allegations. At some point – early on in the investigation – every report was meant to be phoned through to the Crime Information System bureau. That way a crime number was given, the details were entered onto the CIS active database, the offence was registered for bean-counting purposes and – most crucially for Karen – the thing was up there on screen, replete with details and names, accessible on any terminal across West Yorkshire by any supervisor who cared to look. Ready to be managed, opened and interfered with. Until she crimed it, Pamela's story didn't exist for the performance managers, crime analysts and supervisors. Right now, it was all hers.

But that was going to have to change. Nobody cared about the shopping squad, nobody cared how long they took to get enquiries going or register them. But this wasn't just abuse now. Pamela had made it into a murder. If Karen sat on it for too long the dirt would begin to fly.

She had a sort of excuse. Her supervisor, Ricky Spencer, was abstracted to Shade and had left her in charge of the unit. The next level up was Chief Superintendent Max Mclean. He had nominal responsibilities for Child Protection, but he worked out of Wakefield HQ and it would be easy enough to say that she had tried him and got nowhere. None of the Command Team were ever around if you wanted them. The lie would be easy and believable.

But why was she hiding it? Why was she even thinking of lying?

At the end of the interview, as she had stood up to fetch some blank statement forms, Karen had caught Pamela looking up at her. Pamela had averted her gaze immediately, but not quickly enough. What Karen had seen was like a reflection, something refracted back through herself. For a moment it was as if the person sitting there crying had slipped sideways, vanished. She saw someone else staring back through that one good, battered eye, a different person entirely.

That was why she was thinking about lying.

Once she crimed it, it would slide out of her hands. No one else would believe Pamela. That was the nature of the beast. Recovered memory – of murder or child abuse – was something they made jokes about in the canteen. They would have to do *something* with it if it included an allegation of murder, but they wouldn't do much with it – not for long. Not without something to back it up.

Karen didn't want that to happen. She had seen something she recognized in Pamela's expression. Pamela had looked for her and found her. She didn't want to let her down.

In addition, she *believed* Pamela. As soon as Pamela had mentioned the two dead girls, warning bells had gone off in her head. She *remembered* something about the discovery of two dead little girls. She just couldn't place the memory.

And there was no easy way to check. For the last few years – since the inception of the Home Office Large Major Enquiry System (HOLMES, as it was known) – each and every murder enquiry had been given an operational name and registered with Force Intelligence. The details were easily retrievable and cross-referenced against names of witnesses, victims and defendants. But back in 1987 she was almost sure that hadn't happened. For crimes from ten years before, there was no database or other systematic resource through which she could search for details of a double homicide. If she wanted the paperwork she either had to remember it herself, find someone else who was old enough to remember it, or call the press.

She didn't want to call the press – at least, not the *Telegraph and Argos*. To ring Phil Patterson and ask about the double homicide of two teenage girls from the same year as her recent query about a sitting MP would set the dogs loose within hours. No journo would sit on that. So she had to remember. But she had not joined West Yorkshire Police until early 1990 (transferring, according to her largely fictional file, from the Met). If she could remember a case about two dead girls from 1990–1 then that didn't fit with Pamela's chronology.

Her pager went off and she slowed down to look at it, reading an unfamiliar number with a Wakefield code. The message was simple.

'Call 01924 609313. Now.' It looked like a number from HQ, but she couldn't be sure. Could they have found out anyway? From another source?

She ignored it. Whoever it was, they would have to do better than that. She was off duty, a half-day leave. The school had called at 3 p.m. and she had spoken to Liz Hodges, a teacher in Year Three. Mairead was in Year Four and Liz didn't teach her, but she was the closest Karen had to a friend up here. That was why she had called and not Mrs Taylor, who took Mairead's class.

Liz had told her that the same problem they had tried to deal with five months ago had occurred again, but worse. Something had happened between Mairead and another pupil. Mairead had lashed out in some way. Immediately Karen had felt a rush of pressure and guilt. Mairead had seemed fine that morning. She thought things had settled down. The reality of it came back to her. She had responsibilities and she wasn't meeting them. The child needed more than she was giving her.

Yet immediately she felt like trying to get out of it. She considered – disgracefully – calling Neil and asking him to deal with it. But he had rung earlier and said he had a conference at five. He couldn't do the school run, couldn't get out there at all. So she would have to do it herself.

She pulled the Volvo into the school car park at just after 4 p.m. She was late, the playground was already empty. She decided to give Force Intelligence a quick try before she went in. After that drew a blank she could dig out someone on the *Yorkshire Post* tomorrow. If that drew a blank then that would probably have to be the end of it. Crime it and move on.

She got a male DC called Cummins, gave her warrant number then went on to explain a version of the truth she hoped wouldn't attract any queries. Someone had made an allegation of historic abuse, she told him, and she was trying to date it by reference to something the victim remembered from the press about a murder that had happened around the same time.

'When roughly was this?' Cummins asked her.

'I would guess around nineteen eighty-seven.'

'Ten years ago? We don't really have stuff from then. We didn't start giving things an entry until the early nineties. If she remembered it from the press you would be better off trying them.'

She paused, on the point of thanking him and hanging up.

'What were the details?' he asked, presumably out of idle curiosity.

'A double homicide,' she replied. 'Two twelve-year-old girls.'

She listened to a long silence.

'She says they were starved to death. That's what—'

'Yes,' he interrupted her. 'Hang on a minute.'

She could hear him typing something on a keyboard. She waited again.

'I remember it,' he said, finally. 'You're lucky. I was over the other side of the county at the time, but it was quite a big one. Two dead girls . . .' He paused again. She heard more typing. 'Here it is,' he said finally. 'Operation Flight.'

'I thought you said you didn't have entries from back then?'

'Not from nineteen eighty-seven. But your victim must have the dates wrong. The bodies were found in December nineteen ninety.'

Karen shook her head. 'That can't be it, then.'

'It's the only one I remember, the only one we have. Two dead girls. Age estimated early teens. Found in a trench on farmland near Bramhope . . .' She could tell he was reading details from the screen.

'Does it have their names?' she asked.

'No. Case is open. They were never identified.'

She felt her breath catch.

'Also, cause of death was uncertain, but more likely blunt instrument trauma, not starvation. So your victim must be wrong there.'

She tried to get her thoughts together. 'Did they get a time of death?'

'Doesn't say here. But they were badly decomposed. The report actually says "skeletal". So they had been there a while.'

She looked over towards the school, remembering what she was supposed to be doing. 'Where's the file?' she asked. 'Can I look at it?'

'It's in stores at Milgarth. That's where the incident room was. You should check with the SIO first. But do you want the rest of the details?'

'The rest?'

'The best bit.' He sounded as if he were enjoying himself now. 'This is why I remembered it. I'm surprised you've forgotten. It made the national news. They were in a trench with a third body. A man called Eric Pardoe. I don't have the details here but I can tell you from memory that he had been put in there later.'

'Later? Later than what?'

'Later than the girls. He'd only been down there a few weeks when they found him. Check this out: he'd been buried alongside them, deliberately and, this is the best bit, he was buried alive.'

Immediately she remembered it. She had been in West Yorkshire only six months, but the details were so unusual they were hard to forget. Eric Pardoe had been a wealthy MISPER. He had owned a big chain of estate agents. He had gone missing and they had found him three weeks later, buried alongside the remains of two little girls. There had been soil from the grave in his stomach and bowels, indicating that he had been alive when he had been put in there, though, as she recalled now, there were other injuries contributing to cause of death. She took a deep breath.

'Who was the SIO?'

'Mark Harrison, the ACC.'

She nodded. She didn't know Harrison, had never met him. 'And it was never detected?'

'It's got a review date in two months' time. It's still open. The review will be a formality. If it's gone this long they've given up on it.'

She felt her pager going off again, unhooked it and looked. It was the same Wakefield number. 'That's been really helpful,' she said to Cummins. 'I've got somebody paging me from up there,' she told him. 'I'll have to go.' She looked down at the number again. 'You don't know who 609313 is, do you?'

She heard him rustling some papers. 'Hang on,' he said. 'We've got a list here.' 'That's the ACC. Or his office anyway.'

'Which ACC?'

'Mark Harrison. You can ask him about Flight when you call in.'

FIFTEEN

Mairead was sitting in the deputy head's office, on a chair by the wall. Liz was behind the desk, marking work. Karen observed them both for a moment through the door window. Mairead wasn't looking at her. She was looking at her feet, but Karen could see by the redness around her eyes and the defeated slump to her shoulders that she had been crying and upset.

She looked completely different to the kid Neil had taken out of the house that morning. Yet probably this had all started then, inside her head, buried away beneath the smiles. Karen felt a surge of guilt, wondering whether 'the incident' would have happened at all if she had gone back home last night instead of sitting in the local. She realized also that it had probably been a long wait for Mairead. She had not rushed out here, as she should have.

She took a breath, knocked and entered. As she walked in, Mairead looked up at her, searching for help, safety, love – she saw the sudden fear that she would be told off instead, rejected. Karen held out her arms without even looking towards Liz. The shit could wait. She had been here before.

They hugged for a long time, standing in the office, Mairead's face pressed tightly against her neck, her arms around her chest, her legs crossed behind her back. They didn't say anything to each other, but Karen could feel the tears on her skin.

When the tears stopped she gently prised Mairead away and stood her on the floor in front of her. She was tall for her age. Her head came up to just below Karen's ribs. Karen glanced at Liz and saw from her expression – watching it all in silence – that she was meant to do the stern face, stress the gravity of the situation. She saw Mairead looking for it too. She smiled at her.

'Don't worry, Mairead, it will be okay,' she said, and held out her hand to her. Mairead relaxed and smiled back at her, hooking her fingers through her own. She felt again a crushing, terrible sense of guilt. Every time she looked into the child's eyes she saw *his* smile, saw her own reflection in it, saw the whole story. She had damaged the child. She would never ever get away from that.

They sat down together opposite Liz. The teacher was a friend, but Karen could tell she hadn't approved of her actions so far.

Liz was black, her skin a deep, obvious shade of black that was about as rare and curious in Skipton as a two-headed sheep. There were Asians throughout the area, but few blacks outside Bradford and Leeds. Liz had told her she was the only African-Caribbean she knew of north of Keighley. Perhaps if she had been short and inconspicuous the hicks wouldn't have noticed. But she was nearly six five, tall, athletic and striking. She had suffered for it. Like Karen, though for very different reasons, she was an outsider. It was the exclusion that had brought them together, the exclusion that had made them friends. Neither of them belonged here.

From the look on Liz's face Karen suspected that what Mairead had done was serious. Maybe she was even liable to be excluded again.

'There's a lot you don't know, Liz,' she said. 'We need to talk.'

Liz started to say something, frowning, but Mairead interrupted her.

'Do you want me to go into the yard, Aunty Karen?' she asked. 'While you talk?'

Karen smiled again. The name – Aunty Karen – as ever made her wince internally, but there had been a slightly cheeky tone to the offer. Liz would have noticed it. Mairead knew already she was safe, she wasn't going to be told off, not really. No matter what she had done. Karen reached out a hand and stroked a long, stray curl of her hair away from her bright blue eyes.

'That would be good, Mairead,' she said.

'I think it would be better if she remained—' Liz started.

'No, Liz, it wouldn't,' Karen said. 'I will need to tell you things too. Trust me on this.'

Liz looked at her for a moment, wondering what Karen could have to say, then nodded.

'OK. Keep to the yard, Mairead.'

Mairead stood up and retrieved her satchel. She kissed Karen quickly on the cheek and walked out, leaving the door open behind her. Karen stood and closed it, then walked over to the window and watched for her to appear in the school yard.

'It's serious, Karen,' Liz said.

Mairead appeared from a door onto the yard, skipping into the sunlight as if nothing had happened. Karen watched her take a tennis ball from her satchel and begin to play with it against a wall.

'What's she done?'

'There's a boy in Year Five,' Liz said. 'A year older than her – Danny Conroy – he has a reputation. We've had to suspend him three times. He's a bully, or can be. I try not to use the word about kids. He's only ten years old, after all. Nobody is evil at that age.'

How old had Thompson and Venables been, Karen thought, when they had stoned Jamie Bulger? Liz was a good person. One of the few she had ever met. And it wasn't that she hadn't lived in the world. Karen knew about her past. That was how she had come to meet her.

'What happened?' Karen asked. She knew already what kind of story she was going to be told.

'He taunted her in some way. I don't know the detail, because Mairead wouldn't tell me.'

Karen glanced back at Mairead, now bouncing the tennis ball off a wall perilously close to a classroom window, then turned away from the window and sat down opposite Liz. 'Is that it?' she asked.

'No. He tried to steal her satchel ... well, not steal it. I don't suppose he was going to keep the thing. Like I said, he's only ten. She wouldn't let him take it. So he punched her and got her into a head lock. Pulled her to the ground. Other kids saw all this and told us about it. Mairead didn't.' Karen nodded. It was the same as last time. She was holding her breath for the conclusion. 'We were dealing with that, were set to exclude him, in fact. Mairead went to the nurse. She was a bit red in the face and had some marks around her neck, but she hadn't been crying, so I didn't think she was badly hurt.'

'Not necessarily,' Karen said. 'It was the same last time. Don't you remember? Her finger was broken then, but she didn't cry. She doesn't. Not in front of strangers.'

Liz nodded. 'Maybe. Anyway, we sent her off to the nurse and sat him outside the head's office while we waited for his parents to arrive. Mairead came out from seeing the nurse and saw him sitting there. The head was around though. Nothing was said. Not then, anyway.'

'She came back?' Karen asked, not surprised.

'Yes. About ten minutes later she walked up to him and sat down beside him. He had his hand on the wooden bench beside him. He says she asked him to apologize. He says he did, though I don't know whether that's true. Mairead says he didn't. It doesn't matter either way, though. She stabbed him through the hand with a compass she'd taken from a science classroom. Straight through his hand, in one side and out the other. She pinned his hand to the bench, Karen. Left it there for everyone to see, walked off with him howling in pain.'

Karen felt sick. She didn't say anything.

'We will have to exclude her,' Liz said.

'No,' Karen said. 'Let me talk to you first.'

Liz sat back. 'I doubt there's much you could say. She stabbed a kid.'

'You said yourself, no one is evil at that age. Let me talk to you. Let me tell you why she is doing these things. Please, Liz. I've listened to you in the past. Please listen to me. There's things I should have told you, things you need to know. About me.'

'About you?'

'Yes. When you hear you will know about Mairead, about why she does these things.' Karen looked at her feet.

Liz waited. 'Go on then,' she said.

Karen looked up at her. 'I can't,' she said. 'Not here. Not now. it's not that simple for me. There's only one other person who knows – Neil – and he doesn't know the worst of it. It's hard for me ...' She tried to think about it. Why couldn't she just tell her? 'Let me take Mairead home now,' she said. 'I'll talk to her first, find out exactly what happened. I need to talk to her. Then you and I can meet. Let's have a drink tomorrow night, maybe?'

'I'm not sure we should be dealing with this kind of thing in a pub.'

'Let's talk as friends, Liz,' Karen said. 'Let's be honest. For what I have to tell you I will need help. Alcoholic help. I can't do it in a school office.'

Liz frowned, concerned now. 'Are you OK, Karen? There's not something wrong? With you, I mean?'

Karen shook her head. 'Nothing that hasn't always been wrong,' she said.

SIXTEEN

'I'd like your permission to look through your chambers at the Crown Court.'

Bains deliberately looked away from Kenyon and checked the time on his watch.

It was nearly eight o'clock. They were standing in what Bains guessed would be called the drawing room, which was where the housekeeper had put him on arrival. He knew the room already, because he had helped search it the day before.

The housekeeper had looked at him with familiar suspicion, then requested his ID. She was an elderly white woman shaped like a pear. She hadn't been around on Tuesday and looked like she had spent most of Wednesday in tears. Spencer had interviewed her that morning, which wouldn't have helped.

As she opened the door to him she had looked nervously towards the gates, scanning for the pack of television and newspaper reporters who had descended on the place that afternoon. Some were still there, but no longer at the door of the house. The SIO had set up barriers at both ends of the street and put a couple of constables on guard. Kenyon was a judge – there were legitimate reasons why he should be protected.

Satisfied he was on their side, the housekeeper had left him alone in the drawing room and went to find Kenyon. The judge had taken more than fifteen minutes to appear.

Bains would not have recognized him from their meeting eight years previously. The man looked older by at least twice that number of years. As he crossed from the door of the room to where Bains was standing by the window Michael Kenyon walked with a hesitant step, hands stretched out slightly to either side, touching the backs of the furniture, as if to guide himself. There was a blank expression on his face and Bains could see the eyes struggling to focus on him from behind rims of dark, tired skin. He looked strained, disorientated, unsteady. Bains caught a whiff of stale alcohol on his breath.

He was utterly unlike the judge who had pronounced with such confidence on Bains' personal tragedy: '*I am not interested.*'

'It's just a routine check,' Bains added. Kenyon sighed, but it was more an expression of confusion than irritation.

He leaned against a bookcase next to the window and blinked. He was dressed in what appeared to be pyjamas and they looked dirty. His hair was still white, but longer – almost down to his shoulders – stiff and unkempt like the hair of an invalid. As he propped himself against the bookcase, one of his legs began to temble.

'Have you found her?' he asked, his voice almost a whisper.

'No, sir. Unfortunately, that's not why I'm here.'

Kenyon's eyes settled on his own and he watched them take in the details, looking from his face to his hands then back again, frowning deeply, something familiar coming to him, trying to remember it.

'I came to ask permission to search your chambers at the Crown Court,' Bains repeated.

'Do I know you, Officer?'

Bains shook his head. 'No. You don't know me.'

Kenyon looked at him in silence. The frown looked deep, angry. Bains waited, looking straight at him. Sooner or later he would remember.

'Why do you want to search my chambers?'

'Like I said, it's just routine.'

Kenyon shook his head. 'I let you search the house. I didn't even know what you were looking for. It's my daughter.' He stopped, biting on his lower lip and looking away from Bains. He was struggling to hold back the tears. 'It's my daughter that has gone missing. You are treating me as if . . . as if . . .'

'It's all routine, sir. You know it is. You know the score, you're a judge. We follow every line, we eliminate all possibilities. It doesn't mean anything.'

The drawing-room door opened and a very small, oriental woman dressed in a long crimson kimono walked in, her face creased with concern. Bains knew it was Kenyon's 'new' wife and had heard descriptions, but her size still surprised him. She was so small and so thin Bains could easily have picked her up and held her above his head. He guessed her weight at less than six stone. Her face and skin contrasted radically with Kenyon's. She was young, wrinkle-free, underdeveloped, in all respects child-like. She walked quickly to where Kenyon was standing and slipped her arm around his waist. Her head reached the height of his chest.

'You should be in bed, Michael,' she said, her English heavily accented. She was speaking to Kenyon but looking at Bains. The look was hostile.

Kenyon stroked her hair. It looked like the gesture of a father. Bains felt a slight prickling in his scalp. He wondered how old the woman was.

'What are you doing here at this time?' she asked him. 'Have you come with good news?'

He shook his head. 'No. I need permission to search your husband's room at the Crown Court.'

'You *are* police?'

'Yes. I am,' he said. 'And if I don't get permission I will have to get a warrant.'

The recognition flashed across Kenyon's face.

'I remember you now,' he said. His voice was almost inaudible. 'You were the officer that tortured Eric Pardoe.'

Bains struggled to keep his expression blank, fought not to react violently, in tone or in speech. Kenyon had spoken with the same matter-of-fact observational tone he had used eight years before, as if there were no moral import to the accusation. The woman kept her eyes on him, but he was almost sure she hadn't understood.

'I think you should be careful what you say, sir,' Bains said. 'I was neither charged, convicted nor disciplined in relation to those allegations.'

'They sunk the case, nevertheless.'

'No. *You* sunk the case. *You* were the judge. *You* let the man walk.'

They stared at each other for a moment, eyes locking. The anger had come out now. It was between them. Bains waited. Somewhere behind him he could hear a clock ticking in the growing gloom. In his jacket pocket, he gripped the warrant he had already obtained that afternoon. He felt like taking it out, dispensing with the whole charade Spencer and Munro were forcing them to follow with this man, because he was a judge.

Except, of course, that no one else on the team had a clue that he was following this particular line. It was his own little sideline, this one. They had found nothing in the judge's house, nothing to suggest he was a paedophile, or pervert, or connected to such people. Nothing even to help the team exploring the grudge theory – the convict-come-back-to-haunt-him line. And it was when looking through the actions generated by that team, not his own, that Bains had seen why they had found nothing.

Kenyon had told them that he kept little material relating to cases he had tried or been involved with, but what he did have wasn't at home, but in his chambers at the Crown Court. He would look through the material there, he promised, and bring them anything relevant. He had said it would not be appropriate for them to search his chambers – there were issues of legal professional privilege involved. He could not 'allow' a search.

Because the grudge team were cooperating – on the assumption of Kenyon as victim – they had gone along with this and he had duly brought them several boxes of case papers and notebooks, plus several more boxes of court records.

But Bains was looking at Kenyon as a suspect.

The two DCs following the revenge/grudge line – at least until the squad had started to multiply that afternoon – were inexperienced. They came from the CPT. Bains had asked them – casually – whether they had considered getting a warrant to search Kenyon's chambers. They hadn't. It had taken Bains less than thirty minutes at Keighley Magistrates Court to get one. But that was because he knew a wooden-top there who hated everything to do with the Crown Court, because some judge had once upon a time let out a burglar who happened to have turned over his house. Sometimes local knowledge paid off.

Neither Spencer, Munro, nor anyone else on Shade knew he had got the warrant. It was too late to execute it now, so if Kenyon refused permission he intended to keep it secret. He would execute it in the morning, without even informing Kenyon.

He was on the point of turning round and leaving when Kenyon straightened up and looked at him again.

'I remember you well,' he said, voice slightly louder. 'I remember what happened to you. Did you do what defence counsel said you had done? Did you torture that man?'

Bains paused, then shrugged. 'What would it matter if I did?' he asked. 'It's history.'

'It would matter to me.'

'You had made your mind up already.'

Kenyon stared at him, for a moment looking as if he thought he were still in a court room and Bains had been contemptuous.

'You're not in court now,' Bains said, to rub the point home. 'I don't have to answer any of your questions. *I'm* the investigator.'

Kenyon's expression immediately turned to confusion. 'I am not being investigated,' he whispered. 'Our daughter is missing...' He looked down at the woman. There were tears in his eyes again. The woman hugged him tightly, staring at Bains as if she were about to attack him.

'So you'll give me permission?' Bains asked.

Kenyon shook his head. 'No. Not you. You have a grudge against me. I can see it in your eyes. If you had answered my question truthfully I might have let you. I might have believed that, perhaps, you were a good officer to have on our side. Not honest, but brutal and determined. That would be good, if it returned Sophie to us. But I see now that you are not on our side. Not at all.'

Bains nodded. The speech, finally, was what he had expected, even what he had hoped for.

'You had better leave, 'Kenyon said. 'In the morning I will speak to your SIO. I will let *him* search my chambers, perhaps. But not *you*. I will ask him to remove *you* from his team.' He paused for a moment. 'If you have not found her by then.'

Bains found his own way out.

Out on the street he thought about what Kenyon would do now and whether he needed to get into the Crown Court that night, before Kenyon had a chance to clear his chambers. In his mind he was no longer even considering that Kenyon was innocent. He had seen his wife.

No one married someone so frail, so submissive, so tiny, unless it was because they wanted to dominate, because they wanted a child as a sexual partner. It was like men going for women twenty years older. They wanted their mothers really.

But there were more subtle hints too. Kenyon had suggested that Bains might be a ruthless investigator, someone to have on his side, but he had not reacted normally in recognizing him. In his present position, the father of a missing child, a normal reaction would have been to regret the actions of eight years ago, or to have found some empathy for Bains's situation back then.

But the judge had let a paedophile escape. Even if he thought he had done the right thing he must nevertheless have *known* – in his heart – that Eric Pardoe was a paedophile, the exact sort of person who was likely holding his daughter right now. That should have prompted, at the very least, regret. But it had prompted precisely nothing.

SEVENTEEN

Sophie had lost track of time. She was used to waking up at a certain time, eating regularly, going to sleep at eight-thirty sharp. But since he had taken her from the back of the van and pushed the needle into her arm, those things had vanished from her life. Everything had become one long blur. She had to struggle even to recall that her life had once been like that.

Most of the time she felt so sluggish and exhausted that she couldn't even move. The terror – the feeling of panic and fright that had made her tremble, wet herself, cry uncontrollably – all that had gone within minutes and had not come back. Instead her world had become grey, hazy, floating horribly between sleep and wakefulness, limbs so heavy that she could do nothing but lie on the mattress and stare at the ceiling. If she could keep her eyes open at all.

She had no idea whether it was night or day. She had no idea what time it was. Sounds came at her in a rush, distorted like the shapes on the ceiling above her. Sometimes there was no sound and all she could hear was her own heart. Then her ears were swamped with a tremendous roaring noise that made her screw her eyes shut and shrink back inside herself.

Once, when the greyness began to fade from her and her head cleared a little, she heard voices from somewhere. But they seemed far away. She had tried to move her legs to sit up, but something was pinning her, holding her down. She wasn't sure whether it was the 'medicine' he was giving her or something tied around her ankles and wrists. She had tried to scratch her nose but her hand wouldn't move from above her head. She wasn't even sure it was above her head. If she tried to look at the room too long, things began to spin around her and she began to retch. It was easier if she kept her eyes closed.

The man had been gentle with her at first. But she hadn't wanted to let him put the needle into her – even though he was telling her it was for her own good, that after she had slept a little she would see her daddy again. He had hit her then, really hard across the face. She had fallen to the ground and looked up at him standing over her, shouting and screaming. She had felt so terrified she had let him put the needle in. Then everything had faded, even his face. Since then it had never really come back to her.

She knew that she had drunk something; every now and then someone would stand beside her and tell her to swallow. But she couldn't feel anything going down her throat, couldn't see what they were giving her, just that it was wet.

They moved her as well. She could feel hands on her, picking her up, more than one voice talking. But it was like everything was at the end of a very long tunnel. The things that were happening were removed from her, didn't affect her. Once only she felt a sharp pain from inside her tummy. But it hadn't lasted very long.

She had vivid images of her mum, like she was in there with her, keeping her company. Her mum looked so beautiful to her. Mostly she wore a light cotton dress that rustled in the sunlight. She looked down at her with a smile on her face that was like the feeling she got sitting in the midday sun in their garden in Spain, when she had been little – a warmth spreading out over her, through her, everything right in the world, everything happy.

Often she tried to ask her mum questions, but the words wouldn't come out. Her mum would lean over her and run her hand across her brow and through her hair, whispering to her, telling her that she loved her, that she was the best girl in the world.

She missed her mum. She missed her so much it was like a great aching hole inside her. The images seemed real, but she knew they weren't, and inside herself she could feel that she was crying helplessly all the time. If her mum had been alive none of this would ever have happened.

They only mentioned her father once – or at least, she only heard them once. His name pulled her out of the grey and focussed the words in her ears. One of them called him 'the judge' and then used his name. The man speaking had, she thought, a strange accent, like something out of a fairy-tale video from Czechoslovakia that she had seen. Another one – maybe even the one who had put her in the van – said something about 'not touching her *yet*' and 'not hurting her *yet*'.

She heard them laugh, talking about 'damaged goods', but she didn't know what they meant, couldn't even be sure she was hearing the words properly.

Inside her mind she rolled away from them, snuggled herself into a ball, knees tucked under her chin, arms around her legs. If she lay very still and very quiet, her mother would come to her, hold her hand and tell her everything would be fine.

She heard the roaring noise beginning to build up again, from somewhere above the ceiling. She began to whimper to herself, frightened of it, thinking that it was something huge that was rushing towards her to crush her and cut her up.

EIGHTEEN

Karen awoke before four with birdsong loud in her ears. She rolled towards the open window and looked at the dawn light flooding through the room and over her. For a moment she felt confused, not knowing where she was. She sat up, feeling her head pound in protest. The spare room. Not unusual if she had returned late, but she had been in all evening.

She lay back in the bed and closed her eyes, trying to recall. It came to her now – they had argued last night. She sighed and brought her hand to her eyes. The evening had started off well enough. She had cooked for them, they had sat down at the table and eaten together like a family – the thought made her wince, but it had gone well. Except, of course, she had said nothing whatsoever to either Mairead or Neil about events at the school earlier that day.

Mairead had gone to bed happy just after nine. Not surprising. Neil had looked tired, but pleased that she was around, no doubt looking forward to sharing a bed with her. Then she had told him about the incident at the school. They were both drinking at the time – not much, but enough to loosen things up, make it worse.

It had followed a familiar and depressing pattern. He thought Mairead did these things because Karen hadn't told her who she was, because the world she was living in was dysfunctional, devoid of genuine parental reassurance. And the reason for that was because Karen was keeping from her the one most important thing in her life, that she was her mother. Before long he was insisting that '*this time*' she would have to tell her, it would have to come out, be dealt with. Then they could move on, all of them, together.

She had no arguments to muster against this. He was right. But she couldn't do what he was asking, not yet. So she remained silent and gloomy, watching the frustration build up in him. The dynamic was always the same when they argued. He was reasonable, full of suggestions, perceptions, opinions, insights. They seemed decent and undeniable, on the surface, but they weren't where she wanted to go. The thought of them 'moving on' and living happily ever after, 'together', filled her with a dread that made her want to run. But she couldn't tell him that. So she was silent. And nothing was more destructive for him than that. He was, after all, a lawyer.

In the end he had told her that if she did not tell Mairead, he would. That had done the trick. She had reacted at once, explosively. She could see herself shouting at him now: '*You even try it and your feet won't touch the fucking floor on the way through that door! Mairead is my responsibility, not yours. Don't you even think about making decisions like that!*'

She had stepped towards him to shout the words, almost spitting in his face.

As she stepped back she saw the shocked, wounded look in his eyes and immediately felt regret.

'*Yes*,' he had said, quietly, as the tears had begun to well out of her eyes. '*Yes, Karen. As you never tire of reminding me. This is your house. She is your responsibility. You can turn me out anytime you like.*'

But he had still agreed to take the day off and look after her.

Thinking about it brought the guilt back in fresh waves. He had three meetings planned for the day – his boss, he had said, would not like it – but he had still volunteered almost at once to cancel them all and stay 'at home' to care for Mairead. Getting, he said, the priorities right.

Unlike her. She rolled out of bed and searched in her briefcase for the photos and clippings Phil Patterson had given her. She needed to take her mind off it.

Patterson had given her a bundle of fifteen articles – either actual copied clippings or photocopies of the original copy, complete with photos – recording the progress of a reporter called Jack Goulden as he followed in the wake of Geoff Reed's triumphal campaign trail, submitting daily reports to the *Guardian*. Not all the articles seemed to have made it to press for the national paper, but those that weren't were picked up by the *T&A* and the *Yorkshire Post*. Patterson had given her copy from all three papers.

It was early, but she was wide awake. She took her time reading through them all, studying the pictures as she went. As far as it went, what she was looking for was a party of some sort. As a lead, that was about as slim as it could get, but it was all she had to go on. Pamela remembered that Reed had been wearing a red rosette, carrying a champagne glass and 'celebrating'. She had formed the impression that the celebrations were *for* Reed. Her thirteenth birthday had been on 1 June, ten days before the 11 June General Election. She knew the events had happened near her birthday because they had torn from her the dress she had been given on that birthday.

Karen quickly discovered that there were at least twenty-five parties, campaign events (involving booze and champagne) or dinner engagements which might fit the bill. Only six of them, however, involved an element of celebration – five from election night and one from a week earlier when a poll showed Reed well in the lead. The 'poll lead party' had taken place at the constituency office and had been a low-key affair, mainly a press event. Everyone had gone home by nine.

The first party of election night had started – once again at the constituency office (the same converted house, she realized, that she had already visited) – when the polls had closed on 11 June and the exit poll results had come through, predicting a comfortable win for Reed. From there Reed had gone the rounds of friends, supporters and colleagues until shortly after three in the morning when he had been called to the Town Hall to get the official result.

Karen studied the handful of images taken by Goulden for names she might know. There were none. Nor were there any names she recognized given within the articles. After the result had been declared, Jack Goulden had given up and gone to bed, leaving victorious Geoffrey Reed MP to *'make his way to a smaller, private celebration at the house of a close business acquaintance. Finally Geoff Reed could be himself.'*

This last line referred to a theme Goulden had picked up throughout the articles, playing on the subtle differences between the public and private faces of Labour. Reed had escaped relatively unscathed from this line (no doubt in return for allowing Goulden to tail him) – depicted as a sort of amiable, beaming uncle figure, addicted to his nephews and gardening off the campaign trail, but an altogether more devious thinker, populist orator and cunning political operator on the soap box. The theme had run as a more cutting metaphor for a standard critique of the Labour campaign in the wider parts of the articles.

Neither the location of the last party (she suspected the only real one for Reed, all the others having been either to acknowledge campaign debts or put on a show for the cameras), nor the name of the business friend fortunate enough to host the rising star (thinner back then, she noted, but still overweight) were named in the piece. She wondered whether Jack Goulden would remember now, if she tracked him down and paid him a visit.

There was a large photo from somewhere within the Town Hall, showing Reed amidst a sizeable crowd of jubilant supporters. She studied the faces carefully. They were mostly male, mostly early forties to early fifties. They looked like the faces of 'Old Labour', jumping on the band wagon. She didn't know any of them. She made four mental notes: track down Goulden; get hold of remaining clippings about the summer of 1987 from Patterson; show election night photo to a few older officers to see if they recognized anyone; if so, get names, track them down and speak to them.

At five she walked quietly down to the kitchen, hoping not to wake Neil. But he was already at the kitchen table when she got down, head in hands, hair messed up, a tired, defeated look in his eyes when he glanced up at her. She went over to him immediately, putting her arms around him, kissing the top of his head, apologizing. From the look of his face she guessed he had been up a long time and had been upset. That wasn't like him.

'There's no need to apologize,' he said to her. 'It's my fault. I know what you've been through. I shouldn't have said those things.'

She shook her head. 'You're wrong, Neil. It *is* my fault and I *am* sorry.' She sighed, trying to work out what else she could say.

He stood up as she was thinking about it and moved to make her a coffee. She watched him. Whatever she felt for him wasn't enough. There was something missing and because of it she was hurting him. Whatever it was it must have been there in the beginning or they would never have got this far. But right now she couldn't see it, or a way to get back to it. He needed more from her than she could give.

'You take things as slowly as you want, Karen,' he said to her. 'You know how fast you can go with it.' He came and stood behind her, encircling his arms around her waist and pushing his nose into the nape of her neck, beneath her hair. He stood like that for a long time, not saying anything, just hugging himself to her like a child. His voice had sounded calm, but she could hear and feel from his breathing that he was trying not to sob.

NINETEEN

Munro stood at his window looking out into the garden. Not so very long ago children had played here. His own children. Where were they now? Right now?

He sighed. With his ex-wife Louise Robertson and her new partner, playing at happy families in their nice new house. Their 'home' even. They were forgetting about him. In bed, asleep, not thinking of him, probably not even missing him. He was meant to pick them up on Saturday for the weekend. But that wasn't going to happen now. The new man – he couldn't even remember his name – was a banker. Regular hours, kept his promises, was there when he said he would be.

He looked at his watch. It was just after five-thirty in the morning. Up on the moor they would be starting again with the search. Outside the light was bright, the sun climbing above a clear horizon, the air coming through the open window cool and fresh, promising heat for later. He rubbed his hands over his rough, unshaven face. He hadn't slept, not for a single minute. There had been no point in coming home.

Behind him he heard Ricky Spencer cough politely, as if to get his attention. He glanced back at him, at the two boxes full of copied paperwork on the floor beside him. They had been going less than twenty-four hours with HOLMES and already they were drowning in it. There had been a trickle of calls before Harrison's performance for the local TV and then the national TV news in the evening. After that it had gone crazy. Harrison had been right. They were drowning in it. Every call produced an action. Every action had the potential to generate three or four follow-up actions.

'How many now?' he asked Spencer, not looking at him, watching instead two fat wood pigeons waddling across his weed-strewn, uncut lawn. Wood pigeons, he had been told, mated for life.

'Two hundred and sixty-seven, when I left,' Spencer said.

Munro felt the panic starting again when he heard the number. Not even darkness had slowed it down. So 267 telephone calls from cranks, misfits and ordinary members of the public who either did or did not see a distressed kid in a vehicle within the last forty-eight hours. They were calling from all over the country. Munro had to wonder whether Harrison had done this to him on purpose. He turned to Spencer.

'What are we going to do?' There was an edge of desperation to his voice. He saw Spencer notice it and frown.

'Work through them, sir,' Spencer said. He looked at the boxes at his feet, copies of actions that Munro had asked him to bring with him. 'We have a team of forty-six detectives. We'll work through them, the same as if it was any other majority enquiry.'

'She'll be dead before we're even halfway through them. Forty-six isn't enough.'

Spencer ignored the comment. He leaned forward and took a handful of paperwork from the top of one of the boxes. 'There are some things I need you to consider fairly urgently,' he said.

'Did you hear me? Forty-six isn't enough.'

Spencer examined him. 'So we ask for more,' he said finally.

'No use. There will never be enough. I know which way it's going to be. It will be like this without a break now. We will get hundreds of calls, each and every day. We will never keep up with it.'

'We have to keep up with it.'

'The right one will be in there.' He pointed to the boxes. 'But we'll never get to it. Someone will have told us, we'll miss it, she'll die.'

Spencer looked at him for a long time before speaking. 'She's probably already dead, sir,' he said then. 'We probably have all the time in the world.'

'Probably? That's not good enough. She might be alive. She *might* be.'

Munro began to pace along the wall facing out onto the garden. He felt agitated, angry, twitchy. In the bottom of his stomach he was suffering something he had never experienced before on an enquiry – a gnawing gut fear, eating at him, something so acidic it made him double up in pain. Spencer didn't have the same approach. For him it was a career opportunity and that was it. But Sophie Kenyon was out there somewhere, suffering, crying, dying. No one else was going to bring her in. *He* had to organize it, make it happen. It was down to him. Everything. Her life. Her suffering. Her death. A thirteen-year-old kid. He could hear himself breathing heavily, starting to hyperventilate.

'Did you get any sleep, sir?' Spencer asked. Munro ignored him. 'Maybe you should stop drinking the coffees,' Spencer said, trying again. Munro looked over to him as if he were stupid. Spencer shrugged.

'We have to limit it,' Munro said, speaking too fast, words rushed out over his breathing. He stopped walking and took a deep breath. 'We have to cut it down,' he said. 'It's the only way. Like this we could use the whole squad just following up calls. We need to stick to our lines. We have to try to save her.'

Spencer nodded, waiting. Did Spencer think they had to save her? Did anyone on the squad think that, apart from himself? What did they think they were doing? A mere *job*?

'I think we should draw a radius,' he said, bringing his thoughts back, pacing again now, staring at the carpet beneath his feet. 'Assume it's local, draw a radius. Say five miles around Ilkley. Maybe ten, I don't know. Only deal with calls or sightings from within that area, put all the rest on hold.

'Put half the team onto processing those calls, keep the other half following our lines.' He looked over to Spencer to see what he thought.

'You mean a circle?' Spencer asked, frowning.

'That's what I said.'

'You said radius.'

'You know what I meant. What do you think?'

'Is that what we normally do?'

Munro stopped pacing and walked back to the window. 'I don't know,' he said, feeling frightened just saying it. 'I don't know what I'm doing. I don't know anyone who has handled this sort of thing. Not this scale, not with a kid at risk. I did a MISPER that turned into murder eleven years ago, but it wasn't like this. I was only a DC then. I wasn't making the decisions. Half the time I didn't know what was going on. I just chased whatever actions they gave me. There's no "normal" thing to do when it's like this. Not when it blows up. Two hundred calls a night. I need to speak to someone, maybe someone down south . . .'

'Maybe the profiler could help.'

They had put in a request to the National Crime Faculty in Bramshill for a profiler. Someone to work out the psychology, make a guess as to what was going on, whether it was a stranger, someone local, whatever. And then to guess at what he was like, what he did, what the chances were of him killing her. Munro had wanted to see the profiler the first night after Sophie Kenyon had gone missing, but Bramshill had tried to dissuade him. They operated on the same assumption as everyone else – she was safe, she would turn up. So far they hadn't come back to him with a name. He was due to chase them later that day, though he was sure it would all be bullshit anyway. Guesswork.

'We haven't even got a name for the profiler yet,' Munro said. 'But I don't think a *doctor* will know how to run a major enquiry.' He tried to keep the derision out of his voice. Spencer's suggestion had been stupid. 'I'll ask NCF though. I've got to call them anyway today – to get the fucking name they should have given me two days ago.' He turned away from the window and walked back to Spencer. His breathing was more even now, but his heart sounded loud, thumping away in his chest as if he were running. 'What do you need from me?' he asked.

Spencer's features relaxed, reassured his SIO was operational again, not just panicking. He would have to control these attacks. It wasn't good in front of Spencer – or anyone. He could at least pretend that it was all manageable. Spencer passed three sheets of paper to him.

'Three things,' he said. 'Top one is a response from a woman who says she was walking a dog down Wells Road. Right time, right date. Says she saw a girl headed up towards the moor. Description very poor, but could fit. The woman also saw a white van driving up after the girl. That's it. No other detail.'

Munro grabbed the paperwork off him. 'No more detail? She must have more. I'll speak to her later. Get her in.'

'That's already arranged. She comes in to the main incident room at nine. But what I need from you is a decision about the white van. Do we go with that, assume she's accurate, put it out to the press?'

'No. Wait until I've spoken to her. We have to be sure before we limit it like that. Might not even be Sophie. Shit, it's like this every time. Too much to follow up. Have you started to eliminate other school girls, roughly same age?'

'We've started, but without press help that will take weeks.'

'We haven't got weeks. Put a question out through the local papers, the radio stations, the TV, to the heads of all the local schools. Any schoolgirl who walked up Wells Road on Monday, twenty-third of June, between three and six in the evening.'

Spencer took the paperwork back off him. 'OK. The other two things are addresses that have come up blocked on the Operational Information System. I need you to speak to the ACC to get the information released.'

'Blocked on OIS? It means informants live there. Or surveillance. Forget about them. We would already know if they're blocked. How did they come up?'

'One through an informant. The other through the team going through nominals with form for sex offences.'

'What did the informant say?'

'Sound of a child crying. That kind of thing.'

'And it's restricted?'

'Yes. That one is a council block in Bradford. The other is—'

'OK, whatever. You ask Harrison. I can't handle talking to the twat again.'

There was a silence. Munro couldn't tell what Spencer was thinking. He didn't know whether Spencer was a friend of Harrison. Maybe they were grippers together. That was certainly the rumour about Harrison – about all the Command Team, in fact – that they were Masons.

'That it?' Munro asked, impatient for Spencer to be gone.

'For now. What are you going to do about—'

'Ring the NCF. I told you.' Munro walked away from him. 'I'm coming in now anyway,' he said. 'I can't sleep. Not while this is going on. I can't do anything.'

TWENTY

'He said I was a *bastard*. He said Dad was in prison because he was a thief and a criminal. He said I was a bastard because I have no mother.'

Karen looked across the table to where Mairead sat. She tried to work out what was going through her daughter's head. She had said the words calmly, almost matter-of-factly, but the control was hiding something.

It was after nine. Neil had gone to Skipton for food shopping. She would go in to work when he got back. Meanwhile, she was meant to have some kind of motherly 'heart to heart' with her child. At first Mairead had simply continued to eat her breakfast cereal – Ready Brek this morning, despite the weather – ignoring every question Karen put to her. Then she had started crying about it, but Karen could tell the tears were an attempt to stop her asking questions rather than because she was frightened. Finally she got tired of it.

'Look, Mairead. I'm on your side. I don't care what you did. I've done worse, much worse. I just want to know why. I want to know what happened to make you do that. So stop messing around and tell me.'

Mairead had dried her eyes then, shrugging and looking up at her. 'You've done worse?' she asked. Her eyes were glinting with curiosity. 'Like what?'

'Tell me about yesterday first.'

'Then you'll tell me what you've done?'

'Maybe.'

So Mairead had told her. Danny Conroy had taunted her about her having no mother, about her father being in prison. When the taunts hadn't worked he had tried to remove her satchel. He was considerably bigger and heavier than Mairead, but she hadn't let him. So he had pulled her to the ground and punched her.

'He said you were a bastard?' Karen said, frowning. 'Bastard doesn't mean you have no mother.'

Mairead rolled her eyes. 'I *know* that,' she said. 'But he didn't. He's not very bright. He's a bully, a stupid, little boy.'

'Did he hurt you?' Karen asked.

'In what way?'

Karen frowned again, surprised by how intelligent a nine-year-old could be. 'In any way?'

'I didn't enjoy him calling Dad names. Not in front of the whole class. But that wasn't what really bothered me. I'm not the only person to hate him. He steals things from other girls nearly every day. He tried to take my satchel, to get my lunchbox. All I did was stop him. The teachers should be stopping him. I shouldn't have had to fight him off.'

Karen looked into her eyes as she was speaking, trying to see any trace of the hurt that could have so enraged her as to cause her to stab the boy thirty minutes later. But Mairead's eyes were calm, childlike.

'Did he hurt you physically?'

'Not really. Nothing to worry about. I've had worse.'

'Did you feel angry with him?'

Mairead shook her head, considering it. The idea seemed new to her. 'I don't think so,' she said. 'I just thought he needed a lesson. That seemed the best way to do it.'

Karen sat back. She felt a ripple of something like panic in the base of her stomach. She had been looking for pain, she realized, searching for a way to understand why a nine-year-old would stab somebody, but it wasn't there. The attack had been completely cold-blooded.

'Stabbing him?' she asked. 'You thought stabbing him was the best way to teach him a lesson?'

Mairead nodded, looking more nervous now the action had been mentioned. But not that nervous. 'I don't think he'll go around doing that any more,' she said, quietly.

Karen didn't know what to say, didn't have a clue how to deal with it. She stood up and paced around the kitchen, Mairead's eyes following her as she finished off her breakfast. She could give her a lecture, but it didn't seem like that would address the problem. The problem was Mairead didn't appear to be feeling things normal nine-year-olds should feel. What was the best way to deal with that? Wait to see what Liz Hodges had to say, she decided. Maybe they would need to take her back to the psychologist. Liz could tell her about that. She had hoped all that was in the past.

'So are you going to tell me what you've done?' Mairead asked her. There was a slight smile in her eyes. Karen glared at her.

'No. I'm not. Not right now. I'm still thinking about what you've done.'

When Neil got back she drove down through the Wharfe Valley into Leeds, the day already another scorcher by mid-morning. On the radio she heard that in Bradford, incredibly, they were suffering a drought as a consequence of the continuous hot weather and lack of rain. As a consequence of incompetence, she thought. They had enjoyed three weeks without rain and there was no water. There was something stupidly English about it. In Bradford they were having to use water tankers to ship drinking water into Manningham.

She called George Wright to check everything was manageable at the CPT. It wasn't, but there was nothing either of them could do about that. She told him she would be back in after two.

There were two messages on her mobile from the same Command Team number that had paged her twice the day before. She didn't listen to them. Whatever it was that ACC Harrison wanted her for, it wouldn't be good. She was meant to speak to him anyway about Operation Flight. The protocol was that she should get his permission before rummaging through 'his' files. But she had already decided not to do that. How would she explain what she was doing to him? She hadn't even crimed it. Harrison was an ACC now, all he would be interested in was the bean-counting and resource issues.

She had decided that before she spoke to him it would be wise to take a look at the investigation paperwork, preferably take some copies. She might not get the chance to go back. She would probably still have to speak to him about it all, but later in the day. Whatever he was calling her for could wait until then. She didn't want to make two trips to Wakefield.

She got into the rotting seventies dump that was Milgarth Police Station sometime before eleven. Then it was down into the basement again. Only this time the storeman knew exactly where to look.

Flight had been a high-profile failure for the Force. They knew where they had buried it.

There were sixteen crates of paperwork belonging to the investigation into the deaths of Eric Pardoe and two young girls, unknown. She had a quick glance through the property log to see who had extracted the paperwork last: Mark Harrison, signed off as the SIO, over two years ago, when the last review had taken place. She checked which boxes he had extracted and pulled them from the piles. In accordance with best practice his policy logs were there in the first crate, neatly ordered.

She took the first one out, sat down at a wooden bench within the actual property cage and began to read. As she came across references to exhibits, statements or significant lines she followed up anything that interested her by searching for additional material and examining it. Her aim was to spend three hours getting a rough knowledge of his enquiry, enough to see where she should be looking in detail, if anywhere.

In fact, within forty minutes she had something. Following up on references to the post mortem she dug out files of photos they had used while making appeals for sightings during the three weeks of Pardoe's disappearance, prior to his body being found. At that point the enquiry had belonged to another SIO – Harrison had only taken it on when it became a triple murder hunt. The PM photos showed a livid, decomposing corpse, but the photo they had put out on the fliers was a good clear headshot of Pardoe and she recognized him at once.

She opened her briefcase, dug out Patterson's clippings from 11 June and found the photo of Reed surrounded by admirers in the town hall, shortly after his victory. There was no mistaking it. The large, florid man with his arm around the new MP, a big smile on his face, was Eric Pardoe. She rested the photos side by side on the counter, just to be sure. She methodically checked feature after feature. It was him. She breathed an involuntary sigh of relief and felt an intense feeling that only came rarely in an enquiry. It was the thrill she got when – long before she had any rational reason to believe it – she *knew* that she was onto something.

The link to Pardoe, buried beside two dead little girls who might or might not be the same two girls Pamela had recalled, wasn't by itself enough for anything. But it was the first chink of confirmation (of any kind) that she had come across since starting to look into Pamela's story. It was enough to keep her going a little further.

She discovered that Eric Pardoe came from a family who had been selling property in West Yorkshire for nearly one hundred and fifty years. He was wealthy before he even left school, at the age of fifteen, eschewing the possibility of an Oxbridge education (his father had sent him to Bradford Grammar, so it would have been easy enough) in order to join the family business. The list of his assets – compiled by the Flight enquiry team – included fifteen high-value properties spread across the area (all detached residential piles – including his home, a converted farm complex called Lower Woodlands, on the outskirts of Bramhope), a score of lesser properties (from ex-council flats through to parking lots) and other assets (shares, savings, race horses, paintings, a yacht, property in Spain, France, Belgium and Poland) totalling nearly twelve million pounds. It wasn't surprising he had turned down the education.

Pardoe, Philips & Gillespie had eighteen offices in the county and handled over 8,000 property sales a year, according to a background note prepared by a junior DC on Harrison's team. Philips and Gillespie had long since dropped out of the picture, and when Pardoe's father died in 1970 he left Eric (then twenty-eight years old) the entire business. There was a sister – she got a couple of houses out of the will – but the business went to the only son.

Between 1970 and his death at the age of forty-eight, Pardoe brought in eight partners, all with a relatively minor share of the company. His wife inherited (and subsequently sold) his major share when he died. Looking into the financial position and any possible motive for her to have been involved in his kidnapping had been a very active line of enquiry in the first few days after his body was recovered.

From these enquiries Karen learned that Eric and Emily Pardoe had apparently been happily married – despite some obviously large problems outside of the relationship – and had four children, three of whom had still been alive in 1990.

The most obvious spanner in the marital works had occurred a year before Pardoe's death, in 1989. In that year he had been arrested and charged with rape. The case had failed, but not before getting to Leeds Crown Court. Chasing up the possible consequences of this failed rape allegation had been the second most favoured line in

Harrison's enquiry. The first had been based around a possible blackmail/ransom plot. As far as Karen could see, neither line had yielded anything. According to a note within the policy logs, the rape file had been inadvertently destroyed in 1991, someone in stores apparently missing its connection to a live unsolved murder. However, that was the police file. Karen knew there was a chance the CPS would still have theirs. She would ask Neil about that.

She spent some time comparing the list of Pardoe's residential assets to any addresses given in the newspaper clippings as venues for post-election celebrations. There was no match, but there was something about the list of properties owned by Pardoe that bothered her. Half of them were given without street names or house numbers – presumably they were too big for that – so it was difficult to tell what was tickling her without getting out a map and trying to locate the postcodes. A lot of them seemed to be in the LS16 postal area – the Bramhope, Cookridge and Holt Park area of north Leeds.

Pardoe had been reported missing by his wife at 11.39 a.m. on Wednesday, 5 December 1990. He had not returned from the office the night before. A farmer walking across land not two miles from Lower Woodlands had discovered newly turned earth on Thursday, 27 December. The pathologist estimated that Pardoe had been buried within days, if not hours, of his disappearance. Snowfall between 6 and 8 December had made meaningful area searches difficult (the area in which he was buried, at the foot of a hedge between the A658 and Otley Old Road had, in fact, been searched twice in the intervening three weeks, without result). The snows had thawed just before Christmas Day.

The trench he was buried in was over five feet deep. Not easy to dig through the roots of a hawthorn, in midwinter with the soil packed hard and frozen. But the trench had actually been dug out properly some years before, to lay a drainage pipe from the road nearby. The pipe had gone in during the summer of 1984 and tracing anyone who had been involved in laying it had taken up the time of nearly thirty detectives for over four weeks, with no result.

Pardoe's body was actually lying on top of the remains of the two girls, about six inches of soil separating them. The girls were lying alongside each other in a position which – from the photos – made it look like they were embracing. Harrison had brought in a forensic archaeologist – a relatively new breed of fish in 1990 – to estimate how long the girls had been down there. The conclusion had placed their burial anywhere between 1986 and 1988.

Karen looked at the pictures of the bodies as she read this. Pamela was unlikely to have picked up and retained these dates from a newspaper report. Were these the remains of the two girls she had been imprisoned with during June 1987?

Both girls had severe head injuries, blunt instrument traumas that to a layman would have left little doubt as to cause of death. The PM was less conclusive, though. They could 'very possibly' have been clubbed to death, the report said, but, in default of further information and due to the heavy state of decomposition, it was impossible to give an accurate cause of death. Karen picked through the reams of reports until she found what analysis there was of what remained of the girl's stomach contents. 'Insufficient sample to determine,' it read. In other words, they *could* have died from starvation, just as Pamela had said.

Pardoe had ligature injuries to his neck and the remains of extensive bruising across his legs, arms, back, face and head. He had certainly been severely beaten. This, she recalled, had been mooted as a possible contributory factor to his death when she had heard about it herself from the media, back in 1990. But the PM was very clear on this: Pardoe had not died because he was beaten or strangled. He had asphyxiated because he had been buried in five foot of soil. He had been buried alive.

He had been buried alive on top of the remains of two dead girls who had been buried there at least one year before. What was the connection? After a year and a half of enquiries and thousands of wasted man hours, a thirty-five man squad had been gradually wound down and disbanded, having failed to answer this question or discover who was responsible. Every trail they had followed had apparently come back cold, dead.

She ran through the lists of property and forensic enquiries and noted the continuity sheets for the remains of the clothing taken from the two girls. In the photos she could just make out the remnants of colour poking through the wash of wet soil. She thought it might be worth recovering the exhibits from the lab and showing them to Pamela. Maybe she would remember. She made a note of the lab reference numbers.

Before looking through the search logs for Pardoe's addresses she had a rough plan to take Pamela to each and every one of the properties to see if she could jog anything in her memory. It would have been a time-consuming method of taking things on, of limited value and probably best pursued after she had tried to get some independent lead on an address at which both Pardoe and Reed could have celebrated Reed's election victory – possibly from the journalist Jack Goulden.

As it happened, things were simplified the minute she looked at the search log for Lower Woodlands, Pardoe's home address. The statements made it clear that the search teams had discovered cellar areas with 'deep, underground trenches'. There were notes in Harrison's deputy's policy log, speculating as to the relatively recent age of the tunnels, but the enquiry had passed straight over them. Why shouldn't they have? Pardoe's wife had accounted for them as 'drainage ditches'. In any event, Pardoe was the victim in Flight. Why treat his residence with suspicion?

But Karen knew otherwise now. 'Trench' was exactly how Pamela had described the underground chamber in which she had been held. She looked at her watch. It was nearly two and she had eaten nothing. She could do without. If she got the photocopying done in half an hour she could be out at Lower Woodlands by three.

She called George Wright and told him she would be back in the CPT by four.

TWENTY-ONE

Bains half considered skipping morning briefing and going direct to the Crown Court, but thought better of it. If Kenyon had made the call to Munro he would have to face up to it sooner or later. But Munro didn't do the briefing and was nowhere to be seen.

Instead they had to sit through the Ricky Spencer ego show. At the end Spencer explained that Munro was in London, chasing up a psychological profile of the putative kidnapper. As things fell out, Bains was legitimately tasked with continuing the examination of Sophie's family. But Spencer clearly didn't think it was a fruitful line. The team had started off with Spencer (running it) and two others, including Bains. After the Wednesday influx it had grown, briefly, to an eight-strong team. Today Spencer reduced it to Bains, two others and one DS, who also had the team looking into the revenge theory.

He thought about objecting to this disposition on the grounds that it was far too early to rule out the most statistically likely perpetrator – the father. But the scaling down showed Spencer knew nothing of Bains's past and nothing of his visit to the judge. Though he would find out sooner or later – Bains had recorded the judge's refusal of permission for the HOLMES team to input first thing that morning – he didn't want to disabuse Spencer just yet. The tasking left him free to execute his warrant.

He walked over to Bradford Crown Court, expecting Spencer to call him at any point. But the phone was silent as he sat and explained to a civil servant called Crampshaw – the court manager – that he had a warrant, that it was routine and best dealt with sensitively. It was, he said, normal practice to seek a warrant when searching anywhere belonging to a member of the judiciary. Crampshaw seemed to swallow this line. He asked him if Kenyon knew he was there.

Bains nodded. 'Of course. We have the judge's permission. I'm on a team looking at possible revenge motives – someone the judge put away who just got out, perhaps – that's why I need to look at stuff from his chambers. He's already given us most of it. I'm just double-checking. The warrant is a routine precaution to cover legal privilege issues. I'm not looking at the judge himself.' He laughed slightly, as if that idea were silly.

'Well, that's OK, then,' Crampshaw said. 'As long as the judge knows.'

'He hasn't been here this morning?' Bains asked.

'No. He hasn't been in this week. Obviously.'

'Obviously. I saw him yesterday. He's coping, I suppose. You could call him,' Bains suggested, 'but he's in a bad way. Tearful . . .' He looked painfully at Crampshaw, seeking understanding.

Crampshaw stood up. 'That won't be necessary. You have a warrant and you're a policeman. I believe you. Let's keep this quiet.'

The judge's chambers were nothing more glorious than a small office with one desk and a long table. Bains had been in the rooms before for bail applications. The lawyers sat around the long table while the judge – whoever it was – sat at his desk. Down one wall were book cabinets, filled mainly with legal books, the other was bare. That meant the search would be quick. The desk and the bookshelves only.

He set to work with Crampshaw looking over his shoulder. Immediately he found the desk drawers were locked.

'You must have a spare set of keys?'

'I don't know about that,' Crampshaw said, looking more concerned now. 'Didn't the judge give you his keys?'

'I didn't ask. I didn't know the things were locked. Could you check for a spare set?'

He went away reluctantly and Bains sat down behind the desk, took out his pick kit and opened both drawers within five minutes. They were simple locks, designed only to deter.

He looked quickly through the contents. There were assorted items of stationary, drop-down files with case names, a couple of novels, an address book. Anticipating Crampshaw's response, he pulled the files, a blank memo pad and the address book and placed them inside the book cabinets, towards the bottom where more paperwork was piled. Then he closed the drawers and started on the book cabinets. It took him very little time to determine that there was nothing of interest except the judge's video collection.

One entire shelf was taken up with numbered police video boxes, ordered alphabetically, apparently, by case name. He was beginning to take them out when Crampshaw returned.

'There is no spare set,' he said.

'That's OK,' Bains replied, without looking at him. 'I'll speak to Kenyon later. What are these?'

'The judge has a sex ticket,' Crampshaw said.

Bains looked over to him. There was a slight trace of snootiness in Crampshaw's tone.

'A sex ticket?'

'He's authorized to try sex cases. Those are videos of the evidence-in-chief of victims in cases he has tried. He keeps all of them.'

'Why?'

Crampshaw shrugged. 'Why not? In case there's an appeal? To remember? To establish consistency across sentencing? Do you keep no records of cases you've investigated?'

Bains ignored the question. He counted twenty-three videos. 'I'll have to take all these,' he said. 'There may be a clue as to who has taken Sophie here. Maybe it has something to do with one of these cases.'

'Can't you just write down the defendant named?'

Bains stood back and thought about it. Why was he seizing this material? What was he looking for? The truth was that he didn't know. Certainly not the reason given to Crampshaw, because Kenyon had already provided the grudge team with lists of his cases. So why take his videos? He took one off the shelf and looked at it. It was a normal enough police video of a child witness. What he didn't understand was why Kenyon would have kept them all.

'Some don't have the defendant details written on,' he said, looking again at Crampshaw. He held one up to show him. Written on the spine were the victim details only.

'So take only those ones.'

'No. It will be safest to take them all. And all this stuff too.' He pointed to the drop-down files and address book, speaking clearly, in a way that communicated that he had made a decision that was his to take, not Crampshaw's. 'Have you got a box?'

Crampshaw sighed. 'You didn't come very well prepared, did you?'

Bains stepped towards him, fixing his eyes on the man's crumpled old school tie. It meant nothing to him. He didn't even know what school it was. That was the sort of thing Kenyon would know, the sort of thing Bains's parents had desperately tried to achieve for their son by sending him to just such a school. It hadn't worked.

'Don't waste my time,' he said. 'We're rushing around trying to save a little girl's life. Sometimes you don't get to plan things properly.'

TWENTY-TWO

Karen called the lab at Weatherby from her mobile, on the way out to Bramhope and Lower Woodlands. She knew a technician up there from a case way back: Sam Ive. He had made an error and she had covered for him in court, so he owed her. She didn't have to mention it when she spoke to him. He took down the reference numbers and promised to keep it quiet and get back to her when he had located the exhibits.

It took fifteen minutes to get past Headingly in the normal daytime traffic flows. Leeds was so choked with traffic, so difficult to find parking, she found herself taking the trains more than she ever had in London. As she drove past Weetwood it was nearly quarter to three.

Past Weetwood Police Station Leeds turned into open country quite quickly. Bramhope was about five miles further on, on the Otley Road.

The residents of Bramhope liked to think they lived in a village. That was true at least in the sense that the place was separated from the Leeds/Bradford urban conglomeration by areas of open country-side and fields, but Bramhope no longer had support outside of the sprawl. Nobody worked in the village. It was a part of a dormitory system for the top slice of Leeds wealth.

The place was situated on a bend of the Leeds Road, just before it rose to skirt the edge of the Wharfe Valley, ideally placed for fast access to city and countryside alike. Some of the houses were so large that Karen doubted the occupants worked at all.

Between Bramhope and Leeds, to the south, and Bradford, further to the south-west, an area of gently rolling farmland fell down towards the Leeds/Bradford Airport. Karen looked at her A–Z and took a narrow country lane called Moorland Road, leading from the lower outskirts of Bramhope up towards the A658. Woodlands Farm was marked on the A–Z. She guessed that Lower Woodlands was close to it.

As she drew near, a 737 roared above her, turning on the downwind leg from the airport. She looked up as the noise thundered around her. The plane was banking with flaps on full, undercarriage down, no more than 300 metres above her head. The noise was deafening. Immediately she asked herself why someone with Pardoe's wealth would have chosen to live with it. She watched as the machine circled to the west before turning onto finals.

Lower Woodlands was marked – at the turn-off for Woodlands Farm – with a little wooden sign. To get to it you had to drive through the farmyard for Woodlands Farm, turn down into a steep, though not very deep valley and continue for about 500 metres. The slopes of the valley were dotted with tall, mature trees – sycamore, chestnut and ash – so it was difficult to see Lower Woodlands Farm until you were right there at its gates. It was, she thought, nothing if not private.

She left the car outside the gates, put on her shades and walked into the bright, sunlit yard, waiting for the dogs to dash out at her. None came. She began to walk slowly around the place, taking in the detail. The day was hot and still. There was a black Merc parked up in front of the main entrance, but otherwise no sign that anybody was home.

Originally, the farmhouse would have been a relatively small building attached to a much larger barn. From the stonework and the mullion windows she placed the age somewhere in the mid-seventeenth century. The two extensions coming off at right angles to the original barn and house looked to be about a hundred years newer. The effect was to create a large residence (she guessed six to eight bedrooms) with two wings enclosing a stone yard on three sides. Views into the place from the open side were obscured by the trees. One of the wings – the most western – enclosed a large garage space with a massive double door. Easily sufficient to drive a van into.

She walked down a path alongside the east wing and round to the front of the main building. From there she had a view across the shallow valley towards Otley Old Road and, beyond that, the airport. She could see another plane lining up to land. In the cleft of the valley below her, high trees followed the line of a stream. Past that she could clearly see the residence of the closest 'neighbour' – no more than a quarter of a mile away – a similar looking complex, though in need of substantial repair judging by the rickety roof and missing tiles.

From that building there would have been a good view into the front of Pardoe's property. The road down to Lower Woodlands, however, ended at Lower Woodlands. To visit the neighbour and ask what they remembered from eight to ten years ago she would have to drive the long way around, across to the other side of the valley. Undoubtedly, the enquiry would be fruitless anyway. If Pardoe and friends had been abducting children and abusing them in Lower Woodlands – and it was a very large and unwarranted step even to speculate about that at this stage – they would have been more careful than that.

She turned back towards the house and saw a woman at a huge, arched window that had obviously originally been the main barn entrance. She looked about sixty years old, grey hair, smartly dressed in light trousers and a blouse. She was speaking quickly into a cordless phone, probably summoning the constabulary. Karen took out her warrant card and walked up to the window, holding it up for her to see. *What were you doing when Pamela Mathews was here?* she thought. *Closing your eyes and ears or joining in?* Pamela had mentioned a woman coming in to clean her up, brush her hair – making her ready for the men. Again Karen knew she was jumping ahead.

The woman squinted at her warrant card, said something into the phone, then signalled for her to come around to the rear of the building. Karen nodded, smiled at her, then walked back. Keep it friendly, she thought.

The woman was waiting for her when she got round the other side. Karen noticed the diamond necklace at her throat, the clusters of rings on the index and ring fingers of both hands.

'Hello. I'm Karen Sharpe. I'm with the police. Are you Emily Pardoe?'

'What were you doing walking around my house?' The voice was strong, angry, the accent broad Yorkshire.

'I didn't realize you were in. Sorry. Are you Emily Pardoe?'

'You didn't knock. How would you know whether I was in?'

Karen stood about two foot in front of her and flipped out her warrant card again. 'DC Sharpe. Are you Emily Pardoe?'

The woman stepped back and looked past the warrant card into Karen's eyes. Karen met her gaze, still smiling at her.

'What do you want?'

'Nothing urgent. Nothing to worry about,' Karen said. 'I'm doing a review on Operation Flight. I need a favour.'

She watched Emily Pardoe's eyes lose focus, her expression fixing into one of grim resignation. There would be times, Karen knew, when she would go through her life for long periods without even thinking about Eric Pardoe and what had happened to him. That was what happened when you recovered and 'moved on'. But it would never be completely banished. It would always come back. Karen watched her grappling with unseen images for a while, then nod, more to herself than to Karen.

'OK. What kind of favour?'

Karen smiled at her again. 'I just need to look around. Just check a few details in the house.'

Emily Pardoe frowned now. 'Why? What's the house got to do with anything?'

'It's to help me, really,' Karen told her. 'To give me a feel for things. I'm really very sorry about what happened to your husband, Mrs Pardoe.' She pulled a sympathetic face and watched Emily Pardoe register it and soften a little. Enough to let the duff excuse slip by her.

'Come in then, Officer.' She moved away from the door.

Karen stepped into the hallway. 'What kind of review are you doing?'

'It's for Mr Harrison.' She saw a change of expression at the mention of Harrison's name. She couldn't be sure, but it didn't look like Emily Pardoe would have anything good to say about the ACC who had so unsuccessfully investigated her husband's death. 'The investigation is still alive. I wasn't on it originally though, so I have to start from scratch. I like to get a feel for the,' she paused, delicately, 'for the victim, if you'll pardon the expression. It's the way I work.' Pardoe looked at her as if she hadn't understood a word. 'I need to know a little about your husband,' Karen said. 'More than it says on paper. I need to get a sense of him *alive*. I'm sorry. But that's why I'm here.'

'It sounds like a woman's way to work,' Pardoe said. Karen thought there was a trace of derision in her tone. She followed her through a dark hallway into the room with the huge arched window facing out towards the airport. 'Is Mark Harrison your boss, then?'

'Yes. You will have had a lot of contact with him, over the years, I suppose?'

Pardoe stood facing her in the middle of the room. She looked suspicious again now. She didn't answer the question. 'Where do you want to look?'

'I know it will sound strange, but can you just show me around the house? If you don't mind I'll ask some questions as we go.'

'Will it take long? I have to be in Leeds for five.'

'I'll be as quick as you make it.'

She had softened, but not that much.

They started in the cellars, but only because Karen specifically asked her if there were any. 'There are. But I haven't been down there for ages. There's nothing to see.'

'Did Eric go down there much?'

'Not really. He kept wine and junk down there. As you do in a cellar.'

'Can we look, all the same?'

'If you insist.' She didn't move from where she was standing, outside a doorway by a very large kitchen.

'I'd like to,' Karen said, smiling again. Her face was beginning to ache from the effort. 'Did you ever go down into the cellars?'

'Did I? When?'

'When Eric was alive.'

'Not really. As I told you, there's nothing to see.' She opened the door and switched a light on, revealing a set of stone steps, about twenty in all, making it about a ten-foot drop.

Karen followed her down. 'You don't keep wine down here then?'

'I haven't drunk a drop since Eric died.'

When they reached the bottom, she stood aside and pointed to a large empty space lit by a single naked bulb swinging from the ceiling. It was perfectly empty, paved with stone flags and swept clean. Karen searched for cobwebs. There weren't any. Though there was nothing down there, it didn't look like a long-neglected space.

'The cleaner comes down sometimes,' Pardoe said, as if reading her thoughts. 'To clean.'

Karen nodded, pointing back up towards the kitchen. 'Is that the only entrance?'

'Yes. Why do you want to know that?'

'Just curious.' Because if anyone was kept down here they would have to be brought down through the main body of the house, through the kitchen, which probably meant – if Pamela's story was true – that Emily Pardoe had known about it.

Pardoe waited impatiently while Karen walked the length of the space, looking for signs of what might be below the flags. There were no trapdoors, no breaks in the pattern, no sign that there was anything below.

'Are the flags quite new?' she asked, without looking at Pardoe.

'Yes. Why?'

'The reports mentioned some drainage systems down here. I suppose there must have been access to them back in 1990.' When there was no reply she looked up. Emily Pardoe's mouth was shut. She had no intention of answering. But then Karen hadn't asked a question. She didn't need to. The floor had been re-laid to cover the chambers below it.

'Did you fill them in when you re-laid the floor?' she asked, casually, as they walked back up the stairway. 'Or just cover them up?'

'I don't know. I didn't do it. I hired some people. Does it matter?' Her tone was frosty. Karen doubted it mattered. The chances of recovering forensics this far on were slim. But she had wanted to look into the holes, to feel the reality of Pamela's account. Emily Pardoe's reaction to questions about the trenches was more telling than the fact that she had filled them in.

The rest of the tour went quickly and Karen filled in the silences by asking questions about Eric Pardoe, usually getting monosyllabic responses. As they moved into the eastern wing of the house, she could sense, however, that Emily was becoming tenser. They passed through a narrow passageway connecting the old building to the 'new' wing and she asked two questions that Emily didn't even hear. Her thoughts were elsewhere. She was distracted.

Distracted enough, it seemed, to completely omit one room from the tour. When they were heading back towards the passageway into the main building she looked over her shoulder and said, 'And that's it. I hope it's been useful to you.'

Karen stopped by the door she had forgotten to open. 'We missed this room,' she said.

Pardoe froze, not turning towards her for a long time. Karen waited. When she did turn Karen saw that she was trembling slightly and there were tears in her eyes.

'I'm sorry,' Karen said. 'Have I said something to upset you?'

Pardoe shook her head, biting on her lip. 'Not you. No.'

'Is it something to do with this room?'

She nodded. 'That was the children's room.' Her voice broke slightly.

'Yes. I was going to ask you about your—'

'We lost one, you know?'

Karen saw it now. 'Yes,' she said. 'I'm sorry. I'd forgotten that.' The report had said that only three of their four children had been alive in 1990. She remained by the door. She had counted the bedrooms as they were going round, allocating them in her mind to the children. There had been eight rooms with beds in. If this had been another children's bedroom then it would be the ninth. Did they need so many rooms?

'Do we have to go in there?' Emily Pardoe asked her, voice more submissive now. 'It's just ... because ... since we lost Robert ... since he was taken from us ... it's just I've left it as it was. He was our youngest, you know?'

Karen tried to appear sympathetic. Mrs Pardoe had preserved the room as some kind of shrine. 'How did he die?' Karen asked, careful to make the question loaded with concern and empathy. She had read how he had died in the report, but forgotten.

Mrs Pardoe wiped a tear from her left eye. 'He was knocked over.'

Karen remembered then. He had been crushed by a stable hand reversing a tractor, out in the front yard. An accident, everyone devastated, no one prosecuted. Back in 1987. The boy had been nine years old.

'Was this his bedroom?' Karen asked.

Pardoe sighed, seeing that Karen wasn't going to give up, resigning herself to it. She stepped over and turned the door handle. 'No. This was his playroom.'

Karen felt a prickle running down her spine. *His playroom*. That was the word Pamela had used. She stepped into the room after Pardoe and turned to look at the walls. Her jaw dropped.

From behind the door to past the window in the far wall and back towards the door again, running the whole length of the four walls,

127

snaking up and down across the childish wallpaper, someone had painted a dragon. Exactly as Pamela had described it. *'All around the walls, from the door to the window, they had painted a huge, twisting Chinese dragon, with a gaping mouth and flames – not frightening but childish . . .'*

After a while she realized Emily Pardoe was speaking to her.

'Is there something wrong?' she was asking.

Karen closed her mouth. 'No,' she said. 'It's the dragon. I was just admiring it.'

The woman beamed. 'Robert painted it.'

'At nine? He must have been a very talented child.'

'Oh, he was. He was only seven when he painted this. He needed no help.'

Karen ran back through the dates. Nine in 1987. That meant it was painted in 1985. It fitted. She stepped up to it, resisting the urge to touch. The paint had been directly onto the wallpaper, half covering the background pattern of swordfish and dolphins swimming through a sea. Another detail Pamela had got right. Looking at the head, mouth agape, spitting flame, she realized it was the sort of painting that would make a psychologist worry.

Suddenly feeling as if she was contaminating a crime scene, she stepped back towards the doorway and looked at the rest of the room. There wre no beds. But the toys were still there, even the doll's house. She pointed to it.

'It was his sister's,' Mrs Pardoe said. 'He liked it though. He was only young.' She was starting to cry again.

She looked small, exhausted, guilty. Karen felt nothing but contempt for her. She had the beginnings of corroboration now. She knew what had gone on here. Pamela had told the truth.

Karen doubted little Robert had escaped it. She doubted any of Pardoe's children had escaped it. Emily Pardoe was crying for more than her dead child. She was crying because she had been here, because she had known.

'I think I've seen enough,' Karen said, stepping back into the hallway. It was tempting to tape the room off there and then, but she resisted. There would be time for that later.

It was after four before she got back to the CPT and by then George had already left. She sat at her desk and looked with horror at the massive pile of correspondence in her tray. There was no chance of her getting through all of it. George had attached a big sheet of paper to her chair with a message in thick black letters: '**ACC HARRISON WANTS YOU TO CALL HIM. NOW. WAKEFIELD 609313.**'

She tore it off and put it in the bin. There were no doubt more messages on her mobile to that effect. She would deal with Harrison tomorrow. If she started with him now she would probably never get away. She had arranged to meet Liz at seven and she couldn't miss that.

The top item in her tray was a big buff envelope sent from the *T&A*. She opened it and found a brief note from Phil Patterson, then started to flick through the clippings he had enclosed, for the time being ignoring anything that wasn't dated within a week of 11 June 1987. She found what she wanted within half an hour.

The *T&A*'s own reporter had written an article two days after the election on Geoff Reed's local contacts. It was about as savage an exposé as you could expect from a cash-strapped city rag that didn't want to be sued for libel, so the details were likely to be correct. As well as being hand in glove with Eric Pardoe, the article said, Reed was linked mainly to businessmen, union leaders and other local politicians. There was an extensive list – plus others the reporter had refused to name. No doubt the lawyers had been super-cautious when vetting the copy.

The article had run alongside a bigger spread probably culled from a national, setting out the Opposition Leader's 'secret' coterie of friends, hangers-on and followers, all of whom, it seemed, had a holiday home in the Dordogne. The local version was less exotic, but it had the detail Karen wanted.

One throwaway sentence about Reed's movements on 11 June was all it took. She felt like hunting down the reporter and kissing him:

... Reed has been a business partner of Eric Pardoe – of Estate Agents Pardoe, Philips & Gillespie – for nearly ten years. It was in Pardoe's Bramhope mansion that Reed chose to celebrate his election victory, Pardoe hosting a party to which only a small, intimate circle of close friends were invited ...

There it was. She had the crime scene and Reed's presence in it. If she was very lucky indeed she might even get forensics back that would link in Pamela and the two dead girls. That would take time. She would have to get a team in to dig up the cellar as well. But already she had enough to arrest Geoffrey Reed.

She let the adrenalin suffuse her with energy, feeling her scalp tighten, the hairs standing on end, her tummy tingling. She had followed her instincts, stuck with it and got somewhere. That didn't happen often.

TWENTY-THREE

Spencer sat in the ACC's office in Laburnum Grove and watched Mark Harrison logging onto a computer terminal. He couldn't see the monitor. He waited patiently, wondering meanwhile whether he should tell the ACC of his concern about John Munro's health.

Munro had worried him all day. He had left the incident room after two in the morning – leaving Spencer as duty – then called him within hours, asking him to bring copies of the latest actions out to his home address so they could 'discuss strategy'. Spencer had done as asked, but Munro hadn't done anything with the actions and they had hardly discussed anything. Munro had seemed pre-occupied instead with the quantity of information coming in, almost depressed by it. At one point he had said he didn't know what he was doing. Should Spencer tell Harrison that?

Munro clearly hadn't slept since the enquiry had started. Lines were appearing under his eyes and once, today, when he had come out of interviewing the witness Clare Gunnell – the one who had been walking her dog in Wells Road, Ilkley – he had looked like he was about to explode. Gunnell had given all she could, but it was little. She had been paying attention to other things. Munro had looked like he was about to start shouting at her. Afterwards Spencer had watched him trying to calm down in the canteen. One of his eyes was developing a twitch, like a rapid blink. It had still been like that when he had set off for London with DC Cooper to meet the profiler the NCF had arranged.

'Yes,' Harrison said, still looking at his terminal. Spencer watched the beads of sweat forming on his forehead. The window behind him was open and it was a hot afternoon, but not that bad. 'Yes. You can have the Bradford one.'

'Sorry, sir?'

'The Bradford address. Five, Helmsley House, on the Thorpe Edge Estate. That's an old flag. Don't worry about it.' He used the sleeve of his shirt to wipe the sweat from his brow.

'You'll lift the restriction?'

'Nothing to lift. Look . . .' Harrison turned the monitor slightly in Spencer's direction. Spencer stood up and leaned over the desk, getting a waft of stale air from Harrison's mouth as he came closer. He glanced at the screen. It was blank. He moved back to his seat.

'There's no blocked information on the address,' Harrison said. 'We just put the block on as a flag – so anyone looking has to notify us. It was an old drug outlet, as I recall. We had something going on there. I can't recall what. You can go in if you need to.'

Spencer nodded. 'And the other one? The LS16 address?'

Harrison turned towards him, looking directly at him. 'That one is really blocked,' he said. 'You can't go there, regardless of whether the occupant is on the sex offenders' register. Tell John to speak to me about it if he needs to, but I can tell you it's clean. Little Sophie Kenyon won't be there.'

Spencer nodded and made a note in his policy book. God knows what was going on at the address, but if the ACC said it was clean it was one less on the list.

'Now, DS Spencer—' Harrison started.

'DI, sir,' Spencer corrected.

'Detective Inspector. Of course. The reason I wanted you up here is because you were in the CPT over there before being put on Shade. You must, therefore, have supervised DC Sharpe.'

Spencer looked and felt puzzled. 'Karen Sharpe?'

'Yes. What's she like?'

'Good. Competent. I don't know her history. There were things that—'

'Don't worry about that. I know her history. What I wanted to ask you is why she has not been pulled onto Shade?'

Spencer shrugged. 'I don't know. I didn't pick the personnel.' He did know. It was because John Munro didn't like her. They had a history. Some said a personal history.

'I've been trying to contact her for the last day and a half,' Harrison said, irritation in his voice now. 'About something else, as it happens. See if you can get hold of her for me. She's your detective. You must know how to contact her.'

Spencer stared at him for a second. He could refuse, tell him to go through admin, tell him he didn't have a clue how to raise Karen Sharpe, or that he hardly ever knew where she was when he *was* working with her. 'She's often difficult to track down,' he said, instead.

'I've noticed. Find her. Get her up here.' He turned back to the terminal. The meeting was obviously over.

Spencer stood. 'Yes, sir.'

He was about to walk through the door when Harrison spoke again.

'And tell her she's on Shade,' he said. Spencer turned back to object but Harrison spoke again, quickly. 'No arguments. She's on Shade. As of now. John has been asking me for more staff since this started. That's one more. I'll be at the briefing tomorrow if he wants to talk about it.'

Spencer nodded and opened the door. The instruction was clear.

'If there *is* a briefing,' Harrison added. 'Assuming you haven't found little Sophie by then.'

TWENTY-FOUR

Karen got to The Angel in Hetton a little early, giving her further time to worry about the implications of where she was with Pamela's allegations. The evening was still hot and clear so she sat outside at one of the tables and pondered it all. She had not gone to arrest Reed because, almost as soon as she thought about doing it, the problems began to appear.

It wasn't that Reed was a sitting MP, well known in the area, probably well connected, with strings to pull. Justice was blind. There were unwritten rules about arresting politicians, celebrities, journalists and those with connections. But since they were unwritten she had never read them. If this had been purely a child abuse enquiry she wouldn't have hesitated in making the arrest.

But it was now a murder enquiry. Moreover, it was someone else's murder enquiry and that someone was the ACC. What she obviously should do was contact him, tell him what she had discovered. *He* had been trying to contact her for nearly twenty-four hours. Ignoring him was stupid. She wondered why she had done it. There seemed to be no need. Gratuitous insubordination?

Not quite. Sometimes she just found it hard to take the quasi-military command structure thing seriously. It didn't seem to register with her the way it did with others. So Harrison had asked her to call. It didn't mean he had to be *obeyed*, there and then, as if he were her father. Besides, it was a man's world up there, in the top echelons of any police force. Sometimes they needed reminding that instructions were only as good as the authority of the person giving them. And all authority was ceded, given away by people who were happy to obey. She wasn't.

There was in fact little ACC Harrison could do to her. She hadn't committed any provable disciplinary offence. She had simply failed to be as contactable as she should have been. That would be the story anyway. If they wanted to give her a Reg 9 for that then she wouldn't lose any sleep.

What to do about Geoff Reed, however, was more complex. If she told Harrison, he would probably do nothing immediately. What with Shade and all the rest of it the area was strapped for resources, as ever. Harrison wouldn't want to throw man hours at chasing down leads generated by a supposed recovered memory victim. Karen's corroborating evidence would look wafer thin to Harrison.

She watched Liz pull up in her Polo and climb out with the kind of grace she had only ever observed in tall, athletic black women, though that was probably a racist thought. Not for the first time she considered that there were directions she could take their friendship which Liz might find problematic. Though that was guessing. She was no expert at judging these things. Maybe Liz had the same thoughts.

Liz wasn't smiling as she sat down opposite her. Karen looked around. If she was going to tell Liz things they would need to be alone. The table next to them, busy with a group of four, was too close for comfort.

'Shall we go inside?' she asked.

Liz nodded without saying anything. Karen hoped she was going to loosen up a bit.

They bought glasses of white wine and found a table tucked away in a corner, near the kitchen door. It would be too noisy with the traffic from the kitchen for anyone to overhear them.

'I met with the head today,' Liz said, sipping her wine. 'I think we might have to go to the police, Karen. The boy's mother is—'

'She's nine, Liz. Criminal responsibility starts at ten. If you go to the police they will pass it to social services. Do you want that?'

'I don't. But it's not really for me to decide. We have policies for this.'

'OK. Let me tell you what I'm here to tell you first. Then we'll see what you think.' She realized she had interrupted Liz quite sharply. She slowed down, taking a breath. If she wasn't careful she would end up snapping at her. 'None of this is Mairead's fault,' she said. 'None of it.'

Liz nodded, sympathetically. 'I know that, Karen—'

'You don't. You don't know the half of it.' Karen took a long gulp of the wine.

'So tell me,' Liz said.

How much could she tell her? How much was she capable of telling her? Even Neil only knew the bare details. But Liz was different. She had lived in ways Neil hadn't. When Liz had first moved north from London Karen had been assigned to watch out for her, befriend her, be the local contact point, precisely because someone knew that their histories were in some respects similar. But only in some respects. Liz had taken chances and suffered. Karen had taken similar chances, but by and large she had made others suffer. How would Liz react to finding that out?

'It's about me, Liz,' she said. 'All of this is about me. About how I've fucked up her life.'

'I'm sure that's not true—'

'It is. Just listen.'

Liz leaned over the table towards her, waiting for it.

'I'm not what you think I am. I'll start with the top line.' She took a deep, deep breath. 'I'm not Mairead's Aunty Karen . . .' She paused, feeling a mixture of emotions suddenly struggling to get out. Liz was watching her intently. 'I'm Mairead's mother,' she said.

Liz's eyes widened. 'Her *mother*?'

'That's right.'

She gave her a moment to digest it before going on. 'I'm not Karen Sharpe either,' she said, ignoring the shock this produced. 'My real name – the name I was born with – is Helen Young. And I'm not English, despite the accent. I'm from Ireland. Northern Ireland, in fact.'

She sat back, trying to measure her breathing, keep things under control. Liz looked like she wanted to say something but didn't know where to start. Karen went on, not giving her the chance.

'Not many people know all that. Even Neil doesn't know the bit about the name, or about Ireland.'

Liz found her voice, 'But he knows you are Mairead's mother?'

'Yes. That and a little more. But not my name. You're the only person I've told.'

'But Mairead . . . why doesn't she know? Why doesn't she know you are her mum?'

'That's what I'll tell you now.' She drained her glass. 'Mairead told me this morning what that boy said to her,' she continued. 'He was taunting her about her father being in prison, about her having no mother and being a *bastard*. That was the word he used. That's what Mairead told me.' She saw Liz scowling, perhaps in disbelief – which would have been naive – but she went on anyway. 'I don't know whether the boy had heard something, I don't know whether he was making it up. If he was he hit gold. Prison is exactly where Mairead's father is. Durham Jail, in fact – in the high security wing, on remand awaiting trial on a murder charge.'

'Her father? You mean the man you ... the man you ...'

'The man I slept with, obviously. More than that, I shared my life with him for two years. I loved him.' She looked away from Liz. She didn't want to overcomplicate things, not right now, but the use of the past tense was way short of the mark.

'Who did he kill?'

'That doesn't matter. Not least because there won't be a trial. The squad dealing with it – an anti-terrorist unit from Scotland Yard—'

'Anti-terrorist?'

'Yes. He was in the Provisional IRA.'

'Mairead's father?' There was shock in her tone.

'Yes. The squad dealing with it don't know there won't be a trial yet, but it won't be long before they find out. When that happens he will be released.'

'Why will there not be a trial? God, Karen ... I can't believe what you're telling me. I have so many questions. Why no trial?'

'Because Martin – that's his name, James Martin – will tell them that he will call me to give evidence for him if there's a trial. There are people higher up than the ordinary police who will not let that happen, who would rather he walked than have the world know ...' She faltered. 'Have the world know what?'

'The things I have done in the past.' She sighed and sat back, the worst of it out now.

'Maybe I don't need to know what you've done,' Liz said, speaking quickly. 'Maybe I only need to know why Mairead thinks you're her aunty and not her mum.' She reached a hand across the table and took hold of Karen's hand. 'It doesn't matter to me what you've done. I know you. I know already what I think of you.'

Karen felt vulnerable. She had told no one any of this before. She let Liz squeeze her hand.

'Tell me why she doesn't know you're her mum.'

'I was working for people ...'

137

'People?'

'The government. Eleven, twelve years ago. I fell pregnant with her when I was living with Jim Martin. I was in love with him. That shouldn't have happened. He was meant to be an assignment, a target ...' She broke off and looked around her. No one seemed interested. She brought her sleeve across her eyes. 'I had to have the baby ... I don't mean *had to* as if I didn't want ... I mean I'm glad I did ... but at the time I was confused. They made me stay in there, made me have it. If I'd left he would have found out and it would have blown things. They told me people would die if that happened. So I stayed. But I couldn't handle it. I cracked up. I can't even remember her birth. When they told me I could get out I did. I left them both. I walked out on her. I was in a mental hospital for six months. That was in nineteen eighty-eight. I didn't see them again until last year.'

Liz's eyes were thoughtful now. Karen gave her time.

'What happened last year?' she asked eventually.

'They arrested Jim,' Karen said, trying to finish quickly. She didn't want to go into the details of a year ago. 'The police here arrested him for murder. I took Mairead. That's how I have her.'

'Is she in danger?'

'Mairead?'

'Either of you.'

'I don't think so. Not at the moment. There's the peace process in Northern Ireland – if that's what you meant. Maybe if it screws up ... I don't know ... I check the car, check for tails, that sort of thing. If the talks break down it might get worse, I suppose. I might have to move again. Change names.'

Liz shook her head. The expression on her face was hard to read.

'Do you believe me?' Karen asked her.

'Of course I do,' she responded at once. 'Why wouldn't I? You're the only friend I have round here. You've never been anything but straight with me.'

'I was frightened you wouldn't believe it.'

'Don't be mad. Remember how I ended up where I am. I've seen things, Karen. I know what goes on.'

They sat in silence for a moment, Karen watching Liz thinking about it, working out what it all meant.

'So why doesn't Mairead know who you are?' Liz asked, after a while. She still hadn't answered that simple question.

'That happened almost by accident,' Karen said. 'He introduced us like that – Jim did – last year, before he was arrested. I guess if things had worked out differently he would have told her the truth. But last year he told her I was her aunty. I don't know how it got stuck like that. After Jim was arrested she was so upset . . . I don't know . . . I couldn't burden her with that, with telling her the truth . . . not then . . . I thought I would wait a bit. Then we got into the habit. It became comfortable. I was her aunty. She liked it that way. I couldn't bring myself to tell her. Besides, I always knew there wouldn't be a trial. So I always knew he was coming out. I didn't think it would be this long. But when he comes out . . .' She stopped. The thought was suddenly shocking.

Liz finished for her, 'He would want Mairead back?'

'Yes. So I thought it best to leave things like that. She has never known a mother. She thinks her mum had to go away when she was little. God help me, I don't know what I'm doing with her, Liz. I haven't a clue.' She looked at her feet, feeling heavy, depressed. She could feel Liz squeezing her hand tightly.

'Look at me, Karen,' she heard her say. She looked up. 'I've seen you with Mairead. You do know what you're doing. You are being her mother. A good mother. The kid loves you in that way whether you call yourself her mother or not.'

They sat in silence for a while. Eventually Liz broke it.

'What will you do if he wants Mairead back?'

Karen shook her head again. 'I don't know. I don't know, Liz. But I feel I'm not good for her. Maybe she would be better off with him . . .'

Liz watched her, saying nothing. Karen released herself from her grip.

'Thanks for listening,' she said.

Liz shrugged. 'Has she visited him in prison?'

'No. I wouldn't allow it. Neither of us has.'

'What do you feel about him now?'

Karen looked up at her. It was this kind of insight that had attracted her to Liz. Even if she didn't reply, Liz would know.

'It's still there for him,' she said eventually, immediately feeling her shoulders sag. 'It always will be.'

TWENTY-FIVE

She woke with Neil's arms wrapped so tightly around her neck she felt she was being choked. She extricated herself carefully and looked at the alarm clock. It was after six. Mairead would be awake in an hour. She had slept in.

She looked back at his naked, sleeping form. She could see how he would be attractive to most women her age. Physically, anyway. But she had done nothing more than hug him last night. That was all he had asked for. Holding onto her and praying it would not be taken away, no doubt. He felt things when he kissed her, hugged her, held her hand or touched her, things she had thought she could feel too. But she was past that now. She loved him in some way, because he had been good to her, because it would be hard not to love him (like a kitten or a puppy, staring up at her with big wide eyes – what else could she do but pat him?) But his need was too great. The longer she remained with him now, the more hurt he was going to be.

The double bed was hers, of course, the bed she had slept alone in for nearly six years, until he had moved in eight months ago. It felt strange to her now. Like it was his bed. She was getting used to the spare bedroom.

She got up without waking him and went down to the kitchen, checking Mairead on the way. Liz would call later today, after she had spoken to the head. Meanwhile, Mairead was to stay off again. Neil had booked leave already. He hadn't bothered asking her if she wanted him to, which irritated her despite the kindness behind it. He meant well and she relied on him, but Mairead wasn't his child.

Coffee in hand she went up to the room she used as both spare room and study and sat down with the lists of properties belonging to Eric Pardoe that she had copied from the Flight paperwork. Whatever it was about them that was snagging her mind had been there the moment she woke up. She looked through them again, but could see nothing significant. She followed the paper trail put together by a DC Crowther six years ago showing what had happened to each of the properties. Emily Pardoe had sold most of them quite soon after her husband's death. There was a list of buyers, which also meant nothing to Karen. Presumably, they had been looking for connections back to Emily Pardoe, connections that might reveal a motive for the death.

Logging on to her computer, she extracted the press clippings from her briefcase and dug out the name of the journalist who had written about Reed celebrating with Pardoe on election night 1987. Luckily the name was of Polish extraction and relatively unusual: Alex Jablonski. It took her twenty minutes to find it using a normal search engine and then 192.com. If it was the same Alex Jablonski he had moved on to greater things and was working for *The Times* in London. She noted his home number in Chiswick then called it, feeling sure to catch him in at such an hour. She got the answerphone and left a message about needing to speak about Geoffrey Reed and a piece he had written about him ten years ago. She left her mobile number. Then she showered and got ready.

She was out before either Mairead or Neil awoke. She knew what she was going to do. She had thought about it while Neil slept peacefully beside her. She wanted an early start on Reed. It was possible she was going to end up with a lot of paperwork.

Reed lived in Nab Wood, of course – in one of the big detached houses at the mature end of Glenview Road. Huge sycamores and chestnuts, walled gardens, eight bedrooms. No slumming it with the voters.

From what she had been able to find out about him he had married young and his wife had left him not long after. No kids. He hadn't married again, though there had been rumours – that he was gay, that he was bi, that he was shacked up with his researcher, that he liked little boys, that he was alone, single, normal. She came across virtually everything.

Then he was elected in 1987. After that he worked hard at being the harmless, childless uncle figure, sacrificing his life for the good of others, in the public service. And he put on weight. The good life had been good to him, public service or not.

Karen parked the Volvo outside and walked up a short drive. When she got to the door it was nearly seven-fifty. Time enough for him to have left the place, in which case she would look for him at his constituency office. She had accessed his whereabouts from a security unconscious site on the web. He was meant to be here, in Bradford, on 'constituency business'.

There was a long delay after she rang the bell, but eventually he opened the door to her himself, which surprised her. He was leaning on the cane she had seen two days before, dressed much the same, looking casual, relaxed. Until his eyes settled on her. She saw the flicker of recognition, then a brief spark of anger, followed by the automatic smile and the quick conscious arrangement of expression – to give away nothing. But there was a hint of fear lurking behind it all.

'Mr Reed. Karen Sharpe. We met Wednesday. I'm sorry—'

'My memory isn't that bad, Ms Sharpe. What do you want now?'

Something in the tone said he felt a little safer than two days ago. Had he called someone? It wouldn't help him and he was about to realize that.

'I just have a few questions for you. Can I come in?'

'Questions about your problem? The one you spoke to me about?'

'No, actually. This is a separate matter. I'm investigating a crime.'

He frowned at her, trying to work it out, to decide whether he could just shut the door on her. 'I'm very busy,' he said. 'Will it take long? It would be better to book an appointment through—'

'Not for this. I need to ask you now.'

She waited while he came to grips with her tone.

'Come in, then. But you will have to be quick. I've got—'

'I expect this to be very quick.'

He led her, walking slowly through a large hallway to a room with several sofas and a TV. He gestured to a sofa, inviting her to sit on it.

'I'll stand,' she said. 'You sit, if you wish.'

This brought a scowl to his face. It was his house, after all. She took a quick look round it. The décor was much the same as that in his constituency office.

'I called your ACC on Wednesday,' he said, also remaining standing, but turning to face her. 'Have you spoken to him?'

'My ACC?' She looked at him as if she didn't know what the letters signified. He had called Harrison. So that was why Harrison had been pestering her. It made sense. She felt a little glow of self-justification. Ignoring Harrison had been the right move.

'Mark Harrison. The Assistant Chief Constable,' Reed explained.

She shrugged. 'We don't have much to do with him,' she said. 'I'm just serving the public down here. Doing my job.' She wondered if he still had the pen she had given him.

'He hasn't spoken to you?'

She shook her head. He looked momentarily panicked.

'Maybe you should call him,' he suggested.

'I'm sure he'll get me if he wants me,' she replied. 'Can I ask you my questions now? That way we can get this over with.'

She saw him bite down on his lower lip. 'What do you want to ask me about? Should I have a solicitor here?'

She smiled. 'That depends on whether you've done anything. I'm just making preliminary enquiries.'

'What about?'

'An allegation of rape.'

His eyes narrowed. He was concentrating now. 'How could this have anything to do with me?'

'Well . . . I don't know,' she said, keeping her eyes on his. 'This happened ten years ago.' Someone with nothing to fear would probably have relaxed at this point. He didn't. He didn't move at all, didn't change expression. 'I'm looking into the eleventh of June nineteen eighty-seven,' she continued. 'You remember the date, of course?'

He nodded quickly. 'Of course.'

'You were elected then. For the first time, I believe. Do you remember the evening?'

'The night of the election?'

'Yes. Or the early hours of the day after?'

He paused, leaning heavily on the cane. 'It was a long time ago,' he said. 'What has it to do with a rape allegation?'

'Do you remember where you went after you were elected? After the result was declared?'

He stared at her. The moment of truth. There was not a flicker of difference in his facial expression, but his eyes were frantic. She could see the movement there, in the depths.

'I don't recall exactly,' he said, finally. 'Is it important?'

'It might be. Did you celebrate at all?'

Beads of sweat broke out in the centre of his forehead, began to trickle towards his eyes. He brushed them away with his free hand, then looked around.

'I think I will sit down,' he said. 'I have gout, you see.'

She waited while he installed himself on one of the sofas, then repeated the question; 'Did you celebrate anywhere?'

'I'm sure I did.'

'Do you recall where?'

He shook his head. 'No. You know what it's like – or maybe you don't – but there are so many people wanting to thank you, to know you. You follow your agent, basically. He takes you round. You go where you are told.'

She nodded, took out her pocket book and pen. 'The agent. Who was it?'

'Marcus Walsh.' He answered immediately, so quickly she knew what he was going to say next. 'But he's dead. He died a year ago. Cancer.'

She folded the pocket book and put it away. 'So you don't recall where you were?'

'I'm sorry, no. We're talking about ten years ago.'

She placed her briefcase flat on the floor beside her, squatted down by it and opened it. The newspaper report by Jablonski was on top. She took it out, straightened up.

'Did you know Eric Pardoe?' she asked him. She could see his eyes on the paper in her hands.

'Yes,' he said.

'Did you know him well?'

'Yes.'

He was still looking at her hands.

'Was he a friend of yours?'

Finally he looked up into her eyes. 'He was a business partner. He's dead, as you know.'

'Was he involved in your election in nineteen eighty-seven?'

'He supported me. What do you mean *involved*?'

'Was he there when the result was declared?'

Reed pretended to think about this. 'Maybe. I don't know. The place was packed. Why are you asking these questions? Is this about Eric Pardoe?'

'No. It's about a rape. I told you that. Do you think you might have celebrated with Pardoe that night?'

He licked his lips. 'When?'

'That night. Any time that night.'

He was sweating heavily now. 'I might have. Or at least he might have been there when we were celebrating. He was a party member, a supporter.'

'Do you think you could have gone back to his place – Lower Woodlands – to celebrate?'

Reed started to answer quickly, but she stopped him. 'Think about it carefully,' she said. 'This is important.' She moved the hand holding the newspaper clipping and watched his eyes follow it.

'I haven't a clue,' he said finally. 'I don't recall.' It was what he had originally started to say.

'It's possible though?'

He moved his eyes to hers, thinking it through, then shrugged and looked away. 'I don't recall,' he said. She stooped down and replaced the clipping in the briefcase. 'Is that it?' he asked her. She stood up and looked at him. He was lying. He had started lying the moment she had given him the date.

'I want you to come down to Eccleshill Police Station with me,' she said.

He frowned, looking at her as if the suggestion were preposterous. 'I can't. Not right now.'

'You can.'

He started to stand now, getting angry. 'No, Officer, I can't. I have important constituency business to attend to.'

'That will have to wait.'

He stood stock still and glowered at her. 'It can't wait. I'm a Member of Parliament.'

'I'm afraid that doesn't matter. Not now.'

'Are you arresting me? Is that what you're saying?' He asked the question as if the idea was ludicrous, expecting her to deny it at once.

'I am, as a matter of fact,' she replied. 'I'm arresting you for rape.'

The colour drained from his face.

'I need to call people,' he said, his voice suddenly frightened.

'You'll be read your rights at the station,' she said. 'They include a call. But not from here.'

TWENTY-SIX

Bains found a note in his in-tray in the incident room: *'See me before morning briefing.'* That was it. It was signed by Spencer. He looked around him. There were about fifteen people in the room, about half the personnel assigned to the 'search team' Spencer had set up to kick in the doors of anyone who looked likely, starting with those on the sex offenders register.

They had got through twenty-eight so far, according to the check-list on their white board. There were another thirty scheduled for that day. As they turned up nothing, the net was widening. Bains noticed that the last addresses for that day were in Barnsley, off the force area.

Spencer was nowhere to be seen.

He tried his office, then Munro's, then walked up the stairs to the canteen. Maybe they were getting breakfast. The canteen was full, mainly with people assigned to Shade, but not Spencer. He stopped off at the third-floor toilets on the way back and walked in on both Spencer and Munro apparently having some kind of dispute. Both voices were raised as he walked in. He made to walk back out again but Spencer saw him.

'Bains. Wait there. I need to speak to you. Do you have a fucking mobile or what?'

He frowned and turned back. The room was large. Munro was leaning back against a sink, Spencer standing opposite him. Munro looked bad. There were shadows under his eyes and his suit looked shabby, like he had been up in it all night. He had at least a two-day stubble on his face. He was slumped back against the sink and his whole posture spoke of exhaustion and defeat.

'Yes,' Bains said, still looking at Munro, 'yes, I do have a mobile.'

'Well, why isn't it fucking switched on? I've been trying to get you for hours.'

'It is switched on.'

Munro still didn't appear to have noticed him. He had a crumpled piece of paper in his left hand. 'It's useless,' he said. 'Totally fucking useless. She'll be dead now. It's too late . . .'

Spencer turned his attention to Munro. 'It narrows things,' he said. 'What more did you expect?'

'I wanted it to be more specific.' Munro's voice was shaking, almost as if he had been crying. Bains felt a momentary ripple of shock listening to him. He knew Munro from old. He had not seen him like this before. The dynamic between Spencer and him made it seem as if Spencer was in charge.

'What's happened?' he asked.

'If you came to briefings you'd fucking know,' Spencer said.

'I've been to every briefing since this thing started,' Bains replied, keeping his voice calm.

Munro looked up and seemed to see him for the first time. 'Hello, Pete,' he said. 'How are you?'

'I'm fine, sir. You look . . .' He faltered. Burned out, was what he had in mind.

'I'm tired, Pete,' Munro said.

Bains didn't know how to respond. He nodded.

'We went to London to get a profile,' Munro continued, holding the piece of paper up. Bains wasn't sure who he was talking to. 'We got rubbish: *Unemployed, uneducated, abused as a child, etc. etc.* Everything we could have guessed. It takes us nowhere . . .'

'It takes us nowhere *yet*,' Spencer said, clearly irritated with Munro. 'If we have to go wider it will help.'

'If we have to go wider it will be too late. Jesus! It's too massive. There's just too much ground to cover. Not enough time. We haven't a chance.'

'If we have to go wider, we will,' Spencer said. 'We do it. Meanwhile you have to be more positive. You cannot go into briefing sounding like this. Get your fucking self together, for God's sake.'

Bains held his mouth shut, stunned. But Munro didn't respond.

Spencer turned back to Bains, 'What have you been doing at Kenyon's?' he asked. His tone was aggressive.

'What do you mean?'

'He called me last night and complained about you. Says you were rude, disrespectful and threatening.'

147

Munro looked up now, tuning into the words. 'What's this about?' he asked.

'Bains has a history he hasn't told us about,' Spencer said. 'I've had to go dig it out this morning. He was suspended eight years ago after kicking seven bells out of a rape suspect.'

'A *child* rape suspect,' Bains said. Now he knew what was coming he felt calm. It would be different if John Munro was doing the talking. He had respect for Munro. But Spencer was from the shopping squad. He had his head up his own arse.

'Does it make a difference?' Spencer retorted, scorn in his voice. 'You wrecked the case.'

'I was neither disciplined nor charged—'

'So what? We all know how it works. I've seen the paperwork. You held his head under water, then beat him so badly he had internal injuries and was hospitalized.' Spencer sounded mortally offended.

'None of that was proved,' Bains said.

'So did you do it?'

'This is old stuff,' Munro said, his tired voice interrupting them. 'We don't need to go there.'

'You knew about it?' Spencer asked, surprise in his voice now.

'Of course I did. I've known Pete for a long time.' Bains looked at him and saw a trace of compassion in his eyes, an echo from eight years ago, perhaps. Munro clearly remembered *all* the details; he wanted to shut Spencer up before they got to them.

'And you left him on the team looking at Kenyon?' Spencer demanded.

'I think *you* put him on that team,' Munro said.

'You didn't tell me that he had been suspended, that Kenyon had kicked out that case, criticized him. He has a bias against the judge.'

'What makes you think that?'

'He was round at Kenyon's house on Wednesday night. He asked for permission to search his chambers at Crown Court and told the judge he would get a warrant if he refused. That's not how we handle the victims of a child abduction.'

'He was tasked to look at Kenyon,' Munro said.

'That was taking it too far.'

Munro stood up. 'I don't think so,' he said.

'I do,' Spencer said quickly, voice raised now. 'I want him off that team. I think we should think about getting him off the squad.'

'Did the judge say yes?' Munro asked Bains, turning his back on Spencer.

'He said no, sir.'

'What a surprise. Did you get the warrant?'

'Yes. I was in there yesterday—'

'You searched Kenyon's chambers on a warrant?' Spencer asked, almost sputtering. 'Without putting it through me?' He sounded like he was going to blow a fuse. He took a step forward so that he was alongside Munro. His face was red, angry. Bains felt uncomfortable. There was something complex going on between them and he was caught in the middle of it.

'Shut up, Ricky,' Munro said. He sounded like he was speaking to a troublesome child. Bains noticed that Munro's lower left eyelid was contracting in rapid spasms, a twitch. Spencer bit his lip. He wanted to say more, but couldn't, not in front of Bains. 'We'll discuss this later,' Munro said.

'The judge has complained,' Spencer said. 'We have to do something about that.'

'Before he phones Harrison?' Munro said, standing straight and towering above Spencer. 'Is that what you mean?'

'There is that danger,' Spencer replied.

'Fuck Harrison,' Munro said.

TWENTY-SEVEN

Team 2 were on at Eccleshill when she walked Geoff Reed through the backyard and into custody. The custody sergeant was Ray Dance, a straightforward, no-nonsense shift supervisor with over twenty years under his belt. He hardly batted an eyelid in front of Reed, but she had some trouble with him in the custody office once Reed was out of earshot in the holding room. She was still trying to convince him the arrest was safe when Ricky Spencer's number came up on her mobile. She was glad of the interruption.

'Boss?' she answered, turning slightly away from Dance.

'Where are you?' Spencer sounded annoyed.

'Eccleshill. I'm just about to—'

'I've been trying to get you for near enough twenty-four hours. I left messages. Why haven't you got back to me?'

'Sorry, boss. But I've got nothing at this end. No messages, no missed calls.' She let it stand there, daring him to accuse her of lying. Through the silence she could feel his irritation with her.

'So where are you now?' he asked finally.

'I just told you – Eccleshill.'

'I want you in Wakefield in thirty minutes.'

'Wakefield?'

'To see ACC Harrison. In his office. Thirty minutes.'

It had caught up with her. She looked at her watch.

'Any particular reason?' she asked.

'Ask him. He's been trying to get hold of you for nearly two days. You'd better have an excuse ready. A good one.'

She sighed. 'OK,' she said. She thought about Reed sweating in the holding room and glanced at Ray Dance. There was a danger Dance would either refuse detention right now or make a call that would end up with Harrison anyway. It might serve her purposes to get

Harrison out of the way now. She could leave Reed stewing for an hour or so, smooth away Dance's concerns by telling him she was referring it. 'I'm on my way,' she said. 'But half an hour will be pushing it ...'

'So push it.'

'Will you be there?'

'No. It's nothing to do with me.'

'So what is it to do with?'

'I told you – ask Harrison when you get there. Are you leaving now?'

'Yes. I'll set off when—'

'Right now. Are you in your car yet, Karen?'

'I hear you. I'll get there.'

'Good. And when you're done with Harrison come over here.'

'Over where?'

'Bradford Central incident room. As of this moment you're on Shade.'

She frowned, immediately seeing something going on. 'On Shade? Why?'

'Because we need more bodies.'

'Was this your idea? I don't think John Munro would want—'

'This was an instruction from Harrison. Get George to sort the CPT. It will only be a few days.'

He cut the line without saying goodbye to her, stopping her from asking any more questions. She placed the phone in her pocket and let the thoughts bounce through her brain for a little while, before looking over towards Dance.

'I'm going to see ACC Harrison,' she said. 'Right now. We'll let him make the decision.'

'It's not his decision to make,' Dance replied. 'It's mine. But I'll hold Reed until I hear from you.'

She watched Reed being read his rights and searched, then took her car and began to thread her way through the morning rush-hour traffic into Bradford. Reed made no comments at all during booking in. The shock of being arrested was short-lived. He appeared already to have moved on, controlled it. Now he was planning how to get out of it.

He had made his phone call – to his solicitor (despite the fact that custody would have done that for him) – and then shuffled to his cell without complaint. To Dance and anyone else who handled him he was a model of politeness. He had a lot to lose by being the arrogant big shot. What he wanted was for Dance and anyone else who might recognize him to keep quiet, something Dance had assured him would happen. But Karen knew it was only a matter of time. Someone would leak it, no matter how compliant he was.

Past Bradford the traffic didn't let up. The M62 was still choked as she hit it at just after 8.45. It took her nearly forty minutes to get to Wakefield. Harrison kept her waiting a further twenty minutes, which amused her because it would backfire on him once he found out Reed was in custody. She didn't mind. She sat in the wood-panelled ante room and worked out what she was going to say to him.

It seemed the only real option was to tell him everything, to be truthful. She had to convince him that the enquiry into Pamela Mathew's allegations should continue. That wouldn't happen without giving him the detail.

It was after a quarter to ten by the time an ageing secretary stepped through a doorway and asked her to come through.

Mark Harrison was younger than he had looked in the photos she had seen. There was a faint body odour about him, matching the rings of dampness at his armpits, the discoloration of his front teeth. But other than that he looked normal enough, well turned out in regulation black and whites, with a neat, short haircut and a full head of dark hair. The eyes that turned to look at her as she walked to his desk were small, green and tired, surrounded by a mass of tiny wrinkles. She guessed he would be a little over forty, which meant he was a serious high flyer, somehow or other. The means weren't visible on the surface.

She had plenty of opportunity to take in his yellowing teeth because, contrary to Spencer's warning, Harrison was all smiles as she came in. He stood up to greet her, leaned across the desk and took her hand, holding onto it just too long for comfort. He had to lean forward to reach her and as he spoke a fetid gust of breath tickled her face. She stored her disgust, looked him straight in the eye and began to apologize. He released her hand and made a dismissive gesture.

'Don't worry. You're busy, we're all busy. You're here now. That's all I need.'

He was still smiling at her. She shrugged, keeping her face expressionless. When he sat down behind the big hardwood desk she sat down on the chair opposite.

'I've read a lot about you, Karen,' he said, moving his eyes to a fat, buff file on the desk in front of him. 'I've wanted to meet you for quite some time.' Apart from a computer terminal and keyboard, the file was the only item on the desk.

'That my file?' she asked.

'Yes. I've read it all.'

'Which version have you got?'

'The full version. Obviously.'

She nodded, feeling slightly tense now.

He sat back in the chair and smiled again. 'I understand a lot more that you might think, Karen. I'm not being critical. I was in a similar position myself once.'

She stared at him, determined to give nothing away.

'I just wanted that to be clear,' he said. 'I've been where you have been, seen and done the same things.'

She shrugged again. She knew nothing of his history, she doubted he would have made ACC doing the sorts of things she had done though.

'As I recall, sir,' she said, 'my file was leaked last year from this very building. From under your nose.'

He stopped smiling. 'I know it was leaked. I know all about Phoenix. I know all about what is going on now with the case. It's true the file was leaked from these offices, but not when I was in this post. If I had been here that wouldn't have happened. I know what these things mean. I know the value of information. I didn't get here the fast way. As I told you, I was out there too – for a long time.'

This was meant to set up some kind of bond, she assumed, a complicity.

'I don't know what you're talking about,' she said. 'Why am I here?'

He cleared his throat – looking momentarily embarrassed – then tapped something on the keyboard and looked at the monitor.

'We have the press all over us at the moment,' he said, viewing the screen, not her, speaking as if he was chatting harmlessly. 'We need to be careful.'

'Because of Shade,' she said. 'What has that to do with me?'

He looked up at her. 'You are a part of that team now,' he said. 'Did DS Spencer tell you?'

'Yes. *DI* Spencer told me. Why? Why am I now a part of that team?'

He shrugged, looking again at the screen. 'Because we need all the help we can get.'

'So why am I here?'

He smiled again. 'You know why.'

'Because of Geoff Reed?'

'Correct. Tell me what you're up to there. I might need to manage things from the press end.' Still a light, inquisitive tone. Nothing heavy or dramatic.

'Did he call you?' she asked.

'Yes. He said you were asking questions about a police officer involved in child abuse. Is that right?'

'That was what I told him. Why did he call you? Do you *know* him?'

Harrison ignored the questions. 'You told him you were investigating a police officer,' he repeated. 'Was that true?'

'No. I was sounding him out. Is it normal for people to come straight to an ACC when they have a problem with the police?'

Harrison's features were set now. He picked up a pencil from beside her file, opened a drawer, took out a large ringbound pad, opened it at a page where there were already notes and scribbled something. Then he looked up at her, 'So you lied to him. Why?'

'Has he made a complaint?'

'If he had you would be speaking to D&C. Tell me why you lied to him.'

She sighed. 'Because I'm investigating a complaint made against him. I wanted to test his reactions.'

He nodded, as if he understood perfectly. 'So there's no police officer involved? I can relax about that?'

She nodded. He typed something into his computer.

'Tell me about the complaint against Reed.' Once again he spoke without looking at her, as if neither the question nor her answer could be particularly important.

'Someone says ...' she started, but then the door behind her opened, interrupting her.

The secretary who had ushered her in walked briskly to Harrison's desk and placed a note in front of him. 'That's urgent,' she said.

Harrison nodded, looking mildly annoyed.

'You should read it right now, sir,' she said, glancing with something like malevolence in Karen's direction, before leaving.

Harrison waited for her to close the door then smiled apologetically at Karen. 'She runs this Force,' he said. 'I do what she tells me.' Karen didn't smile. 'Continue,' he said.

'I have a complainant who says he raped her,' she said. She watched Harrison take this in then glance quickly at the note the secretary had left him. He started to ask her a question while he was still reading it, but stopped halfway through. She saw the colour leaving his lips, then one of his cheeks twitch slightly. When he looked up at her his brow was creased with annoyance, the pretence at politeness gone,

'Have you already arrested Reed?' he asked, his voice a tight whisper.

'Yes,' she said, looking straight at him. 'He's at Eccleshill waiting for me to interview him. I had to come here instead.'

He stood up suddenly, so quickly his thighs struck the desk, moving it forward. '*You stupid fucking woman! Are you totally mad?*' The words were hissed so forcefully from between his teeth that she flinched involuntarily, before she could control the reaction. She rose immediately.

'*Sit down! Sit down now!*' he yelled.

She began to walk towards the door, listening for movement that would show he was following her.

'*I told you to sit! You are going nowhere until you have explained this to me!*'

She got to the door and placed her hand around the handle, then paused and looked back at him. He was still standing behind the desk, face bright red, features twisted with rage.

'I'm not your child,' she said, calmly. 'Nor even your dog. I am a thirty-six-year-old adult. I will leave now unless you speak to me professionally. We can take up the dispute with the Federation, the press, a court or D&C. But I won't tolerate you shouting at me.'

She watched something like shock enter his expression. The reaction quickly gave way to one she had seen many times in short-tempered males – confusion.

He swallowed, took a breath, then looked away from her. His

shoulders relaxed a little. She stood by the door, waiting. He was quicker than she expected. Within half a minute the colour had left him and he sat down. When he looked up at her again he appeared embarrassed.

'I'm sorry,' he said finally. 'You are right. I should not have reacted like that.'

She let go of the door and walked back to the chair. When she had sat down she raised her eyebrows. 'What would you like to know, sir?' she asked.

He took a breath. 'Have you charged Reed?'

'No. I told custody I would come here and discuss the arrest with you.'

'He's an MP. Did you think about that? Did you *for one minute*...' He stopped himself. His voice was going up again.

'I don't care what he is,' she replied.

'No. I can see that.' He flicked open her file and looked at her photo on the front page. 'It's all in here,' he said. 'I should have expected something like this.'

She kept quiet.

'What did you arrest him for and when?'

'This morning, about eight o'clock. For rape.'

'The rape of whom?'

'Caroline Dunn.' The lie slipped straight out, without her even having to think about it.

'This morning I've looked at all the offences you've crimed in the last six months. I don't recall seeing that name anywhere.' He turned to his computer and she watched him move the mouse around the screen, click on an icon, wait, then type in Dunn's name. 'Date of birth?' he asked.

'Twenty-third of November nineteen seventy-four.' Again she lied without pausing, hoping her maths were good.

He typed the date of birth, waited, staring at the screen, then looked up at her. 'She's not known,' he said. 'When did you take her statement?'

'A couple of days ago. It's sensitive – because of Reed. I thought it better not to put it on CIS.'

'But didn't think to mention it to anyone a couple of days ago?'

'I tried to get Max Mclean, without any luck.'

'He's been here all week.'

She shrugged. 'I tried.'

He frowned. 'Don't lie to me. What exactly is the allegation and what is the evidence?'

'It's a recovered memory case ...'

His mouth twisted into a sneer. 'You arrested a sitting local MP on the basis of recovered memories?'

'Yes. Good memories. Very clear.'

'What does she say she remembers?'

'She saw him on TV and remembered him raping her. I believe her.'

'You would. You're the investigator. Try to think like a juror next time. When does she say it happened?'

'Ten years ago.'

'That it – ten years? No day, month, time?'

She didn't pause for a second, 'Winter of nineteen eighty-seven. She recalls snow.'

'Where did it happen?'

'A house. That's all she recalls. Maybe Reed's own house. She gave me some detail and some of it matches up.'

'Anyone else involved, aside from Reed?'

She shook her head.

Harrison sat back, calmer now, contemplating her, weighing her up. 'Caroline Dunn,' he said, as if he were trying to remember the name. He stood up and walked to a grey three-drawer standard issue filing cabinet beside the window. Opening the top drawer, he consulted an index card, running his finger down a long list of names. Karen could see drop-down files with name tabs. He turned back to her. 'She's not an informant,' he said. 'So who is she?' He slid the drawer shut.

Karen shrugged. 'Why would you think she was an informant?'

He ignored the question: 'She's not on the PNC, not on OIS, not an informant, not known to us. So who is she?'

'A normal citizen.'

He nodded, looking sceptically at her; 'Any witnesses to this incident she alleges?'

'No.'

'Any MISPER reports?'

'No.'

The expression on his face turned to something near disgust. 'I can't believe you,' he said. He turned back to his computer terminal and began to type.

She sat for a while watching him. When it didn't look like he was going to say anything more, she spoke, 'What do you want me to do?'

'I want you to get out of here,' he said, not even looking at her. 'Get back to Eccleshill and release him. Do not interview him. Do not even speak to him again. Pray he doesn't put in a complaint.'

She sat for a while, angry, but not surprised.

'That's it,' he said, still without looking at her. 'Get up and go. Send all your paperwork to me. It's no longer your case.'

'That's it? Just like that? You expect me just to ditch the thing?'

'I'm *telling* you to ditch it. *Ordering* you. You know as well as I do that you haven't a hope in hell of getting a charge on the evidence you've told me about. Who is custody sergeant over there?' He looked at her now.

'Ray Dance.'

'If necessary I'll call him and tell him. But I don't want to have to do that. I want you to do as you're told. Do you understand?'

She stood up without answering and walked to the door.

'DC Sharpe,' he called to her as she was opening it. She looked back at him. 'When you've released him, go to Shade. I don't know what you were trying to do arresting on such crap. I know that I would like to start disciplinary proceedings against you now, but I can't. We've too much flak as it is at present. But you haven't heard the last of this.'

He turned back to his machine. She waited until she was sure he was finished, then stepped out and closed the door behind her. Safe on the other side she allowed herself a smile.

TWENTY-EIGHT

Neil had promised to make phone calls to find out if the CPS still had the file for Pardoe's ditched 1989 rape case. In the car park within Laburnum Grove she used her mobile and called him. He told her Liz Hodges still hadn't called. They were in the fields behind the house, he said, looking for wild flowers. She could hear Mairead shouting something to him in the background.

'That's not what you called about, is it?' he asked.

'About Liz? Yes.' She felt guilty again.

'You want to know about the rape file,' he said.

'If you've got round to it,' she said. 'But that wasn't why I called.'

'I have got round to it and you are in luck,' he said, the reproach gone out of his voice at once. As ever, he believed her. 'If you go to our building in Wakefield and ask for Malcolm Barber he should have it for you already. Show your ID, mention me.'

'How come you still have it?' she asked.

'The suspect for your rape – Eric Pardoe – was murdered in nineteen ninety. Did you know that?'

'Yes. I thought I'd said that.'

'No. You didn't. Anyway, we gave advice on the murder file. The rape file is attached. There is no destruction date for the murder, because it wasn't solved.'

'What advice did you give?'

'No idea.'

'Am I getting the advice file as well?'

'Yes. Don't lose it.'

She heard Mairead shouting again. She was sure she was calling him 'Daddy'. She wanted to ask him about it, then thought better of it and told him she hoped to be back early again. She had hung up before she remembered she had been put on Shade and might not get back at all.

The CPS file came in a large plastic sack. She put it on the back seat of the Volvo and drove back to Eccleshill, thinking about her exchange with Harrison. She had no idea why she had lied to him. It had been obvious from his first reaction that nothing she could have said about evidence would have got him to authorize continuing with the enquiry. So there had been no reason to lie.

Yet she had made up a false name for Pamela, moved the date of the offence a few months and completely omitted any reference to the two dead little girls, Pardoe's murder and Harrison's own enquiry. Something automatic had kicked in without her having a choice in the matter.

She was still trying to decipher her actions when she got back to Eccleshill. Before going back to custody she went up to the CPU to try to find George, to give him the bad news. But the squad room was empty. She checked her desk and found a message from Sam Ive, the lab tech at Wetherby she had asked to dig out the forensics from Flight. The message said simply: 'Have result. Please ring.' She called him at once.

'You're not going to like this,' he said. It sounded like he was whispering.

'It's all been destroyed?' she guessed.

'No. It's gone missing.'

She asked him to clarify.

'I've searched through that section, and the shelving where it should be is labelled up correctly, but there's nothing there.'

'Empty shelves?'

'Exactly.'

'It doesn't sound unusual, Sam. Did you look elsewhere?'

'Of course. I looked all over. The exhibits are gone. All of them.'

She thought for a moment. 'Are they booked out to anyone?'

'No. There is no reference to them in any of the logs, except for the entry when they were booked in, back in nineteen ninety.'

'You sure they're not just misplaced?'

'Not one hundred per cent. I'd have to search the entire lab to be sure – and people would notice that. You told me to keep it quiet. I see why now.'

She frowned. 'Why?'

There was a moment's silence.

'Work it out, Karen. Who has access? Only people on the inside.'

It sounded too conspiratorial to her. She had been up to the lab stores herself. They were not exactly well organized as far as old cases were concerned.

'Can you search again for me, Sam? I need to be sure.'

'I've already looked round three times.'

'You said you would need to search the whole lab. Can you do that? There's no real rush. This time tomorrow would be fine.'

She heard him sigh. 'I'll do it, Karen. But I'm telling you, they're gone. They've been removed and they haven't been booked out.'

'That's not so very suspicious. Stop worrying about it. Maybe the Flight SIO removed them and forgot to sign them out.'

'You know that's impossible.'

The mention of Harrison brought something else to mind. 'When did you first look, Sam – at the shelves, I mean?'

'Yesterday.'

Before she had met with Harrison. But then, since she hadn't mentioned the connection to Flight to Harrison it couldn't have been him anyway.

'Do you have a record of any work done on them?'

'Yes. That's filed separately.'

'Did they do any DNA from Pardoe to the girls?'

'Are you kidding? The girls were dead two years when they dug them up. We didn't really know how to extract it like that then. We could do it now.'

'If you had the exhibits.'

'Yes. But why do it? Pardoe was buried with them.'

'To see if he raped them.'

It would have been a standard line for any SIO, she thought, given Pardoe's past.

Down in the cell block she stood at the booking-in counter and spoke briefly to Ray Dance. She wanted to ignore Harrison and interview Reed, though she knew that by now his brief would have got control of it and the only likely result was a series of 'no comment' replies. She couldn't do that without lying to Dance, however, because the first question he asked her was what Harrison had decided. She didn't want to get Dance into trouble.

She was in the middle of explaining it to him when Dance indicated a short, elderly black woman in standard lawyer clothes – black skirt, white blouse, black jacket – approaching her from the holding room.

'His brief,' Dance whispered.

Karen turned to her.

'Are you the officer who has arrested my client?' she demanded. Her voice was harsh, full of genuine outrage and heavily inflected with some kind of West Indies accent.

'I don't know,' Karen replied. 'Who is your client?'

'Geoffrey Reed. I want to know your grounds and what evidence you have. Right now. They'd better be sound or you will suffer for this, young lady.'

Karen smiled at her. 'He's being released without charge or interview,' she said. 'Courtesy of ACC Mark Harrison. Be sure to tell him that, so he knows where the favour came from.'

The woman turned to Dance. 'Is this true, Sergeant?'

'Yes. I'm doing the paperwork now.'

'I still want your grounds,' she said, turning back to Karen. 'This will not be the end of this. I will make a complaint at once.'

'You should ask your client about that, I think. Now that he's walking he might not want the publicity. And I don't think I'm obliged even to speak to you now that he's leaving.'

'Do not tell me how to do my job, Officer—'

'If you want to speak to *me*, however,' Karen interrupted, 'here's my card.' She handed her one of the standard West Yorkshire Police contact cards. It didn't even have her name on it. 'You can book an appointment. Right now I'm busy.'

She left without waiting for the response. As the security door slammed behind her she could hear the woman just beginning to start on Dance.

TWENTY-NINE

DC John Markham was sick of Shade already. Standing inside the hallway of Flat 5, Helmsley House, on the Thorpe Edge Estate in Bradford, he tried to shut out the sound of the heavy machinery demolishing the adjacent block. It was difficult. When the crane began with the demolition ball, clouds of dust floated down from the cracked ceiling, caused by vibrations so strong it felt like a minor earth tremor. The walls in the place were laced with cracks and fissures and most of the windows were broken and boarded up.

For that reason, no one was meant to be living there. He surveyed the hallway as the dog team hurried past him, the dog panting excitedly. It had taken them nearly ten minutes to break down the door. It had been fortified and reinforced from the inside with breeze blocks and metal brackets. A drug outlet, that meant. Or at least it had been. There was a loose scattering of used syringes on the boards below him.

The intelligence on the place was nearly two years old. There had been an old block on the details, which the deputy SIO had got the ACC to remove. Other flats in the same block had been 'live' more recently. They had checked the place as much as was possible before going in and it had seemed thoroughly empty, but you could never be sure. It was only midday. If the place was a live outlet, it would be populated and run by addicts. The owner wouldn't come near the place. Addicts would seldom be up and about before midday. It was just after midday when the door went in.

The dog team called out pretty quickly – confirming the place was vacant – and then they all walked in – himself, Atkinson (who was meant to be his sergeant), Spoofer and McCormick. This was a low-priority, low-risk Shade action. None of them was expecting to find little Sophie Kenyon curled up waiting for them on the other side of the door.

That was what it had been like since he had started on the squad. Nonstop, low-risk, helpless tasking, often depriving him of sleep and rest. The sort of actions you knew would yield nothing before you even started them. It wasn't his kind of policing. That was why he was sick of it. The whole squad knew the kid was dead, yet everything was being done on a twenty-four hour clock, as if they could save her.

Two rooms in they solved the puzzle of how the door had been bolted and secured when nobody was at home. There was an escape hatch. Markham thought he should have warned Atkinson. This – cracking heroin chains, turning over outlets, setting up surveillance on the owners of places like this – this *was* his kind of policing, and he had been in fortified outlets like this many times. There was often an escape hatch.

He stood beneath the jagged, gaping hole in the ceiling, looking up into the flat above, while Spoofer and McCormick scurried around to try to get into the place from the floor above.

'An escape hatch,' he said. Atkinson was at his elbow.

'This was a drug hole,' Atkinson said, 'not a porn den.'

Markham nodded assent. In one of the other rooms the dog sounded excited.

'It'll be the drugs,' Atkinson said. 'It won't be able to smell a fucking thing with the drugs.'

The dog had been trained – allegedly – to recognize the scent of little Sophie. They had taken something from her house and conditioned it to look for the scent on it. But in its other life the dog was a standard drugs sniffer. The force only had two dogs that could really sniff out people. But Shade was so big they had made a desperate, dubious effort to 'convert' the drugs dogs to people dogs. So confusion was more than possible.

The dog man – someone called Archer – appeared holding what looked like a piece of tissue. 'Maybe this,' he said. He was holding it up towards them in his bare hands. He hadn't bagged it or handled it right. He was contaminating it there and then.

'How do you know it's not something to do with drugs?' Atkinson asked.

Archer looked confused. 'Drugs?'

'This was a drugs den,' Atkinson explained. 'An outlet. We told you that in briefing.'

'You said that was two years ago.'

'We said the intell was two years old. But that's all these blocks are used for now. That's why they're pulling them all down.'

Markham thought the dog man didn't look very confident that his dog could distinguish between heroin and a little girl. He left them to it and began to look around. The information that had brought them here had come through on one of the incident room public lines. Beneath the deafening racket of the pneumatic drills, one of the builders knocking down the block next door had thought he heard a little girl crying. He hadn't dared go into Helmsley to look for himself, because he knew it was 'full of dealers'. Nobody had asked him whether the noise might have been cats mating in the ruins.

There had been a separate report about a dirty van pulling away from the place on Wednesday night, but that was by a 'neighbour' trying to report on the drug trade, most likely a rival dealer. The report had been anonymous, phoned in from a callbox about 200 metres away.

Within seconds Markham had decided that, though there was an abundance of evidence to show the place had been used to trade drugs through the letterbox, it was all old. No one had been doing anything like that recently. On the other hand, someone had been here recently. He took Atkinson through into the kitchen area and pointed to the evidence, shouting above the machine noises coming from outside.

There were dirty cups and plates in the sink, a working kettle, a jar of coffee and some teaspoons. In the wastebin were wrappings from fast food outlets and chip shops, not smelling so bad as to be that old. Markham picked up one of the used coffee cups and held it up for Atkinson to see. There was an inch of liquid swilling around in the bottom, but no mould. Mould usually formed on coffee dregs within a few days. On the sides there were saucers that had been used as ashtrays – the crushed butts didn't look very old either.

'Plenty of DNA here, if we want it,' Markham said.

'For what, John? This proves nothing. Someone was here. That's it.'

'Not selling drugs though. Not this recently.'

'A squatter then. Who cares? The kid isn't here.'

Markham nodded again. Atkinson – who was on temporary promotion – was in charge. He didn't want to argue with him. They had a tight schedule to get through that day and Atkinson was as bored of it all as he was. If they didn't finish their tasks they wouldn't get home, wouldn't get any sleep. That was the way it was working.

In a smaller room with boarded windows he examined an area of floor that was cleaner than the rest, then brought Atkinson in again.

'There was a mattress here, I think,' he said, pointing to the pattern of dirt and dust.

Atkinson nodded. 'So somebody slept here once. Big deal. Put it in the report, John. The HOLMES team will decide if it needs a chaser. We're out of here now. We have four more to do before four. We're looking for a kid, not evidence.'

THIRTY

There was an encampment of reporters outside the Tyrls, bristling with hardware – cameras, booms, lighting, masses of cables leading across the pavement to location vans parked up in what was usually a bus stop. Karen counted maybe thirty of them, crowded behind barriers that were meant to keep access to the police station clear. Around and about them Bradford was getting on with life as if they weren't there. Most people who passed by didn't even look at them.

She had parked in the car park by the Crown Court and walked down through Centenary Square, stopping off at the news kiosk there to pick up a tabloid. The 'news' had gone over her head during the last few days. She had been so wrapped up in Pamela's allegation she hadn't noticed how big it all was.

Shade was everywhere she looked. Huge banner headlines on every front page. Photo spreads showing pictures of Ilkley, the moor (dirty black and white, made to look more like Brady and Hindley's Saddleworth than the tame stretch of grassland that it actually was), Munro and Harrison, lists of local paedophile suspects. The broadsheets were just as bad. The 'nation' appeared to be 'gripped' by 'little lost Sophie Kenyon' and the quest to rescue her.

She read a few choice, dramatic quotes from Munro as she passed the reporters, then dumped the rag in the bin on the way in.

By contrast, the incident room was empty. A huge marker board at one end showed columns of daily dispositions for about ten teams of detectives. Her own name wasn't anywhere to be seen. She guessed there would be a de-brief at five and she would learn more then.

She spent fifteen minutes trying to locate Spencer elsewhere in the station, then returned and found a desk with access to a HOLMES terminal. There was a TV/Video player set up beside the terminal and a stack of videos littered the desk. She cleared them onto the floor and logged on using the passwords written up on the whiteboard, then began to work her way through Munro's latest enquiry, looking out for anything that caught her eye.

In nearly an hour and a half she was interrupted only five times by detectives wandering in and out. No one asked her who she was or what she was doing. By four o'clock she reckoned she had got through a third of the material they had collated without anything jumping out at her. The material on Sophie Kenyon's home life brought a sense of panic to her and she avoided it. She didn't want to know about the real child behind all this. It made her think of Mairead.

Her thoughts there were too complicated to be comfortable. She could think, like any parent, of the horror involved. She could feel the dread creeping up her spine. But when she posed the usual question – *'How would you get over a loss like that, as a parent, how could you possibly cope with it?'* – she ran up against a wall of guilt so high she felt something like claustrophobia coming on. Nine years ago she had taken herself from Mairead, voluntarily. *She had placed herself in that position.* Until Jim Martin had showed up with their daughter last year, Karen had got on with her life as if the child had never existed. Though she had suffered for it every day of every year, she was not entitled to feel what other parents would feel. Not without guilt.

Needing a break, she walked out to the car, retrieved Eric Pardoe's rape file and took it back up to the desk to read it.

Pardoe had been accused by a fourteen-year-old schoolgirl called Laura Cowgill. Karen read her statement with some detachment. Probably she was going to have to return this file to Neil and send everything else she had off to the ACC without being able to do much more about it. If the forensics had come through for her – or even if they had retained a patch, or a description, of the dresses the two dead girls had been wearing – she would have had something concrete to work with in terms of corroboration. Pamela might have recognized the dresses. The link would have given credence to her memories. Forensic possibilities, though a long shot, would have been even better. But all that was out of the question if the lab couldn't even find the exhibits.

There were other lines she wanted to follow, the most obvious being to locate (possibly through the reporters) other people who had been with Reed the night he had been elected. Also to run checks against MISPERS named Anna and Kirsty, the names Pamela recalled for the girls. The original Flight team had worked without names, so she might be able to turn something up from around the right time frame. But it was time-consuming legwork.

Then there was Pamela herself. She needed pushing on her past. She had been kidnapped and had escaped, so someone would have been told about it – parents, teachers, social workers, police – and it was inconceivable that she hadn't gone to a doctor. But to get at that Karen would have to find out why she was lying, what she was trying to conceal.

She doubted Harrison would be shouting for the file with much urgency. He had other things on his plate. If Reed didn't complain, which was likely – with sex accusations a little of the mud always stuck and he wouldn't want it sticking in public – then there was a chance Harrison would forget about the problems Karen had posed him. But she would have to forget about Pamela Matthews in return.

That was probably going to be easy in the short term. Pamela had been kidnapped and raped ten years ago. Karen was meant to be trying to locate a thirteen-year-old who had been kidnapped, raped and possibly murdered that week. The priorities were easy enough.

At least until she read Laura Cowgill's file.

It was a normal enough child rape file, to a point. She got through Laura's statement, the recent complaint statements, the medical and the 'no reply' interview quite quickly. Back in 1989 DNA wasn't as certain. If you raped someone in 1997 there was no chance of running a mistaken ID defence – the traces were recoverable and they were recoverable whether you used a condom or not, whether you ejaculated or not, even if you killed and buried the victim afterwards. Karen had worked cases where the victim's body had been burned to ashes but DNA had been recovered from the scene. The only viable rape defence nowadays was consent. But back in 1989 it had been open to Pardoe to exercise his right to silence. With one key exception he had done so.

According to the statement of a DC Bains, Pardoe had made two unsolicited comments when being booked back into his cell from an interview room. Both had been said in front of the custody sergeant and recorded on the custody record. This had then been offered to Pardoe for him to agree and sign. He had refused.

Not surprisingly.

The first read: '*You should look into her past. She's done this sort of thing before.*'

According to Bains he had immediately cautioned Pardoe and advised him that if he wanted to speak they could arrange another interview. A by-the-book response, though the book on so-called 'verbals' – unsolicited comments made backstage, off the tape – was still being written in 1989. Now it was impossible to get any such comment admitted in evidence. Back then – with taped interview procedures still new – the law was less clear.

By itself the first comment wasn't particularly harmful to Pardoe. He had gone on though, each word witnessed and noted by the custody sergeant:

'*I don't need to go back in there. I'm tired of this. She knew what she was doing. That's all I'm saying. Look into her past and you'll see. She's no angel.*'

Bains had then asked one further question: '*Are you saying she consented?*'

To which Pardoe had responded: '*You know what I'm saying.*'

The combined effect was damning, firstly because, taken together, the words amounted to an admission of sexual activity, secondly because the reference to the girl's past tallied with things Laura Cowgill had told the enquiry, but which no one had passed on to Pardoe.

Laura said she had been babysitting for the Pardoes, at the house Karen had visited – Lower Woodlands – for a number of months, once every two weeks or so, when one night Pardoe had returned home early, without his wife, and raped her. The detail caught Karen's attention. Not the blow-by-blow account of the suffering involved, recounted very poorly by Laura in a typically sterile CJA statement, but the location: Pardoe had taken her to the children's playroom to complete the act. This tied in precisely with the detail Pamela had given Karen. Already, there in this file, there was a kind of corroboration for Pamela's account. Maybe not something a lawyer would accept, but enough to keep Karen's attention.

She noted in passing that the investigation had been lax enough not to search the cellar areas. Normally, for any rape, the place would have been turned upside down.

Laura had been tied to an iron-frame bed placed in the playroom. She had not cried out and had not struggled because she had been petrified, literally frozen stiff. Pardoe had not even had to threaten her. There was a good reason for Laura's lack of reaction and it appeared in the unused material section – Laura had been the victim of previous serial abuse by her stepfather. She already knew what to expect, already knew how to react in order to minimize the damage. This detail tied in perfectly with Pardoe's alleged admissions made to Bains.

By itself the past sexual abuse would have been evidentially damaging to the case – it meant a jury would be more likely to believe that Laura had the conceptual tools to invent the whole incident. It also meant, because it led to such a complete lack of resistance, that the medical evidence didn't help. Laura had no corroborative injuries at all.

But Bains's verbals took some of the sting out of this. Instead of the defence leading out Laura's past history, the admissions would allow the prosecution to bring it up and, better still, to allege some kind of collusion between Pardoe and Laura's previous abuser. How else could Pardoe have known? It was open to him to suggest Laura had told him, but this would entail a level of intimacy between them which would itself be damaging.

The DNA came back as inconclusive, but there was forensic evidence of semen in the playroom, on the bed in question. On that basis the CPS had run the thing.

The case had come unstuck when the defence – on a Section seventy-six submission at the trial – had alleged that Bains had beaten the admissions out of Pardoe. They had doctors' reports and medical evidence to back up the claim. The judge had ruled out the admissions – it was for the prosecution to prove they were voluntary – and then kicked out the case because, without the verbals, the whole thing fell apart. Karen read the judgement three times, carefully. It was faultless. Then she put the file down and sat back.

Without the brutality allegations it was already a normal, dead-end rape file. Most likely it would have failed anyway for lack of corroboration. Probably it should never have been run in the first place. But two details were ringing in her head now like alarm bells. She knew they were not going to go away. She couldn't now put Pamela's file aside and get on with the Shade.

On the surface there was nothing untoward about the case. To anyone else, what she was looking at would be a coincidence. But she knew better than that.

The feeling she had as she looked again at the judgement was one she had learned over the years not to ignore. The details setting the adrenalin thrilling through her blood were that the SIO on the case had been Mark Harrison and the judge who had kicked the whole thing was Michael Kenyon.

She barely had time to think the implications through, however, when she noticed that someone was standing beside her, looking over her shoulder.

She looked up, annoyed. Almost immediately her features relaxed slightly, despite herself. The man's appearance was striking. He was probably about her own height, dressed casually in jeans and a T-shirt. She noticed his arms first, one of them resting on the back of her chair. He had dark, muscular arms, dense with hairs, a bright ridged golden bangle on one wrist. A Sikh.

His hair was cut short to his skull and he wore a neat goatee beard. The bone structure was attractive – high cheekbones, thin lips, the shape of the eyes slightly Asiatic, the skin a rich, tanned brown. In his goatee and in his hair she could see streaks of grey and white. She guessed he was slightly older than her.

She caught his eyes and felt something inside her pause. They were dark, brown eyes, attractive in themselves, but she saw in their depths a gentleness that could only come from pain. She recognized it at once.

'You're at my desk,' he said. He had some kind of southern accent she couldn't place.

'I'm sorry,' she said, smiling at him. He didn't smile back. 'Do we know each other?' she asked.

'I'm Bains,' he said.

She swallowed and glanced automatically at the papers in front of her. 'Pete Bains?' she asked.

'That's right.' He made no move to hold out a hand to her. The eyes held her own, unwavering, the expression patient and totally devoid of interest in her. He didn't even ask who she was.

She looked down at the *kara* on his wrist. Was it the same person she had just been reading about? She had assumed that 'Pete Bains' was white. She recalled now, with slight embarrassment, that Bains was a common Sikh name too.

'Pete?' she asked, not wanting to just get up and move. 'Is that your original name?'

He sighed, as if he had been asked the question too many times. 'Why?' he asked, still standing behind her, still leaning on her chair. Behind him she could see the incident room beginning to fill as people returned for briefing.

'Just curious,' she said. 'I'm not trying to be rude.'

He frowned and his eyes left hers, moving across the videos she had placed on the floor. He was annoyed about that, she could tell.

'Sorry,' she said. 'I needed a terminal.'

His eyes glanced across hers again and then across the paperwork she had been reading. She felt like covering it with her arm, without knowing why. If he noticed what it was his expression gave nothing away. Finally his eyes came back to her.

'Who are you?' he asked.

'Karen Sharpe.' She held her hand out to him. She could see that he had heard of her. He shook her hand briefly, a surprisingly gentle grip. She was looking into his eyes still, not moving. Behind him she heard someone saying something about Geoff Reed. She frowned. 'What did they say?' she asked.

'Geoff Reed,' Bains replied. 'The MP.'

She stood up in front of him. He was exactly her height.

'What about him?' She felt her pulse quickening.

'They're up at his house now. He's killed himself.'

THIRTY-ONE

There were no barriers, no tapes. One uniformed constable stood at the gates to Reed's house. That was it. But he was there to keep back the press, not preserve the scene. It was a short drive from the Tyrls to Nab Wood and the press had made it already, in force, shouting for quotes from anyone who walked into the building. Little Sophie Kenyon would get less attention tonight – they were all here doing the dead MP instead.

She counted two uniform cars and maybe two others that looked like CID vehicles. Not many men for the death of someone so prominent on the local scene. But that was because they weren't treating this as a crime scene. You were entitled to kill yourself. And they had decided already that Geoffrey Reed had done just that. If this had been a murder scene she wouldn't have been able to get near it. There would have been cordons at the end of the road.

She walked straight up the driveway and through the open front door. The smell came at her immediately. A sharp, raw odour, like nothing else on earth, fresh and fetid all at once, unmistakeable. Somewhere upstairs she could hear a female weeping softly. She passed through the room Reed had taken her to that morning and into another hallway. She was following the sound of murmuring voices. Though the house was full compared to this morning, already it had a different atmosphere to it, an emptiness. This morning it had been somewhere private, it had belonged. Now it was open to anyone.

Ahead of her she saw two doors, both with uniforms standing beside them, chatting. Through the one that was open she could see a crowd of suits. She stepped into it and the smell intensified. One of the uniformed bobbies was holding a handkerchief to his mouth and nose, but the stench didn't affect her. She had experienced it before, too many times. As she entered the room she felt perfectly calm. She knew already what she was going to see.

He was sitting at a table much like the one in his constituency offices, back towards a large bay window. There were men around him, some in white steriles, others in suits, still others in paramedic green overalls, though she hadn't noticed an ambulance outside. They wouldn't need one. It didn't take her more than ten seconds to put it together.

Reed had sat at his desk and rested a single barrelled shotgun on top of it. He had pushed the barrel far into his mouth and pulled the trigger. The shotgun was dangling at his side now, the thumb of his left hand still caught up in the trigger guard.

She knew he had pushed it deep into his mouth because his face was intact, even down to the lower jaw. It was intact, but distorted, resembling and yet not resembling the face she had seen that morning. The bay windows were no more than three feet behind him. The blast had taken all of the back of his head away, showering it out through the broken glass in a tight pattern of blood, bone and brain matter.

Even with the stench, even with him sitting there in front of her, close enough to touch, the whole scene looked surreal, like a special effect from a film. Nearer to the body, beneath the warmer smell of congealing blood, she could smell faeces and urine.

As she stepped forward, everyone in the room turned to look at her. She ignored them and tried to take in all the details she could. Soon they would kick her out. She wouldn't get a second chance.

There were no sheets on the flooring, no guides to stop them wandering wherever they wanted, nothing to preserve the scene at all. One of the men in green overalls had been leaning against the desk Reed was sitting at as she came in. Even as they turned to her she could see their hands, all over the place, touching everything, contaminating.

There were four of them in uniform, two in sterile suits and two in green overalls. Nine people including herself standing in a room the size of an average study. The crime scene was ruined already.

Her eyes scanned along the walls of the place; mahogany shelving crammed with books, African ornaments, tiny, tasteful oil paintings of nudes. Nothing looked out of place or disturbed, but she had never been in here before, so she didn't know. Reed sat in a chair that lined up perfectly with the copious blood spatter pattern behind him, fat thighs tucked under the desk, preventing the whole chair from tipping backwards as the gun went off. The desk in front of him was completely clear. No paperwork, no notes.

She stepped around one of the paramedics, intending to go through the drawers of his desk there and then, but one of the men in suits reached out and held her by the arm.

'Can I ask who you are?' he said. His voice sounded deep, morose, tired.

She flicked her warrant card at him and he let go of her arm.

'DC Sharpe,' he said. 'Good. I'm DI Firth. I'm deputy SIO here. I need to have a word with you.'

She nodded. She felt slightly dazed now. *Had she had anything to do with this?*

'Is the gun his?' she asked, focusing on the dead man's eyes for the first time. They were clouded, sightless, like the eyes of all dead things she had ever seen. She looked up at Firth. Behind him she could see that everyone else was watching her.

'We don't know,' Firth said. 'I expect so though. He went shooting in Scotland. There's photos in the hallway . . .'

'Is there a gun case?'

He shrugged. 'I don't know. We haven't found one yet. Can you come with me please? I really do need to speak to you.'

'Has Harrison spoken to you?'

He nodded. His eyes were rimmed with dark bags. She looked into them and saw that he wasn't going to be aggressive with her, no matter what Harrison might have wanted.

'It's not your fault,' he said quietly to her. There was sympathy in his tone.

'I know,' she replied. 'That's not what I'm concerned about. You should be treating this scene as a murder until you know otherwise.'

She looked behind him at the other detectives. They were smirking.

'That wasn't my decision,' Firth said. 'The ACC decided that. It's his enquiry.'

'Harrison was here?' she asked. 'It was his decision?'

Firth nodded, waving something in front of her face. 'It hardly matters,' he said. 'Have you seen this?'

It was a newspaper – the evening edition of the *T&A*. The banner headline across the front page read: 'LOCAL MP ARRESTED FOR RAPE OF CHILD.'

'No,' she said.

'This was on the desk in front of him,' he said. 'I think we know what happened here. I just need you to fill me in on some details.'

THIRTY-TWO

Bains had heard of Karen Sharpe – almost everyone had – because of Phoenix, because of Phil Leech. But he had suffered enough from rumours in his own past to have long ago ceased taking an interest in gossip. Consequently, he couldn't remember much of what he had heard. Which was irritating, now that he needed to know.

She had been reading his file – the file on the 1989 rape case against Eric Pardoe. Presumably she had pulled it from the stores in Milgarth. Why? She hadn't made a secret of it, hadn't covered it when he had stood behind her. But then, she hadn't mentioned it either. And it was too much of a coincidence that she had been sitting at his own terminal and reading it.

He sipped carefully at the iced lemonade he had made earlier that day. It was nearing nine o'clock and the windows were wide open, but it was still too hot. They had released him early – insisted upon it – allegedly as a way of controlling the overtime budget. He had been on since seven-thirty, a long enough day, but he still had plenty to do. The orders had come from Spencer, sending him a message. No one else had been sent home early.

So he had brought the material seized from Kenyon's chambers home with him. He sat back in the armchair his wife had chosen over fifteen years ago, sipped his lemonade and watched the images flickering across his TV screen. It was easy enough work. First he checked – by watching part of it – that the video was what it said was on the label. Then he skipped through it at fast forward pace to make sure that was all it was.

Most of them were the evidence of abused children, recorded by the CPT in video form so the kids wouldn't have to give live evidence in court. But eight had nothing written on the boxes and a further three were labelled by defendant name and contained recordings of CCTV footage of offences. He didn't really know what he was looking for.

He was operating blindly, methodically, following through all the possibilities that would usually be left untouched. He had done the same with Kenyon's phone numbers – including his mobile – and with the memo pad taken from his desk drawers. The phone numbers had gone off for subscriber details on all calls to and from each phone. The pad he had sent off for an ESDA test, just in case. It was the only way to do it. It annoyed him that he was the *only* person who was doing this, the only person on the squad who seemed to think Kenyon *ought* to be a suspect.

He thought about Karen Sharpe as he moved through the videos. He had tried to check her out by asking around, without much luck. No one even knew whether she was on the Shade squad. It was possible she had simply walked in and started interfering, pursuing some line of her own. That was about as much as he had got out of his DS, that she was 'trouble', unmanageable. He hadn't wanted to pry too much, as it would get back to her. He had searched through the enquiry database for references to Pardoe and found nothing. Then, when she had exited at a run on hearing that Geoff Reed was dead, he had searched through the enquiry for the MP, with similar result.

Had she known who he was? She had double-checked his name, even making an enquiry about his English nickname. Outside his family, everyone called him Pete these days. There had been a time when the name – invented for him by a geography teacher at school, without his involvement or permission – had annoyed him, the very sound of it grating. But even he had got used to it now. It amused him only slightly that it concealed his ethnicity. More often than not people held that against him too, as if he ought to be broadcasting his origins in advance, so as not to shock in the flesh.

Sharpe had been attractive. He had noticed without it registering in the parts of his brain, emotions and flesh that it was meant to affect. He noticed it as if it were a neutral fact, without relevance or interest to him. He saw that this lack of interest had communicated itself to her, despite himself. He didn't want to be like that. It was part of a problem he was trying to move away from.

When she had stood up she had been his own height. Tall and slim, wearing a pair of faded, close-fitting blue jeans and a pure white T-shirt. A small chest, a bone structure that looked strong, especially in the face, the cheekbones, the jawline. She looked exactly proportioned, as if she worked out, watched her weight, led a life full of nerves and anxiety. Yet her eyes had reflected only calmness, control, an easy comfort with herself, with her body. The way she spoke had given the same impression. Slightly ironic, playing with him ever so slightly, flirting. He could detect no accent at all. Which made her from somewhere down south.

There was a pair of expensive shades resting on her head, but apart from that he saw no accessories at all – no rings, bracelets, earrings or necklaces. Similarly, no make-up. Her hair was just past shoulder-length and pulled back into a ponytail. Dark hair, green eyes. The eyes had met his own, stared into them and remained there, long past the point where it could have been comfortable for her. In the end he had looked away.

He flicked the video off with the remote control, stood up and paced over to the windows. Had she had no effect on him? He was nervous about her. She had sat there reading *his* file as if she wanted him to know. Why else sit at his terminal? But were the nerves all he was feeling? He walked through to the kitchen, picked the cordless up from its rest and dialled up the ACR. When he got an operator he gave his number and asked for DC Karen Sharpe's contact details. He told the operator he was working on Shade. He wrote down Sharpe's address and mobile number, then went back to the videos, still thinking about it.

The eight unlabelled videos clearly came from child pornography cases. He watched them in silence with his muscles tightening. They were movies of people having sex with children, of varying quality and length. The children's ages varied. The worst showed a child who could have been no older than six. In all but one there were no shots of the perpetrators. At least, none useful for identification purposes. The one which showed more than close-up penetration shots was poor quality and showed some kind of gang rape scene. He watched it through because he knew it would affect him. These things always did. He needed to cultivate that anger. It was what kept him going.

The downside was that the images pulled him to Millie. He could not even imagine children suffering without thinking of her. The thought was always the same. He saw himself sitting there, in this very chair, talking while it was happening to her not one hundred yards away. He imagined her last moments of panic and fear. She would have been shouting his name, he knew that, shouting for him to get up and help her. She had been dying but he had not heard. He had been on the phone.

When the video was finished he stood up and stared out into the garden. He wished he could smoke a cigarette, or drink. But if he started on that route he wouldn't stop until he was six feet under.

THIRTY-THREE

Driving back up the Aire Valley, Karen felt little. Outside of the enquiry that had brought her to him, Reed meant nothing to her. He was – *still* was – a suspect in an historic child abuse enquiry. Whether he was dead or alive was irrelevant to that status. It did mean the end of the enquiry though. That left her feeling irritated. His death didn't produce closure. Legally, it left all the questions unanswered.

On the other hand, it was one less headache. One that had already cost her in the eyes of people like Harrison. And that wasn't over. She had stalled with Firth, giving him vague answers, giving nothing away about Pamela Mathews, wanting instead to think more carefully about how to extricate herself from the mess her (now unnecessary) lies to Harrison had created.

That she had somehow 'killed' Reed had no impact at all on her, once she had time to consider the thought. If it was true that he had committed suicide then *he* had chosen it. There had been other options. All *she* had done was her job. What worried her more was the relationship of cause to effect? Why would someone kill themselves over an allegation that had got nowhere?

She took out her phone and considered trying to contact Pamela Mathews to pass on the good news. Pamela had reluctantly conceded a set of contact numbers at their last meeting. She imagined Pamela would take the death for what it seemed – proof of guilt, vindication. It had happened to Karen before that suspects had chosen to opt out. A bitter, angry satisfaction was the usual response from the alleged victims.

There was a voicemail message on her phone from a number she didn't recognize, another mobile. Pamela could wait until the morning, she decided, to bask in righteous fury. She would look for her and tell her face to face, if she hadn't already caught it on the TV news. She listened to the message.

It was short. The caller was Alex Jablonski, the journalist she had rung that morning. He was, he said, in Yorkshire covering the Kenyon disappearance and the suicide of Geoff Reed. They could meet tomorrow, if she wished. She had probably walked right past him as she had left Reed's home. He left hotel details. Irrelevant now, she thought, but she saved the message automatically.

She was still distracted by Harrison's decision to run the scene as a suicide when she got home, so she didn't see the car parked by the dry stone wall opposite until she had stopped her own engine and stepped out. She looked over to it then, feeling immediately a sense of unease. Visitors were almost unknown. She thought fleetingly that it might have been Liz Hodges, come to deliver bad news in person. Or the head of the school, which would be even worse. Thinking of Liz reminded her that she had forgotten about Mairead entirely. She should have called Neil before now and asked him what had happened.

The car was a Range Rover, beige, slightly battered in appearance. Not Liz's and probably not the head's. She walked over to it to check the plate, but didn't recognize that either. As she moved back towards the house she heard the front door open and saw Neil standing there, waiting for her. The look on his face immediately told her something was up.

'A Mr Sutherland is here,' he said. 'Says he's an uncle of yours.'

'Sutherland?' She felt her heart jump. 'You let him in?'

'Of course. He says he's—'

She pushed past him without waiting for more. In the front room her limbs froze. Eric Sutherland was seated on one of the sofas, Mairead on his knee. They both looked up as she came in, but Mairead made no effort to move towards her. There was an uneasy look on her face, as if she had already picked up what Neil clearly hadn't – that Eric Sutherland was someone to be wary of. She looked uncomfortable on his knee. Sutherland had an arm around her waist.

'Mairead,' Karen said quietly, trying to control herself, 'come over here to me.'

'This man says he is my Uncle Eric,' Mairead said, frowning.

'Hello, Helen,' Sutherland said, smiling at her.

Mairead looked angrily at him. 'She's called Karen,' she said.

'Is she now?' Sutherland said, eyebrow raised. 'We used to call her Helen.'

'Shut up, Sutherland,' Karen said, stepping towards them. Her hands were clenched into fists. She tried to relax them. Sutherland took his cue and moved his arm from Mairead. Mairead immediately got off his knee. Behind her Karen could sense that Neil had also caught the tone in her voice.

'Shall I take Mairead outside for a bit?' he asked. 'To leave you two alone?'

'That won't be necessary,' she said, still looking at Sutherland. 'You're leaving now,' she said to him.

He made no attempt to move. 'I think that would be a good idea,' Sutherland said, looking at Neil. 'I will only be a few minutes with Helen.'

'Helen?'

'He knows my name as well as you,' she said to him. 'He's fucking around.' She turned to Sutherland again. 'Get out, Sutherland. I don't want you here.'

'You shouldn't swear in front of Mairead,' Sutherland said, still not moving. Mairead walked past Karen and stood by Neil's leg.

Karen caught her breath. Suddenly she realized she didn't know what to do. Sutherland was a face from her past, but not one she had met way back, not someone she had ever known when she had been Helen Young. He had cropped up a year before when she had been trying to track down Phil Leech's killer. He hadn't known her then and he didn't know her now, but he was still from that world. It brought complications. She didn't know what government department he was with, but whether it was military, police or security, she couldn't just throw him out of her house. It wasn't that simple. She took a breath.

'OK,' she said, glancing at Neil. 'Give us fifteen minutes, Neil.'

Neil knew not to ask questions. He took Mairead's hand and started to explain something to her, leading her towards the back of the house. Karen watched Sutherland's features, as Mairead put her shoes on. He was in his fifties, she guessed, thin, white and tense. A ramrod straight military back. A year before he had been clean shaven. Now he had a handlebar moustache, making him even more conspicuous. She waited until the back door shut behind Neil and Mairead before allowing herself to relax. Sutherland didn't know her, but he knew about her. He knew details she wanted to keep from

Mairead and Neil. His use of her real name had been nothing but a deliberate reminder of that. He had leverage.

'What do you want?' she asked.

'To give you some information,' he said. Now that they were alone she registered the distaste on his face. Uncle Eric had all but vanished. She wondered what he had been saying to Mairead. He didn't like Karen, of course. When he had first met her – a year before – he had been guarding secrets she wanted access to. She had tricked him effortlessly and he wasn't going to forget that.

'I don't want it,' she said.

'You don't know what it is.'

'I don't want anything off you.'

'I'll tell you anyway,' he said. 'We are making a decision about James Martin tonight.' He looked at his watch. 'I've been sent to try you one last time.'

'I thought you came to give me information, not ask for things.'

'The information is that the decision will be made tonight.'

'I thought the CPS had the conduct of Martin's case,' she said. 'What decision do you have to make? And who do you mean by "we"?'

'The CPS will do what we tell them to.'

'I wouldn't count on it.'

He waved a hand dismissively. 'Of course we can count on it.' He smiled. 'We spoke to the Attorney General some time ago. He understands the position.'

'And what is the position?'

'You know what it is. That's why I've come here. One last chance. Karen. That's what I'm offering.'

She ignored him. 'You haven't answered my question,' she said. 'Who do you mean by "we"? Who are you with?'

'You know who I'm with,' he said. 'The same people you are with.'

'West Yorkshire Police?'

He sneered. 'Hardly, Karen. You're with us.'

'I'm not.'

'You always will be. You know that. It's not a club. You can't just opt out.'

'I *am* out.'

'That's how you like to think of it. But that's not reality. Information binds us for life. Once you're in, you're in.'

'Not me.'

'Yes. You, Karen. Even you.' He smiled his thin, tight smile. 'I wish I could just forget about you, believe me. You have caused me many sleepless nights over the last year. I have had to stay alert since then. You caught me out once. It won't happen again.'

'Have you been watching me?'

'Don't be pathetic. I watch *over* you. You are still in danger. You do realize that?'

She sighed. There was a noise starting in the back of her head. Eventually it would turn into a headache. She wanted rid of him.

'What do you want?' she asked again.

'To try you again. One last time, before we decide.'

'Try me for what?'

'You met a colleague of mine four months ago.'

'Bill Heaney.'

'Yes. He is our liaison with the Law officers. He asked you if Martin was serious about calling you to give evidence for him. You said he was.'

She waited.

'How did you know that?' he asked. 'Have you seen Martin?'

'You would know if I had.'

'Have you spoken to him?'

'You would know that too, I suppose. I've neither seen nor heard from him. I guessed, that's all. I knew him well, remember?'

'And you still think he will do this?'

She nodded. 'He has nothing to lose.'

'And everything to gain. Do you think he cares for his daughter?'

She bit her lip and stared at him. She knew what was coming.

'If he is released he will want her back,' he said. 'He has been writing her letters.'

Her mouth fell open.

'You didn't guess that?' He was obviously pleased he had surprised her.

'We've received nothing.'

'We intercepted them. Saved you the trouble.'

She moved forward, suddenly angry. She wanted to lean into his face and shout at him. She saw him smile again. She caught herself.

'We assumed,' he said, 'that you would not want the child communicating with a murderer and terrorist.'

She said nothing.

'We also assume you would not wish her to go back to him. The best way of achieving that is to work with us.'

She put her hands in her pockets and waited for it. Heaney had come out with the same offer. They wanted to try Martin for the murder of Phil Leech and they had enough forensic evidence to do it. They did not wish her to give evidence for the Crown. She had given a statement, but it said nothing useful. They had tried to find out from her what she really knew, but she had said nothing.

Which was fine. The worst thing that could happen – in their eyes – was that Martin was given the chance to question her in a court of law, either in cross examination (if she gave Crown evidence) or as his own witness (if he called her, which he had promised to do). By questioning her Martin could expose more than they ever wanted public about covert operations against the IRA during the mid-eighties.

She knew James Martin would never call her to give evidence. He loved her. He was the father of her child. His threat was bluff. Tragically, it was *because* he was incapable of ever doing anything to hurt her that Phil Leech and Fiona Mitchell had died. But she would tell them nothing of this. Which left them only the option of removing her from the country – disappearing her – until the trial was over, making it impossible for Martin to call her. They needed her co-operation for that. She wasn't going to give it.

'I'm not working with you,' she said. 'Not on this. Not on anything. Never again.'

Sutherland nodded quickly, apparently not inclined to force the issue. He stood. 'Your choice, Karen,' he said. 'And one I understand, in a way.' He smiled at her again. It almost looked genuine. 'You know the consequences. We will instruct the Crown to drop the charges against him sometime next week. He will be released at once. Thereafter you will have to fight your own battle over the child.'

She frowned, looking at the carpet under her feet, feeling suddenly confused. Outside she could hear Mairead shouting something to Neil.

'It will be too late to change your mind once we've instructed the Attorney,' he said. He was standing very close to her. He had a small piece of card in his hand. 'These are my numbers,' he said. 'I want things to work for you, Karen. We haven't gotten along very well, you and me. We got off to a bad start. But I know what you did for us. I know everything.' She reached up and took the card from him. He rested his hand on her shoulder. 'Whether I like you or not is immaterial. I mean that. I will look after you if you ask me to. We never forget.'

She looked up into his eyes. Grey, sharp, devious. Everything was a game for him. It was the same for all of them. They were not worthy of an ounce of trust.

'I don't want you to look after me,' she said. 'I don't need your help.' She could hear Mairead laughing now. She saw that Sutherland heard it too.

'She is a lovely child,' he said. 'What her father is, what he did, doesn't matter to us. Because you are one of us. Because we know how these things work. Life is rarely straightforward. We understand that more than most, don't we? Besides, we put you there. We put you in that terrible position. It wasn't your fault. And your courage saved many lives. That means we owe a debt to you. To show you that I mean what I say I have arranged things with the school.'

'What?' She felt the colour leaving her face.

'I have arranged things with the school Mairead attends. I did it today, as soon as I heard—'

'Heard? Heard what?' She felt the anger rising.

'About Mairead's difficulties.' He pulled a pained face. 'Like father, like son. Forgive the sexism, but I fear she has inherited your tendency towards violence. Don't worry though. She will not be excluded. She can return on Monday. The incident will not be mentioned again.'

'How did you find out? I want to know.' He stepped away from her, cautiously. He knew what she was capable of. 'You have my numbers,' he said. 'If you need anything – anything at all – no strings of course, then please call.'

'How did you know?' she demanded again.

He shook his head. 'You know better than that, Karen.'

As he moved to leave she felt sick. She knew his source already. It was obvious.

THIRTY-FOUR

Sophie cowered in the corner and watched it all happening above and around her. A blurred nightmare of obscure shapes, sudden and devastating violence.

First she had awoken with a pain between her legs. She had begun to cry at once, more frightened of what it meant than the actual discomfort it was causing her. Though she could feel the pain, like everything else the sensation was dulled from the drugs they were giving her. Her head spun with a nauseous dizziness, her eyes struggled to focus. She pushed herself into a sitting position and fell at once off the bed and onto the floor, banging her head and slipping immediately into semi-consciousness.

When her sight returned she felt as though she were swimming through something viscous and clinging. A welter of confusing sounds and shapes spun around her. The pain was still there, dragging her to the surface, a sharp stabbing that ran from her groin to her stomach. She tried to hold her eyes open, the sound of her voice echoing in a scream of fear even as she looked down to see blood welling out between her legs.

Something had happened to her. She knew. While she had been buried in unconscious oblivion they had done something to her, they had hurt her. She felt fear ripple through her body and began to cry in earnest, shouting uselessly for her mummy.

Then the door opened and they came in. Three of them, moving with a slow, blurred movement, faces and forms unclear, like monsters in a horror film, arms swishing around them, feet thundering on the floor and in her ears. They began to shout at each other at once. She could hear it like something coming at her through liquid, filled with a strange, distant bubbling.

But she knew what it was. They were arguing. She shrank back into the corner and felt the pulse of blood seeping out of her. As she watched, the drugged haze began to lift and her head began to clear. One knelt down beside her and began to stroke her hair, but only for a moment.

When he stood up, his movements became sudden, sharp, loud. She saw him move towards one of the others, shouting at him. She still couldn't work out what he was saying. Then suddenly the other was on the floor and the one who had hit her in the beginning was standing over him, hitting him with something black and long. She listened to the blows and watched the one on the floor moving, as if in slow motion, trying to protect himself, at first shouting out things in a foreign language she did not understand, then, as the blows went on, crying and grunting in pain.

She watched the blows raining down on him. Sometimes she could hear things cracking. The man was hitting him in the head. She could see it more clearly than she had seen anything since they had brought her here. It was happening so close to her that she could feel warm drops of blood spattering her face and body. Behind the man doing the hitting she could see the third one, just standing there, motionless, at the door.

After a while the man on the floor stopped moving but the other kept going, pausing only to stoop and pull the man's arms away from his face. The man's arms flopped to the floor and she watched his features flatten and turn red, a huge stream of blood spreading across the floor, flowing towards her.

The man on the floor began to writhe in tiny, rippling spasms. His blood met her own on the floor and the two streams began to mingle. In her nostrils there was a strong smell she didn't recognize. The one who spoke English was panting and gasping with the effort of hitting the one on the floor. He paused and leaned against the wall, then began to shout at the other. She could just make out the words now:

'*I said to leave her,*' he was screaming. '*I said to fucking leave her. You do what I say. Do you understand? You do what I fucking say.*'

She felt suddenly ice cold and began to shiver. The one on the floor said nothing and was perfectly still. The English one straightened up and pointed at her.

'*Look at the blood,*' he was saying. '*Look what the fucking idiot has done to her.*' He seemed to be crying as he looked down at her. '*What* are we going to do now?' he yelled. '*What are we going to fucking do about it?*'

The other looked at him, then said something in broken English about a doctor. The English one moved to hit him, but stopped.

'*We can't get a fucking doctor, you idiot. We can't.*'

She saw them both looking at her, looking at the blood. She began to sob uncontrollably. The pain was getting worse.

'*Give her the drugs,*' the English one said. His words were getting clearer. For the first time the haze inside her eyes began to clear. '*When she's out I'll clean her up. Maybe try to stitch her . . .*' They were speaking about her as if she couldn't hear them. The shivering in her legs increased. '*If she doesn't make it, she doesn't make it,*' she heard him say. '*It's fucked now.*'

They walked out and closed the door behind them. She stopped crying and looked over at the one on the floor. Where his arm was stretched out she could see a small black tattoo, smudged with blood, just above his wrist. It was a swastika – she knew because they had taught her about it in history lessons. The arm was perfectly still now. The blood had stopped running out of him and he wasn't breathing.

THIRTY-FIVE

Ricky Spencer thought he should have seen it coming. From that morning in the toilets – Munro swearing at him, criticizing Harrison in front of Bains, allowing Bains to continue investigating Kenyon when he clearly had a grudge – it was all there. Even the day before he had seemed panicky, distracted. Spencer had the chance to tell Harrison and he should have. He regretted his loyalty now.

At nine-fifteen he found Munro alone in the office they were sharing in The Tyrls, hunched over his desk, head in his hands. As he came in Munro remained like that, not even bothering to look up. Spencer stood in front of the desk and politely cleared his throat, but Munro was either asleep or worse. In the end Spencer reached over and shook his shoulder.

Munro looked up with black, tired eyes. They were open – not like he had been sleeping – but the expression in them was one of dejection and defeat. He asked Spencer what he wanted. His voice was hard, hostile. But that wasn't what concerned Spencer. He was almost sure he could smell alcohol on Munro's breath.

'Have you been out for a drink?' he asked.

Munro sighed and sat back in the chair, looking away from him, out through the window. It was still light outside. A mild summer evening. Through the open window Spencer could hear a babble of voices drifting up from the plaza, two floors below.

The media circus had regrouped, but not focusing on Shade. An MP had shot himself. They were saying it was because Karen Sharpe had gone after him for an ancient child abuse allegation – the sort of frivolous, wasteful chase he would have closed down if he'd still been over at the CPT, still been in a position to watch her. But it was too late now. They would hang her out to dry if she'd put a foot wrong.

They'd been waiting for the excuse to do it for over a year. It wasn't his problem now.

'What do you want, Ricky?' Munro asked him.

Spencer swallowed his concern. Munro didn't seem drunk. He seemed tired, depressed. Maybe he was wrong. Spencer wondered whether he had slept at all since this started. He had even had difficulties himself.

'They are having problems with a defence solicitor downstairs,' he said. 'I want you to exclude him.'

There were certain circumstances in which a suspect could be denied legal representation by a specific individual. He couldn't remember what they were, but knew it needed at least the authority of a superintendent.

'Do you know how long it is now?' Munro said.

Spencer frowned. 'How long what is?'

'One hundred hours and thirty minutes, at least, since she disappeared. One hundred hours at nine this evening. Assuming she vanished at five on Monday.'

Spencer nodded, still frowning. The calculation took them nowhere. He would rather Munro was down in the incident room directing things than slumped across his desk computing futile calculations of loss. He wondered whether he was always this awkward to work with.

'Do you still think she's with a relative?' Munro asked him, voice heavy with bleak sarcasm.

Spencer shrugged. Wherever she was, they still had to get on and find her, dead or alive.

'You don't care, do you?' Munro asked, an edge to his voice. 'None of you fucking care. They even want me to call off the searches on the moor. They haven't been up there two days and already they want to stop. They don't care. That's why we're still missing her.'

Spencer looked away from him. It wasn't worth an argument. He waited in silence until he was sure Munro had finished. 'Will you exclude this solicitor, *sir*?' he asked again.

Munro let out a long breath, than ran his hands through his hair. 'It's too fucking late for all that, Ricky,' he said. 'I've told you before. We're too late. I should have gone to Harrison and told him. I don't know what I'm doing. I haven't a clue. No one knows. They couldn't give me a single name of an SIO who has recently handled this sort of thing. Not this big. Not with HOLMES fucking you up in the background. In the entire country they couldn't give me a name. We have so many actions that—'

'We're working through them,' Spencer interrupted. He didn't have time for the angst again. It had been bad enough that morning. 'That's what we're meant to be doing. You're tired. You should exclude this brief for me, go home, get some sleep.'

Munro stared at him in silence.

'You're fucking useless like this,' Spencer said, looking right at him.

Munro took in the insult, stood up, reaching behind the chair for his jacket. He didn't say anything in response. He knew it was true.

'What do you want me to do?' he asked, when he'd got the jacket on. Spencer thought he sounded almost tearful.

'Exclude a solicitor.'

'Oh,' Munro said, as if he had only just picked up the request. 'Who is it?'

'Alastair Bateman.' He was local, well known.

'He's normally OK,' Munro said, looking puzzled.

'He won't let us question the suspect,' Spencer said.

'He can't stop you,' Munro replied, focusing, it seemed, on the problem.

'He won't let the client answer, I mean. Says we have no grounds to hold him and haven't disclosed enough. Says we haven't even got a charge in mind.'

'Which is true?'

'Obviously.'

'Who's the suspect?'

'Thomas Ritchie. He's from Wakefield. He's on the register. We got two anonymous calls pointing to him.'

Munro nodded. 'Anonymous. A waste of fucking time. Someone who knows he's a paedophile and wants him off their estate.'

'Undoubtedly. But we still need to question him. He hasn't got the girl, but he might know who has. His conviction was for Internet child porn, a year back. It's a tight little virtual world out there. They all know each other. They all know what's going on. Those were your words, I think – at the first briefing.'

'All right. I'll speak to Alastair. He knows the score.' Already he was walking to the door.

'You should just exclude him,' Spencer tried.

'Can't do it. Not for that reason.'

On the way down Spencer thought he had recovered. They passed people from the squad and Munro greeted them, said encouraging words, sounded normal again. But as they came through the cell block doors, Munro stumbled and steadied himself against the wall.

At the custody counter, there were beads of sweat running from Munro's hairline to the nape of his neck. Spencer leaned towards him to ask him quietly if he was OK, but Munro anticipated his movement and put a hand up to stop him.

'Fuck off, Ricky,' he said, under his breath. 'I've had just about enough of you.'

Spencer stepped away, trying to think what he had done wrong. When Munro turned to look at him Spencer thought his pupils looked dilated, the lids straining to stay open. He was falling asleep on his feet, but by the time Spencer realized it was too late, Alastair Bateman was already coming up from behind them.

'I've been asking to speak to you, John,' Bateman started. He looked pleased to see Munro. They obviously knew each other.

Munro turned and shook his hand, grinning.

Bateman frowned. 'You look tired, John.'

'I am, Alastair. Not enough football in the diet. You still supporting the scum?' Munro explained to Spencer: 'Alastair's a Man U fan. He's not from Manchester, of course.'

Bateman laughed politely. He was a young man, thin and unshaven, with a face devoid of fat and a suit full of creases. He was a good foot shorter than Munro. 'But you're a Man City man, aren't you?' he asked Munro.

'I am. For twenty-five years. That's loyalty, you see.'

'You're Scottish though.'

'I am. So I shouldn't criticize, right?' Munro laughed. The sound echoed down the cell corridor. 'You're making things difficult, Alastair,' Munro said then, face straightening. 'That's what Ricky here tells me. Let's have a chat, shall we?'

They walked to a spare interview room and sat down in the windowless, airless space. The fluorescent tube in the ceiling was flickering disturbingly. Munro looked as if he was about to shut the door on Spencer, but Spencer walked past him before he had the chance. Munro sat opposite Bateman across the small desk. There was no third chair, so Spencer stood behind Munro.

'We want to talk to your client, Alastair,' Munro started. 'That's all. He's not under suspicion of anything. We're looking for a little girl here. We want him to help, if he can. That's all.'

Bateman took out a pad and began to write things down.

'Why are you doing that?' Munro asked. 'This is all off the record.'

'Not for me it's not,' Bateman said. Spencer saw Munro tense. 'I want to know why you arrested my client.'

'Can't we just talk about this, Alastair, man to man?' Munro was trying a wheedling why-can't we-be-buddies tone. It wasn't working. 'We don't have to get legal about it,' he said. 'Your client hasn't done anything to bring him under suspicion. We just need his help.'

Bateman scribbled again. Spencer watched Munro's eyes following the pen. He saw the involuntary flexing of the jaw muscles he had noticed earlier.

'So why is he arrested?' Bateman asked finally, looking up.

'So we can talk to him.'

'What were your grounds to arrest him?'

'So we can talk to him. No big deal.'

'I'm writing that down,' Bateman said. 'You have told me you have no grounds to arrest him. Yet you have done so and are holding him, therefore, illegally.' He began to write again, looking up at Spencer after a pause. 'You are my witness,' he said to Spencer.

'Shut up, Alastair,' Munro said, voice harder. 'I could take that pad off you if I wanted. I don't have to speak to you. I don't have to explain anything. I could exclude you if I wanted. Do you want to play this as friends or do I start using other methods?'

Spencer held his jaw tight. He saw Bateman sit back, surprised, trying to compute what Munro's words might mean.

'I am trying to save the life of a little girl here,' Munro continued. His tone was rising, but still Spencer thought he was in control, on top of it. 'I don't have time to fuck around. Your client is a child-abusing little pervert who shouldn't be out on the street. I want him to tell me what he knows, that's all. Are you going to block that?'

Bateman leaned forward and wrote onto the pad again, then looked up, eyes perfectly calm. 'I'm not your friend, John,' he said. 'I'm here to represent someone. Because he's on the register doesn't give you a reason to kick his door in and haul him down here. What I want to know is when you're going to release him.'

'Fuck this!' Munro said the words in a barely audible hiss. Then he was up and moving before Spencer could react, rising from the chair and reaching across the desk. Bateman automatically moved backwards. But Munro was quick. He had the pad of paper out of his hands before he could protect it. While Bateman was still stunned, Munro straightened up and began to turn towards the door.

Then Bateman realized what he had done. Shouting something incoherent, he reached forward and took hold of the pad still in Munro's left hand.

Munro swivelled towards him, eyes blazing with rage. 'Let go!' he shouted. His voice was tense, high-pitched.

'I will not,' Bateman said. 'You'll give me it back now or—'

'Let fucking go. I'll only tell you once more.'

Spencer could see it coming.

'That is *my* pad,' Bateman shouted. He started wrenching at it, face red with anger. 'DI Spencer is a witness to this—'

'*DI Spencer is my deputy SIO*,' Munro spat the words at him. '*He won't see a fucking thing!*' He let go of the pad. Bateman fell backwards, suddenly released. Spencer watched Munro's body tense, saw his right arm pull back. He moved to try to stop him – but too late, too slow.

Munro stepped into Bateman's space and snapped his arm out, striking Bateman a clean, heavy blow into the middle of his face. Bateman stumbled backwards into the cell wall, his hand to his nose, eyes wide with shock. The pad dropped to the floor.

Munro stood to his full height in front of the lawyer, took a breath, then calmly stooped down to pick up the pad. As he bent foward, blood began to well from between Bateman's fingers. Spencer cursed under his breath and Munro turned very slowly towards him.

'What did you see, Ricky?' he asked. 'Did you see anything?' His eyes looked mad.

'You stupid fucker,' Spencer said. 'Get out of here now.' He moved past him towards Bateman, but Munro wasn't taking the hint.

'What did you see?' he asked again. There was worry in his voice.

'I saw you hit this solicitor, John,' Spencer said. 'I need to get him a doctor. If you don't get out I'll have you arrested.'

He turned back to Bateman, whose eyes were screwed tight with pain now. The blow had been hard. Munro was a big man. Behind him he heard the door open.

'Leave the notepad,' he shouted, but when he turned to check, Munro was still standing there.

There were tears in his eyes.

THIRTY-SIX

In the bar of the Midland Hotel Karen ordered a pot of coffee and tried to keep her eyes focused. The clock on the wall said 8.55. She had been up all night, mind filled with thoughts of James Martin and what his release might bring. About five minutes after the birds started – at 4 a.m. – fatigue caught up with her. But she knew from experience that to give in then would simply make her more tired later, so she had got up, made coffee and toast, steered her mind towards Geoff Reed, Pamela Mathews and Michael Kenyon. At 7.30 she had called Jablonski, waking him. She had left the house before Neil and Mairead were up.

Jablonski had agreed to meet her here, the hotel where he was staying, a vast, crumbling Victorian railway hotel in central Bradford. The bar was closed, but she didn't want to sit alone and order nothing in the breakfast restaurant, so she asked for coffee in the bar. She was slightly early.

Saturday. Over four days since Sophie Kenyon had disappeared. She had thought of the girl she had neither met nor seen as she had kissed Mairead's forehead before leaving the house. Mairead had got to bed late and had been deep in slumber. Karen had spent too long talking to her about Sutherland the night before, about what he had said to her. In the end it had precipitated another argument with Neil. She had slept alone again.

She hadn't seen Sophie Kenyon in the flesh, but she knew what she looked like. There were huge blow-ups of her all over one wall of the Shade incident room. The child was older than Mairead and different in appearance. She had long blonde hair, which fell down to almost the middle of her back, a rounder face, blue eyes and a wide mouth. She didn't look like Michael Kenyon, her father, though Karen had only seen the recent picture of him they had used in the *T&A*.

She shared something with Mairead though – a sadness to her expression. The picture they had taken for the enlargements showed Sophie in her school uniform staring fixedly at the camera. Where there should have been innocence in her eyes, Karen saw knowledge, though she didn't know of what. It was the same with Mairead; even her cheeky grin had a depth Karen didn't see in other kids, a premature knowledge of limits.

She emptied her coffee cup and sighed. She was neglecting both of them. She should have been in the Tyrls, checking in with John Munro, not meeting a journalist to ask questions about an enquiry without a suspect. And she was neglecting Mairead, leaving her too much in the care of Neil. All that was going to have to stop. The whole Neil thing was going to have to stop. She knew that. Martin's release would change everything, when it happened.

Jablonski appeared ten minutes later than arranged and quickly found her. He was a tall, well-built man, probably in his late thirties. The only thing remotely Polish about him was the long, hooked nose, though Karen knew so little about Poland that for all she knew the nose was atypical – she was guessing, and using some vague racial prejudice to do so.

'Why did you change your mind?' he asked as he sat down.

'Change my mind?' She frowned at him.

'You said you weren't going to bother calling me since Reed was dead. Then you changed your mind.'

'Oh.' She nodded. 'Just trying to tie up the loose ends.'

'Good,' he said, helping himself to the coffee she had ordered. 'It's nice to meet you, Karen Sharpe. I've heard about you.'

She waited for the inevitable.

'You were the officer involved in the death of that drug squad guy last year, weren't you?'

'Involved in?' she asked.

'There was a connection,' he said, sipping the coffee. 'Weren't you going to be a witness then dropped out?'

He was well informed, to a point.

'I was never a witness,' she lied. 'I worked with Phil Leech – the deceased – on the drug squad. That's all.'

He smiled at her. 'That's not what I heard.'

She smiled back at him. 'What have you got to tell me about Geoff Reed?'

His face grew serious. 'Not much, really. But I'll tell you what I know. Are you still investigating him?'

'Who said I was investigating him?'

'The newspapers . . .'

'Well, you know what they say about—'

'. . . and also, in your original message you told me you were interested in Geoff Reed's whereabouts on election night in nineteen eighty-seven.'

'Yes. I did say that, I suppose. You did a little piece for the *T&A* back then. About cronyism. Geoff Reed's friends. You probably don't remember—'

'Oh, but I do. The article cost me goodwill. It was part of a bigger piece the editor pulled. Too dangerous for a small-town rag. What do you want to know about it?'

'Whatever you can tell me.'

'What's your angle? Why were you looking at him? They told me you were on Shade – is that right?'

'I am. But this isn't about that.'

'What's it about? Reed is dead. How could it matter what he was doing ten years ago, or who he was with?'

'It probably doesn't matter. Like I said, I'm just tying things up.'

'You arrested him yesterday for rape. An old rape allegation, from ten years ago – at least that's what the *T&A* ran with. Was it something to do with election night?'

Karen looked unblinkingly at him, face impassive. He was quick on the uptake. She would have to be careful. 'I've already read what you wrote about election night,' she said. 'What I'm interested in is who Reed was mixing with back then.'

'Eric Pardoe?'

'Yes. Who else?'

Jablonski sat back, frowning now. 'I can see where you're going,' he said. 'We should talk about this.'

'Talk about what?'

'You're making connections.'

'Am I?'

'I think so. Big connections.'

He sat in silence, sipping from the cup. She waited for further explanation, but none was forthcoming. She tried to work out what connections he might guess that she was making. She couldn't, so instead she let herself settle and get used to the silence. It wasn't a game he would win with her.

'I need something from this,' he said, eventually. 'I need to be in on it.'

'You know I can't do that. I need your confidence right now.'

'You have it. But if you get anything decent I want it.'

'Done.'

'Just like that?'

'Why not? I don't expect to get anything. Reed is dead and I'm tying up loose ends.'

'So why do you need me to be quiet?'

'Because this enquiry already cost *me* goodwill. I wasn't popular on this force to start with. Now the ACC thinks I virtually killed Geoff Reed. And for no good reason.'

'I see. The loose ends are important to you because you still want to prove things against him. For your career?'

'Not quite.'

'What then?'

'Tell me what you know. We'll take it from there.'

'Have you heard about Eric Pardoe?'

'Yes. I've been to his house, in fact.'

'You've been digging, then. What do you make of him?'

'You know he's dead?'

'Of course. I covered his death from London. I tried, in fact, to run the same article I wrote in nineteen eighty-seven but from down there. Updated. They still wouldn't let me.'

'Why the reluctance? What did you write?'

'I'll show you.' He pulled a folded piece of paper from inside his jacket pocket and passed it across to her. 'I printed it off last night from my laptop. That's the updated one – the one I wanted to run when Pardoe was found buried on top of two dead girls.'

She unfolded it. The article was perhaps 1,500 words long, with photos. She scanned the photos, finding Geoff Reed and Eric Pardoe quite quickly. She didn't recognize the others.

'I would have thought,' Jablonski said, while she was still looking at it, 'that if you were a politician or a judge, Eric Pardoe would not be the sort of friend you would want to have. A man accused of raping a fourteen-year-old girl who is subsequently found buried on top of two dead teenagers. That's not good publicity. You might go to some lengths to hide such connections.'

She looked up at him. 'What do you mean – if you were a politician or a judge?'

'Third picture from the right,' he replied. 'Recognize him?'

She looked at it. A young man with white hair, a thin face.

'That's Michael Kenyon,' Jablonski said. 'The picture is from nineteen eighty-seven. He wasn't a judge then. He was a young silk, going places. He made judge the year after that photo was taken.'

She saw the resemblance and held her breath, keeping her eyes on the page and away from Jablonski. Silently, she ran the possible links through her mind, testing them, doubting them. But they were there. They were real. If Jablonski was correct she had it in black and white.

'What's the connection?' she asked, still careful not to look at him. She could feel the information releasing adrenalin into her blood-stream. She would have to control it or he would see.

'Pardoe invested for him, bought him properties.' Jablonski said. 'They go back a long way. The details are all there. Solid stuff. Good sources.'

'They were friends, or business partners?'

'Is there a difference at that level? Reed and he were connected in the same way.'

'And they wouldn't let you publish this?'

'The *T&A* was just too cautious. They cut nearly all the names because the lawyers told them to. Pardoe looked like a pillar of society back then, so it was a bit stupid. All they put in was one reference to Reed going back to Pardoe's on election night. But when I wrote the updated piece Pardoe had already been charged and acquitted of child rape and then subsequently murdered. Things were different. It should have been a good story, a good set of connections to flag up. It would have made Reed look dirty even if he wasn't. But someone got the editor to pull it. I was in London, by then, with *The Times*. I was junior staff. I let it go.'

'Did they give you reasons?'

'It doesn't work like that. Not if you're nobody. What I didn't know then was that Kenyon was the judge who pulled Pardoe's rape case. Did you know that?'

She looked up at him. 'I did. What else do you know about that case?'

'It was meant to fail because some DC had a go at Pardoe—'

'Bains?'

'I don't remember the name. I remember he had just lost his kid and his wife. He was under pressure. He lost it with Pardoe and had a go at him. That was how the defence ran it.'

'Lost a kid *and* a wife?'

'The kid had some kind of accident. The wife killed herself subsequently.'

'This is DC Bains you're talking about?'

'I don't recall his name. Asian guy. Anyway, it looked safe to throw the thing. Kenyon had all those reasons. But he didn't ever say he was a friend of Pardoe's. To me that stinks badly.'

Karen folded the piece of paper. 'Kenyon looks different now,' she said. 'Older.'

'His wife died, I think,' Jablonski said, 'two years after he made judge.'

'You have a good memory.'

He shrugged. 'That's the job.'

'Can I keep this?'

He nodded. 'That's why I printed it off. You going to tell me where you're going on this?'

'I don't know where I'm going,' she said. 'I'm not meant to be looking at it at all.'

'Funny that, isn't it?'

'What?'

'How the thing gets closed down.'

'You're seeing too many conspiracies. It's just a manpower thing. I'm meant to be looking for Sophie Kenyon.'

'And you think that's a coincidence?'

'What?'

'That Kenyon's kid goes missing, you arrest Reed for a ten-year-old child rape and he kills himself, then you get pulled from the enquiry? You think all that is coincidence?'

She stared at him.

'In my job that kind of coincidence doesn't exist,' he said.

She stood up. 'I have to go,' she said.

He stood with her. 'Remember the deal.'

'I will. Thanks for this, but I doubt anything will come of it.'

'Now why does that not surprise me?'

She paused. 'Was there anyone else?' she asked.

'Anyone else in what way?'

'Besides the names you have listed here. You hear of anyone else connected to Pardoe that I should know about?'

He shook his head. 'There were rumours about other politicians, policemen, that kind of thing. But they didn't come to anything.'

'Policemen? Any names?'

'None that I got to.'

She considered this for a while, then reached out and shook his hand.

'We must talk about Phoenix someday,' he said, smiling again. 'Before it all goes pear-shaped. You should get your side of the story down before then.'

'*Is* it all going pear-shaped?'

'You know it is.'

The Shade incident room was filling up for morning briefing. There was a buzz in the air, some kind of rumour about Munro. It was big enough to eclipse whatever interest Karen's arrest of Reed might have generated. The only person she saw looking at her was Bains. He was at the terminal she had used. He looked up at her almost as soon as she entered. She caught his eyes and saw immediately the sadness she had seen the day before. But she knew the reason now. She smiled at him, she hoped with some kind of understanding. He looked away.

She searched across the whiteboards for Kenyon's number, wrote it down, then – as they all filed into the conference room for the briefing – walked up to the canteen to call him.

She let it ring until the exchange cut her off, then called again. Eventually it was answered by a male voice.

'Yes?'

'Is that Judge Kenyon?'

'Yes. What do you want? Who are you?' He sounded half deaf, disorientated.

'I'm sorry, Judge. Perhaps I woke you up.'

'Who is it?'

'It's DC Sharpe. I'm investigating your daughter's disappearance. I need to come out and speak to you. Today.'

'What about?'

She paused. The question was strange and she hadn't expected it. Surely people from the enquiry were talking to him all the time?

'I don't want any more police round here,' he said, not waiting for her answer. 'I've told Munro that. I'll speak to John Munro. That's all. Who do you think I am? Do you *realize* who I am? There are security implications, for God's sake.'

She waited until he was silent. The message was clear. She was below him, not important enough. Either that or he was a brick short. There were no security implications she could think of.

'I'm looking at some lines from ten years ago,' she said, irritation getting the better of her. She had not wanted to warn him.

'Ten years ago? Who are you?'

'I'm DC Sharpe, sir. I just need to—'

'Did you hear me? If you want to say something say it to your SIO.'

She took a breath. 'Did you know that Geoff Reed has died?'

Silence. She decided to continue.

'He killed himself last night. Perhaps you haven't caught the news. I arrested him yesterday for rape. An old allegation—'

'What are you going on about?'

'An old rape allegation, sir. From nineteen eighty-seven.'

'What has this to do with Sophie?'

'I need to talk to you about Eric Pardoe.'

Again, silence.

'Are you still there, sir?' She listened to him breathing. 'If we could just book a time sometime today . . .'

'*Who are you? Are you with Bains?*' The words were almost whispered down the line.

'Bains? No, sir. I'm just trying to—'

'*You're trying to kill her. You don't know what you're doing.*'

The line went dead.

She stood for a while looking at her mobile. He had definitely hung up on her. She looked at her watch. She had missed the start of briefing. She took out the article Jablonski had given her and calculated quickly what she needed to do that morning. First priority was to contact Pamela Mathews and show her the photo. If Pamela recognized the young Kenyon she was going to the judge's house whether he liked it or not.

THIRTY-SEVEN

'Why have you pulled me off Kenyon?'

'You heard the dispositions. I need you on the team looking for Ritchie. I'm putting DC Lawrence onto Kenyon. You know why.'

Bains stood in front of Spencer and wondered what was the best way to play the man. He had announced the changes at the morning briefing without any warning at all. The ACC had been standing right next to Spencer and, though Bains had been near the back of the room, the ACC had found him, looked at him and nodded, the meaning clear. He had either instructed the action or approved it.

'Rachel Lawrence is inexperienced. I don't think—'

'I didn't ask for your opinion, Pete. I've moved you because we have to look squeaky clean as far as Kenyon goes and also because I need experience on the Ritchie angle. That's all there is to it. I don't want to argue.'

The 'Ritchie angle', as Spencer referred to it, was exciting the whole squad except Bains. Thomas Ritchie was someone they had pulled in on anonymous info the day before. The story was unclear and neither Spencer nor Harrison had said anything to clarify it, but the rumour mill had it that John Munro had sensed something about Ritchie and tried to work it out of him. He had personally decided to interview Ritchie, only to discover that Ritchie's brief was closing things down. They were saying Munro had totally lost it with the brief. He had attacked him in an interview room, hospitalizing him. Harrison had suspended him at once.

He hadn't appointed a replacement. At briefing he had given a short speech saying he was now personally responsible for the enquiry, then had handed over to Ricky Spencer. Spencer's finest hour. Bains wondered whether he really wanted the job. He wasn't up to it and, whatever else he might be, he knew his limitations. Sitting at Munro's desk, he looked harassed and worried.

Either Harrison or Spencer had then released Ritchie – neither was owning up – after Munro had exploded. Ritchie had walked from the station at 10.20 the night before. Just under an hour later a well-known Bradford prostitute called Leigh-Ann Kiltie had come into the station with new information about him.

They had played coy with the information at briefing. Something about it being sensitive and too much had already been leaked to the press. They had Kiltie in a cell downstairs 'for her own protection'. She claimed to be having a relationship with Ritchie. Whatever she had told them lit fuses. Within an hour and a half of releasing Ritchie they wanted him back. But by then it was too late. Ritchie had disappeared.

'You know I've worked with Kiltie before,' Bains said.

'Lots of people have worked with Kiltie,' Spencer said. She had provided low-level information in return for unofficial immunity for the better part of ten years. 'What do you want to say about her?'

'She's unreliable. She would say anything for a tenner.'

'Or do anything, right?'

'Right.'

Spencer wasn't going to listen. 'Well, I have the info and you don't, Pete. And I'm telling you, if this line pans out we could have the kid rescued by this evening. All we have to do is find Ritchie. That's what I want you to help with.'

'I'll need time to hand over to DC Lawrence.'

'You won't. She can read it all on HOLMES. That's what I've done. That's how I've run this enquiry. So move all your stuff into here and I'll hand it on to her. If you're quick I can do it just now. Along with about twenty others she's waiting out there to see me.' He looked back behind Bains at the doorway, signalling that Bains was holding him up and the interview was over.

'Hand all my stuff to you?' Bains asked, still reluctant.

'You heard. I already told you Kenyon complained about you. I want to return everything you've seized and I want to do it today. All those videos. You found nothing on them anyway. You forget that Judge Kenyon is a victim in this enquiry. That's where you went wrong. Understandable, in the circumstances.'

'There are some things that—'

'Just do it, Pete. I don't have time for this.'

Bains gave up. He would find another way around it.

Outside he passed Rachel Lawrence in a line of other officers waiting to catch Spencer after briefing. He said nothing to her.

At his desk he began to plan damage limitation. He had no intention of complying with Spencer's order. From under his desk he pulled out the box he had used to move the videos from the Crown Court. He started moving exhibits into it. On top of his desk he found the return from Force Intelligence analysing Kenyon's phone usage. He pulled his chair out and sat down to read it.

He focused quickly on the usage from both the mobile and the landline during the two days prior to Sophie's disappearance. Force Intelligence had identified and analysed the frequency of contact to all numbers. Only two stood out. Bains made a note of them then turned to the page listing the subscriber details for each number called.

One number was an 'unregistered' mobile and came up as unlisted. They could do more work on it, but that would take time. The subscriber for the second number was West Yorkshire Police. He frowned. The number had been called on five occasions during the two days prior to Sophie's disappearance. He searched back through a longer time frame and found that the number had been called, in total, fifteen times in the nine days prior to Monday, 23 June and on eleven occasions in the two days subsequent to that.

He pulled the list of telephone numbers from his drawer and looked up the number. When he read it he thought he had drawn a blank. The number was for Mark Harrison's office. But then he thought again. Kenyon had called Mark Harrison when Sophie had vanished. That much was known. But why call him before? And why call him so many times?

He looked at the mobile number. There was similar usage to that number, over a similar time frame. For both numbers there was not a single returned call from either of those numbers into Kenyon's landline or mobile. On a hunch he looked up at the whiteboards listing all the enquiry numbers. It was there. It was Mark Harrison's mobile number.

He sat back in his chair, puzzled. He wanted to think about it, think about what it meant, but already he could hear Spencer's voice out in the corridor. He needed to move camp before Spencer got hold of everything.

He scooped the sheets from Force Intelligence into the box along with the unlabelled videos from Kenyon's chambers. For the time being the stuff could stay in his car. He would move it all to his house when he got the chance later.

THIRTY-EIGHT

Karen left urgent messages on both numbers Pamela had given her, but by eleven she hadn't responded to either. One of the numbers was the Priestley Road address she had already been to – the only address she had for Pamela. She thought she would try it anyway. It was possible Pamela was there, but just too drunk to answer. It was also possible the boyfriend was there. But she was in a hurry now. She needed to get to Kenyon today and she needed some form of ID from Pamela before she could do that.

Her plan before meeting Jablonski had been to come in that morning, crime the thing and wait for the flak. But Jablonski had set her running again. With the consequence that she was *still* purusing a murder inquiry linked to Operation Flight without Harrison being aware of it, *still* hadn't crimed it and *still* had to face Harrison's real wrath when he found out about her lies. She had considered tearing up all Pamela's statements and re-doing them in the name of Caroline Dunn. It was unlikely she would be caught. But not impossible.

She got to Otley before midday with no response from Pamela. The address looked empty, the road outside it clear of cars. She parked directly outside the house and walked straight to the door. Before knocking she called the number again and listened to the phone ringing on the inside. She left a message saying she was at the door and about to knock. She looked through the letter box at an empty hallway, then she knocked.

She spent over five minutes knocking, then walked to the end of the street and threaded her way along the access snicket to the rear of the properties. She counted down to twenty-seven, found a broken garden gate opening onto an overgrown lawn and picked her way up a cracked concrete path to the rear of the property. Most of the gardens she had passed were empty, but she could hear children playing further down the row.

The curtains to twenty-seven were open onto a dining room littered with dirty plates and a kitchen in a similar state of disarray. The sun was hot on the back of her head and she could smell the stink of rotting rubbish through the kitchen door. She looked up to the bedroom windows and shouted out Pamela's name. She heard a door open from the property adjacent and a woman in a bathrobe appeared from the back door of the neighbouring house.

'There's no one in, love,' the woman told her.

Karen walked to the small wire fence separating the properties. 'I'm police,' she said. 'I'm looking for Pamela Mathews.'

'Like I said, love, there's no one in. They've not been in for a couple of days now. Since you were here last, in fact.'

Karen nodded, smiling to herself. 'You saw me here? Can I ask your name please?'

'Helen Mawson. I'm the neighbour.' The woman indicated to the house behind her, to prove the point. Her name rang bells immediately. Karen thought about it, looking at the woman for clues. She was probably in her early forties. She looked clean, average size, plain face. Her hair was gathered up into a towel. The garden she was standing in was well tended, with flowers and shrubs and a carefully mowed lawn, in stark contrast to Pamela's own plot. Helen Mawson? She had heard the name recently.

'Have we met before?' she asked her.

'I doubt it. I've never been in trouble in my life.'

It came to her. Helen Mawson was the name Pamela had given her as the woman she said had recommended Karen to her. The woman who had suffered domestic violence – a broken jaw – at the hands of her boyfriend. Pamela had said Karen had investigated him and he had been imprisoned. Karen hadn't recalled the name at the time. Now she knew why.

'No fights with boyfriends?' she asked. 'You're not *that* Helen Mawson?'

'Not me. Happily married for fifteen years.'

Pamela had lied to her again.

'What do you know about Pamela?'

'She's a drunk. You'll have noticed that yourself.'

No love lost, Karen thought. 'I need to find her. Quickly. Can you think of anything?'

'Try the pubs. Is she in trouble?'

'No. But she may be in danger. Does she have any regular pubs?'

She looked disappointed that Pamela wasn't in trouble. 'I don't know her that well,' she said. 'What's she in danger from? That boyfriend?'

'Maybe. Do you know whether it was the boyfriend that hit her recently?'

'I hear things. The walls are thin. But I never saw anything. They keep themselves to themselves, apart from the noise. It's usually bad around closing time. I don't want any trouble though, so I don't ask questions. They haven't been here that long, anyway.'

'No? How long is that then?'

'Two months maybe? Maybe less.'

Karen was surprised. Pamela had told her she had been at the address for over two years. 'Do you know where they came from?'

'Abroad. They came from Germany, or somewhere like that. That's what she told me.'

'Germany?'

She looked back at the house, still silent, still empty. Pamela hadn't mentioned any such thing. Had she lied to Mawson?

'Both of them?' Karen asked.

'I think so. They moved in together. They rent it—'

'We're talking about the boyfriend I saw when I came earlier in the week? He was about—'

'Yes. You spoke to him by his car.'

Karen smiled at her. She hadn't seen a single clue that anyone in the street had noticed anything. 'Do you recall his name?'

'Simon, isn't it?'

'Yes,' Karen said. 'Simon Devereux. Do you know anything about him? He told me he didn't live here. If I could find him I might find Pamela.'

'I don't know anything about him. But I wouldn't cross him. Not seeing what he's done to her.'

'I thought you weren't sure whether he hit her?'

'Who else would it be?'

Karen nodded. 'Can I leave you a number? To call me if she shows up?'

'Of course you can.'

Karen took out one of the generic cards and scribbled her mobile number onto it. 'Do you have a phone yourself?' she asked.

'Yes. Do you want the number?'

'Please.'

The woman disappeared inside, then returned with a piece of paper. They exchanged card for paper.

'You've been very helpful,' Karen said. 'If she calls, don't tell her I was here. Just call me, day or night, whenever it is.'

'You sure about that? They sometimes keep strange hours.'

'I'm sure. Do you know if they have any other cars, besides the one I saw two days ago?'

'He has a van. A dirty white thing.'

'You wouldn't have the registration number?'

The woman shook her head. 'You sure they're not in trouble?' she asked.

'Not that I know of.'

'Pity,' she said. 'They're a blight on the entire street.'

THIRTY-NINE

Back at Shade she found, yet again, an almost empty incident room. Presumably they were all out kicking in doors. She didn't know because she had skipped briefing. She felt a twinge of regret. It was time to check in and do some of the work they wanted her to do.

But on the tasking whiteboard at the end of the room she searched in vain for her own name. Had they simply forgotten about her? Or did John Munro really not want her anywhere near it? She wondered what gossip she had missed about him. She looked around the room. There were three people working at terminals. One of them was a young DC she knew vaguely from the Drugs Squad, though she couldn't recall his name. She walked up to him and asked him.

'He's been suspended,' the man told her, matter-of-factly.

'For what?'

'No one knows. The rumour is he lost it with a defence brief. Hit him. But they weren't saying anything at briefing this morning and he hasn't showed up.'

She let this information sink in. It was surprising. She couldn't imagine John Munro losing control. 'Did the press get it yet?' she asked.

He shrugged. 'No idea.'

'So who is in charge?' she asked.

The man shrugged again. 'Harrison was there this morning. But we haven't seen him since. Ricky Spencer probably. Why?'

She looked down at the terminal he was working on. 'You on the HOLMES team?' she asked.

'Yes. What do you need?'

'I don't know,' she said. 'I need to know what I'm meant to be doing.'

'You're on Ritchie, with everyone else. Did you miss briefing?' There was reproach to his tone.

'Yes. What's Ritchie?'

'It's in the briefing sheets. Read one. You're meant to be on Jim McPherson's team, I think.' He obviously knew her name.

'I'm not up on the board,' she said.

He shrugged. 'They called the names out at briefing. Maybe they think you're sick.'

She frowned at him. 'Why?'

'You were involved with that suicide yesterday, right?'

'Involved with?'

'You found him, they said.'

She shook her head, but wasn't surprised at how far wide of the mark the jungle drums could be.

'Maybe they thought it was upsetting and wrote you off. I don't know, Karen – I'm just guessing.'

She thanked him, wishing she was better with names, then found a spare desk with access to the PNC and ran Simon Devereux through. The result came back negative. No criminal record. She logged onto OIS and ran the same name with the date of birth he had given her. He was there, but there was a problem. He was blocked.

She sat back in the seat and stared at the screen, trying to think what that might mean. Usually it meant the subject was an informant. But an informant was unlikely to be handled by an ACC. The wording on the block told her: '*All enquiries to ACC Harrison.*' That wasn't standard. Standard wording would either be a reference to the director of intelligence or to the individual handler or controller. Assuming he *was* an informant.

She ran the name through all the other systems she had access to, but the result was the same. Someone didn't want anyone prying into Simon Devereux and that someone was the ACC. She couldn't think of a way to get round it.

As she sat thinking about it, something else slotted into her mind. When she had logged onto HOLMES yesterday and begun to trawl through the enquiry, two other things had come up as blocked with a reference to the ACC. At the time it hadn't even registered with her consciously. Now she realized that it had been sitting there in her head like a little thorn, even before she had come across Devereux as similarly blocked. She tried to remember the details and logged onto HOLMES to look for them.

It took her nearly thirty minutes. They were two addresses. She read them to herself. The first was called Dean Head Farm. The address was on Dean Lane, with a postcode in the LS16 area of north Leeds. As soon as she read the words she could feel something pulling at her. It meant something. She had seen the words before, or heard them.

She sat for a long time trying to bring it back, with no luck. The write-up indicated that an action had been generated to request ACC Harrison to remove the block as the address had come up in the enquiry and the SIO wished to search the premises. The response revealed that Ricky Spencer had requested the removal on Thursday and the ACC had refused. The address had not been searched.

The second block was against an address on the Thorpe Edge Estate. That meant nothing to her. The block had been removed and the premises searched with no result.

She didn't know where it was taking her. She looked through the system to find out who would know about Kenyon – assuming they had searched his premises and ran him as a suspect (the standard thing to do) – and found that the sole officer tasked with investigating the judge was DC Bains. She searched for his mobile number on the whiteboard and rang him. He answered almost immediately. He was in his car, he said, about to leave.

'I need to speak to you about Kenyon,' she said.

'Why me?'

'It says on HOLMES you're the man looking at him.'

'It needs updating. Spencer kicked me off it this morning.'

'Even better. Can we talk?'

He was silent for almost thirty seconds. She waited.

'Why?' he asked, finally.

'I have some interesting information. I need to know what you've got. I think we should pool it.'

'Why would I be interested? That's not my tasking now.'

'You know why.'

Another long silence. Then: 'Do *you* know why?'

'Yes,' she replied.

'How?'

'A journalist told me.'

'It's bullshit,' he said. 'Whatever he told you is bullshit. I was *tasked* to look at Kenyon.'

'And now you're not. You going to speak to me, or not?'

His car was in the Jacob's Well car park. She walked up there, found him and got in. She had imagined he would be twitchy, from the sound of his voice, but as she pulled the door shut and looked over at him, he looked as calm as he had the day before. She looked over at the box on the back seat.

'That your copies?'

'Copies?'

'Of your enquiry into Kenyon?'

He narrowed his eyes at her. 'What do you want, Sharpe?'

'I've been looking at something that has led me to Kenyon,' she said. 'I need to know whether you found out anything about him. I might need some help as well.'

'Help?'

'Yes. I need to locate someone and I need to speak to Kenyon. I can't do both.'

'You've got some nerve,' he said, frowning slightly. 'You'll be in deep shit if you try speaking to Kenyon.'

'Was that what you tried?'

'Not really.'

'He recognize you?'

He paused, weighing her up. 'You're the one who got Phil Leech killed,' he said, deliberately trying to provoke her, perhaps.

She shrugged. 'So they say. Probably Geoff Reed too. There are rumours about both of us.'

He nodded. 'Fair enough.'

'Shall I tell you a story?' she asked.

'What kind of story?'

'About some rich people, a general election and some little girls. I'm still working on the plot, but I'll give you what I have.'

'For what?'

'If you like it you can help me finish.'

It took her forty minutes because he started interrupting with questions almost at once. From the beginning he was interested, focused, intent. She told him everything she had discovered, all the lies she had told to Harrison, all the theories she had about it. His questions were sharp, raising queries she hadn't even considered.

When she was finished he told her everything he had done in looking at Kenyon, ending with an analysis of phone calls made from the judge's phones, mobile and fixed line. From which she learned that the judge had called Mark Harrison nearly twenty times in the nine days prior to his daughter's disappearance and nearly fifteen times in the two subsequent days.

'What else?' she asked him.

'I took a notepad from his office desk. They don't know I took it because I had to do the lock to get in. I sent if off for ESDA tests, on the off-chance. They're due back today.'

She nodded. He was thorough. 'That it?'

'In that box,' he said, pointing to the box on the back seat, 'are videos I took from his office. He had a whole stack of them. Child abuse or child porn cases he had tried. That was the explanation for the collection. I've watched them and found nothing. Maybe you should look at them.'

'Why?'

'I don't know.' He held his hands up in the air. 'Because when you're following a hunch it's best to cover everything, even if it looks stupid.'

'I'll look at them,' she said. 'Why do you have the hunch?'

He looked out of the open car window, but didn't respond.

'Because of what he said about you?' she asked. 'In court? That long ago?'

'Maybe,' he said, speaking quietly. 'I can't tell. I hate the fucker. But I know it's irrational. I hope that's not it. I'm just trying to do what you would normally do, I think. He's the dad. He's the number one suspect. Spencer doesn't want me looking at him. Doesn't really want anyone looking at him. I don't know why.'

'Because of Harrison?'

'Maybe. Maybe Spencer just isn't very good. He's got them all chasing after a lead put down by Leigh-Ann Kiltie, for God's sake.'

'The prostitute?'

'The same. She's totally unreliable.'

She watched his profile for a while, thinking that he was attractive, feeling something unfamiliar stirring inside her. His appearance had caught her yesterday, but not like this. It was stronger now and she knew why. It was what she knew about him, what Jablonski had told her about his dead wife and child. She had a weakness like that. She was attracted to sadness. She had to keep away from it.

'Will you help me?' she asked. 'Will you try to find Pamela Mathews while I speak to Kenyon?'

He looked at her. 'You're not going to ask me about it?'

'Ask you about what?'

'Whether I beat Pardoe. Everyone asks that at some point.'

She shook her head. 'Not me. You don't ask why I killed Phil Leech; I won't ask why you tortured Pardoe.'

He smiled. She watched him and smiled back, thinking that it was something rare in him, that he would smile.

'You'll have to give me more detail about her,' he said.

Once she had left him she walked back towards The Tyrls, but paused by the magistrates court in the very middle of the broad square they had created there, complete with rubbish-strewn fountain. She was in full view of both the police station and the court, but somehow the public openness of it made her feel better about what she was going to do.

She dug out the card Sutherland had given her. She stood in the sunlight for a long time staring at it before calling his mobile.

He answered without it seeming to ring at all, greeting her immediately by name: 'Karen. How can I help?'

She realized he must already have her mobile number programmed into his phone, though she had never given him it. She swallowed the tightness in her throat. 'No strings,' she said. 'You said no strings.'

'Of course. You're part of the family, Karen. How could there be strings?'

He was lying. They all lied and did it well. They were trained to.

'I need to find out about someone,' she said.

'Give me the name. I'll do my best.'

'He's on a police system and he's blocked. I need the info unblocking today, without reference to the person who has set up the block.'

'And who is that?'

'An ACC called Mark Harrison.'

Sutherland didn't pause. 'That's not a problem. What's the name?'

'Simon Devereux.'

FORTY

It was after two by the time she got out to Ilkley. She was surprised that the road blocks had been removed and she could drive through to the judge's door unimpeded. She expected at least a uniform at the garden gate, but no one was there and no one bothered her. Either Reed's death really was pulling the press interest away or they were finally losing steam on poor little Sophie Kenyon. Either way it was still surprising that Munro – or Spencer – had pulled the protection.

She didn't know what she was going to say to Kenyon, but was working on more or less the same plan she had used with Reed. Whatever she had done with Reed, it had worked. She felt uneasy about that, however. Not because he was dead, but because they were treating it as suicide. Maybe she hadn't done anything. Maybe she had merely been at someone else's convenience.

She hung on the doorbell for a good ten minutes before getting out her mobile and calling again the number she had for Kenyon. Once again that day she listened to a phone ringing inside an empty house. She followed a path to the side, through a tall gate into an extensive garden. When she came round to the rear of the property she saw the kitchen door was wide open. She stepped in and called out Kenyon's name. No response.

She thought about it only momentarily. She had an excuse, because he had left his door open. If he returned she could say she had stepped in to make calls to secure the premises. Wasn't that her duty, as an officer of the law?

She didn't pause in the kitchen. It was neat, clean, free of the slightest sign of recent use. The next room was a lounge of sorts, lined with bookshelves. Past a certain income level, she thought, all houses were the same. The place didn't look very different to Reed's home in Nab Wood. What was she looking for?

She realized she didn't know. Moreover, Bains and his team had already been in here, four days ago. If there was anything to find they would have taken it then. She was in the main hall behind the front door and in the process of deciding that what she was doing wasn't worth it, when suddenly she felt it. A prickling at the back of her neck. She turned quickly, thinking she was being watched. But she was alone. She caught her breath, thought about it. Then sniffed the air. Inside she could feel the beginnings of panic.

The odour was slight, but she had a good nose. She followed it, climbing two flights of stairs without even bothering to stop at the rooms on the way. All the time her heart was picking up speed. On the top floor there was a choice of two rooms. One was a bathroom, empty. The door to the other was closed. She stepped up to it and listened. There was no sound, but she wasn't expecting any. She had been here before, many times. She had felt this before. She knew what was about to happen. Instinctively, she crouched behind the door, bracing herself. Then she turned the knob and kicked it open.

She took in the view at once, checked the corners and dark spaces, exhaled. Then she straightened up and stepped in. Her heart was already beginning to slow. There was danger here, but it wasn't immediate.

He was swinging from a rope fixed to a hook driven into a beam in the ceiling. The hook was a large solid thing. It looked like it had been placed there deliberately, for just this purpose. The beam was solid too, easily enough to support his weight. He wasn't a large man. Beside him a chair was overturned, kicked away. The body looked stretched, long, though she knew that could not have been the case. It was swaying slightly in the draft created by her entry. She knew who it was without seeing the face, which was turned away from her. But she had to check.

She walked around it, resisting the urge to reach out a hand and steady it, to stop the movement. The face was only a few inches above the level of her own, the tongue protruding black/blue, the eyes rolled up and opaque, a trickle of blood snaking down from one nostril. The skin was livid. She looked down at the floor and noted that the clearance was less than three inches. There was a damp puddle beneath the feet where he had wet himself. That was what she had smelled. That and death. Death had its own smell, something almost imperceptible that set in and was apparent – if you knew it – long before the corpse started to rot.

She looked carefully at the face. It was Michael Kenyon. He was wearing some kind of silk kimono, which had fallen open at the waist, no doubt as he was kicking out and struggling. Even when this was chosen, the body struggled for life automatically. A bigger drop and it would have been faster, snapping the neck. But like this he had died slowly, from asphyxiation or hypoxia. She could see his protuberant, hairless stomach, his groin, his pubic hair, his half-erect penis, filled with blood that would never get out of it now. She turned away.

There was a desk and chair in the room and she walked over to them. She didn't want to sit down, she didn't want to touch anything. She wanted to get out of there, run. But her legs felt weak, her head light. She sat down carefully and bent forward, letting the blood rush to her brain.

When she was sure she wasn't going to pass out she looked up at him again. *Someone is doing this to me*, she thought. *First Reed, now Kenyon. It cannot be coincidence.* Jablonski was right.

She looked at the desk. It was some kind of study she was in. There were bookshelves and, on the desk, writing paper. Face up, right in front of her, there was a single sheet of white A4, unlined. Towards the back of the desk she noted the pad it had been torn from. She looked at the pen on the floor beside her feet, a cheap biro. To the right, in a wastepaper basket, another source of odour – an empty half whiskey bottle. She stared at it then bent over the sheet of A4 and read the words written onto it:

This is the only way I can think of to save her. She shall not suffer for my sins. I pray only that she will live and know that I loved her.

She read it three times, committing the words to memory, then she looked back at the dangling corpse. If he had killed himself, he had done it to save his daughter. That was what the note said. She didn't know what logic would make that work, but she saw the intention clearly enough. She felt a constriction in her chest and stood up. The room was airless, stifling, the midday heat intense within the confined space between the eaves. There were no windows. The room was at the very top of the house, a part of the roof space. The ceiling sloped down on either side of her. She needed to get out.

She looked at what she had touched. With her fingers, nothing except the doorknob. She wiped it with the edge of her T-shirt. She had kicked the door in with her foot. She felt a need to erase all traces of her presence. She felt – without knowing why – that someone was setting her up, that everything had been planned. She inspected the door. There was no mark that she could see. She was wearing training shoes, but she knew better than to think they had achieved traceless contact. She would have to ditch them, burn them, bury them. She felt the panic welling inside her.

She took deep breaths, listening to the peculiar dead silence in the house. Then she stepped out of the room and pulled the door shut behind her, first wrapping her hand in the bottom of her T-shirt.

She paused on the stairs, listening again. She could hear nothing. She walked down carefully, leaving by the back door and leaving it open, exactly as she had found it. There were no CCTV systems she could detect, nothing to say she had been there.

On the street she walked casually to her car, got in and paused. She checked the mirrors, fighting a surprising urge to gag. The street was empty. She started the engine and pulled away.

FORTY-ONE

She called Bains's mobile as soon as she was clear of Ilkley.

'Where are you?' Her voice sounded high-pitched, frightened. Her arms were shaking and her breath too shallow. She tried to control it.

'At home.' He sounded pleased to hear from her. 'I have things you need to see,' he said, starting immediately to tell her something. Then she heard him pause as he picked up on her tone. 'What's happened?'

She resisted an urge to whisper and instead pulled the car into a lay-by just past the Cow and Calf pub. In the rear-view mirror she had a good line of sight back down the road she had just taken from town. She watched for traffic, but saw nothing suspicious.

'Why do you ask?' she said.

'You sound breathless. Did you run from somewhere?'

'No. But we need to meet. Now.'

He didn't say anything.

'Can we meet?' she asked again. There was a hint of panic to her voice.

'Do you want me to come into The Tyrls?' he asked. 'I was going to suggest that anyway. I have the ESDA results on Kenyon's notepad.'

'No. Not there,' she said. 'We need somewhere private.'

She could almost hear him thinking.

'Don't tell me anything over these phones,' she said, realizing immediately that it would sound mad to him. He didn't reply.

She counted and watched two cars drive up the road and pass her. She had taken the Baildon Road out – up and over the moor. To her left, through the passenger window, she had a clear view across the width of the Wharfe Valley. Over her shoulder she could see the town, shimmering in the heat. She thought she could hear a siren.

'You can come here,' he said, finally. 'You can come to my house.'

'Good. Where are you?'

He gave her an address in Heaton.

'I'll be twenty minutes,' she said. 'If anyone calls for me, don't let on I've been to Ilkley.'

'Why would they call here? And who are "they"?'

'I don't know. Just do that for me.'

Another pause.

'You'll understand when I get there,' she said, then thought about it. 'Maybe,' she added. 'Maybe I'm just being paranoid. But will you promise me that?'

'Promise what?'

'That you won't say I'm in Ilkley.'

He was silent again. She grew impatient.

'OK. Forget it,' she said. 'I shouldn't be asking. I won't come if—'

'OK. I won't say,' he said, quietly.

'You sure?'

'I'm sure.'

'Twenty minutes.'

She cut the line.

His house was vast, one of the detached Victorian mansions off Park Road, set in a good three acres of walled land, filled with towering, mature chestnut and beech. She pulled through two huge gateposts onto a neglected driveway and walked up to the front door. There was no bell. She knocked gently, waited a few minutes then walked around the side of the property.

The rear garden sloped down through trees, across an overgrown lawn filled with weeds. There was a kidney-shaped swimming pool by the bottom wall – empty, unused and surrounded now by vegetation – and a view out towards Bingley through the gaps in the foliage. Bains was dressed in jeans and T-shirt, standing by the pool. She called out to him and he began to walk towards her.

'Can we go inside?' she asked. 'I need to tell you things.'

He nodded, face inscrutable, then said, 'No one can hear you out here.'

'You'd be surprised,' she said, looking around. She was being stupid, overreacting. She took a breath.

'What's happened?' he asked.

She stood in front of him in the knee-length grass of the lawn and looked into his face. 'Can I trust you?' she asked.

He moved his head to the side slightly, trying to assess her. 'What have you done?'

'I haven't done anything. But it might not seem like that.'

He nodded. 'Yes. You can trust me. Tell me about it.'

She sighed. 'I've just been out to Kenyon's. He's dead. Swinging from the rafters in the top room.'

Bain's expression didn't alter. He glanced briefly at some movement in the trees – birds taking off – before looking back at her.

'He hanged himself,' Karen said. 'At least, that's how it looks.'

'What are they saying?' he asked. 'Are they treating it as suicide?'

'They're not there yet. At least, they weren't when I left.'

He frowned. 'You found him?'

She nodded, waiting for him to judge her. 'The house was empty and open. I found him then left.'

'You called it in?'

She shook her head, licked her top lip. 'No.'

'Why not?'

She thought about that. Her eyes fell on the swimming pool over his shoulder. It looked like it had been drained a long time ago. There was a layer of soil in the bottom and a tangle of bushes and grass sprouting there, destroying it.

'It's something to do with my past, I think,' she said. 'I'm overreacting. Reed shot himself yesterday – or was shot. Kenyon was hanged today. As far as I can see, I'm the only link.'

He was still looking into her eyes. She could see him trying to work this out. He didn't have enough information though. Not to make proper sense of it.

'It's hot,' he said. 'Let's go up and get a glass of lemonade. Before you tell me more I think there's something you should see.'

She followed him through the grass, her mind trying to work through the possibilities created by Kenyon's death. They entered through some open patio doors and she stepped into some kind of lounge. She wasn't taking in the detail. He disappeared into another room and she stood in the middle of the floor, listening to the drumming of her pulse. After a few minutes he called out to her.

She walked into another room. There was a TV and video in front of a low, cream couch, videos strewn across the floor. He was

227

crouched by the video machine, setting up a tape. As she entered, he pointed to a glass of cloudy yellow liquid on a table behind him.

'Drink that,' he said. 'It's good. I made it this morning.'

She felt like something a little stronger. She remained where she was, watching him. He seemed too calm.

'Did you hear what I just told you?' she asked.

He held a finger up without looking at her, then stood up. 'Watch this first,' he said. He pressed a button and images appeared. 'I watched it again after you spoke to me. Something you said tripped a connection.'

The images that appeared were poor and there was no sound. There was a long lead in of flickering, unclear track, filled with interference. Then she could make out people moving around in a poorly lit room.

'What is this?' she asked, slightly irritated. 'Why do you want me to watch it?'

'It's one of the tapes from Kenyon's collection. There's no label. Just watch. You'll see.'

After about a minute someone must have switched on a light. The image became marginally clearer. She could see beds and male figures beside them, people on the beds. The camera angle was awkward – high up in a corner of the room – and it was difficult to make out anything other than the heads of the people involved. She counted perhaps four or five individuals moving around in the room, all male, from their dress. She tried to make out detail, but the quality was so poor she doubted it would ever be useful for court or identification purposes.

'There are three girls on the beds,' he told her. He had obviously watched it many times.

'What is it?' she asked again. She could see the smaller figures on the beds now that he had pointed them out.

'I thought it was child porn,' he said. 'A tape of evidence. See that figure there.' He pointed to someone at one of the beds. 'You see what he's doing?'

'Not really,' she said. 'Is it an old tape? It's terrible quality. It would be no good for ID.'

'Not this bit. But watch.'

The tape ran on, then suddenly there was a bright flash of light, illuminating everything. Bains pressed a button, pausing it.

'Someone just took a picture using a flash,' he said. 'There are four people in frame here. The photographer is out of sight.' He pressed another button and the tape rewound. 'I'll run it the slowest I can. Watch.'

The tape inched forward, frame by frame in the same poor light, until the flash went off, then suddenly there it was, lit up like daylight. He paused it and she looked with unease at the images in front of her. There were four men in view. Whoever was taking the flash photo would be number Five, not visible in the frame. One and Two were stood beside one of the beds. She could see a young girl on the bed and she could see number Three on top of her. Number One was pinning the girl from behind. She was grateful she couldn't see the girl's face, though evidentially that would have been better.

'Don't look at the action,' Bains said. 'Look at the walls.'

She moved her eyes and felt a shock like electricity. Her heart began to race. Only one wall was visible in the frame, but the painting on it was crystal clear in the light of the flash – a childish painting of a dragon, curving round towards the door. She was looking at the room in Pardoe's house, the playroom.

'Jesus Christ,' she said, whispering.

'Is it your dragon?' he asked her. 'The one you told me about?'

She nodded. 'That's Pardoe's house,' she said. 'This was in Kenyon's chambers?'

'Yes. Look now to see whether you can see him.'

She sat down on the sofa and scrutinized each of the men frozen in the frame. Nearest to the camera, visible from a very foreshortened angle, she could make out number Four; a man with white hair, sitting in a chair in the corner, an empty champagne glass dangling loosely in his hand. He looked, from the slumped position, as if he were asleep.

'Probably that one,' she said, pointing. 'If any of them. But it's difficult with the angle.'

'They will be able to enhance the darkened parts as well, at the lab. Is that Geoff Reed?' He pointed to the man on top of the girl. His back was to the camera, but he looked large.

'It could be,' she said. 'He's large enough. But no jury would buy it. It's too unclear.'

'But this wasn't an evidence tape,' he said, standing up. 'From the cassette, it's a recent copy of something older. Nor do *we* need it as evidence. Both Reed and Kenyon are dead. Look at this. He picked something up from the table by the untouched glass of lemonade and passed it to her. 'It's the ESDA test from the pad that was in Kenyon's desk. We struck lucky.'

She started to examine the report, but he spoke over her thoughts.

'It's part of a letter. We've only got fragments of it.' He started to read it for her, looking over her shoulder. She looked up at him briefly. He was standing so close their thighs were touching.

... would precipitate the kind of reaction it has. God will be my judge. You know what happened. I take satisfaction that I am so far from being like him that ... In any case this will be the last time this is held over me. What I did in 1989 was evil and I cannot now ... So I am passing it to you. Soon all this will be known. I cannot bear this pressure any longer. I make this decision for me alone, but I am warning you because as clear as I am on this film, so too are you. There will inevitably be wider consequences. Whether I shall face them to ... is ... but certainly to attempt to extract pathetic sums of money in return for an illusory sense of security when I would in any case know that this record would always be there, ready to use again, has done nothing but the reverse of what he intended. I am beyond this now ... my conscience will guide me and I hope only that the end result will include his removal from decent society ... would be ... penalty ... so be it ...

When he was finished she looked again at the frozen picture on the TV screen. There was new sense to it now. As a blackmail tape, it didn't have to be clear. For the participants – who already knew they had been there – their images would be damningly obvious. It was only if you didn't know what to look for that the thing was useless.

Immediately an idea fell into place for her. She leant forward in the chair, scrutinizing the frozen frame, checking the appearance of each of the males in turn. She felt a chill running along the inside of her veins. She looked up at Bains. It was starting to make sense, to resolve itself. She had the beginnings of a line.

'A blackmail video?' she said.

'I assume so. But if I'm reading the fragment correctly, Kenyon has not sent it – with this note – to the blackmailer. He has sent this to someone who is also at blackmail risk – someone else in that image.'

'He also wrote a suicide note,' she said. 'Assuming that he killed himself . . .'

'What did it say?'

'*"This is the only way I can think of to save her. She shall not suffer for my sins. I pray only that she will live and know that I loved her."* Sound like a confession?'

'Maybe.'

'Maybe it was meant to sound like a confession. Maybe I was meant to find him, read the note, assume that he had killed himself.'

'You think he was killed?'

'How do we know otherwise?'

'Reed as well?'

She shrugged.

'But how would they know you were going to be there, at Kenyon's?' he asked.

'I don't know.'

She looked back down at the ESDA report. 'Was it a letter to Reed?'

'I spoke to someone working with Greg Firth earlier. Because they were treating it as suicide they didn't search Reed's house. So there's no way of knowing.'

She sat back in the sofa and her eyes fixed again on the image on the TV screen, on what she had seen the moment she knew what to look for. She looked around her at the empty house. She had been right. There had been reason for caution, reason even for fear. Bains stepped away from her.

'Nice house,' she said, watching as he walked back towards the TV. 'It's big.' She felt the beginnings of calmness coming to her. It was always the same once the danger was identified. With knowledge came necessity. There was no room for fear. Just a simple calculation of means to end.

Bains frowned at her, the change of subject unnerving him.

'You save a lot when you were younger?' she asked, smiling slightly.

'My family are wealthy,' he said, almost apologetically. 'We're a close family. I only own a part of this place.' He waved his hand around him, taking it in, then looked embarrassed that he had even felt the need to explain it to her.

'Do you have anything stronger than lemonade to drink?' she asked.

He shook his head.

'No alcohol,' she said, nodding to herself. 'A religious thing?'

'A control thing,' he replied. 'I don't have any religion.' He picked up the glass of lemonade and handed it to her.

'You sure the ESDA findings are referring to this video?' she asked him, though the question was as much for herself as for him. She was testing the thought, but she already knew the answer. In her mind – in the very back of it, in the part where she kept the suspicions and fears – she already knew who Kenyon had sent his note to.

She sipped the ice cold drink. It was pleasant, bitter, not sweet like she had expected.

'I'm not sure about anything,' he said. 'When I find Pamela Mathews we can show her the video and ask her if it's her. We can ask her if it's Kenyon too. But we should go through Shade with this now. If it's blackmail there must be connections to Sophie Kenyon's disappearance. We need to take it all to Spencer, get the manpower onto it.'

She stood up. 'We can't do that,' she said. 'That's why I asked if I could trust you. We're on our own with this.'

He scowled at her. 'Why? There's a fifty-man team out there.'

She stepped over to the TV screen and bent down, placing her finger on each of the four males in turn. 'Kenyon, Reed and possibly Pardoe,' she said. From the angle it was difficult to be sure about Pardoe. 'Of those we can see that just leaves this one.' She rested her finger on Number Two, the man standing behind the girl on the bed, holding her head in his hands, controlling her.

'We're on our own,' she said. 'Because I think I know who this is.'

FORTY-TWO

Ricky Spencer felt excited and frustrated all at once. Sitting in the car with Harrison he realized he had been entrusted with something that could blow up in his face, something other officers of his rank would either shun like the plague or grab with both hands, depending upon how ambitious they were.

He was ambitious. Moreover, it wasn't going to blow up on him, because the prostitue Leigh-Ann Kiltie had given them the key to getting somewhere with the whole sorry mess.

That he might actually pull it off – that he might actually find the Kenyon girl where Munro had cracked along the way – *that* excited him. That success was dependent upon finding a child perv scroat that Harrison himself had insisted on releasing not an hour before Kiltie came to them was more frustrating than he could bear. It wasn't lost on him that Munro himself would have hung onto Ritchie. Harrison, in suspending him, had overruled him and ordered that Ritchie be cut loose.

'So run me through it,' Harrison said to him. He didn't seem bothered about his error.

'She's been having a relationship with Ritchie for nearly six months—'

'I thought he was into kiddies?'

Spencer looked over at him. Did he know that little about it?

'Most of them have normal relationships too, sir,' he said. 'Most of them look normal, in fact.'

Harrison scowled, as if he thought Spencer was being facetious. 'Go on,' he said.

They were in Harrison's official car, complete with driver, on the way back to the Tyrls from Wakefield. Spencer had a press conference booked and waiting for him and they were late because

Harrison had insisted on introducing him to the chief constable, which Spencer could have done without.

The press conference was important. He had a photo of Ritchie – supplied by Kiltie – and he was going to release it, go public. That wouldn't be so good for Ritchie because the whole world would assume he was the actual abductor. But it would help find him where every other lead was so far failing.

'She says he's done nothing while she's been with him,' Spencer continued. 'Nothing with kiddies, that is. But he has connections still. He tries to hide them from her, but she finds things—'

'What kind of things?'

'Photos, letters. We've seized them all. He's been taking photos from outside three schools in the area. We don't know what he does with them yet, but the guess is it's some kind of targeting system operated across the net. We've got his computer and should have a result by tomorrow morning.'

'Is that it? He's your number one suspect because of that?' Harrison smoothed a hand across his crumpled, sweat-stained shirt.

'He's not a suspect at all,' Spencer said. 'She's given a good alibi for all relevant times and dates. It's because of something he told her that we need to get hold of him.' He paused, just to see if Harrison would urge him on. The ACC just stared at him, however. 'She says he told her he knew who took Sophie Kenyon. She says he said he had known the man, way back in the past.'

The car came up to Jacob's Well junction. They were almost there. Spencer checked his watch. He should have been ready at three and already it was fifteen minutes past. The driver had stuck to the speed limits all the way from Wakefield.

'Don't worry,' Harrison said. 'They'll wait for you.'

'Yes,' Spencer said, not feeling so sure. He wasn't used to this kind of thing. 'Anyway, she tells us she thought Ritchie might have met this man recently, *since* Sophie was taken. She said his words were: 'I know who is *holding* her.'

'When did he say this to her?'

'Tuesday evening, when they were watching the news. You were appealing for witnesses.'

'She took her time coming in. She's a prostitute, right?'

'Yes. Well known in Bradford.'

'Did we offer her money? Did she ask for any?'

'No. She says she thought he was bullshitting her at first. Then changed her mind when we kicked his door in.'

'Why would he say that to her?'

'Exactly. That was my point. Why would he lie about it to her? It's not exactly something that would impress her.'

'That's what I'm saying. Why tell her at all?'

Spencer shrugged. 'I don't know. But it's the best lead we've got.'

'Did he give her a name?'

'Yes. She even questioned him for detail. She did well. She says he called the guy Starsky. It's a nickname, she says, not a surname. Starsky drives a white van. Thinks he used to live in Addingham, but that was years ago.'

'A white van? Didn't that come up before?'

Spencer was surprised Harrison remembered. 'Yes, sir. Thirty-two calls from different parts of the country feature white vans. None from West Yorkshire, but there's a witness from the actual time of the kidnap who thought she saw a white van in Ilkley. We're doing our best with it. But it's not much to go on. We need to find Ritchie.'

'Starsky? What could that be short for?'

'Starsky and Hutch? The TV cops? I don't know.'

'Or something foreign,' Harrison said. 'Starkolski. Starkovski. Have you checked Polish names?'

'We've got someone working on all that.'

The car swerved into the back of the Tyrls and pulled to a stop to the side of the main entrance. Spencer quickly climbed out – his press briefing pack clutched to his chest. Imaging had done blow-ups of Ritchie and he had those in a roll under his arm. He began to walk towards the doors, not waiting for Harrison.

As he went through he saw the empty press barriers in the plaza outside. They would all be upstairs, waiting for him. He walked across the lobby, slipped his pass and popped the inner door. On the other side of it a DS called Cox was waiting for him, face anxious.

'Sorry,' Spencer said. 'I was with the ACC. He's behind me. Can you wait for him?'

Cox caught hold of his arm. 'That's not it, sir,' he said, whispering urgently in his ear. 'I need to speak to you *now*, before you go in.'

Spencer paused, annoyed. 'I'm late,' he said. 'Unless you've found the kid it can wait.'

'It's her father,' Cox hissed.

Spencer looked around them. The ACC was coming through the main doors, but apart from that he could see no one else in earshot. 'What about him?' he asked.

'He's killed himself.'

Spencer felt his head jerk back, as if he had been hit. '*Killed* himself? Are you sure?'

'The maid came back and found him swinging from the rafters.'

'When?'

'Not half an hour ago. There's a team up there now.' Cox looked away from him as Harrison came through the inner security door. 'Hello, sir,' Cox said.

Harrison ignored him. 'Is there a problem?' he asked Spencer, about to walk past him.

Spencer sighed. 'Kenyon has killed himself,' he said.

Harrison stopped in mid-stride and turned to Cox. 'Did you know about this?' he asked.

'Yes, sir. I just found out.'

'Why didn't you call me?'

'I just found out,' Cox repeated.

'Jesus!' Spencer said. 'What do we do now?' Harrison looked shocked. He didn't reply. 'The press,' Spencer said. 'We can't tell them. We might—'

'Stop panicking,' Harrison said, raising his voice slightly. 'You need to cancel your conference until you know enough about this.'

Spencer shook his head. 'I can't,' he said. 'This is urgent. We have a chance of finding the kid with this.'

'I've just *told* you to cancel it,' Harrison said. 'Who is in charge at the scene?' he asked Cox.

'There's a uniform PS up there at the moment, sir. That's all.'

'Go and find me his number.'

Cox looked confused for a moment. He wasn't used to being a substitute for directory enquiries.

'Did you hear me?'

'Yes, sir.' He walked off in the direction of dispatch.

'We have to keep it from them,' Spencer said, thinking aloud. 'What if the kid's alive? What if she's being kept somewhere where there's a TV? We couldn't do that to her.'

'You have kids yourself, Spencer?' Harrison asked.

Spencer nodded.

'It shows,' Harrison said. As if it were somehow an expression of weakness.

FORTY-THREE

Karen was on her way to the Tyrls when Sutherland's number came up on her mobile. She pulled over on Manningham Lane and took the call, locking the doors and winding up the windows despite the heat. She had watched for cars behind her since leaving Bains's home.

'You are nothing if not interesting,' Sutherland told her. She watched the cars pass her, mentally noting the registration numbers of the first five. 'You've certainly been digging in some interesting places.' He sounded almost chatty.

'What have you got for me?' she asked him, her tone flat and unresponsive.

'Tell me what you're looking into first,' he said.

She took a breath. 'You said no strings,' she said. She cut the line. It took all her willpower to do it. She wanted what he had, but she didn't want him down her neck.

She waited, watching the traffic in her mirrors, marking the seconds on her wristwatch. It was a gamble, but not a very risky one. It took him two minutes and forty seconds to call again.

'Yes?' she said.

'You're too impulsive,' he told her, irritated. 'You always were. If you do that to me again I'll write you off.'

She wasn't sure what kind of threat that was. She ignored it. 'What have you got for me?'

'Not much,' he said. 'I will have more if we can have longer.'

'What have you got *now*?'

'Are you working for Mark Harrison on this?'

She considered whether she should answer. His tone sounded cautionary. It didn't sound like he knew Harrison.

'No. Should I be?' she replied.

There was a pause before he answered. 'I don't think so,' he said.

'Like I said, I haven't much. Your man Devereux is blocked and the block is controlled by Harrison. There's a story to it all, but we didn't have time to get it.'

'Who can tell it?'

'A man called Berne would be a good start.'

'Berne? Who is he?'

'He's a retired DCI. His name crops up in several places.'

'Where?'

'I don't know. I didn't do this myself. All I get is the report I ask for.' He sounded impatient now. 'I thought you knew how it worked.'

'I know you will have *all* the detail in the report,' she said.

He was silent for a moment. 'Do you want more, or not?' he asked. 'I have other things to do.'

'Yes. I need it all,' she said.

'You can't have it all,' he replied. 'Make do with what I give you. You deserve less.'

She frowned and clamped her teeth together, forcing herself not to cut the line again.

'Berne will be able to tell you things. That's where we would have gone, had we time,' he said.

'What's his connection?'

'I'm not sure. But there's a link to Harrison. So be careful.'

'What kind of link? Why should I be careful?'

'A casework link. And you should always be careful. You need to ask Berne about something called Operation Candy.'

She rifled quickly through her memory for the name, drawing a blank. 'What is it?'

'It's a Regional Crime Squad operation from nineteen-eighty. Berne was the SIO. It resulted in the detection of a child pornography ring with links to East Germany and the Balkans. One of the lesser players was called Simon Stark. He was given a three-year sentence for unlawful sexual intercourse and indecent assault on a twelve-year-old.'

'Simon Stark?'

She had heard the name before. But where? Somewhere in the paperwork she had already gathered. She looked at her watch. She would have to get up to Eccleshill and check.

'Yes,' Sutherland continued. 'Simon Stark. Does it ring any bells?'

'Maybe. I'm trying to remember.'

'It's Devereux's real name. His real date of birth is eighth of January nineteen fifty-eight. You won't find his antecedents on the PNC because they're blocked. The block goes back to Mark Harrison. We have managed to get past it, of course.'

'Without Harrison being aware?'

'Don't be obtuse.'

She took that as confirmation. 'So what is he?'

'He's a child abuser, a rapist, a car thief. He has a firearms tag too. He came out in nineteen eighty-three and was back inside by nineteen eighty-five, on remand for some kind of sexual assault on an eleven-year-old girl. The case failed—'

'Hang on,' she said. She took out her notebook, balanced the phone against her shoulder and began writing down what he was telling her. 'Go on. Tell me more.'

'In nineteen eighty-six he was arrested for ringing high-value cars for export to Eastern bloc countries. That case failed as well. He resurfaces in nineteen-ninety in Germany where he is convicted of rape. An eighteen-year-old girl. He beat her as well, judging by the range of charges. He served six years of a ten-year sentence and was released last year on their equivalent of Home Office licence.'

She recalled Pamela's neighbour had said Devereux and Pamela had arrived recently from abroad.

'You told me his date of birth was twentieth of April nineteen fifty-six?' Sutherland asked.

'Yes.'

'That's Hitler's birthday. A joke, I think, though I don't think he belongs to any political grouping. He is intelligent however, despite being from Liverpool. He started a pharmacy course in nineteen seventy-eight. The conviction ended that. He has a diploma of some sort. Probably from prison.'

'What's the link to Mark Harrison in all this?'

'Ask Berne.'

'Why shouldn't I ask Harrison?'

There was a slight pause. 'Do what you want,' he said. 'But I'd advise you to go to Berne first.'

'And say what?'

'Ask him about Candy. But be careful. I don't know where Berne stands in all this. I don't know where anyone stands.'

'So why don't *you* tell me about Candy? Fill in the gaps for me.'

'Because I don't know. I told you – we didn't have enough time to run it all down.'

He was lying, she was sure. But there would be no point in pressing it.

'OK. Do you know where I can get Berne?'

She wrote down the address he gave her. It was near Harrogate.

'That might be out of date,' he said. 'He retired in nineteen eighty-three.'

'No phone number?'

'No.'

She looked over the notes she had taken, checking the detail. Either Pamela Mathews had a very damaged memory or she had been lying from start to finish.

'Is that it?' she asked him.

'Yes. For now. We could—'

'Thanks. That's helpful,' she said, interrupting him. She cut the connection before he could start with the demands.

She called Bains straight away and passed everything on to him. Then she did a U-turn and watched her mirrors again as she headed for Eccleshill. She tried to dislodge the name Simon Stark from her memory. She had seen something in the material relating to the investigation of Pardoe's widow. She was almost sure of it.

It was after four when she parked up in Eccleshill. The CPT was empty. She walked through the long office and went straight to her desk. Looking down at it, the feeling she had was the same one she had experienced when her car was stolen, five years back. Then she had stared at the empty space in Park Square and immediately thought that she must have forgotten where she had parked it. She had looked helplessly up and down the street, trying to work out her error, knowing all the time, in some part of her brain, that there was no error, that she had left it right there.

A confrontation with emptiness, where there should have been a solid object.

The night before, after leaving Reed's house, she had stopped at Eccleshill and left all the copied paperwork from Flight and everything she had so far gathered investigating Pamela Mathews's allegations in three cardboard boxes on the surface of her desk. They were gone. She searched under the desk. She searched the entire office. But she knew even as she was doing it where they had gone.

Harrison had requested them and she had delayed. So he had sent someone to get them. She listened to her phone messages and found the one she wanted. Harrison's staff officer telling her he would be at Eccleshill that afternoon to collect everything ACC Harrison had asked for.

Depending upon the time he had arrived, depending upon Harrison's schedule, it was possible that the ACC already knew everything she had tried to keep from him.

FORTY-FOUR

There was no answer from Pamela Mathews's address. Peering through the letterbox, Bains looked at an untidy hallway, reeking of damp, and listened to the profound silence that only thoroughly empty houses could produce.

He started with the neighbour – Helen Mawson. Karen Sharpe had questioned her, but not in detail. He did it thoroughly. He interviewed her for nearly forty-five minutes, teasing out detail about the lives of Pamela Mathews and Simon Devereux. He approached it as if Mathews was a MISPER and covered all the angles.

Before he was halfway through, Mawson was bored and irritated with it, but he kept on. He had a theory about witnesses. What they thought they remembered was less than half of what they had seen. With persistence and the right questions, you could get half again out of them. In the case of Mawson, Bains guessed she had kept most of what she knew from Sharpe not by accident, but deliberately, because she was frightened of Devereux, because she had been warned off.

By the end of the session he had learned that Mathews and Devereux had a fight – literally – almost every day of the week. Not just weekends or once a week. Every day. Usually it was about alcohol. Mathews was the loudest – screaming at Devereux for trying to control her, for ruining her life, for damaging her, for not giving her enough money and for many, many other things. Always her words were slurred and she sounded drunk. Always it sounded like she had started the argument.

Devereux was seldom audible until the blows started. Then he could be heard punctuating the rhythmic banging or slapping noises with small grunts. Sometimes he lost it and screamed at her. Usually by then she was wailing uncontrollably, crying out in pain with each and every new noise. But it didn't stop her the next night. However bad it sounded, Mathews was soon yelling at him all over again.

About once every fortnight it sounded like Devereux was tearing the place apart – an explosion of violence that carried straight through the paper-thin walls and terrified Mawson so much she had once called the police. Once only.

It had taken them over half an hour to show, by which point both Devereux and Mathews had left the premises. But one way or another Devereux found out about the call. Bains called up a DC in his old office at Keighley and got him to bring up and check the IBIS log for the night in question, right then while he was sitting in Mawson's living room. But there was nothing on it to suggest how Devereux had found out she had called it in – the complaint had simply been 'no crimed' and written off at the end of the night shift when the occupants had not been located. But a day later Devereux had come round to Mawson's house and told her never to do it again.

'Did he hit you? Or threaten you?' Bains asked her.

'No. He didn't need to. I'd already heard what he was capable of. I'd already seen the results. That woman was never without a face that was black with bruising. I don't recall ever seeing her without bruises.'

He also found out that they had no friends and no visitors, that when Devereux was not in, Mathews could be heard sobbing to herself, that Devereux had a white van with the letters 'PCH' in the registration, that he was always dressed smartly and that Mathews was prohibited from bringing alcohol into the house. Which meant that most of the time she was out and only returned drunk. Mawson didn't know which pubs she used, but said she usually returned in a taxi.

He tried all the local taxi firms and drew a blank. Then he started on the local pubs. It took him an hour trawling through an ever widening circle of Otley pubs before he found someone who recognized Mathews's photo. A woman sitting at the bar in the Golden Fleece said she had once shared a cab back from Bradford with Mathews. She couldn't recall the pub, but she could recall the taxi firm. They were Bradford based.

When he rang them they had never heard of Pamela Mathews. He drove down to their offices next to Foster Square station and waited while the controller listened with half an ear as he ran through a comprehensive description of Pamela Mathews. The controller was Asian – Mirpuri Pakistani, by his facial appearance – and too fat for the chair he was sitting in. He spoke difficult English. Whenever a call came in he simply ignored Bains and dealt with it. In between calls he picked at his back teeth with a bent wooden toothpick.

'It might be Cheryl,' he said, eventually. 'She's been a regular for about two months.'

'Where does she drink?'

He shrugged. 'We pick her up from all over town.' He looked at his watch. 'This time of night it's a bit early for the bigger places. Try The Rose Tree.'

The Rose Tree was halfway up Little Horton Lane, a long way from the cab office. It seemed a long shot to Bains, but he drove there anyway. When he walked through the door it was nearly seven o'clock. He heard her immediately.

It might have been Saturday night, but it was way too early for The Rose Tree. The place was almost empty. He looked quickly round its brown, un-themed interior, the ceilings the colour of cigarette smoke, the bottle-glass windows, the cheap posters on the walls advertising quiz and karaoke nights, the bored barman leaning on the beer pumps with a sour face, massive beer gut and drooping moustache, then took in the handful of locals standing in the entrance to what was euphemistically entitled 'The Lounge Bar'. There were six people there and they were all looking into the other room, bemused smiles on their faces. They were all male. He walked towards them.

As he drew alongside them, she came into view. The others glanced at him then looked back to her. It wasn't worth missing the show just to scrutinize a stranger. And it *was* a show.

She was standing by the bar in the further room, the pool table between her and her audience. She had a karaoke microphone in her hand and she was singing at the top of her voice. The microphone was switched off and there was no backing track. He noted the tight mass of frizzy black hair on her head, the old bruises on her cheeks, the bright, fresh shiner closing up her left eye, the high heels, the trousers dripping with some kind of tassel, the top that barely covered a third of her bare, intensely freckled flesh, and the row of fake diamonds strung around her neck. Bruised or not, she seemed to be having the time of her life.

She was singing a pop song he knew. The notes were so far off pitch that he realized it couldn't just have been that she was tipsy. To get it so risibly wrong she had to be totally tone deaf. Or maybe Devereux/Stark had been whacking her around the head too much. As she sang she smiled, winked and pouted at the six males watching her. They giggled every now and then, laughing at her, not with her. She didn't notice. He had the feeling it wouldn't matter anyway. She had their attention. That was all she wanted.

As she sang she paced back and forth, dancing to a track running through her head. It might have been the one she was trying to sing, it might not. From the noise she was making there was no way of telling. She danced better than she sang though. The coordination in her movements made Bains think that, despite the gross exhibitionism (the audience were clearly unknown to her) she wasn't really that tipsy. 'I was happy,' was how they usually described it in their statements. Meaning pissed, but not legless. The top she was wearing was hung so loosely on her shoulders that every time she turned it flapped open, revealing for an instant her breastbone, breasts and nipples, to the obvious delight of the assembled males. He couldn't see a glass anywhere near her.

He excused himself and pushed through the men watching her. Her eyes caught his as he walked towards her and he saw her pause and frown. He thought then that without the bruises, sober, she might once have been pretty. She was too thin though, almost emaciated. He glanced back at the males, wondering if any of them was Devereux. They didn't match the description Sharpe had given him. One of them booed him, because his presence had shut her up.

He stepped over to her and took the microphone out of her hand, flipping his warrant card in front of her face with his other hand. Then he put the microphone down on the pool table and spoke quietly to her. 'Pamela Mathews? Are you Pamela Mathews?'

She nodded, looking slightly afraid.

'You're under arrest, Pamela,' he said. 'For kidnap, sexual assault on a child and perverting the course of justice.'

FORTY-FIVE

When he got her to his car he cuffed her, to make it look real, then drove her out to Shipley Police Station, a part-time satellite nick with no custody suite, no custody sergeants and no facilities to book in prisoners. There were cells though, from the days when it had done all that. He took the cuffs off her before using his pass to get them in. It was unlikely there would be anyone significant there at this time on a Saturday evening, but he didn't want to take a chance. The questions might be awkward to answer.

On the way over she didn't ask him a single question. He kept an eye on her in the mirror. She started crying the moment he got her out of the pub and kept it up all the way through Bradford. He had neither tissues nor comfort to offer so he just ignored her. She wiped her eyes on her top when he came to get her out at Shipley.

He kept hold of her going into the station, because he didn't know how much she had drunk. But she seemed steady enough. Her breath was heavy with the sweet, stale odour of cheap red wine.

He put her in one of the old cells, shut the door on her and walked to the end of the corridor. He stepped outside to get a better signal and called Sharpe, getting the messaging service on her phone. He left a message saying he had Mathews at Shipley. Then he moved a TV and video player from a deserted office on the first floor into one of the interview rooms, set up the tape from Kenyon's chambers and returned to the cell corridor. He sat down on a chair in the kitchen the traffic wardens used and listened to Mathews's muted sobbing, drifting to him like whale noises through the heavy metal door. He left her to it for fifteen minutes longer before going in.

'You're in trouble,' he told her, standing at the door. She was sitting on the edge of the bunk, face in her hands. 'I'm going to interview you now and if I don't get answers I'm going to leave you here until Monday morning. Then I'm going to charge you with child abduction and assault, take you to Bradford Magistrates and get you remanded in custody for the next six months. Do you understand that?'

She looked blankly at him, bottom lip trembling, then whispered, 'What is this about? What is all this about?'

He took her up to the interview room, put her in a chair in front of the TV screen and sat down at an angle from her.

'It's about this,' he said. He switched the video on and watched her face. She had told so many lies to Sharpe he needed to know quickly where he was with her. This was the best way he could think of to do it.

He watched her trying to discern the images and finally getting there, leaning towards the screen to be able to see better. When it came to the flash explosion he froze it exactly as he had for Sharpe and then sat back and waited. Immediately, he began to feel guilty.

Her face was riveted to the images, her eyes wide with something like shock. He didn't have to point anything out to her. She turned towards him. 'I know this place,' she said, voice still a whisper. 'Why are you showing me this? Where does it come from?'

He leaned towards the screen and placed his finger on the white-haired male seated in the chair. 'This person here,' he said. 'Do you know him?'

Her frown became an intense furrow. He could see her whole body gradually tightening up. Her eyes widened so much he could clearly see the whites. She began to jerk her head from side to side. As she looked towards him, he realized she was seeing something else. She was looking right at him, but not seeing him at all.

He pulled out the picture of Kenyon that Sharpe had given him and placed it on the table in front of her. She looked down at it automatically.

'I think this is the same man,' he said. 'Do you know who it is?'

He let her stare at it for nearly three minutes then placed his finger on the image of the large male, hunched over the girl on the bed, back towards the camera.

'This might be Geoff Reed,' he said to her. 'The MP. Did you know he was dead?'

She moved her chair back suddenly, looking at him as if he had struck her.

'He shot himself,' he said. 'Yesterday.' He pointed again to the white-haired male. 'This man hanged himself today. Only hours ago. Do you know him?'

She was beginning to shake, the movement working its way up her from her legs. She crossed her arms over her chest and hunched down over her knees, swaying slightly, as if she were freezing cold.

'All these dead people. Is that you on the bed?' he asked her. 'Is that you, Pamela?'

Suddenly she sat bolt upright. '*Switch it off! Switch the thing off.*' Her voice was rasping, rising quickly in pitch. '*I don't want to see it. I don't want to look. Switch it off, please.*'

He clicked the TV off and moved the photo, then pulled his chair towards her.

'That white-haired man is Michael Kenyon. His daughter is Sophie Kenyon.' He waited for recognition to flicker in her eyes. It didn't. 'Have you heard of Sophie Kenyon?'

She shook her head slightly. Her eyes were still wide open, swivelling about like a frightened horse. She looked as if at any moment she might start screaming hysterically. She looked terrified.

'She was kidnapped on Monday evening. She's thirteen years old. That's what I've arrested you for. I think *you* kidnapped her.' He poked a finger into her chest, hard enough to make her flinch and gape at him. 'I think you have taken her because this man, her father, raped you when you were thirteen. I think you know where she is. I want you to tell me.'

She looked at him for a split second, disbelief written all over her features, then suddenly she was falling, collapsing off the chair and onto the floor. Before he could even get off his own chair and step out of her way she was on the ground and curling into a tight foetal ball at his feet. She began to cry with a terrible gurgling noise, from deep within her chest, stricken with grief or fear or misery. For a moment he was paralysed and could do nothing but watch her. A high-pitched animal wailing rushed up from her throat and her hands moved into her hair and began pulling at it. She began to tremble and twitch as if she were having a fit.

He stooped over her and tried to pull her up. She tightened against him and lashed out with a hand, pushing him away. He stepped away and stood by the door. Whatever lies she had told Sharpe, whatever she had kept from her, what he had triggered was genuine. He didn't know what to do to stop it.

'I need to know where Sophie is,' he said, desperately raising his voice above the noise.

She sounded like she was choking. She began to rock back and forwards on the floor.

'You have to tell me. If you don't tell me it will be worse for you.' He squatted down beside her and placed his hand on her shoulder, gently.

The contact paused her. She looked up at him, eyes streaked with tears, face contorted. '*I don't know . . . I don't know . . . you have to believe me . . .*' She was blubbering. '*I know nothing about that. Nothing.*'

'You have to tell me everything,' he said. 'Not just what you told DC Sharpe. I believe you have done this with Simon Devereux – the two of you together. Do you know where Simon Devereux is?'

She began to shake her head furiously.

'I know his real name is Stark,' he said. 'I know everything he has done. Did you get him to help you? If you did we will—'

Suddenly she was sitting up, wiping her eyes. '*Did I get him to help me?*' She was almost screaming, '*No .. no . . . no . . .*' She shook her head so violently he thought it would damage her. '*I had nothing to do with this. Nothing. You have to believe me. I would not do that . . . you don't understand . . . I would never ever ever do that . . .*'

Her face was soaked with tears, but though she was still trembling he could see her struggling to control it now, a new kind of expression on her face. The eyes were fierce, determined, no longer frightened of him. She was angry.

'*I will tell you a story,*' she shouted at him. '*I will tell you a fucking story . . .*'

She pushed herself to her feet. He stood up after her and she pulled the chair away from the table and sat on it. He stood beside her, wondering what she was going to do, worried she might lash out at him.

'Sit down,' she said, her voice loud. 'Sit down and I'll tell you something I've told no one.'

She pushed the other chair towards him and began to wipe the tears from her face. He sat down on it, watching her carefully. She looked at the cheap wristwatch she was wearing, then bit at her bottom lip and sucked in a long, deep breath.

'I hope you have nothing to do for a while,' she said. She was looking straight at him. For a split second her lips formed into an embarrassed smile. On her bruised face it appeared like a flicker of light, animating her eyes, then gone in an instant, replaced by something innocent, nervous. Her voice broke into a slight sob. 'You have me all wrong,' she said. 'It will take time to put you right.'

FORTY-SIX

Karen was delayed getting out to Berne's place because she couldn't get an answer from Neil's mobile or the house, so she drove out there. Not so long a detour, but one she had been hoping to avoid. At home, in an empty house, she read a note he had left her on the kitchen table. He had taken Mairead to his parents' in Nottingham. They would be back tomorrow.

She felt angry reading it. Her plan – as she had clearly told him – had been to get back early. Though that wasn't now going to be possible, she hadn't called to tell him that. In effect he had just gone without consultation, taking her daughter with him. She called his mobile again, immediately. This time he answered.

'Neil?'

'Yes.'

'Where are you?'

'Nearly there.'

'Where?'

'My parents' house. I left you a note.'

She took a breath. He was being short with her, not his usual self. 'We have to talk about this,' she said.

'You're right about that.'

'What do you mean?'

He didn't reply.

'Is Mairead there?' she asked, worried now.

'Obviously.'

'Can I speak to her?'

'Of course. You're the primary carer, Karen. Did you forget that?'

She bit her lip and listened to him asking Mairead to take the phone. After a while he came back on the line.

'No. She's busy with something. She says she'll speak to you later.'

'I want to speak to her now.'

'You know what she's like, Karen. Look, I'm driving. Can we leave this until later?'

She was in the process of thinking about it when the line cut, she assumed because of a gap in coverage, but he might just as easily have actually hung up on her.

She resisted the urge to call him back and instead sat in a chair in the darkness of the front room, looking at the home he had made of her house. When there had once been blank walls and empty space he had hung pictures and bought sofas and chairs, standard lamps. Where she had a mess of books piled up on the floor he had brought in old bookcases and put up shelves. There were even flowers in vases – willow herb and foxglove – picked with Mairead out in the fields, no doubt.

He had painted everywhere, laid new carpets, fixed the units in the kitchen, filled the place with the smell of baking bread and homemade stews. He had given to her selflessly for nearly a year. She had returned nothing. Now, finally, perhaps, he was getting sick of it.

She sighed. It didn't matter, not as far as it affected Neil and her. But Mairead had called him Daddy two days ago. She had not misheard that. For the last eight weeks Mairead had seen more of Neil than her own mother. It had to stop.

What she ought to do now was ring Bains and tell him she was off, that she had to go to Nottingham for the night. She stood up and walked over to the phone. Then looked at her watch. It wasn't seven-thirty yet. Berne lived near Harrogate. If she was quick she would be able to see him then get down to Nottingham.

FORTY-SEVEN

'My name is not Pamela Mathews. Simon gave me that name to come back here. I grew up as Elaine Williams. That's my real name. That's who I am. Elaine Williams.'

Bains nodded at her, encouragingly. But she didn't need help now. She wasn't even looking to see if he was listening.

'I grew up in Liverpool. Well, not Liverpool – Crosby, actually. You probably don't know it. It's a dump. It's just outside Liverpool. We had a council flat on an estate there. I don't have the accent now, but I can do it, if I need to, if you want me to. I've been trying to forget about it. Forget about Liverpool, forget who I was. Forget Elaine Williams. Most of my life I've been trying to forget things. Sometimes remembering things can kill you. I mean that.'

She paused and fished around inside the small black handbag she had been carrying.

'Can I smoke?' she asked. 'I've just started again . . .'

She didn't wait for a reply. He watched as she lit up some kind of foul-smelling menthol cigarette, took a drag into her lungs and then continued.

'Remembering things can drive you mad. For instance, my mother was a prostitute and a drug addict. I know that now, though at the time – as an eight- or ten-year-old – that wasn't clear to me. Not like it is now. I don't know how she came to have me. There was never a father figure in my life and I have no idea who he was. I never asked, she never told me. Always, throughout my childhood, it was just me and her.

'I don't know what she really felt for me. I thought I did, at one time. Now I don't know. She hit me a lot, shouted at me. She didn't have much time for me, not when she had other things to think about. She had a lot of other things to think about. I used to watch her injecting heroin into her arms. I didn't know what it was then. She told me it was medicine. Then she used to collapse onto the bathroom floor and I couldn't get through to her, couldn't wake her for a long time. After that – when she came round – she wasn't always fun to be with. As you can guess.

'It wasn't a happy way to be, I suppose. But I didn't think that it was so bad that she would need to do what she did. I suppose I thought she loved me. You do when you're little. No matter what they do you think they're your mummy and you love them. It takes a long time to realize that they might not be feeling the same things in return.

'I recall few good things. I remember once – once only – her playing with me, when I was little. She pretended she was Chinese and made faces at me. That's it – that's the single thing I can recall. Maybe she loved me during that one moment. She never brought clients home and that must have been because of me, to try to protect me from them. I don't know. I suppose I thought she was doing her best. But that wasn't true.'

She sucked on the cigarette again, frowning slightly at the thought.

'When I was twelve I started to get interested in boys. She didn't like that. I can try to explain it away for her, but I don't want to. Why should I now? She beat me when she found out I'd been speaking to them, she read my diary, forbade me to meet them, kept me in. Maybe other kids go through this. Maybe it had nothing to do with what happened. But because it happened when we were arguing about a boy – Bill Pennington, he was called – I always thought the two things were connected.'

She gently tapped the long line of ash from the end of her cigarette onto the corner of the interview table.

'A man I didn't know came and took me away from her. I wasn't kidnapped. She gave me to him. I think he bought me. I think he actually gave her money for me.'

For the first time she looked up at him, questioning, waiting for some kind of judgement, as if what her mother had done to her would somehow reflect upon her, make her dirty in his eyes. He gazed back at her, eyes blank, until she looked away again.

'That was Simon Stark – Starsky, they called him, because back then he had thick curly hair, like the American TV cop, and because the name was similar. I had known of him vaguely, from the estate.

He was someone you kept away from. When this was happening he would have been about thirty and I was thirteen. I remember my mother looked at me with kind eyes as she gave me to him. She told me she had to go away for a while, but she would be back. Meanwhile this man would care for me. She was a good liar. Only as she turned away did I see her face change. I saw the lie then, but it was too late. He took me to his flat and injected me with a drug. I don't know what it was. Heroin, I think. I tried to fight, of course. It's hard for me to imagine it now. I can't remember any pain. I can't remember any confusion or fear, but I suppose there must have been a lot of that. I must have been terrified. I just can't recall much of it. For a long time I couldn't recall *any* of it. It's funny what your mind can do to stop you going mad.'

She looked at him again. This time he nodded. Her eyes were dry and her voice was flat, almost deadpan, as if she were describing something that had happened to someone else. He had seen the effect before. He had no doubt that what she was telling him was true.

'The rest of what I put in my statement for Karen is true,' she continued. 'Everything. This was in nineteen eighty-seven. They kept me somewhere with two other little girls. They raped me. There were five of them. Starsky and four others. The MP was one of them, the other two I'm not so clear about. It was in that room, on that video you showed me. If the judge is the person sitting there then he did it too, because they all did it. They did it to all three of us. They were drunk, drugged, high. Except for Starsky. Starsky knew what he was doing. He had set the thing up, I suppose. Some of the others could hardly stand up though. Maybe they didn't know what they were doing, what he had got them into. I don't know. I remember them snorting lines of coke – there, in that room. They really hurt one of the other little girls, so much that she was bleeding. A woman came in and cleaned her up. I never saw the woman again and I don't know who she was, but she must have known what was going on and done nothing to stop it.'

She sat back in the chair and sucked the cigarette down to the butt, then looked for somewhere to put it. He pointed to a wastebasket and she dropped it in, reached into her handbag and took out another.

'They kept us in a hole in the ground,' she said. 'I told Karen all about this. It's all in my statement. Have you read it?'

He nodded. Her tone was almost conversational.

'The other two starved to death. Right there beside me. I don't know why it happened. I'm sure they didn't intend it that way. I can talk about it now because I've got used to it. But I hadn't remembered any of this until two weeks ago.'

She placed the unlit cigarette between her lips.

'Do you believe what I'm telling you?' she asked him.

He didn't hesitate. 'I believe every word,' he said, quietly.

She paused and looked into his face, finding his eyes, holding them for a moment, weighing him up. Then she nodded quickly to herself. 'Good,' she said. 'Because that was just the start of it. The rest I haven't told anyone. Mainly because I didn't think anyone would believe me.'

She lit the cigarette, sucked and exhaled.

'I was the only one to live. He came back to me. He saved my life. Simon Stark. So I owe him, see? That was what he always told me and I believed him. There's a part of me still believes that. I was only thirteen. I couldn't work out the complications. Did it matter that he had put me in there? Someone else was meant to feed and clothe me, someone who forgot. That's what Simon said. He rescued me. I remember now him pulling me out of the hole, hugging me, cursing and swearing under his breath because the others were dead. Then he took me away somewhere in a car, washed me, gave me a bed, fed me. He looked after me until I could walk again. But I couldn't speak and that annoyed him. Maybe if I had been able to say something it would have turned out different. Maybe he would have let me go.' She looked up at Bains and smiled again. 'But where would I have gone? There was no one for me. No one to look after me.' She fell silent, staring at her feet.

Bains cleared his throat. 'What do you mean you couldn't speak?'

'I'm thinking about it,' she said. 'I only just remembered that.'

He waited. Eventually she started again.

'I lost my voice. I don't know why. Maybe because I was starving, almost dead. Maybe because your mind does things like that. But I couldn't speak when he pulled me out, couldn't say a thing.'

Another silence.

'Did that last long?' Bains asked. He didn't want her to stop now.

'I'm not sure how long,' she said. 'But I was like that all the time they kept me in the van.' She looked at him as if he would understand, as if she had told this part before.

257

'The van? You haven't told me about that.'

She took a lungful of smoke, head down. 'No. I haven't, have I?' She was whispering again.

'Do you want a break?' he asked her.

She shook her head. 'No. It's just I'm remembering things all the time.' She smiled. 'I'm remembering who I am. What I have been. What he has done to me.'

Bains thought about getting up and getting her a coffee anyway, but she continued without it.

'He took me abroad. He put me in the back of a van – the same van he has now, in fact – he put me in that, tied up and gagged, just in case, and we drove abroad. We went to Germany first, I think. The images are hazy. It doesn't matter. We ended up in Poland. My idea of how long we were there is blurred, but I was kept in the back of the van the whole time – I know that.'

'Months?' he asked her. 'Months? Weeks?'

She shook her head and sighed. 'No. We left in nineteen eighty-seven and I didn't get out until he left me with Dieter and came back here. Then Dieter let me out.'

'When did he come back here?'

She looked up at him, biting her lower lip again, trembling. 'He came back in nineteen-ninety.'

Bains nodded, keeping his features impassive, as if what she had just told him was something he heard every day. 'You're sure? That's three years, almost.'

She nodded. She looked like she was about to start crying again.

'Why?' Bains asked. 'Why keep you in the back of a van?'

A single tear spilled out of the eye that wasn't freshly bruised. 'Because I couldn't speak,' she said. 'He said I was no good for anything because I couldn't speak. It made him mad. He tried to hit me to get me to talk at first, but that didn't work, so he kept me in the van.'

'No good for anything? What did he mean?'

'No good for anything. I think he was going to sell me.'

'*Sell* you?'

'Yes. That was his plan. To sell all three of us. But two died and that left just me. And I couldn't speak.' She began to sob. 'They were going to make films with us.'

'Films?'

'Porno films. But because I couldn't speak they didn't want me.'

'They? Who were they?'

'The people he had sold me to – or was going to. I don't know. They were Poles, I think. It was a business thing. Dieter was his business partner.'

'So he kept you in a van for three years instead?' He tried to keep the disbelief out of his voice. He knew just by looking at her what she was saying was true. But the story was crazy.

She nodded, wiping her tears with the back of her hand.

'Why? Why not just let you go?'

She dropped the cigarette onto the floor and stubbed it out with her foot, then looked up at him. 'Because I was still good for some things,' she said. 'I was still good for clients.'

He tried to fill in the gaps. She was having difficulty with it. He didn't want to force her to have to recount everything.

'So he used you for sex, Pamela. Is that what you're saying?'

'Not him,' she said. 'He has only had sex with me once. Once only – back then in that house. He's not interested in women like that. When this was all going on I was fourteen, fifteen years old. Older, before it was all over.'

Bains thought about it. 'Are you saying he kept you in the back of a van and sold you for sex?'

She nodded, then bent over and placed her face in her hands.

'He did this for three years?' Bains asked.

She nodded again. She couldn't look at him. What had happened was shameful to her, as if she had something to do with it, as if she had been a willing part of it all.

'Three years?' He couldn't stop himself asking her again.

'You don't believe me, do you?'

'I do believe you. Please. Don't think I don't believe you. It's just—'

'What? You think I could have escaped?'

'I don't. No. I'm only asking you these questions to get at the detail—'

'Because everyone else will think I could have escaped?'

'No because it's horrible, Pamela. Because it's one of the most horrible things I have ever heard.' He reached out and rested his hand upon her shoulder.

She didn't respond. 'I couldn't escape,' she said, speaking into her hands now so that the words were muffled. 'He kept it locked. If I had shouted or screamed he would have beat me until I couldn't walk. But I couldn't shout anyway. I was mute – isn't that what you call it? It was like I didn't have a tongue. During the night he tied a rope around my wrists and fixed it to a hook in the floor. He let me out to go to the bathroom, to wash myself, sometimes to eat. That was it. We were parked up usually. He had an apartment, somewhere. He shared it with Dieter. Dieter always liked me. When Dieter was with me – in the van, I mean, when we were, you know, doing it – he was always gentle with me. Dieter didn't like what Simon was doing to me. He told me so. But he didn't dare change anything.'

'Did no one get suspicious? Surely people must have realized. Three years is—'

'The police came three times. I remember each time. The first time he simply paid them and they looked in at me and left. The second time I thought they had come to rescue me, but it wasn't like that. They pretended they had found me but they were joking. It was all organized with Stark. They had paid him. I had to go with them . . . you know . . . do it . . .'

Bains looked away from her. He could feel a tightening sensation in his chest.

'The third time he got me out of the van and they spoke to me in a house somewhere. They gave me a pad and paper to write replies, but I wrote nothing. He told me before they came that if I did anything he would kill me. I believed him. He had told them I was deaf and dumb – his deaf and dumb sister – and he was looking after me. They went away, apologizing to him.'

'This was all in Poland?'

'Not all of it. We moved around a bit. Some other countries. I don't recall. East Germany, I think. Maybe Yugoslavia. He was in business with some Russians by the end of it all. They gave him some kind of protection. I was like a side show. He used to bring them down to the van to have a go with me when he was doing deals. I did whatever he wanted, whatever he said. You don't understand the worst of it, you see. The worst of it was that I didn't *want* to escape. What could I do out there? Out in the outside world, in a foreign country, unable to speak? I had no education. I knew nothing. How long would I last? What could I do? At least Simon looked after me, fed me. What did I have to escape to?'

'You don't have to justify not escaping to me, Pamela. I believe everything you are telling me.'

She nodded, looking doubtful.

'You said he went away, in nineteen-ninety. What happened then?'

'Dieter released me. Simon had to come to England. He wouldn't say why. Dieter thought he was sent over to put a hit on someone.'

'Put a hit? You mean to kill somebody?'

'That's what Dieter said. We were guessing though. Dieter moved me into the house as soon as he was gone. He was a big man, Dieter – like a huge skinhead. You wouldn't have thought he could be so kind. He had bad acne on his back . . .'

She stopped, remembering things.

'Anyway, Simon never came back. He was in England nearly three months. When he came back he was arrested in Berlin, for rape.'

'You were in Germany when this happened?'

'Yes. The place was near Dresden, near the border, in a huge estate full of refugees and illegal immigrants. They were doing something with cars – Dieter and Stark. Stealing them, I think. Then running them through to Russia. I think Dieter set up Simon's arrest, so he wouldn't come back. I can't imagine Simon raping an eighteen-year-old. He couldn't do it with me, so why with anyone else that age? He was interested in younger girls, always. But a woman in Berlin said he had raped her six months before. She gave evidence and they convicted him. He was sentenced to ten years, I think. I'm sure Dieter set it up. Poor Dieter. He did it for me, for us. So we wouldn't have to be frightened of him again.'

She started to cry again. Bains watched, feeling helpless now.

'When he was gone things got better. That's when I learned how to talk again. It just came back to me, one day, as if it had never stopped. Dieter asked me a question one morning and I just answered him.'

She began to laugh to herself, remembering it, for a brief moment almost managing to look happy, despite the tears.

'Dieter looked after me then. He even let me go to a local college. The one the immigrants used. Then I went to a technical college for a year. I learned French and German. I lived with Dieter. He let me go out and do things provided I was back for a certain time. Things were almost normal . . .' She had to stop, realizing what was coming up.

Bains could guess. 'Go on, Pamela,' he said. 'Finish it for me.'

'They released Simon last year. He came for us straight away. We were living in the same place. We should have moved really. We should have done something to hide from him. He turned up at the door and wouldn't speak to me. He was thinner, with short hair. He looked older. Dieter was frightened of him. He kept telling Dieter he had forgiven him, that the past was the past, but we knew he wasn't like that. Dieter let him stay, for a few days only, he said...'

She began to cry uncontrollably. Bains stood up and walked to the kitchen area, returning with some kitchen roll a few minutes later. She was still crying. He gave her the paper and let her wipe her eyes and calm down.

'What happened?' he asked.

'Dieter disappeared one day. He went out and just didn't come back.'

'You think Stark killed him?'

She nodded. 'Maybe. Maybe just frightened him. Dieter was so good to me...'

He let her cry again, patient now they were near the end.

'Then we came over here,' she said. 'He changed my name to Pamela Mathews, got me some false documents. We came back.'

Bains sat back in the chair.

'So you see,' she said. 'You had me wrong. I would never ever do those things to a little girl. Ever.'

He looked at her, sure she was telling the truth, but sure she had left something out too.

'Maybe not you,' he said. 'What about Stark?'

She looked away from him, then spoke calmly. 'I don't know what he's doing.'

'Could he have kidnapped Sophie Kenyon?'

She didn't reply.

'Would you have known about it if he had? You are living with him.'

'I don't know anything. He's never there. I don't know where he is half the time. I thought he was getting into drugs, but I don't know...'

'Is he still forcing you to have sex for him – for clients, I mean?'

'No. He doesn't force me to do anything. Not any more. It hasn't been like that since he got out.'

'So what do you do for money?'

'I don't do anything. He gives me money. He looks after me.'

'For nothing?'

'For nothing? Is that how you see it? I think I've done enough for him already.' She was starting to shiver now, her face full of confusion.

'Is that how he sees it?'

'He feels guilty. He thinks he's responsible for me.'

Bains felt surprise registering on his face.

'Is that so surprising?' she asked, voice barely audible.

'It doesn't sound like him.'

'He's not a monster.'

Bains felt his brow creasing. 'He *is* a monster, Pamela. If you don't see that then—'

'You haven't met him. He looks like you, or me. He looks normal. He gives me money, cares for me. He's not a monster. He's human, just like—'

'Appearance is nothing. The worst ones always look normal. Did he do that to your face?' He pointed to the bruising.

She looked away from him and he could sense, suddenly, some kind of new distress building up in her.

'Why are you still with him?' he asked her.

She looked quickly at him, eyes filled with fear. 'I don't know,' she whispered. 'I don't know why I just don't walk out. There is a part of me that doesn't want him hurt, that still thinks he rescued me, pulled me out of that trench, saved my life. But then – as I remember more and more – there is a part of me that knows the truth. That's why I went to Karen, I think. I knew it would come to this. I saw her picture in the local paper. She did an interview about child abuse. I liked the look of her face. I knew if I went to her then this would happen.'

'Tell me where Stark is,' Bains said. 'I will arrest him for all of this. You need never fear him again.'

She shook her head. 'I don't know where he is. I haven't seen him in three days.'

'Do you know where he might be?'

'No. I have no idea.' She didn't look at him as she replied and her voice was harder. He was sure now that she was lying.

'You can tell me,' he said. 'Don't be frightened.'

She shook her head again. 'I don't know.'

He sighed. 'Why didn't you tell DC Sharpe about him? Why did you only mention Geoff Reed?'

Her head was facing the wall now. When she said nothing he reached over and gently turned her to face him.

'Why, Pamela?'

Her face creased into a childish expression of guilt and fear, her lips trembling, her eyes evasive. 'Because I couldn't,' she whispered. 'Not then. I don't know why.'

FORTY-EIGHT

It took Karen a while to pinpoint Berne's address from the map. Once she got there she discovered that he lived near Blubberhouses, on the road between Skipton and Harrogate, in a cottage overlooking the USAF radar station. The station dominated the view for miles around and the view from Berne's front window would be no different – thirty white domes of varying sizes, each shaped like a massive golf ball.

The cottage was so small Karen had to stoop to enter and remain slightly stooped once she was inside. It wasn't a problem Mike Berne had. The man who opened the door to her was about five foot three, so short she found it slightly embarrassing to stand over him. She felt like a giant visiting the world of the little people. How he had got into the police at a time when height restrictions were in force was a mystery.

'DCI Mike Berne?' she asked, smiling down at him, remembering Sutherland's words of caution.

'Yes. I *was* DCI Berne,' he said. 'Who are you?'

She introduced herself and held out her warrant card for him to see. He didn't look at it or react to her name.

'I can tell you're in the job,' he said. 'I don't need to look at that. I was a copper for nearly thirty years.'

'I know. That's why I'm here. Is there somewhere we can talk? In private?'

She looked behind him at the two sofas placed in front of a flickering TV set. On one of them a woman who looked very much older than Berne was sagging inside a pile of cushions, cardigans, blankets and woolly hats. Karen was wearing only a T-shirt and had still been too hot outside. Inside the cottage, however, the place was still roasting. All the windows were closed, the curtains drawn.

Outside the air had been close, stifling with the build-up to an electric storm. She touched a radiator behind her. It was on full blast. Behind the scent of a commercial air freshener she could detect traces of something more rotten. Incontinence, illness, decay.

'Forgive the temperature,' Berne said. 'My wife has an illness. She can't hear you. So it's private here. But we'll go out the back anyway. That way I can smoke.'

The woman didn't blink as Karen followed Berne past her and out the rear door to the property.

They walked through a short garden to a gate in a hedge. Berne opened it, extracting at the same time a packet of cigarettes from his pocket.

'We'll walk up the hill a little way,' he said. 'I rarely get out these days. She's been dying for nearly three years. I wish sometimes she would just peg it and have done with it.'

'I'm sorry,' Karen said. The amosphere inside had been depressing. She could understand his thought, but didn't like him saying it.

'That's what happens to love,' Berne said. 'Fifty years down the line you have to watch them die.'

They walked up a slight incline and Berne sat down on a dry stone wall with a magnificent view out over the golf balls. In a wide sky beyond them, in the far distance, heavy, rolling storm clouds were approaching. The air was prickly with static and her skin was beaded with perspiration. She sat beside him and watched him light a cigarette. She didn't comment on the view.

'So what do you want to know?' he asked her. 'I get visits about once a year these days. It's crazy we had no better recording system then. I suppose everything is recorded on a computer these days.'

'I'm here about Operation Candy,' she said.

He blinked and took a drag on the cigarette. 'I'm not sure I recall that one,' he said, eventually.

'Are you sure?' She sighed to herself. He wasn't a good liar. 'What about Simon Stark?'

He stared at her for a moment, then feigned recognition. 'Stark? Oh yes. I remember him. What do you want to know? And why?'

She started with the tale she had thought up earlier. 'I'm on Shade. It's the operation looking into the disappearance of Sophie Kenyon. You might have seen it on the news?'

'I have. Isn't Mark Harrison running that?'

She nodded, watching his expression. 'Yes. He's SIO.'

'He didn't send you here?'

'No. He's SIO, but he hasn't much to do with it. A DI called Ricky Spencer's running it.'

He nodded, as if he understood that, though things had been very different in 1983, when he'd retired. 'And you're here about Simon Stark?'

'Yes. He's come up in connection with some historic allegations that might be connected to the girl's disappearance.'

'And who told you about me?'

She looked away from him. 'Someone on the squad,' she said. 'A DC Bains?'

He smiled at her, harmlessly. 'I don't know him. Does he work for Harrison?'

She stood in front of him. 'We all do,' she said. 'He's the SIO. What are you worried about?'

He frowned at her, thinking about it while he smoked the cigarette. After a while he pointed to the thunder clouds. 'There's going to be a big one tonight,' he said. 'It's long overdue.'

She looked over at the clouds. 'Mr Berne,' she said. 'I have a kid I should be with. I haven't got unlimited time to stand around out here. You know how it works. I was given a task to ask you about Candy and Simon Stark, so I'm asking you. If you can't say anything just tell me and I'll go.'

He chewed at a fingernail, looking at her. 'And Mark Harrison knows nothing of this?'

'No. Not that I'm aware of. Why the concern about him?' She tried to make her tone sound innocent.

He smirked slightly and looked at his feet. 'Tell me how Stark is connected to this missing girl.'

She took a deep breath, as if his caginess were merely tedious. 'I don't know,' she said, for once telling the truth. 'Stark comes up as someone else who might have had a connection with the missing girl's father and who had a paedophile history. Someone called Simon Devereux. I was told Devereux's real name was Stark—'

'By your source? By DC Bains?' He smiled at her now, a peculiar smile that meant something she couldn't for a moment fathom.

'Yes. He said he'd heard about you doing an operation back in the early eighties—'

'Bullshit.' He got down off the wall.

Now she grasped it. He didn't believe a word she was saying. He stood in front of her, so close she felt intimidated despite his size.

'What do you want, Sharpe? Did Harrison send you out here? To test me?'

She took a step backwards, but didn't reply.

'Because if he did you can fuck right off.' He turned and pushed past her, walking quickly back down towards the cottage. She paused only briefly, thinking about it, then ran after him.

'I'm sorry,' she said. 'I lied to you.'

He stopped, swivelled to face her and waited.

'I wasn't sure what it was safe to say,' she said.

'Why?'

'I wasn't sure where you stood with Harrison.'

His eyes narrowed. 'Who sent you?' he asked. 'If Harrison didn't send you, who did?'

She licked her lips. 'A man called Sutherland,' she said. She saw him trying to remember. 'You won't know him. He's not with the police.'

'So who is he with?'

She shrugged, thinking hard about the ways in which a man so short could have gotten into a police force over forty years ago.

'He's with the security services,' she said.

He inclined his head, looking straight into her eyes, taking his time, waiting for her to react. She stared straight back at him.

'Did he approach you?' he asked, eventually.

'No.'

'So you approached him?' He said it as if he couldn't believe that would happen. She nodded and watched understanding gradually come to him.

'You're the one who worked with Phil Leech,' he said, after a pause. It wasn't a question. 'I keep up with things. I've heard about you. I read between the lines on that one. What did this Sutherland say to you?'

'That there was a story between Stark and Harrison. That you would tell it.'

He nodded. 'Why did you go to him in the first place?'

'Because Devereux and Stark's details are blocked and—'

'You can't get past the block without going through Harrison?'

'Yes. How did you know?'

'I've been expecting this,' he said. 'In all the years officers have been coming to my door, no one ever asked me about Candy. I'm surprised it's taken so long to come out.' He turned and began walking towards the wall. 'Come on,' he called after her. 'I'll have another fag. That's about as long as it will take. If you'd been truthful with me I'd have told you straight away.'

She leaned on the wall as he spoke to her, looking out across the tops of the golf balls, waiting for the thunder to start.

'Candy was a novelty back then,' he said. 'We knew about child abusers, we knew there might be rings set up to make it systematic. But there weren't any easy ways to get into them. That's all changed now, of course. The Internet makes it easier for both sides. Back then there was only one way to do it.' He looked up at her.

'An undercover officer,' she said, suddenly seeing everything he was about to tell her.

'That's right. It was my operation and I picked him myself. I planned the whole thing for six months. I can't remember how we got our lead in now. It looked good, but it's the same with all these things. There's no quick hits. It takes time to give someone the identity, put them in, build up the trust. Do you know what I'm talking about here?'

He turned and looked at her. She looked away. 'I know,' she said, quietly. 'I know all about it.'

'I'm sure you do,' he said. 'There's a type. I don't know what it is, or how it works. But that was my skill – to recognize the type. The sort of person who could do that. I saw it in you the moment you knocked on my door. That's how I knew you were bullshitting me.'

She stepped back from the wall and turned to look in the other direction, back up the hill. She felt uncomfortable.

'I needed someone who could do it properly, for a long time,' he said. 'You know what I mean. Someone talented, committed, incapable of corruption. I got two of those qualities. His name was Mark Harrison. He was a DC in Greater Manchester at the time. I don't know why he came forward. He'd never done the work before. It can't have been the subject matter, the nature of the operation, because, of course, we didn't tell them that when we put out the feelers. When we'd got past a certain stage and it was down to a list of three, we told him it was child abuse and he tried to back out. Now, I should have seen it for what it was then and there. No male copper backs away from that sort of thing. Because those are the people you most want to take down. He was frightened, see? Right then he knew it, knew that it was there, inside him – the potential. But I wasn't looking for that sort of sign. So I persuaded him to stay. So maybe it's all my fault, really. Who knows?' He dropped his cigarette on the ground. 'He was under for over three years. Do you know what that means?'

'Yes. I do know what it means,' she said. 'Tell me the rest of it.'

'You know what I'm going to tell you,' he replied.

'I do. But tell it anyway. So we're sure.'

'He did a good job. In the strike phase we netted twenty-two of them, from all over the country. We passed details on thirty more to Interpol and other national forces. We convicted eleven. On the Continent they were less efficient. They binned only three. But it was a good result. It ended the ring and put fear into the whole network. Harrison gave evidence from behind screens.'

'What was the MO?'

'They were buying media – film, tapes, photos. Whatever. They enticed, lured or kidnapped kiddies as young as seven and filmed them all. Boys and girls. The stuff was made on demand, most of it from the Continent, most of that from Eastern bloc countries. Harrison took the whole thing down.'

'So what was the problem?'

He hesitated. 'What I'm going to tell you is nothing more than rumour really. It came from the mouths of the perverts we pulled in. So they had an incentive. They needed to discredit him. They even tried it at the trial, but the judge wouldn't let them . . .' He broke off, still reluctant to tell her.

'Tell me,' she said. 'I'll make my own mind up.'

He shrugged. 'They said he went native.'

'Meaning he indulged?'

'Meaning exactly that.'

'How many of them said that?'

He swallowed. 'Enough to make it worth investigating.'

'How many?'

'All twenty-two.'

'Twenty-two witnesses. It doesn't sound like rumour to me. *Did* you investigate it?'

'Yes. It went up through the Force solicitors and was knocked back from a great height.'

'How great a height?'

He shrugged again. 'I'm not sure. Certainly the chief constable. Maybe there were politicians behind him. I don't really know. I did as I was told. The Force didn't need that kind of publicity. It would have undermined the entire case against the eleven we convicted. So we sat on it, buried it. I did what I was told.'

She sighed. It was exactly as she had thought. 'What about Stark?'

'He was minor. On the edge of things. But he went down with the rest of them on Harrison's evidence. How has he come up again?'

'I'm not sure yet. He's led me to you, one way or another. So there's something there. What do you think now?'

'About what?'

'About Harrison.'

'You mean whether he's safe?'

'Yes.'

'They're never safe. You know that. Child abuse isn't something you stray into. It's a lifelong affliction. We put him there, sure. We made a mistake. We put him right into the path of the thing, gave him an identity that pulled it out of him. He found out things about himself he didn't know were there. But they were there before we used him. They didn't get invented by us. Don't you think?'

She looked at her feet, bothered by the question. 'I don't know,' she said. 'I hope not.'

She was back in her car and halfway to Skipton before the full effect of what Berne had told her sank in. She hit the brakes and pulled into a lay-by, the beginnings of panic fluttering in her stomach. She pulled out her mobile to call Bains and saw she had two messages from him. She listened to them, hoping that he had found Mathews.

The first message calmed her. He had caught up with Mathews and had her at Shipley Police Station. She checked her watch. There was time to check on her, then continue on to Nottingham.

She had actually started the car and started off again before she listened to the second message. She slowed at once, watching a fast-moving low-profile car approach rapidly from behind. She switched her hazards on, watched it overtake and speed off – a Porsche – then tried to think clearly. Bains had released Mathews.

The message was long. He gave a short account of what Pamela had told him, confirming everything Karen now thought and feared, then said he had been forced to release her because there was no offence he could think of to hold her on. Karen cursed aloud and called him back at once. She started talking as soon as he answered, voice raised.

'Where did she go?'

'I took her back to Otley—'

'Where's Stark?'

'She didn't know. I tried to—'

'Was he at Otley?'

'No. There was no one there. I walked—'

'Did you check? Are you sure?'

'I walked to the door with her. What's up, Karen? Has something happened?'

'Did you check inside the house?'

'It was empty. It looked empty.'

'*Could* he have been there?'

'No. Yes. Maybe. I don't know. She seemed safe enough with it.'

'How long ago was this?'

'Forty minutes. I've just got back.'

She depressed the accelerator, switched off the hazards and took the speed gradually past ninety on the long stretch down to the Ilkley turn-off. She had to get to Otley quickly. As the fields stripped by her in the incipient dusk she told him quickly what Berne had told her. When she finished he was silent.

'You know what this means?' she asked.

'No. I thought you hadn't put anything on CIS. How would Harrison know about Mathews?'

'He sent his staff officer over to Eccleshill today. He took away all the paperwork. He will have read everything, including her name and address . . .'

Bains was silent again. She waited, steering around the Porsche that had passed her earlier. She had a brief glimpse of a youngish man on a mobile phone. No one she knew.

'You want me to get over there now?' Bains asked.

'No. I'm ten minutes away from Otley. What are you doing now?'

'I'm in the Tyrls. Spencer has pestered me all day to check in for this Ritchie thing. I thought I'd better show my face.'

Already she wasn't listening.

'Did she give you anything on Stark's whereabouts?'

'No. She was lying, I think. Stalling. She's frightened of him.'

'She has good reason to be.'

'I couldn't get anything useful from her. She told me she'd already told you where he lived. She told me to ask you.'

'She told me he lived with her.'

'Well, maybe that's it, then, the Otley address.'

The junction for Ilkley appeared at a bend in the road. There were four cars stacked up to get round an articulated truck that was lumbering along at a snail's pace. She hit the horn and pulled into the opposite carriageway. She didn't have time to be polite.

'I'll call you if I need you,' she said, and cut the line.

FORTY-NINE

As she walked the short path to the front door, the sky above her was black with thunder clouds, the air stagnant, full of bottled-up heat and static. It would burst soon, bringing the short summer to an end. The darkness had caught the summer evening by surprise: the street lighting was still off. Consequently, she could see nothing by trying to peer through the net curtains at the windows, so she went to the door and knocked, quietly.

There was no answer. She looked through the letterbox, and saw nothing. She felt uneasy, nervous, thinking they had made a mistake in letting her go, whatever the law was. She was hoping Pamela had given in and gone out again, in search of booze, but her heart was telling her otherwise.

She moved down one, to Mawson's house, but there was no answer there either, so she walked quickly around to the rear of the place, heart faster than normal, aware of the fact that she was reacting too quickly, with as yet no real reason to be afraid.

The gardens at the back were silent, everyone indoors, waiting for the rain. She could hear a single bird – probably a starling – singing a crazy chromatic pattern somewhere in the trees at the end of the row of gardens. She stepped through the open gate at the back of Pamela's house and saw immediately that the kitchen door was open. She slowed and checked the shed at the end of the path, then walked to the door. The air was so close it felt as if it were pressing against her skin.

She could see a wedge of floor space through the three-inch gap where the door was left open. Nothing suspicious, except the open door. She pushed it open a little further, hoping it wouldn't creak. Then she stepped in, paused and listened. Immediately she felt a prickle of sweat break out at the back of her neck. The place was silent, but not with the silence that came from emptiness. She knew instinctively, without any good reason, that the house was occupied.

She took a long, silent breath, wondering whether to call out for Pamela, walk out and shout for back up, or investigate alone. She had already entered two houses in two days to find bodies waiting for her.

She decided to shout out. She cleared her throat and spoke into the silence: 'Pamela Mathews? It's the police. If you're in here could you speak out now please?'

She waited for three or four minutes, listening for sound. She had an irrational suspicion that someone was standing just out of sight, holding their breath. She stepped through the kitchen and into the dining room, calling out again: 'Is there anybody here? It's the police.'

She heard a car pass, slowing, on the front street. Then another. She waited until the noise had stopped then stepped into the hall, glancing quickly up the stairs at the empty walls. She could smell something now, something so faint it was just below the level of conscious recognition. But she picked it up. She felt her pulse quickening and stepped alongside the open door to the living room, looking in.

Pamela was flat out on the floor, face down, a pool of blood gathering around her head. Karen froze.

The body looked perfectly still, but Karen could tell she was alive. She couldn't see the face, couldn't see any movement in the chest. But she was still sure it wasn't a corpse she was looking at. Not yet.

You knew a dead body the moment you saw it. There was something stiff about them, a lack of animation that even unconscious human beings still possessed. That didn't mean Pamela Mathews wasn't in the process of dying, right there in front of her. It just meant Karen had less time than she would have liked. If Pamela had been dead she could have backed out, called in the cavalry and taken all night. Now she had to do something.

She held her place. She didn't move towards the body, didn't say anything. She waited, listening out for the sounds. Someone else was here. She was sure of it.

Nothing changed. She took a breath and stepped into the room, scanning the spaces quickly, hands ready, fists clenched. She took in the cushions pulled from the sofa, the pattern of blood spattered up the wall by the fireplace, the dirty beige carpet, scuffed, blood-stained and threadbare in places. She saw the wound to the side of Pamela's head, gently pulsing with fresh blood. She could see no weapon.

She stepped back into the hall and listened to the silence from the floor above. She took the stairway slowly, back tight against the wall, head upwards. She wished fleetingly that she had extracted the gun from its place beneath the floorboards back in her house. In England they weren't used to the comfort guns gave you. Most men she knew felt nervous holding one. But in this kind of situation she would never quite get used to being without one. She felt naked.

The landing creaked beneath her feet and she waited again, senses turned up, tuned in for the slightest movement. When she was sure she could hear nothing she searched each room, methodically, carefully. She checked in the loft space. The house was empty. She let her breath come more freely, relaxing slightly, pulled out her mobile and started back down the stairs, quickly keying in the emergency number as she went.

She had got to Pamela's body and was bending down to feel the strength of her pulse before she realized something had changed. She froze for a second, the mistake registering like a door slamming in her brain. Then she was turning quickly, her mind reacting automatically, bringing up her arms to protect her head. She had just enough time to see the figure closing in on her.

Something black flashed down at her. As it struck her face, the room lit up with a blinding white light. For a fraction of a second it felt as if her head had been split in two. Her legs gave way beneath her and she was spinning, falling backwards. She felt her body connect with something, then the light was out and she was gone.

FIFTY

Ricky Spencer sat in John Munro's office, in John Munro's chair, at John Munro's desk and felt the desperation building to a scream within him. In less than fifteen minutes he had passed from a state of total elation – more elation that he had ever felt in the fourteen years he had been doing this job – to a violent, uncontrollable frustration. He rested his head in his hands and tried to get his thoughts onto a rational track.

His squad had done everything he had asked of them. They had been fantastic. In less than three hours they had split up, reorganized and set about processing the twenty-eight tip-off calls his delayed TV press conference had almost immediately began to generate. Twenty-eight calls had yielded precisely twenty-eight different locations for the whereabouts of Thomas Ritchie, but it hadn't daunted them. The sergeants had been spot on – fired up, motivated, moving heaven and earth to get in the manpower to run each and every lead into the ground, dead, within three hours of dividing the total calls between eight geographical teams.

They had processed twenty-one before hitting gold. In a tiny DSS bedsit in the heart of Bradford itself they unearthed Ritchie seated nervously before a TV screen watching the news coverage about the hunt to find him. They had brought him immediately to The Tyrls.

Spencer had met the search team at the rear entrance, punching the air briefly with a triumphant clenched fist as the car pulled up to the back doors. The DS directing the team had not been out with them and had come down with him. Spencer had watched him shaking the hand of the DC who had kicked in Ritchie's door – Neil Evans, he was called – and had felt then something like the sort of pride he had felt when his wife had delivered their first child.

It was the most significant thing he had ever pulled off in his career.

But within twenty minutes it had gone to shit. Ritchie was installed in the cells and immediately requested legal advice. Before Spencer could control the issue – at the time he had been in Munro's office on the phone to Harrison, passing on the good news – the custody sergeant, a fat, lazy time-server called Bill Nott, had put through a call to Bateman and Co., the very same solicitors that John Munro had clashed with.

When Spencer got down to the cells and tried to get Ritchie into an interview room, Bill Nott had refused him access, insisting he wait for the arrival of Ritchie's solicitor. Spencer had stood at the booking-in counter shouting at Nott, almost spitting the situation into his face: Ritchie had the information they needed, information that might save the life of the kidnapped child, they could not wait for Bateman to arrive.

He was still arguing with Nott when Bateman's lackey – a spotty law student called Khan – came through the gate, demanding to speak to Ritchie at once, in private.

Spencer backed off, retreating to his office and calling Harrison, exactly as he had previously called on Munro, in an attempt to get authority to exclude the representative.

Harrison blanked him with a deadpan voice: 'You play it by the book, Ricky,' he said. 'We play by the rules. That's what we always do. This enquiry will be no different. Standards will be maintained. There are no grounds to exclude the solicitor. Get in there and get on with your interview. Tell me what comes out of it.'

Spencer had slammed the phone down, anger rising like bile in his throat. Then he called for DI Murphy and they walked down to the cell area and interviewed Ritchie with the representative present. They took forty minutes at it, carefully and slowly putting to Ritchie exactly what they needed out of him, exactly where they had derived their information.

They needed an address and a name for the man he knew as Starsky. They started hard, but by the end of the forty minutes they were begging for the details. Ritchie stared back at them throughout, a slight smirk forming at the corners of his mouth. After each question the solicitor's representative repeated the same answer, like a mantra: 'My client exercises his right to silence until you have told him which offence he is suspected of.'

Finally Spencer lost it, jumping up from his chair and shouting down at the man standing between his entire squad and Sophie Kenyon: '*You little prick. You're taking a kiddie's life here. Do you care about nothing?*'

Khan had flinched, then stood up. Murphy had both hands on Spencer's arm, pulling him back into the chair.

'I feel physically unsafe here,' Khan said. 'I request that you terminate this interview at once and give me a copy of the tape.' He pointed to the tape machine, still running, recording everything.

Spencer had called Harrison again. Harrison was patient with him, sending his blood pressure through the ceiling as he questioned him about the detailed grounds for arresting and holding Ritchie.

'There are none,' Spencer had said. 'We had no grounds. If we hadn't have arrested him he wouldn't have come in.'

'Then let him go.'

Spencer waited thirty minutes at Munro's desk, trying to control himself. Then he called down to custody and asked where Khan was.

'On the benches, right in front of me.' The speaker wasn't Nott but a replacement called James. Nott, Spencer discovered, had gone sick shortly after he had shouted at him. He was putting in a complaint.

'Get Khan out of there,' Spencer told the new man.

'I beg your pardon, sir?'

'Get him out of the custody area. Do your fucking job. He can wait out front like anyone else. When we interview his client we will come for him. We're not here to provide him with comfort.'

Since then a further ten minutes had passed. Now it couldn't wait any longer. He stood up. Until he did something the anger was just going to build.

He walked down through the station and looked at Khan, pacing around the front lobby on his mobile, obviously worried. Probably he would be calling Bateman, asking him what he should do. Bateman himself hadn't come out because John Munro had broken his nose.

Spencer took the lift down to the cells and walked straight up to the new custody officer. 'I want the keys to the exercise yard,' he said.

'For what, sir?'

'Don't be insubordinate.' He stared into the man's face, forehead creased with suppressed rage.

'I'm sorry ... I was just ... I just need to ...'

'I want to go for a smoke. What else?'

'Should you do that, sir? There are prisoners out there.'

'Just give me the keys and shut up.'

The man was young, a PC acting as sergeant from Nott's shift, not used to the job. He looked dubious and reluctant, but he handed over the big bunch of keys. Spencer took them and walked down to Ritchie's cell.

It took him a couple of minutes trying each key to find the right one. He turned it in the lock, pulled the door open and saw Ritchie sit up on the narrow bunk and look at him, curiosity then fear in his expression.

Spencer pulled the door closed behind him. 'You called for something, Thomas?' he said.

Ritchie shook his head, standing up suddenly and backing towards the wall. Spencer walked towards him.

'My mistake,' he said. 'But it's time we had a chat anyway. Just you and me.'

FIFTY-ONE

The world returned abruptly to Karen – consciousness bursting to life as suddenly as it had been extinguished. Her thoughts flooded back in a tide of images and sounds, rushing at her without sense or control. For a while she was lost in them, her mind swamped. She felt weightless, floating on a cloud of disconnected sensations, suffering a panicky need to get back to earth, to anchor herself. She could hear herself panting for breath.

She struggled to regain her sense of body. For a while she could feel nothing. Then parts of it began to prod her with tiny needles of pain. As the weight of her limbs dragged at her, the reel of images racing through her head started to slow and take shape, forming into memories. Though she could feel pain now, it was still something in the background.

The things she was watching had happened many years ago, when she had been a child. It took her a while to realize that she was watching only three scenes, over and over again.

One was an image of her mother, moving from her bedroom to the bathroom, a long, dishevelled nightdress clinging to her thighs and breasts. She was moving in slow motion, her long hair flying around her like something alive, her thick limbs slow with peasant move-ments, the floor thundering beneath her. Her mouth was open and twisted into a silent scream. The image repeated over and over and Karen could see herself moving quickly through her peripheral vision, close to the ground, a small child. She was trying to get out of the way.

The image passed quickly to a single scene of millisecond duration, revealed in an explosion of frozen white light, as if an old-fashioned flash bulb had gone off, throwing everything into black and white. She could see herself sitting on a bed, hunched over her knees, making no effort to protect herself as someone rained blows upon her head. The image was so fleeting it was difficult to discern detail, but the child she was looking at was small, perhaps no more than five years old. She could see her own head moving with the blows, bouncing towards her knees, returning, waiting for the next blow. She couldn't see who was striking her, but she knew that it could only be her mother.

Then she was above herself, watching from somewhere in the ceiling above her bed, back in Cross, County Down, when they had lived in the old converted barn on the edge of the village, the fields scattered out to either side of her beyond the house walls, the tiny lines of hedgerows and dry stone walls making an intricate pattern across the gently undulating land.

She was lying back on the bed, smiling with a drug-induced serenity, an open, empty pill bottle tumbling from her outstretched hand, a thin trail of saliva coming from the corner of her mouth. Her breathing was heavy and laboured, but she felt a peacefulness she could recall now as if it were the languid torpor of a daydream, suffusing her with a sense of well-being. On the bedside table beside her she had left a note, but the words were vague and she could no longer read them. As she tried to make them out, the image switched back rapidly to her near-naked mother, the sweat running from beneath the nightshirt, the hair matted and greasy, writhing like snakes as she screamed her way past a fleeing child ...

The sequence disturbed Karen. She was unsure now whether she was seeing dreams or memories. She tried to move her head, but the pain exploded inside her at once, overpowering her with a fire that flashed along every nerve in her body. With its onset real life returned to her with shocking definition.

Her head felt like a balloon, filled with a throbbing of such intensity that for a long while it overwhelmed all thought. But as she became accustomed to it she traced the line of its progress down her back and into her legs. Her torso felt like a shell within which every single organ had become ruptured. She couldn't breathe without suffering a stabbing pain that ran like an electric current from one side of her chest to the other. She opened her mouth to gasp and felt her lips sticking together.

She realized she was lying on her face. Her legs were twisted, but in contact with the ground. She allowed herself mentally to check the parts of her body. They were all there. In her ears there was an intermittent crashing noise, so loud it was making her flinch. Her eyes, she understood now, were closed – stuck together with some sticky, warm liquid.

She lay still, not trying to move, with no sense of the passage of time. When she knew for sure that the noise she could hear was thunder, that she could hear nothing else, she opened her eyes. There was blood in them and for a few seconds everything was blurred. Very slowly she moved her right hand up and wiped the stuff away. In front of her she could see the pattern of the carpet in Pamela Mathews's front room. She rolled slowly onto her back and gasped for air.

Though she couldn't be sure, she thought the blood all over her face, neck and chest was her own. She reached her fingers up to her head and felt around the contours of a sizeable gashed swelling running from about half an inch above her right eye into the hairline. There was still blood seeping out of it. Her right eye was completely closed, the lids swollen together. She wasn't sure whether it was damaged. She pushed herself into a sitting position and looked around.

The night was dark around her, the lights off. She was alone. Where Pamela's body had been on the floor there was now an empty space. The throbbing in her head was a continuous drumbeat of blood. From outside, in the distance, the thunder rumbled through the night sky. She looked at her watch. It was after ten. She had been out for over an hour and a half. She stood up, leaning against the fireplace in the room. She tried to steady herself, but wanted to bend over and vomit. For nearly ten minutes she concentrated on simply remaining upright while the room expanded and shrank in her vision, the furniture spinning like she was drunk. She took deep breaths.

He hadn't even bothered to tie her. He had dragged Pamela from the room. She could see the trail of blood where her head had banged across the floor to the front door. She walked to the front door and opened it. Past the doorstep the street was empty, dark, silent. He had got a bleeding body out to a vehicle and no one had seen, no one had reported anything. If he had hit Karen only slightly harder she might have died before anyone saw fit to check the place.

The thought set a shivering in her limbs. Then came an anger of such intensity that it blotted out the pain. She forced herself up into

Pamela's bathroom and looked at the mess he had made of her face. He had struck her with something that had opened her scalp in a three-inch wound, intersecting her forehead. Beneath it, from the pain in her skull, he had probably fractured the bone. Concussion would set in within the next few hours. She knew how it worked, she had been here before. She needed hospital treatment.

Like all scalp wounds the injury had bled profusely. Her T-shirt was drenched in congealing blood, her face streaked with it. She washed it clean, then tore a green towel into long strips and bandaged herself, just above the right eye. With the blood rinsed from the eye she was able to check it. The swelling came from the head wound – he had not damaged her eye.

He had done other things to her though, while she was flat out and defenceless. She stripped carefully and inspected the areas of tenderness. He had kicked or punched her body, mainly around the ribs and breasts. Nothing permanent, but it was an invasion, something deliberate. She squinted at her image in the mirror and tried to slow the anger. She needed to control it if she was to be effective.

She had been careless, stupid. She had walked into it like an idiot, like a novice. Stark was a nobody, yet she had let him take her down. Probably he *had* left her for dead. She had dealt with people ten times more dangerous than him and lived. Yet she had allowed him to get into a position from which he might easily have killed her. She felt the violence swelling inside her.

She checked her watch again. She knew what she had to do. The hospital would have to wait.

FIFTY-TWO

She drove to Wakefield carefully, taking her time, trying to keep a straight line on the road. It was difficult. The motion of the car set her head spinning and during the first fifteen minutes she had to stop twice. But she got used to it, pushing the pain into the background. Worse things had happened to her.

But she felt strange, disconnected – as if the blow had knocked her out of herself. Concussion was dangerous, but blood clots under the skull were lethal. She would need to get to a hospital if she wanted to be sure.

The air was thick with the impending storm, the sky unnaturally dark for the time of night. In the distance she could see sheet lightning shorting between layers of cloud. She counted to thirteen or fourteen between each burst, then the thunder came to her, rolling through the night in a long angry growl, like a trapped animal. The moisture was dense in the heat, soaking her skin. Sooner or later it was going to erupt.

She had two messages on her mobile from Bains, but she didn't pick them up. The details were irrelevant now. She was going straight to the source.

Harrison's office was in the HQ complex at Laburnum Grove, in Wakefield. She parked her car in the car park, showing the night-watch guard her ID and ignoring the way he looked at her face, her clothes, the blood staining her T-shirt like some kind of tie-dye experiment.

She walked up to the back door and let herself in by swiping the card through the security system. The building was part of a cluster of Victorian terraced houses, bought up and converted.

The Command Team – from the Chief Constable down – was on

the top floor of the oldest building, the only one in the series that stood alone. She walked straight up, switching the lights on as she went. The place was empty, the wide, wooden stairway creaking beneath her. The interior design and fittings retained an air of former grandeur – like a country mansion, except now hung with cheap glass chandeliers and oil portraits of past chief constables.

Harrison's office was locked. She bent down and examined the mechanism. She could pick it easily, if she had brought the equipment with her – but she hadn't. She walked through the open doorway leading to the Command Team secretariat and hunted through drawers for keys, watching with detached interest as drops of fresh blood dripped from her chin onto the desks of the secretaries. Her head was throbbing as if an infection were already setting in.

She found three bunches, took them back and spent about three minutes trying different ones before she found it. Then she stepped into his office, switched the lights on, closed the door behind her and looked around.

Apart from the usual assortment of management bullshit posters (neatly framed to match the wood panelling) his choice of wall art revealed only a standard interest in golf. There were pictures of him with trophies, in full swing, posing beside other players who were presumably golfing celebrities, though the faces meant nothing to her. It was a large room and she had seen it all before, not seventy-two hours ago. But she hadn't been looking then. This time things were different.

She walked over to his desk and tried the drawers. They were locked. The computer screen, which was the single item on the surface of the desk, was switched off. She had seen him look through a list of informants searching for Caroline Dunn, the false name she had given for Pamela. The list had been in the top drawer of the filing cabinets by the window. All she wanted from his desk was the keys to that. She sat down in his chair and tried to force the drawers. They were too strong. She stood up and tried the cabinets. They too were locked.

She stood by the desk, feeling a peculiar irritation with it, then took hold of it with both hands and tipped the whole thing onto its side, not bothering to move the computer monitor before doing so. The monitor hit the floor with a loud crash, but didn't break. The exertion made her so dizzy she almost fell over. She stood for a while looking at the mess, waiting for her balance to return. She could feel the warmth of blood on her face. Beneath the makeshift bandage the wound was still bleeding.

She rolled the desk onto its back until she had access to the underside of the drawer unit. There was a computer terminal under the desk and she knocked it aside. She began to kick the drawer unit apart.

The wood looked strong, dark, expensive, but it was only cheap stained stuff. It took her less than a minute to break the unit apart and then kick the drawers open. As the contents spilled onto the floor, she looked down at them without surprise, trying to keep her eyes steady. She felt an effect like nystagmus, as if she were drunk. It wasn't just the blow to her head, nor even the blood loss – she was tired too. She hadn't slept properly for over two days. In amongst the clutter of stationary that had fallen from the drawers she could see no keys.

But there was a gun – a standard issue H&K, as used by the force firearms squad. Less standard was the silencer lying a little apart from it. She picked them both up and checked them, slipping out the magazine, pulling the slide back and inspecting the breech. There was a round chambered up and a full clip. The safety was on. She pushed it off and ejected the chambered round, placing the 9mm bullet inside the top pocket of her jeans. The gun might have been standard issue, but she doubted he had a licence for it. The serial had been burned off. She screwed the silencer onto the barrel and put it on top of the filing cabinets.

Then she left his door open and walked back down to her car, saying hello to a uniformed sergeant passing through the yard. He too stared at her face and looked about to say something. She walked past him without giving him the chance. She took a large red crowbar from the boot of her car and went back up. The security in the place was appalling. Harrison wouldn't be relying upon it. But she guessed he would be relying on something.

She jammed the crowbar through the thin gap at the side of the top filing cabinet drawer, buckling the metal to do so. Then she snapped it back and forced one side of the drawer to push past the lock. She pulled the crowbar out and slid the drawer open. On her belt she heard her mobile chirrup as if it were receiving a message. She checked it, but nothing had come in.

She reached her fingers under the top of the filing cabinet and felt carefully along the sides, immediately finding the wires. She slid the drawer completely out and placed it on the floor. Then she leaned into the cabinet and looked for the thing that had set off her mobile.

It was a simple cell phone transmitter, such as could be bought in any one of a number of private security shops in the area, taped to the top surface of the cabinet. The largest part of it was the battery. She followed the wires back to the lock. Her phone had buzzed because the mechanism had sent a signal when she had opened the drawer. Probably it was programmed to call Harrison's mobile automatically. That meant he would know someone was here, know someone was into his files. She had limited time.

She squatted on the floor and dug out the index card. There were about one hundred and fifty names listed. She did what he had done and ran her finger down them. There was a chance he had used a different name for Stark, so she wanted to check all the names, searching for anything similar. But there was no need. He was listed under 'S' exactly as he should have been: 'Simon Stark'. She followed the reference then dug into the second drawer and extracted a thin buff file evelope. She walked over to his upturned desk with it and sat down in the chair.

It took her about twenty minutes to take in the details. Even as she was finishing reading she heard his footsteps in the stairwell past the door. She closed the file, picked up the gun and waited.

FIFTY-THREE

He came up the stairs and through the door at a rush, clearly expecting the burglar to have already flown. He was halfway into the room before he could stop his progress and take in what he was looking at. She saw a moment of surprise on his face, not just at the mess or that someone was there, but that *she* was there.

'Who were you expecting?' she asked, calmly. She cradled the gun in her lap, not pointing it at him.

He caught his breath and looked quickly behind him, for a moment contemplating some kind of escape.

'Shut the door,' she said. She brought the gun up and waved it momentarily in his direction. He looked at it but didn't move. She watched him adjust, thinking quickly. He was dressed in civvies, a pair of black trousers and a checked open-neck shirt, black leather brogues. All looking like they came from M&S. His hair was wet and slicked back against his skull, as if the alarm had dragged him out of a shower or bathtub.

'Sharpe,' he said, voice cracking. He swallowed, still computing the possibilities. 'What are you doing here?'

'I said shut the door,' she repeated. She saw his attention focus on the silenced gun. 'Don't worry about trying to get your gun,' she added. 'This is it. I found it in your desk.' She waved it casually towards the overturned desk. His gaze took in the mess, the crowbar, the jemmied drawers, as if noticing everything for the first time. And I got *this* from your filing system.' She held up Stark's file with her free hand. 'You have some explaining to do.'

'Explaining?' He still hadn't remembered his rank. He blinked, struggling to fit the pieces together.

'This is Simon Stark's file,' she said. 'So before you consider pretending to be the outraged assistant chief constable, before you even think about calling in security, just think about what I might tell them.'

She watched as he ingested the thought, eyes moving quickly from the file to the gun, then back up to her face. Then she saw the realization flicker behind the surface. He licked his lips but said nothing. His eyes narrowed, the expression hardening. He turned back towards the door, contemplating his options. Then he stepped over and closed it. Something about the way he moved made the action deliberate, almost threatening – as if *he* was shutting *her* in. When he turned to face her again the fear had left him.

'We can talk about this, Sharpe,' he said, running a hand through his wet hair. His voice had an edge now, a suppressed anger. She had crossed him and revealed herself – he knew now, what he had to deal with. 'I'm sure there are reasons why you have done this,' he said. 'But I also know that you are mistaken.'

'The clock is against me,' she said, interrupting him. 'So listen carefully. I don't care what you've done, Harrison. I don't need an explanation. I'm only interested in where Simon Stark is. If you tell me that now then I'll get up and leave. It's as simple as that.'

He stared straight at her, his eyes sharp with resentment.

'Did you hear me?' she asked.

She watched him lick his lips again, then make an effort to compose his features. 'Simon Stark?' he said. 'Isn't that the name of an informant?'

She stood up and walked towards him. His eyes followed her, focusing on the bandage. She could feel wetness trickling across her forehead, over her nose, into her lips. She reached a hand up and brushed away a line of bright red blood.

'Stark did this to me,' she said. 'I will need hospital treatment. I haven't got all night.' She stepped right in front of him, as if he were no physical threat to her at all. She stared into his face for a few moments, then turned away and pulled a chair towards him. 'Sit down.'

He looked nervous again, her proximity affecting him. His eyes kept moving from her face to the gun, obviously bothered by it. She knew why. He thought there was a round in the breech and could probably see the safety was off. He sat down slowly, carefully – eyes constantly on her, as if she might do something violent if he let them drift. He knew about her past, had read her file. She walked behind him, the gun pointed at the floor. His head swivelled to follow her.

'I'm offering you a deal,' she said. 'It's the best you're going to get. You tell me where Stark is and I walk out of here and leave you. When I'm gone you can do what you like.'

She rested a hand on top of his wet hair and felt him stiffen. Gently gripping the top of his head, she applied pressure to turn his head and eyes away from her, then brought the gun up and rested it against the back of his head.

'What do you think?' she asked. He started to say something but she pressed the gun into his skin silencing him. 'I feel dizzy,' she said. 'Like I'm not really here.' She began to stroke the top of his head. 'You think you know all about me, but you don't.' She stepped back from him and his head and body twisted immediately to look up at her. There was uncertainty bordering on open fear now.

She wiped her hand on her jeans then walked around him and pulled another chair from the wall, lining it up about four feet in front of his own. She sat on it, leaning forward, the gun hanging between her legs.

'I've done some terrible things,' she said. Her voice cracked slightly. 'Whatever you've done, I've done worse. You know how I started out?'

He didn't respond. His face was immobile, streaked with sweat, flushed from the run up the stairwell.

'I started out with Loyalist paramilitaries,' she said. 'I feel comfortable talking to you about it because I know you will understand what I'm saying. They were filth. Pure filth. I started out living with filth, living and breathing their dirt, their filthy ideas and prejudices, so steeped in it I thought I'd never get the shit out of my eyes.' She shuddered. 'It makes my skin crawl to remember,' she said. 'This must be making sense to you? Am I right?'

She waited for him to answer. He shifted uncomfortably in the chair, eyes still on her, but saying nothing.

'I'm sure it does,' she said. 'You were trying to tell me that when I was here . . . when?' She tried to think back to when she had sat here with him. Two, three days ago? She couldn't be sure. 'My head's gone,' she said. 'I'm losing track of time. But you remember. I was in here. We sat here . . .' She pointed at the overturned desk. 'You and me. Assistant chief constable and pathetic little female DC. Remember? You shouted at me. I know why now.'

She looked down at the gun, then changed her grip on it, releasing the trigger and holding it by the long silencer, allowing it to dangle between her fingers. When she looked back at him he pretended he hadn't noticed. Assuming there was a round chambered up, if she dropped it like that there was a good chance it would go off.

'None of that matters now,' she said. 'Things have changed. That's why I'm telling you about myself. I want you to know how low I have sunk. Even now, when I think about it, it is as if there's a stench in my nostrils. Do you know what I mean?'

His breathing was slightly faster now, but he was still in control.

'They were into drugs,' she continued. 'All the Protestant groups did that sort of thing. At least that's how it seemed. They had no ideals. That's how I got into them. Through crime, through selling drugs to them. Usually heroin.

'I was a Protestant, you see. My family were all Protestants, all either Scottish or English by descent. In my file it says I'm Irish, but I'm not. Being born in the North doesn't make you Irish. So I would never have got anywhere with the Republicans if I hadn't known James Martin. You remember him? He's the one locked up for the shooting of Phil Leech and Fiona Mitchell. Shortly to be released, without charge.'

She watched blood dripping from the bottom of her chin onto his carpet. Her head felt fuzzy, the throbbing beneath the bandage growing in intensity.

'Martin knew I could get in with the crowd I'd gone to school with. The filthy white trash who were bombing out Catholic families in Newry, cutting throats in Belfast, killing kids, women, young men, whatever – all on the simple grounds that they were of a different religion. None of the Republicans I knew would ever have done that, you see. They were into ideas. And I had no religion. And Martin loved me . . .' She looked into his eyes and smiled, briefly. 'So he took a chance. Wrong choice, of course. The little girl he thought he knew had been picked off already – in England. She was already bought. So, you see, nearly all my life I've been manipulated by someone or other for purposes I barely knew about. Any of this ring bells? I'm guessing it's the same for everyone who does what we've done . . .'

He cleared his throat, looking for a moment as if he were about to say something. She didn't wait.

'You know how it is – you adapt quite quickly. For me it wasn't that hard. I'd grown up with Loyalists. I ended up living with one of them on an estate in North Belfast. That was probably the worst time in my life. He wanted some kind of relationship with me, but I was already in a relationship with Jim Martin.'

She looked up at him and waited for his eyes to meet hers.

'That was the only problem, though, because other than that I found the guy attractive. That's possible, isn't it? When you get in there, when you sink yourself in it so deep that you're not even sure who you are – then that's possible – that you find the most despicable things attractive, unobjectionable. After a while you cease *pretending* to be like them. You stop acting and *become* them. You and I know that.'

Harrison shifted his eyes away from her. He had started to sweat so that she could smell it now. She took a breath, struggling with thoughts she hadn't allowed into her conscious mind for over ten years.

'His name was Gerry Walsh,' she said. Her voice shook. 'He was as bad as the rest of them, but he liked me. That allowed me to get something going. They used me, I used him. Except, when you're the one in there, it isn't that simple, is it? I'm talking about over ten years ago now. When I think about it I realize I don't know who that person was. Who was it? Who was I? Who was it that took me over and did all those things?' She shrugged. 'Not someone I chose to be. Someone I *had* to be, in order to survive.'

She saw him nod, quickly, the slightest of movements. She smiled.

'Sooner or later it was going to happen, of course,' she said. 'Walsh and I were running in and out of the north-west, loaded out with gear, using the ferries. We couldn't have done that without inside help, of course. But it was always like that for the Loyalists. They had the backers.' She paused, remembering it. 'At some point I was going to run into someone who would blow me. I was passing back names and details all the time. And people were being picked off because of it. Because of what I gave the Republicans, or what I gave to the English without them knowing, or because of what the Republicans, in turn, gave to the police, or because they did it themselves, directly.

I knew three who were shot while I was doing it. That can't go on for long without someone putting the pieces together.'

She paused and let the gun slip from her grasp, sliding gently onto the carpet at her feet. She watched his eyes taking it in, computing the distance he would have to lunge to get at it.

'We did a deal with some kids from Liverpool,' she said. 'It had all been set up from Belfast by people I didn't even know. The exchange was to take place in an industrial estate somewhere off the motorway on the way to Wales. It was in the middle of winter, snow on the ground, the dead of night. Walsh and I parked up and walked into some kind of shed. They came out and we started to go through the checking. We had cash – a lot of it – they had about three kilos of high-grade brown. So it was a big enough deal. But they wouldn't exchange.' She paused and tried to read his expression. 'You know where it's going?' she asked. 'You know that fear?' A muscle twitched slightly in his cheekbone, under the left eye. 'Do you?'

He swallowed and moved backwards in the seat. 'Yes,' he said. 'I know it.' His voice was high-pitched, strung out with nervousness.

She nodded. 'I remember the one who popped it,' she continued. 'He was called Errol and had dreads, like he wanted to be black. He kept looking at me all the time and smiling. Even as he was doing it I knew why. But there was nothing I could do. There were two others with him. They both had weapons, so did I, though Gerry Walsh didn't know that.'

She wiped a drop of blood from her left eyelid, sat back in the chair.

'*Your woman there is filth.*' That was what Errol said to Gerry. Somehow or other, from somewhere, he had clocked me. Gerry didn't believe it, but he was slow. One of the others – I don't even recall his name – was moving to come behind me and search me. I couldn't let that happen, so I ducked and rolled – meaning, I suppose, just to ride with it, let it be blown and get out of there. But as soon as I went to run, the guy pulled the gun and started shooting. Trying to kill me.'

She took a deep breath, the memories twisting in her head. In front of her Harrison moved forward in his chair, nearer to the gun. But his eyes were on hers now, attention focused, listening.

'Gerry whacked him,' she said. 'Hit him with something as he was firing at me. Gerry saved my life.' She nodded to herself, acknowledging the debt. 'But I knew it was too late.' She sighed. 'There was a fire fight then. The other one went down. I suppose I must have hit him. Everyone was shooting except Gerry. He wasn't armed. So it must have been me. Then the one called Errol ran. I had to make a decision. Leave him or go after him. I got up and went over to where Gerry was hiding. But even as I looked at him I knew he had worked it out. Probably something about the way I was shooting – shooting and moving at the same time. I don't know. He hadn't even known I had a weapon . . .' Her voice trailed off and she cleared her throat. Her breathing was too fast. She tried to control it, counting out the breaths until she was certain she could speak with a clear voice.

'I made a mistake then,' she said. 'You will know why. Because I'd known Gerry, because I worked with him, because he liked me, because I'd spent so long getting under his skin, building the trust, listening to his sad little stories about his kids and ex-partner, because I was soft.'

She looked up and her vision blurred momentarily. 'I told him to leave. I let him go.' In her stomach she could feel the beginning of the concussion nausea.

'Then I went after Errol,' she said. 'But not to arrest him.' She took a long, deep breath and held her hands out in front of her, palms upward. 'Why? Why did I do that?'

He didn't answer. A flash of lightning lit the wall behind him in electric blue and a second later the thunder cracked across the rooftop like an artillery shell, so close the noise was deafening.

'At this point any normal person would ask me why,' she said. 'Why chase him down? Why not just let him go, get out of there? My employer, ultimately, was Her Majesty's Government. I was a police officer. But you won't ask will you?'

He cleared his throat, frowning, the twitch a rapid flutter now, almost constant. 'No,' he said. 'I wouldn't ask you that.'

'Because you know how it is,' she said. 'You know that at that point I had stopped being a police officer. I had lost track of myself. I had become something else.' She took a breath, held it in, counted to twenty, then slowly exhaled. 'I caught up with Errol getting into his car,' she said. 'I pulled him out, made him kneel on the ground and questioned him at gunpoint. I was trying to find out who had blown me and who he had told. If he hadn't passed anything back to Belfast,

I could continue with my undercover life. I was thinking in that way even though I knew Gerry was onto it now. So you see, it *was* a survival thing, an automatic, irrational survival impulse. For that woman, for what I had become, it was a question of survival. But it's difficult to tell whether you're getting the truth or not in that kind of situation. The guy was scared shitless. I think he would have said anything.'

She stopped talking and looked out through the windows at the night. She could hear Harrison breathing in front of her, hear the thunder moving into the distance, hear her own heart slowing, hear the steady drip of blood running out of her.

'I killed him,' she said, her voice flat.

She looked back at him. He was biting at his lower lip, sweat running into his eyes, making him squint.

'Do you know why I did that?' she asked.

He shook his head, too quickly and too vigorously to look anything but frightened.

'I did it because he tried to kill me. Because *in that world* those were the rules.'

She pointed at her forehead, touching the injury. 'Simon Stark tried to kill me this evening. That's why I've told you this. Not because I want you to be frightened of me. But because I want you to understand what I'm like. I want you to understand that I really don't give a fuck what you've done. I know how it is. I've been there. All I want is Simon Stark. So you better tell me where he is.'

FIFTY-FOUR

Suddenly, the rain came. It didn't start with a few drops. There was the silence between thunder claps, each drawing progressively into the distance, then it was there, hammering against the windows like hailstones. Within seconds whole sheets of it were lashing across the building, drenching and battering the window panes as if someone had turned a fire hose on them. She watched him looking at it, his brow creased with worry. She didn't wait for him to answer.

'Let me tell you what I know about you,' she said. 'It will help with what I'm offering.'

The noise on the glass was so intense she had to raise her voice. He started as she spoke, moving back in the chair, away from her. His mouth had been open, either to say something, or just because the rain was so fierce. He closed it, then brought up a hand and wiped the sweat from his eyes, blinking compulsively.

'First I'll trace the connections between you and Simon Stark,' she said. 'All this started when you were a DC in Manchester. You volunteered for something called Operation Candy, though you didn't know what you were volunteering for at the time. They didn't tell you until you were in, did they?'

He swallowed, seeing for the first time that she had more than just the file on Stark.

'They always have little tricks to pull you in,' she said. 'Tricks and lies. I've been there . . . Stark was one of the people you fingered. He was a minor player then. Your evidence put him inside on abuse charges. He was in prison for a while, but not for as long as you were undercover on Candy. Three years. Three years living and breathing the filth, sharing their dirt, pretending to be a child abuser.' She raised her eyebrows appreciatively.

'Who told you that?' he asked, the words so faint she could hardly hear.

'Does it matter? I've been investigating you, Harrison. I know a lot more than that. For instance, I know that you made contact with Simon Stark after he was released . . .'

'Not me. I didn't initiate the contact. He came to me.'

'It says all that in here.' She pointed to the file she had removed from his filing cabinet. It was about an inch thick, stuffed with informant logs detailing the contacts between Stark and Harrison over a period of nearly eleven years. 'You should have destroyed this,' she said. 'Why didn't you?'

He looked at her, squinting, thinking about it. 'Why should I? It's an informant log. That's all. There's nothing to destroy.'

She nodded. The action made her vision blur. 'That was a big mistake,' she said. 'But you can take it with you when you tell me where Stark is. There's no copies, so it will be *our secret*.' She smiled at him and felt a trickle of blood run between her lips. She saw his eyes looking at it. 'According to this log you started running Stark as an informant in nineteen eighty-six, when you were a DI at Eccleshill. You were given the Yorkshire end of a SERCS operation cracking a ring running stolen high-value vehicles into Eastern bloc countries and the Gulf. One of the people arrested was called Simon Smith. That was what he was calling himself then. I assume you spotted him, recognized him and—'

'No. It didn't happen like that. I did not look for him. I didn't even have anything to do with the arrest. Two DCs on my team had it. Stark was offering to cooperate. They had him sitting in the CID room and he saw me from there. *He* recognized *me*.'

She shrugged her shoulders. 'Why are you telling me that?'

He looked away from her.

'Are you feeling guilty? What are you trying to justify?' she asked.

He looked at the gun, still lying on the carpet about a foot in front of her feet. One of his legs had started to tremble.

'It doesn't really matter,' she said. 'From then on he appears as an informant. One way or another you had the case against him dropped and he walked.' She didn't wait for him to contradict this. 'A fruitful relationship began.' She picked up the bulky file and held it in front of his eyes. 'He was a good source of information. In that same year he led you to Eric Pardoe, a pillar of the local community. But you knew what he was really up to. Stark was telling you from mid-nineteen eighty-six onwards. Pardoe was a paedophile. But you didn't do anything about it, did you?'

'The information was poor, unsubstantiated—'

'Instead, you became a business partner. Maybe even a friend.'

He cleared his throat. 'The information was nothing but rumours.'

'So you met up with Pardoe and became friends?'

'It doesn't say that there.' He pointed to the log.

'No. But I have a journalist who wrote an article about it. He will tell a court – if necessary – that Pardoe and you were business partners and friends.' She counted the lie in her head. It was the first she had told him.

'Not friends,' Harrison said. 'I bought a few houses off him. That's all. That doesn't mean we were partners.'

Through the fuzziness she felt a small thrill. He had given her a link. She could evidence it later.

'You bought property from someone a high-grade informant told you was an active paedophile? You must have been ACC material even back then.'

'We didn't know whether he was a paedophile.'

'No? So what information was he selling?'

She saw a moment of panic in the back of his eyes – enough to confirm her guesswork.

'You didn't destroy this,' she said, pointing to Stark's file. 'But you destroyed Pardoe's file.'

He shook his head vigorously. 'No. The papers for that enquiry are still—'

'Not Flight. I have copies of all the paperwork for Flight. I'm talking about Pardoe's informant file.'

He looked at her, trying to keep his features still, trying to guess where she was guessing, where she was lying, what information she had. But he didn't deny it, and that was all she needed to push it one further step.

'Pardoe was giving you information throughout the time you were buying properties from him. I'm guessing he's the informant referred to in Stark's file as Eric Davis. Stark led you to him. References to him start in the same log as references to Pardoe. I'm guessing the three arrests of child pornographers made towards the end of nineteen eighty-seven – all on info given by this Davis – were all little gifts from Pardoe. Because you had something on him.'

He stared at her, chewing furiously at his lower lip, hatred in his eyes.

'The links to him are all in here,' she said. She picked up Stark's file again. 'Like I said, you should have destroyed this. No point in getting rid of Pardoe's logs if you leave references to them in other files.'

'You're guessing all this,' he said, but he was jumpy now.

'There's none of this in the Flight paperwork,' she continued. 'No mention of it at all. You led an enquiry into the death of someone you had bought houses from and ran as an informant and you told no one. *No one.* Is that how they taught you to investigate homicides at training school?'

'You're guessing he was an informant. You don't know that.'

'Worse than that,' she added, 'you investigated him for rape a year before Flight. Your informant, friend and business partner.'

She saw the shock register in his eyes.

'The rape of Laura Cowgill,' she said. 'You were SIO. That file is gone, of course. Along with all the exhibits from Flight. But I got a copy from other sources.'

She could see him thinking frantically, trying to put together a way out of it.

'What did you do to get the case dropped?' she asked him.

'That case failed because an officer attacked Pardoe and—'

'*Before* that. What did you do *before* they found out about DC Bains's attack?'

He stopped in mid-sentence, mouth opening and closing in silence.

'You know what I'm talking about,' she said. 'Making cases fail is a speciality of yours. Stark's case in nineteen eighty-six – for the rung cars—.'

'He was never charged. It had nothing to do with me.'

'You made sure he *wasn't* charged. Then again in nineteen eighty-seven. Stark was picked up again by SERCS. This time for involvement in an international child porn ring reaching back into Russia. You bailed him out.' She leafed through the file on Stark and pulled out the relevant log. 'It says that right here,' she said. 'You made the call to SERCS, bailed him out...'

'That was normal practice. He was a valuable informant. I was doing nothing but protecting the source. The evidence for the Moscow thing was weak. We discussed it and made choices.'

'Is that also why you arranged for Kenyon to be the judge in Pardoe's rape trial?'

He began to stutter, for a moment unable to get any words out of his mouth.

'Don't lie to me,' she said, raising her voice. 'You knew Kenyon was a friend of Pardoe's. You knew Kenyon. The three of you were all friends together.'

She watched his jaw quivering as he tried to remain calm, to maintain the act, belatedly to remember that he was the assistant chief constable.

'I have photos of Kenyon with Pardoe,' she said. Assuming Kenyon was the man in the video, it wasn't strictly a lie. 'I can prove business and social connections between them well before the Laura Cowgill rape trial. Are you denying you knew the judge?'

'I didn't know him,' he said. He was taking chances. 'I didn't know him then or subsequently.'

'So why would he call you when his daughter disappeared?'

'Because I'm the chief constable—'

'*Assistant* chief constable. Don't get above yourself. Would that also explain why he called you fifteen times in the two weeks *prior* to his daughter's disappearance?'

He closed his mouth, then screwed his eyes shut. He brought his hands up and covered his ears, shutting her out. She saw his muscles tense, from his thighs through to his neck. He was holding his breath, forcing himself to *not* respond to her. When he finally opened his eyes and looked at her, she saw the beginning of understanding, of real fear.

'I've been busy,' she said. 'When we're finished here – if it comes to it – I'll take all your phones and do what I've done to Kenyon's phone. I'll find out whether you called him back. But even if you didn't I have more than enough. Kenyon sent you a note. I did an ESDA test on the pad he used. I have a copy of it.' She watched the colour draining from his face. 'In the note he talks about nineteen eighty-nine,' she said. 'What did he do in that year?' He didn't look at her. 'He stopped the case against Pardoe. But he did worse than that two years before. In the note he tells you about a video. Do you know what video he is talking about?'

'I have received no note from him.' The words were whispered from between his fingers.

'You know I have a witness, Harrison, Pamela Mathews. You stole the paperwork relating to her. Pamela will say that she was kidnapped and raped, at the age of thirteen, by five men. Three of them are dead. She recognized Geoff Reed herself. He shot himself – or was shot – two days ago. I myself traced the links to Michael Kenyon. He too is dead. Because you are SIO for both Reed and Kenyon I wouldn't now have a clue whether they killed themselves or were murdered. You told the investigators to treat both cases as suicide.'

'They left notes—'

'Eric Pardoe died in nineteen eighty-nine, but I have photos of him to show Pamela Mathews. I also have photos of you. She has already seen them. She says she recognizes you.'

'*No. No. No.*' He stared up at her, tears in his eyes.

'She recognizes you as one of the men who raped her in nineteen eighty-seven.' Lie number two.

'No. She is useless. She's a drunk. She's a drunk who claims recovered memory. She isn't credible.'

'You've read her papers, then? Didn't take you long.'

'No prosecutor would run with the evidence of Pamela Mathews.' So he didn't know that Stark had taken her.

'They don't need to,' she said. 'Not *just* with that evidence.' She paused, watching his lips quivering. In his heart he already knew what was coming. The fear in his eyes confirmed everything.

'I have the video,' she said.

Suddenly he was moving. The change was so quick he was down and reaching for the gun before she had even moved in the chair. As she straightened to face him he was already in front of her, eyes wide, filled with desperation, the gun at arm's length and pointing directly at her face. She saw him squint against the noise, closing his eyes to the image, saw his finger tightening on the trigger. The barrel was no more than six inches from her face.

He didn't hesitate.

She heard the merchanism click on the empty chamber, then she was sliding off the chair, hand closing around the gun. She moved sideways as he opened his eyes. His face was filled with confusion and surprise. There had been no shot, no explosion, no bullet crashing through her face.

She slipped her other arm behind his elbow and snapped his arm back against her own. She felt his elbow pop, the bone cracking apart. A shriek of pain slipped from his lips, the grip on the gun loosening at once. She changed her position, took it from his grasp and turned it in her hand, the whole movement smooth, controlled. He looked up at her, still on his knees, still yelling with pain as she brought the butt straight down into the middle of his face.

The blow was so powerful she staggered backwards, head rocking as though she had been struck. As she steadied herself she saw that he was splayed backwards on the floor, his useable hand covering his nose, a stream of frothy red blood spurting between his fingers. The arm she had snapped was lying uselessly at his side. She changed hands, pulled the slide back on the gun, slotting a round into the breech, then stepped over him.

'Stupid fucker,' she said. 'You tried to kill me.'

FIFTY-FIVE

He began to cry at once. But not like an adult would. The noise coming out of him was a terrified bawling, the sort of reaction she would have expected from a child.

'I spoke to Mike Berne,' she said, shouting above him. 'I know what you were doing on Candy.'

He began to roll from side to side on the floor, hand still covering his face.

'Is that how it happened? Did Stark know about you? Did he know what you had been doing?'

She couldn't be sure if he could even hear her. The crying broke into long sobs. He pulled himself onto his side, curling into a foetal ball. He was shaking from head to foot. In between sobs he was trying to say things, but the words were muffled, garbled, full of blood and saliva. His breathing was out of control.

She tried to keep herself from shouting with frustration and annoyance. She would get nothing out of him if he remained like this.

'*Don't hurt . . . please don't do it . . . not to him . . . don't hurt Mark . . . please don't hurt Mark. . . .*' His voice was high-pitched, like a child's.

'I'm not going to hurt you,' she said. The words had no effect. She said them again. 'I'm here to help you. I can help you, Mark. I won't hurt you.' She kept repeating the words, trying to get a soothing tone into her voice.

She knelt down on the floor beside him and began moving her hand in a stroking motion across his matted hair. Almost immediately it began to subside. The convulsions became less violent, he stopped pulling away from her and began to gasp for breath. He rolled to look at her, then immediately rolled back as if he couldn't face the image. Several seconds passed before he turned back again, eyes filled with confusion, as if he were struggling even to recognize her. She kept the gun low, out of his line of sight and began to say senseless things, not even words, exactly as she would do a distressed child. She wiped the blood from his eyes and moved closer to him, stroking his head with a firmer motion.

'You can tell me all about it,' she said. 'I won't hurt you.'

'*It wasn't me,*' he said. '*It wasn't me. I didn't do anything.*' He was shivering uncontrollably, but the movement was different to the involuntary jerking that had creased him into a ball moments ago.

'I know it wasn't you,' she said. She tried to pretend she *was* speaking to a child. 'Tell me who it was.'

'*It was Simon. He threatened me. He said he would hurt me.*'

'What did Simon do?' she asked, keeping her eyes on his.

'*You won't tell Daddy?*'

The words were virtually inaudible. She stared at him, trying to keep her face free of reaction. She felt disgusted. She repeated what he had said to herself, hardly able to believe it. But even as the meaning sank in, she saw pain jump through his arm again, pulling him out of it. His eyes clouded. He was staring straight at her, but not seeing her. She saw the thoughts dancing across his sight, moving so rapidly his eyes began to jink backwards and forwards, following them. Then the images were gone. His eyes cleared, focused, settled on her face. He was looking at her again. He was Mark Harrison.

At once his expression knitted with profound confusion, passing quickly into shame, as he realized what he had said to her. He started to move to get away from her, wincing as the pain shot through him. She brought the gun up and rested it against his face, stilling him.

'Keep still, Mark,' she said. With her free hand she began to stroke his head again. 'Remember where we are. Remember what's happening. If I have to I'll use this. You just tried to kill me. You're dangerous. But I don't think you want to create any more problems for yourself. On what I have you're going to prison for life...'

'I've done nothing,' he said, still whispering, eyes trying to twist to see the barrel of the gun, pressed against his cheek. His nose was smashed almost flat, so wrecked he was breathing through his mouth, a fine spittle of blood spraying up at her with every word. She could see the tears welling into his eyes again.

'Remember our bargain,' she said. 'Remember that I don't care.'

'He was blackmailing me,' he said, voice trembling. 'Stark. I didn't know what to do. I've hurt no one. I've tried to hurt no one. Ever since they pulled him in and he saw me – I've been trying to stop him. I swear it's true.' There was a naked desperation in his tone.

'I believe you,' she said.

'He was going to make things up about me. Rumours . . . rumours about what I had done when I was undercover . . . I tried to keep him happy and at the same time to run him for information, but in nineteen eighty-seven it went too far. They were kidnapping children, putting them in vans, sending them to Eastern bloc countries, the Gulf. I couldn't keep control of them.'

'Them? Who were they?'

'Pardoe and Stark. They were both in it.'

'Not you?'

He shook his head and tried to move into an upright position. She placed her hand on his forehead, holding him in position, head against her thigh.

'Who did they kidnap? Give me names.'

'They took a little girl in November nineteen eighty-six. I can't remember her name. She disappeared from Fleetwood. Her mother was a prostitute, a crack addict. She was fourteen years old . . .'

Inside her chest she had a feeling like something was gripping her heart.

'I didn't know about her until afterwards. By then it was too late. Stark took three girls the year after. Mathews was one of them. Pardoe was throwing a party for his politician friends. You know about it. They had the three little girls locked in the cellar.' He was crying uncontrollably now, the sobs breaking up his words, tears mingling with blood in his mouth. 'They took video footage. They got people drunk. They put a drug in the wine, in the food . . . I didn't know what I was doing. He told me they were prostitutes from Bradford that Reed had laid on . . . to celebrate. He didn't say how old they were. I swear to you . . . I didn't know. The girls said nothing. They just lay there. It was all a set-up – so they could get the video of us, in there, to blackmail us. . . .'

She didn't believe a word. She had seen the video, had heard Pamela's account. The figure she had rightly guessed to be Harrison was so unclear that the footage would have been useless to identify him, but Harrison *knew* it was him. In his eyes, the footage would clearly show him *in action*. It was the same effect that had hooked

Kenyon. The facial features were unclear, but the recorded activities were not. And, unlike Kenyon and Reed, Harrison had gone into the room with two people he had *known* were paedophiles.

'And then they used it to blackmail you?' she asked, keeping her voice sympathetic.

'Yes. On the Cowgill rape . . . on other things . . . they threatened all three of us. The video was their protection.'

'What happened to the girls?'

He started to sob again. 'They starved to death. Two of them starved to death. Stark was arrested. He was arrested days after the whole thing. They were meant to take the girls out of the country, sell them for films. They weren't meant to die. But Stark got pulled by SERCS for that Hamburg porn job. I couldn't believe it. Pardoe was meant to feed the girls while Stark wasn't there, while I was trying to get him released. But he didn't.'

He looked up at her helplessly.

She looked back at him. The blood was pounding in her neck, the hairs on her scalp standing on end.

'They died,' he said. 'They died in that hole. Mathews was the third. She survived. Stark pulled her out. Pardoe had gone on holiday, to Spain or somewhere. He had just left the place, left them in there. Stark was furious with him. He wanted to kill him there and then. I got him out of the country, persuaded him not to. I was trying to control him, trying to keep in with him so that I could control him.'

'But he killed him anyway?'

Harrison swallowed hard, the muscles in his face trembling. 'He came back. In nineteen-ninety. He came back and killed him. He buried him alive . . .'

'How convenient for you.'

'I knew nothing about it.'

'I've seen Stark's log. You were in contact with him in nineteen-ninety. You knew he was in the country.'

'I didn't know why.'

'He told you that Pardoe was giving information to another DI, behind your back. I've seen the log. Don't deny it. You couldn't allow it. You knew what he might say about you.'

'I didn't ask Stark to do it. Not *that*.' He was pleading with her.

She cupped her hand around his jaw and pressed the gun against his neck, shutting his mouth. 'Why is he back now?' she asked. 'Why is he here? I don't believe he came all the way here to look for Pamela Mathews.' She eased her hand away, allowing him to reply.

'He wanted money. He tried to blackmail Reed, but Reed blanked him. So he went to Kenyon. He sent him the video. I couldn't control him. I tried, but he's a monster. He has no fear.'

Suddenly she saw it. What had only been a suspicion – driving her forward without her even knowing it – was there now, suddenly out in the open, the final missing link.

'What did Kenyon do?' she asked, but she already knew the answer.

'He said he couldn't take it any more. He called me. He said he was going to confess everything. He *told* Stark that. He told him . . .'

'So you had to kidnap his daughter to stop him?'

'Not *me*. I have done nothing . . .'

His protestations faded into the background. Now Kenyon's suicide note made sense. She stood up quickly, letting him drop away from her. She could hear him yelling in pain as his head bounced off the floor. She didn't care. She pointed the gun down at him, telling him to remain where he was.

'Where is Stark?' she asked. Her voice was calm, but her heart was racing now. She knew what was at stake.

He crawled back to the wall of the room and pushed himself into a sitting position, resting against it. 'You said you would let me go.'

'And I will. If you tell me now where Simon Stark is.'

He paused momentarily. She saw a glint in his eyes, because he too knew what was at stake. He had known all along.

'Dean Head Farm,' he said. 'That's all I know. He was at a place called Dean Head Farm. It's near the airport. It's a place that—'

'I know it,' she said

It was the address the Shade team had asked him to unblock. He had prevented them from searching it.

She pulled out her mobile phone, keeping the gun trained on him. She dialled Bains's number.

He answered almost at once. 'Karen? Where are you?'

'Wakefield. Where are you?'

'The same. I'm with DC Jones. We're trying to chase down a lead from—'

'Forget that. And lose Jones. I need you here. Now.'

'Where?'

'Laburnum Grove.'

She thought she might be slurring her words. There was a momentary silence.

'Harrison,' he said.

'That's right. How long before you can be here?'

'Less than ten.'

'Do it.'

She cut the connection and looked over to Harrison. His face was smeared with blood and tears, contorted into a grimace of open hatred.

'*You told me! You fucking told me! You gave me your word!* he was hissing at her.

'I can't let you go,' she said, keeping the gun on him. 'You would call Stark and warn him.'

'*You fucking lied to me!*' He struggled into a standing position against the wall. He looked drunk, arm hanging limply at his side, shirt covered with his own blood, eyes wavering about as he tried to keep his balance.

'You're under arrest, Harrison,' she said. 'Try one step towards me and I'll shoot your fucking legs off.'

FIFTY-SIX

It took only two punches to get two addresses out of Thomas Ritchie.

The first Spencer landed in his gut as he brought his hands up to protect his face. He doubled up immediately, face turning an instant pink, eyes agog. Spencer waited for him to sink to his knees then took a long swing at his face, catching him with all the power he could put into it, somewhere around the left cheekbone. Ritchie's head snapped off the wall and a muted gurgling noise came out of his throat. He fell onto all fours and Spencer stepped back, looking for a suitable spot to kick him.

He didn't need to. Before he even had time to bring his leg back Ritchie was talking, not just telling him he would cooperate, but actually doing it, right there and then – giving him addresses. Spencer listened, catching his breath. It was the first time ever that he had assaulted a prisoner.

The first address was somewhere up near Leeds/Bradford airport. Ritchie said it was the only one he knew for the man he called Starsky. He spoke in a strangled, pained voice. He had barely enough wind left to speak at all. He kept his head down, not looking at Spencer, expecting him to strike again.

In the past, he said, Starsky had lived there. That was all he knew. He had heard he was living there again. The place was a ruined farm – Dean Head Farm, just off a dirt track they called Dean Head Lane. Spencer realized at once that he recognized the address. One way or another it must have already come up in the enquiry. He would have to check.

The second was Starsky's girlfriend's place – an ex-council semi in Otley. Priestley Road – Ritchie didn't know the number. He had a name for the girlfriend though. She was called Pamela. It would be enough for Spencer to find the place.

He reached down and wiped his hands on the back of Ritchie's shirt. There was no blood and they were perfectly dry. He was not sweating, his breathing was calm, controlled.

'You're a little fuck, Ritchie,' he said. Then he turned and left the cell.

Back in his office he called the three sergeants he had been relying on and told them to pick a team of three detectives each and three cars.

'I have addresses for Starsky,' he said. 'We're going there now. Keep it quiet though.'

Only Ron Coombs asked him how he had got them. He ignored the question.

While he was waiting for them he fired up the terminal on his desk and searched the Electoral Register for Priestley Road. There was no 'Pamela' living there. He checked OIS with the same result. He rubbed his knuckles and looked at the names of all the occupants he had information on. His knuckles were red and sore. He wasn't used to hitting people.

Nearly all the occupants of Priestley Road were families with children. Only three premises had a single couple living in them. He wrote down the names and numbers – twenty-seven, twenty-nine and seven. It would do to start with. If necessary he could get the whole squad onto it, do the entire road in fifteen minutes.

But he wanted to start with the farm address.

Dean Head Farm. He ran it through HOLMES and it came back at once. It was an address that had come up as blocked. He had gone to Mark Harrison to ask for the block to be removed. Harrison had refused. He reached for the phone to call Harrison, to ask again, to tell him what he knew. Then he paused. Something clicked into place in the back of his mind. He felt a slight shiver running up his spine.

He was still thinking about it when his mobile went off. The number came up as Karen Sharpe. He didn't want to talk to her. She had been AWOL from her team and was in trouble, but he didn't want to deal with it now. He clicked the little green phone symbol and held it to his ear, intending to tell her he was busy, that – whatever it was – it would have to wait.

FIFTY-SEVEN

She drove furiously through the night, the rain lashing around her, in the distance diffuse lightning dancing between the clouds. The fuzziness in her head had converted itself into a headache now, a heavy throbbing behind her eyes. She felt a continuous sensation of nausea and was conscious that at times she was having to struggle to keep the car in a straight line. As she drove through the centre of Leeds cars began to sound their horns at her.

Once on the Headingly Road she pulled over and looked at the A–Z. The Dean Head Farm address was not just familiar because she had noticed it as blocked by Harrison, she had already seen it on the map when she had been looking for Pardoe's address. It didn't take her long to locate it. Knowing where it was – that she could be there in under ten minutes – calmed her slightly. She set off again at a slower pace. The last thing she wanted was to be stopped by a traffic patrol. Or crash.

She had left Harrison with Bains, telling him a shortened version of nearly everything that had happened. The crucial thing wasn't so much to process Harrison – to get him to a cell block and custody suite – as to stop him using any phones. Baines had agreed to hold him at Laburnum Grove until he heard further from her. He hadn't needed the gun to do this, though she had offered it. He had refused, looking at it as if it might burn him merely to touch it. Consequently, it was sitting on the seat beside her, the silencer unscrewed and discarded. She hadn't given Bains time enough to argue about it.

As soon as she was driving she had called Ricky Spencer. After three attempts she got through to him. He had wanted to get rid of her at first. But that had changed when she told him she had arrested Harrison and that she knew where Sophie Kenyon was being held.

The silence hadn't lasted as long as she had thought it would. Instead of all the questions he had cut straight to the point.

'What's the address?'

'Dean Head Farm. It's a place that—'

'I know it.' He cut her off. 'It was blocked by Harrison. I have that address here as well. I'm setting up teams to get in there right now.'

'I'm halfway there already. I'll be there in fifteen minutes max.'

'Stop now.'

'Stop? Are you mad? Time is against us, Ricky. We have to go for it now. I'm almost there.'

'Are you drunk, Karen? You sound drunk.'

'I'm fucked. My head is fucked. I might be concussed. I don't know if—'

'Stop now. That's an order. Stop and wait for us. I'm bringing twelve men with me. Don't go in there alone.'

'How long will you be?'

'Half an hour at most.'

She looked over at the gun on the seat. 'OK,' she said. 'I'll wait on Dean Head Lane.'

He wanted more details from her, but she told him she couldn't drive and do both.

'Call Pete Bains,' she said. 'He'll give you the detail.'

'Bains? What's he got to do with this?'

'He's holding Harrison for me.'

She cut the line. She had no intention of waiting.

The rain was coming down in dense sheets as she turned off the A660 and began to pick her way through narrower country lanes, all heading towards the airport. She turned left on Moor Road, then right onto Otley Old Road. The road climbed through woods, or gardens filled with trees – she couldn't be sure in the dark – then she was over the crest of a hill and looking across at the runway lights, less than three miles across the valley below. Squalls of rain drove through the headlights in front of her, making the flight path markers intermittently flicker and vanish.

She pulled over and looked at the map. Above her the thunder had started again, nearer this time, the same angry rumbling that had greeted her return to consciousness.

It took a while for her eyes to settle sufficiently to be able to pinpoint where she was. She found the Pardoes' house first – the lights were on, though she was too far away to see anything more than that. She followed the line of a dotted dirt track leading off Otley Old Road until she could see a rooftop somewhere in the darkness between Pardoe's house and the road. It was the property she had seen from Emily Pardoe's front garden, no more than half a mile away. There were no lights on that she could see.

She took her time on the dirt track, driving carefully, windscreen wipers on full. She had covered only half the distance before a clap of thunder exploded directly above her, the blast immediately accompanied by a surreal electric blue illumination that threw everything into blinding contrast. For a moment she had a glimpse of the trees she was driving through, the building at the end of the lane, the dirt track in front of her, then the earth shook beneath the car and the water burst through in great, torrential sheets, striking the windscreen with a deafening clatter. Wherever the bolt had struck, it had been close.

The quantity of water was so great the pot holes in the track were filled within moments. The road became a series of pools and troughs, difficult to see in the thickening layers. She slowed to a crawling pace and switched off her headlights. Ahead of her, lightning was forking to earth in long, jagged lines, creating enough light for her to see her way along the path.

When she thought she was about two hundred yards away she stopped, pushed the gun into her jacket pocket, took the flashlight from the glove compartment and got out. Within moments she was drenched through. She stepped off the lane onto the mud beneath the tree line and began to move slowly forward. She had picked her way a hundred yards further before she could see the edges of the buildings. She listened.

There was an irregular banging noise, like an unfastened door slamming shut in the wind. Apart from that, nothing. But the wind and rain were strong. She moved on, repeatedly sinking up to her shins in puddles and holes as she tried to keep her eyes clear of water, tried to remain alert to the sounds and movements around her. The towel she had used as a bandage became saturated with water, so she took it off and dropped it in the mud, not daring to check whether her head was still bleeding.

Where the trees stopped she came upon a narrow walled yard,

abutting the rear of the property. No cars parked up. No signs of life. She could see the loose door now. It looked like the main back door to the place, flapping against its hinges with every gust.

The place had been a farm once and there were about three sets of solid, stone buildings. The roof tiles on all of them were patchy – and on one completely absent – she could see streams of rain water running through the holes, into the spaces below. There were glass panes in some of the windows still, mainly the mullion windows to the main building, the farm house itself.

There were trees growing up through the roofless vault of what had once been a decent size barn, so she decided she didn't need to check that. Then she caught herself. She had made stupid assumptions all day. She followed the edge of the tree line to the doorless entrance to the place, pulling the gun before she ran quickly to the wall.

Inside was little different from outside – a soaking pile of collapsed rubble, overgrown with vegetation. She looked through the doorway but didn't step in.

The adjoining building was some form of wide stone outhouse. It had a door, but it wasn't locked. She pushed it open and shone the torch into the blackness within.

There were two abandoned, rusting cars, both without wheels and still on blocks, one with the bonnet open and the engine out, lying on a patch of gleaming, oil-stained earth alongside it. There were no floors between the ground level and the roof and rain was pouring in and over everything. She shone the torch carefully around the darkened corners – a disused work bench, a series of gaping cupboards, shelving. She backed out.

It was a short run from the outhouse to the main building and even as she was crossing the distance, rain whipping into her eyes, she thought fleetingly, for the first time, that Harrison was maybe laughing at her now. The entire address might be a red herring. She stepped straight through the swinging back door, gun in one hand, torch in the other.

She was in a kitchen. There was a table – something cheap and dirty, covered in dust – a number of chairs, a sink with a tap that was gently dripping, spaces where the oven and fridges should have been. She stopped and reached for the light switch, on the wall beside the door. She could see a naked bulb in the fitting hanging from the ceiling and the place looked watertight, but the light switch didn't work. She found the fuse box with her torch and walked quietly over to it. As she did so, the smell came into her nostrils and she stopped, her heart sinking.

The odour had become bitterly familiar to her during the last twenty-four hours. But this time she knew whose body it would be. She didn't want to find it. She bent down by the fusebox and felt the pulsing at her scalp. She was bleeding again, contaminating what was without doubt a murder scene. Outside another peal of thunder made the place shake. From somewhere in the house she could hear the steady, heavy drip of water.

There was a meter by the box and it was clear from examining its silent mechanism that the electricity into the place wasn't switched on. She stood up and walked to the door to the next room. It would have been the living room, when the place was occupied. Now it was empty, the floor littered with a mound of old syringes and fast food cartons. Behind the smell of the body she could smell stale, spilt alcohol and urine. But the body wasn't in this room.

She walked through, listening. The place had the silence of somewhere that had long been empty, but she had noticed fag ends and ash tipped down the sink in the kitchen, crushed beer cans under the table. The fag ends had not looked so old as to be negligible. She needed to be careful, not make the same mistakes twice.

She had a flashback of herself falling, Gerry Walsh standing over her, the bar bouncing off her head, the first blow already delivered, the world lit up with white light. Everything too late.

She had let Walsh go. That had been the mistake. She had told Harrison only the surface of the tale. For Errol's death she felt nothing, but she had given Walsh a chance, made the mistake, trusted him without even thinking it through. She should have killed him. For not doing that she had paid dearly.

She waited for the image to fade – the afterglow like something burned into her eyelids – then she walked through to a hallway, her feet creaking the boards slightly at the entrance. She could tell from the smell that the body was in the room directly opposite. She stepped away from it, towards the stairs. She walked up them, gun extended in front of her, flashlight poking into the dark crevices. There were three bedrooms and a disused bathroom, water dripping through the ceiling into all of them. Two wire bedframes in two of the rooms, but no mattresses. When she tried the cold water in the bathroom she found the taps dry, despite the dripping tap in the kitchen. Already she knew there was no living thing in the place.

All the same, she walked back down the stairs, then checked all the rooms she had already checked again. Then she checked outside, just in case. Finally she stood by the remaining room listening to her heart, feeling the horror building within her, her mouth drying. She had wanted to find Sophie Kenyon, but not like this.

She stepped in and shone the torch around the floor, finding the body at once. It was right behind the door, almost flush with the wall. She took in the shape as the odour rose powerfully into her nostrils, sticking in the back of her mouth like a finger pushed down her throat. Then she felt her heart flutter slightly. It was a man – a fully grown male corpse. She let the breath out of her lungs and covered the rest of the room quickly with the light.

There was a bed in the corner, a kiddy's bed raised about two foot off the floor, once again without a mattress. Between the corpse and the bed she could see a long black tongue of dried blood. There were blood stains on the bed frame too. But no other body. She sucked at the fetid air, head swimming with pressure, but relieved, then turned back to the corpse, feeling vaguely guilty that she was relieved.

She was crouched beside it, counting the head injuries, noting the stage of decomposition, the position of the limbs, the small crude tattoo of a swastika above his left wrist (like something a convict might do with an improvised needle and ink), the sheer quantity of blood, when she heard Ricky Spencer shouting a police warning from over at the back door. She stood up.

'There's only me in here,' she shouted to him. 'Karen Sharpe. It's clear, Ricky.'

She stepped back to the door, hearing him curse and then mutter instructions to someone else. She pushed the gun back into her jacket.

He came through quickly. 'I told you to fucking wait.'

She nodded. There was nothing she could say to him.

'Have you searched the place?'

She nodded again. 'It's empty. He fucked me over.' She looked at her feet. 'There's a body in there,' she said. 'But it's not the girl and not my witness.'

He walked in and shone his own flashlight around, then stooped behind the door. Others were coming through. They walked past her, following him in. She heard him tell them to search the place and cordon it off. Then he called out: 'Gordon, Jim and Alex only. Search this place. Everyone else out. Now. This is a murder scene.' She heard people leaving behind her, murmuring to themselves. When she moved her head to look at them there was a millisecond delay whilst her senses caught up, like something was loose within her skull, jangling around.

She felt crushed, defeated. She wanted to sit down in a heap and sleep, pass out, forget about everything. She had played all her cards with Harrison and he had got past her, tricked her, kept the vital information to himself. He had signed the girl's death warrant. She looked up to find Spencer staring at her, face quivering with anger.

'That includes you,' he said, spitting the words at her. 'Get out, Karen. Get out and get to hospital.' He glanced at the wound to her head. 'You look like shit. Maybe that thing will save you ...' He pointed at the wound. 'Maybe you can say you weren't yourself. Be sure that something will have to save you. You've fucked up big time.'

She frowned, feeling suddenly and unfamiliarly like she wanted to start crying. She was unsteady, her stomach constantly turning over. She didn't want him to shout at her. She turned away from him and began to walk towards the door.

'I'm telling Bains to let Harrison go,' he called after her. 'To minimize this fuck-up you've caused.'

'He admitted offences to me ...' She began half-heartedly.

'He admitted what? Tell me one clear thing he admitted. I've spoken to Bains. I hear nothing strong enough to act on. Worse than that you broke his nose and his arm. Which jury do you think is going to listen to that and convict?'

FIFTY-EIGHT

She stood outside in the rain, the water running freely over her head and down her shoulders. When she felt too weak to stand she leaned against the house wall, watching them getting on with it, cordoning the place, searching the buildings and rooms she had already been through.

Spencer came out, but he didn't see her. He was talking with two detective sergeants about leaving the place with an SIO, about getting on with what they had. She heard him mention Pamela's address in Otley and thought about walking over and telling him that she had already been there, that it was a waste of time. But he started saying something about her. She couldn't hear it clearly, just her name. She saw one of the others point her out to him, warning him. Spencer shut up long enough to shout back at her, 'I thought I told you to fuck off, Karen. Your car is blocking access. Leave your details for the team and go. I don't want you around my enquiry.'

She pushed herself off the wall and walked slowly past them, back up the lane to her car. She didn't say anything.

At the vehicle she sat in the driver's seat and for a moment couldn't remember what she needed to do to drive. She got the key in eventually, then tried to reverse back down the lane. An unmarked car was backed up behind her, doing the same thing, the headlights too painful in her eyes. Behind that there was a van full of uniforms. She ran the car into the ditch six times.

On the main road she pulled in and switched the engine off, forcing herself to find the pieces that had bothered her. Everything had fitted together to point the way – firstly to Reed, then Kenyon, then Harrison, with Pardoe along the way. She had found everything, she had got the information, she had worked out why Sophie Kenyon had been kidnapped, why Pamela Mathews had gone the same way. What pieces didn't fit?

Something about the addresses. She looked back down the lane. *Dean Head Farm.* She rolled the words around her woozy brain like a ball bearing. She knew the address as soon as Harrison gave her it, because she had seen it on HOLMES, had seen that he had blocked a search. But was that all? She switched the windscreen wipers off. The rain was slowing now, the thunder gone.

She watched Spencer drive his car out of the lane onto the main road. He turned without noticing her and sped off. She wondered what he would make of the blood-staining at Pamela Mathews's address. She looked in the rear-view mirror at the blue flashing lights of a uniform car pulling up behind her.

She stopped trying to remember and after a few moments it came back to her. She had seen Dean Head Farm in the paperwork from Flight, in the list of properties that Pardoe's widow had sold off. But why was that significant? Because she had noticed something about the addresses *then*, as she was looking.

There had been another address.

She felt a mental pause, as if her brain was taking a deep breath. Then suddenly it was all with her, every detail, everything slotted into place as if it had all always been there, ready for her to read off like newsprint. Stark's name had been entered against Dean Head Farm in Pardoe's widow's papers. She had sold or given this property to Stark. But his name had been against another property as well – a flat on the Thorpe Edge Estate.

She frowned as she started up the engine. She could feel her head pounding as the adrenalin rushed through her. Pamela *had* told her. That was what she said to Bains, that she had *already* told Karen where he lived. The very first time Karen had asked her about Stark, Pamela had told her that he would be at Thorpe Edge.

She pulled out into the road and started up the hill, the car swerving slightly as she tried to control her reflexes. There had been two addresses blocked that had been referred to Harrison. Dean Head Farm and five, Helmsley House, on the Thorpe Edge. He had let them search the latter, but not Dean Head Farm. Helmsley House was the address she had seen in Emily Pardoe's papers. She was sure of it. Harrison had unblocked it and called Stark to warn him. That had to be it. The team had searched the place and found nothing because Harrison had got to them first, because they had moved the girl before the search team got in. Probably they had moved her to Dean Head Farm and then back out again.

What better place to conceal something? A premises already searched.

Harrison would call and warn Stark, just in case. If Bains released him he would call. And once Stark knew the balloon had gone up whatever reason he might have had to keep Sophie Kenyon alive would be gone.

The thought came to her like a shot of pure adrenalin. She floored the accelerator and felt her head reeling as the car veered across the carriageway.

FIFTY-NINE

She called Bains as she was climbing the north side of Eccleshill at over twice the speed limit. If she saw a car in her path she hit the horn, flashed her lights, then pulled straight into the opposite carriageway to get round it. She had no time to be careful, no time to ask, no time to wait. In front of her she saw cars braking and pulling over. They could see her coming from a long way up the hill. She was swerving all over the road. At the speed she was going she was less than two minutes from the estate.

Thorpe Edge. A condemned sixties project. Low, five-floor blocks built across a steep hillside that took the worst of the winter winds and frost. The place had been a collapsing crime haven ever since she had been in West Yorkshire. Earlier that year Central Government had finally donated money to demolish and rebuild it. The bulldozers had moved in a few months ago. If Stark owned a property on the estate the council would be buying it off him.

'I've been trying to call you,' Bains told her as he answered. 'He's gone. I was ordered to release him.'

'How long ago?'

'Fifteen, twenty minutes. I don't think he was going to a hospital. He made me drop him off at the services on—'

'Listen. I need to tell you something. I haven't got long.' She held the phone with her right hand and steered with the left. She felt sick. Worse, her head was doing something strange now. It had started somewhere between the airport and Greengates. At first she hadn't realized it was happening. The effect was rapid, like watching a film in which there were tiny, millisecond cuts in the footage, not frequent or long enough to make things jerky, but enough to make it seem that something was wrong, enough to alert her.

'I'm at number five, Helmsley House, on the Thorpe Edge,' she said. She took the main access road too fast and had to grind the brakes, skidding. She waited until the car had straightened out then spoke again. 'Helmsley House. It was another blocked address on the enquiry. They searched it, but I think Harrison warned Stark. I think they moved her from here to Dean Head Farm earlier in the week. This place was empty when we searched. I think they probably moved her back again afterwards.'

'Did you tell Spencer? You should be in a hospital.'

She slowed down as the housing blocks came into view. 'Spencer didn't want to know. You don't need to come, you don't need to tell anyone. You just need to know I'm here. Just in case . . .'

The cuts were getting longer. It was like falling asleep at the wheel, but with no warning at all – just a moment of blackness, the shutter closed, then the world resumed, a fraction of a second lost to her. A fraction of a second during which she had no awareness at all.

Bains had said something to her, something in reply – but she had lost it. She cut him off and pulled the car over. She was hot, sweating profusely, her heart already racing.

She put the gun in her jacket and stepped out of the car. The rain had stopped completely. She sniffed the ozone rising from the wet leaves of the few trees bordering the access road, the overgrown weed-choked lawns surrounding the blocks. She noticed that she had parked the car at a crazy angle, one of the wheels on the verge, half on, half off. She thought about what her brain and body were telling her.

Intermittently, her consciousness was closing down. But her body didn't sag or collapse when it happened. When the lights came back on she was where she had been, a split second later, still doing what she had been doing moments before. Except she hadn't been there to be doing it. She was suffering blackouts – instant and total – and they were getting worse.

She looked at the fast-moving trails of cloud rising above her in the night sky. Then over towards the nearest block on the estate. Her vision narrowed. She saw dismal concrete blocks, ringed by slanting terraces on the hill above, a rubbish-strewn wasteland, dotted with burned-out cars and garbage skips. Everything was orange, bathed in the flicker of phosphorous, surfaces soaked and gleaming from the rainfall. Orange-washed concrete interspaced with pits of darkness.

She knew which one was Helmsley House, she had been here

before. Beside it now she could see there were cranes and a demoliton site. They had already taken one of the blocks down. There were a few lights on in some of the other blocks, but not in Helmsley. The place was condemned, next on the list. She didn't know whether it had electricty still. She could see a handful of cars strewn around the site, a white van, lights on, engine running, no one behind the wheel. Was there something about a white van she needed to remember?

Her body was telling her to stop, to get to a hospital. Before long she was going to pass out completely.

She started to walk, realizing only after she had gone ten paces that she had left the car door wide open. She kept going. She was going to do this now. Her head would have to wait.

She looked at her watch as she was passing the van. It was parked right outside the block, the driver's door open, but no one there. It was nearly two in the morning. What had happened to the night? The memories were slipping away from her.

She took the stairwell two at a time, banging clumsily off the walls as she rounded the corners. A litter of discarded syringes and used condoms got beneath her feet, making her slip. She turned the corner leading to the landing for number five, stepped out onto it and took the gun from her jacket pocket. Then something happened.

She saw her feet find the landing, saw her head turning to stare along the corridor, saw the door to number five, registered that it was open, glimpsed the darkness within, the shape of a man moving through it – then she was there. She was standing in the doorway.

In her mind, the movement was seamless, instant. She stepped onto the landing, saw the man coming through the door, then she was standing in the doorway with the gun raised in front of her. The man was gone. She was in the hallway, standing on a damp, discarded mattress, pushing the door away from her with the hand that held the gun. She was flooded with light, a naked bulb swinging from a fixture above her. From within she could hear raised voices, screaming, movement. The wound in her head was throbbing with pain, her face felt shiny, wet. Her right arm was aching as if she had been striking something. Her eyes were squinting against the brightness. In her chest she could feel her heart pounding. Something had happened.

She stopped, reality spinning around her. She was disorientated, confused. She glanced back over her shoulder and found the man who had been in the doorway. He was crawling away behind her, trying to push himself to his knees, whimpering with fright. She placed her hand against the half-open door to stop herself from falling. The man's face was covered with blood. He was skinny, young. She looked down at the gun. It had not been fired, but the bones in her hand were ringing. The man got to his knees, tears coming from his eyes. She turned the gun towards him and watched as he staggered away from her.

She had come the distance from the head of the stairwell to the door. The man had been standing here in front of her, coming out of the flat. Things had happened – but she had lost it all.

Ahead of her, from within the place, someone was shouting at someone else – male voices. Then a woman's scream, short, cut-off. She turned back and stepped towards it, the gun extended in front of her, her arm wavering. She was in a narrow hallway leading to an open doorway. The walls around her were cracked, fissures running up and across them, bulging plaster peeling off in huge chunks, huge patches of spreading rot. The stuff felt crumbly to the touch. The bulb in the ceiling was swinging like someone had used it as a punch bag.

In her head she saw images of herself being dragged across a patch of waste ground by Gerry Walsh and two others, her mouth hanging loose, incapable of speech, the jaw broken.

She looked down at the mattress she was standing on. The man she had seen in the doorway had been carrying it. She fitted it together. Harrison had called, they were moving out. She had caught them trying to flee. Her hand was on the frame of the door – a huge re-inforced thing, braced with iron bars and metal cross struts. If they had not been coming out at the moment she arrived she would never have got in. Harrison had done her a favour.

She stepped forwards, moving towards the open doorway of the next room. The door began to shut as she came up to it. She could hear herself shouting something, calling out, but it was all automatic. She had no idea what she was saying.

She kicked the door open before it could close, stepped into a larger room and pointed the gun at the first person she could see.

It was Stark. She recognized him at once. In a split second she took in the scene in front of her.

She was in what would have been the living room. The ceiling was hanging down in chunks of plasterboard, exposing the beams and joists. The floor was covered with rubbish. There was one grimy sofa against the furthest wall, rodent holes eaten through it, another naked bulb dangling from exposed wiring in the ceiling, a flickering portable TV on an upturned box near the sofa.

There were six people in the room, including herself. The place was small and filled with the stink of human sweat. Everyone was shouting at once.

Everyone except the little girl huddled up against the woman on the floor.

A part of her she had no control over listed the child's condition, methodically, without emotion. She couldn't tell if the girl was conscious. Her chest was moving, heaving. But her eyes were closed, or so bruised they looked closed. She could see that there was an injury to her lower body somewhere – the trousers she was wearing were covered in blood. Her fingers were clenched up, trembling. She was injured, but she was breathing. She was alive.

The woman holding her was Pamela Mathews. Her face looked twisted, distorted, as if someone had struck it so heavy a blow they had knocked it out of shape. There were tears streaming from her eyes, blood running out of her hairline, her mouth was open and moving, shouting things at Karen, her eyes on her, full of fear, imploring.

But Karen could hear nothing of what she was saying. The whole thing was like white noise, a single high-pitched blur of screams and rage.

A second man was standing with his back to Karen pulling at Pamela's hair trying to get her away from the child.

The man was taller than Stark and held an automatic in the hand furthest from Karen. He looked young, foreign – short, cropped blond hair, high cheekbones, well-defined muscle structure – like a weightlifter.

She kept the gun on Stark, then took in the third man. He was moving towards her, a weapon of some kind in his hand. She had him in her peripheral vision only. She needed to shift priorities. He was coming at her, he was armed. Stark was not.

Suddenly the words rushed at her ears. Stark was giving instructions, telling the man coming at her to take her gun, telling him to get her on the floor. The man was shouting back at him in a language Karen didn't understand.

'*She's a fucking pig. She won't use it,*' Stark shouted.

He was concentrating on the girl and Pamela. He wasn't even worried about her. '*This is not Germany. Do as I tell you. The police don't shoot here. Take it off her and get her on the fucking floor.*'

Suddenly Pamela's voice rose up behind Stark's, a higher-pitched wail fractured with sobs of fear, '*They are going to kill us. He says they are going to kill us.*'

Stark seemed to erupt with movement. Three quick paces towards Pamela. He was screaming at her, features creased with hatred. '*SHUT. THE. FUCK. UP. BITCH.*'

He punctuated every word with a stamping movement. The first two blows hit the side of Pamela's chest, the second her neck. The third missed her and struck the child's legs.

Karen took a breath and felt her consciousness stutter again, another flashback. She could see Gerry Walsh and the others pushing her into the boot of a car. She was watching it happening to her as the man to her left was closing on her. Everything was speeded up, thoughts flashing through her head too fast to track. Walsh and his friends had kept her for three days, working on her. She could remember no pain at all now, none of the detail.

The third man was almost on her. He had his gun pointed at a lazy angle, towards her feet. He was no more than a yard away from her, reaching out to take her gun.

She brought the gun up to the height of his waist and pulled the trigger.

She saw Stark and the blond man jump, shocked by the noise. The room was small. The shot expanded quickly, a deafening percussive explosion in the enclosed space.

Then there was silence, all the noise and shouting over.

The man closing in on her staggered sideways, towards the blond weightlifter and Stark. His mouth was wide open, gulping at the air like a fish, the gun hanging loosely from his fingers. He went down onto one knee, then fell over backwards, arms pawing at the air, legs bent, hit somewhere in the chest. The expression on his face said he was screaming, but no sound was coming out of him, not even the sound of his breath. One of his legs began to jerk around, a reflex movement. The blood began to run out of him, gathering in a puddle on the dirty floor.

Karen followed him down, moving with him as he fell, not giving them time to react. She went onto one knee beside him and brought the pistol up again. She held his shirt with one hand, pulling the upper body slightly towards her. With the other she placed the gun against his temple. His eyes were open, but there was no understanding there. She could see the shock setting in already.

She paused, holding the position, looking up at Stark and the blond. They were frozen with disbelief, staring at her. She paused just long enough for them to know that what she was doing was deliberate. Then she pulled the trigger again.

The noise seemed louder, shattering the silence, reverberating off the walls and ceiling. The top of the man's head broke up, erupting across the room and spattering the blond and Pamela. The wall and ceiling behind them were streaked with a long, ragged line. The smell was suddenly intense. She saw the blond gagging and brought the gun up to point it at him.

She began to speak. Her voice was calm, assured, but she could only hear it like something coming from a long way away from her. She was looking at the blond, but speaking to Stark.

'Simon Stark. I'm arresting you for the kidnap of Sophie Kenyon . . .'

He began edging backwards towards the door leading into the next room. The blond man's gun was still pointing at Pamela, but the look on his blood-flecked face was one of stunned confusion.

Karen stood up. Stark was in the doorway now. He was going to run.

'You!' She pointed her free hand at the blond.

'I don't know you. But I will not hurt you if you put the gun down and walk away. Now.'

She moved the gun up and covered his face with the sight, using both hands to hold and steady it. Pamela was nowhere near his head. She had a clear shot. But his gun was still wavering. She couldn't risk it.

'I have a clear shot at you,' she said. 'If I wanted to I could take you now.'

He blinked, trying to understand the words.

'Move away. Walk out of here. Do you understand?'

Out of the corner of her eye she saw Stark turn and run.

'Walk,' she shouted. 'Walk now!'

The man stepped backwards, limbs shaking, moving the gun up

and away from Pamela's hair, letting go of her. He stepped over her body. The look in his eyes said he was unsure.

'Drop the gun,' she said, enunciating each word carefully.

It clattered to the ground.

'Now leave.'

She kept the sights over his face. He was moving slowly, carefully, creeping towards the entrance, keeping his eyes on her. She thought about Gerry Walsh, thought about how she had made this mistake before. She could see herself hanging by hooks in the basement of a bar in South Manchester.

She waited until he had his back to her and was turning to walk out, until the gun sight was directly over the back of his head. Then she pulled the trigger. She closed her eyes against the blast, heard it echo and expand. Then the sound of the body hitting the floor.

Pamela's eyes were open, staring at her. There was an expression of disbelief, of horror, despite her injuries. Karen moved her gently away from the child and felt at the child's neck for a pulse. The child's skin was hot, feverish, but her heart was still going strong. Karen felt her consciousness flicker again and leaned over on all fours to stop herself collapsing. When she was steady she reached out a hand and stroked the child's cheek. It was Sophie Kenyon. She recognized her from the incident room pictures. Her breathing was heavy, uneven.

She pulled out her mobile and gave it to Pamela. 'Call for help,' she said. 'I have to leave you. But you're safe now.' She looked at the doorway Stark had run through. 'I won't be long.'

SIXTY

In the first room she saw the ladder at once. It was leaning against a hole in the roof, into the flat above – an escape route. She ran to it, placed her foot unsteadily on the first rung, then stopped. She listened into the darkness above for a few seconds. She could hear nothing. She turned and looked back at the room she was in. It was empty, no light, no furniture, but along the back wall there was a row of plastic petrol containers, all full. They had been intending to torch the place.

There were two doors – one leading back from where she had come from, the other closed. She stepped away from the ladder. If Stark had gone up the ladder he would have pulled it up after him. She moved quickly to the door, pulling it open without hesitating, stepping through.

The world exploded with fire and noise. She felt herself spinning backwards, struck somewhere, her legs kicked away beneath her. She fell against the door, her gun going off. One shot, two, three – she fired without aiming, in a panic, without being able to see. The flashes in her face were blinding, scorching her eyes with pain, but they were not coming from her own weapon. Someone was firing at her with something bigger, from close range.

As the shots stopped the blackness rose to meet her. She was on the floor – she knew that – but she could still feel herself falling, the world circling around her, receding, slipping away . . .

She was entering another world. One that had been waiting for her all along. A place of calmness. This is what it would have been like if the tablets had worked when she was a teenager. Everything slowed down, peaceful, out of her control. Things were still happening to her, but she had a sense of safety. Nothing could affect her any more.

It was like she was floating above it all, untouchable. Turning gently through space and watching herself. Everything that was happening was happening elsewhere. It had nothing to do with her. She could hear her heart beating, pumping furiously, could feel the blood surging through her veins.

She remembered Mairead walking into the attic room in the cottage. Karen had been alone, sitting at a desk sorting out the paperwork she stored up there. A scorching July day. The sunlight was bright outside and she had drawn curtains across it. She had been trying to concentrate.

Mairead had been wearing a long dress, made from a light cotton material. Bright red. She had smiled, walking over to the window with a confidence and grace that already took Karen's breath away. She could remember thinking, *That is my daughter . . .*

Mairead had stood there, looking at the drawn curtains, frowning. Then she had pulled them back. The sunlight flooded in, filtered through the folds of her dress, blazing across the dirty walls, washing the entire room with the colour of her clothing. As she moved the crimson pattern had shifted across the peeling wallpaper, moving with her. Her arms were outstretched, the light refracted through her like she was an angel . . .

Stark had fired perhaps five times. She couldn't be sure how many hits she had taken. One to the thigh. She could feel it pulsing. There was no pain.

She lay on the floor and waited.

He was about fifteen feet away from her. She could hear him. The sound was faint, like something at the end of a long pipe. A low moaning. Pulling herself along the floor, she inched her way towards it.

Her fingers found the blood first. A hot stream of it flowing away from the noise. Then a leg. As she gripped the leg there was no reaction. Stark was on the floor. He wasn't standing. She pulled her way up the wall, standing as best she could. The room was pitch-black. Either she was blinded or she had hit the door as she fell, closing it.

It was difficult to balance, with one leg hanging like lead. She had to lean against the wall. When she had a stable position she began to stamp him with her good leg, leaning against the wall, feeling the body with her shoe first, trying to locate the head, the gut, then stamping down. The anger she felt rose quickly above the growing pain. She could feel it venting through her as she kicked and shouted.

With the first few blows there was a reaction from the body. She tried to continue but the pain was too much to bear. She bent down, resting the leg. She began to hit out with the butt of the pistol. She tried to find the head. The world was spinning now. An inky blackness. She felt nauseous. It was difficult to coordinate her movements. Soon she was going to collapse, pass out completely.

The noise was still coming out of Stark's mouth. It wasn't a very loud noise but she had to stop it. She threw the gun away and started to punch where she thought the face would be. At first she could feel that his hands were moving, trying to protect his face. But after a while they fell away. She tried to head butt him once and heard bones cracking. But the effort knocked her to the floor. When she could think again she pulled herself up and staggered back against the wall.

She began to grope her way around the walls of the room, searching for the light switch or the door. She found the light switch first.

The single bulb in the centre of the ceiling lit a room bathed in blood. She saw now why Stark had been lying there, why it had been so easy. As she had gone down she had been firing. At least one of her shots had got him in the chest. There had been no need to kick him at all.

She hobbled over to where he was lying. Her head was spinning out of control, threatening to topple her at any moment. Blood loss. She had two flesh wounds, one to her head, the other in the muscle at the top of her thigh. The thigh wound would kill her if it had severed the femoral artery. Judging by the blood gushing down beneath her jeans, it might have.

She looked at the room. The only piece of furniture was a bare iron bed frame. Everywhere she had moved across the floor she could chart her progress in a three inch wide trail of blood. She needed help, quickly.

She bent over Stark. He was still alive, his eyes open, but rapidly closing up. His expression was dull, devoid of understanding. He was deep in shock.

She eased herself down the wall beside him and took hold of his wrist, moving the hand away from where it had been clutching at his chest.

She held it tightly, feeling the pulse there, watching his face. *Die*, she whispered. *Die*. She looked for a sign of recognition, of consciousness. There was none. The chest heaved, the body sank back into itself, the eyes became sightless.

She placed her hand over his heart. She could feel it racing, thumping away inside the chest, still fighting. She counted the beats, felt it pause, flutter, resume, then stop. She held her hand over the nose and mouth, blocking the airways until there was no breath left.

SIXTY-ONE

Bains had been telling her where he was when she cut the line. She could have only been a few minutes ahead of him. He was driving along Valley Parade, the roads deserted. He turned at once towards Eccleshill and accelerated.

He saw her car as soon as he came into the estate, stalled on a grass verge, door open. A white van was pulling around it, leaving the estate. At the wheel a thin, white youth, blood on his features. Bains felt his heart freezing. Something had already happened. He was too late. He drove past the van at full speed and screeched to a stop outside Helmsley House.

He was getting out of the car when he heard the shots – a whole volley of them, one after the other, from somewhere inside the block. The sound was muted, dull whip-like cracks in the night, muffled by the masonry. He heard a woman scream and began to run for the building.

He took the piss-smelling stairs three at a time, running. As he turned onto the balcony for number five he heard another shot. He sprinted to the door.

It was swung up against the hinges, but open. He could see light through the crack. He paused. He had no weapon. Nothing. He had nothing that could help him. If he entered now and they were shooting he was dead. He took a breath, then stepped forward.

Suddenly the door opened. A woman staggered out, stumbling towards him, something held in her arms. He moved to catch hold of her, then realized who it was. Mathews, with a child in her arms. He grabbed hold of her, stopping her from falling, glancing at the same time into the open hallway behind her. There was no movement or noise. He looked down at the child she was holding. It was Sophie

Kenyon. He could see her chest moving. She was breathing. He felt for her pulse. It was there, but it was weak.

Mathews's eyes were black, her lips split, the breath hissing between them. She was holding her right arm as if it was broken. Her face looked twisted out of shape. She was trying to give him something – a mobile phone. He looked away from her again, into the flat, worried about what might still be in there.

'Where's DC Sharpe?' he asked her. 'Where's Karen?'

But there was nothing but shocked fear in her eyes.

'I'll get you help,' he said. 'Stay here. Hold the child. I have to get Karen out of there. Is there anyone armed in there? Do you know who is in there?'

Her eyes looked back at him, no sign that she had heard anything he had said. He couldn't wait. He stood up and stepped into the place.

It stank like an abattoir. He had to take out his handkerchief and cover his nose to stop himself retching. He knew what the smell was – fresh blood. Old blood he could take. He was used to it, the sweet rotting smell. But the stuff getting up his nose now was still warm, still running.

In the first room he saw Sharpe straight away. He saw her because she was the only thing alive in there, the only thing moving. She was lying on her back, hands clutching at her leg. The blood coming out of her was pumping across the floorboards in rhythm with her breathing. He could see a trail of it leading away from her, towards a room she had crawled out of. She was taking huge gasps of air, her whole chest rising and falling as she tried to get more of it into her lungs. She was going into shock. Around her there were two other bodies, blood all over.

Bains stepped quickly over the first body – a tall male, no face – and knelt down beside Sharpe. She was looking at him, her face still bloodied from the head wound, but he couldn't be sure whether she was seeing anything. He stroked her head and spoke quietly to her while he checked quickly for wounds.

There was a thigh wound, a gun shot. It was bleeding badly. He stood up quickly, and moved into the next room. He saw rows of petrol containers along the wall, a ladder leading through a hole in the floor to the flat above. He stepped through the open door to the next room.

There was blood all over, a body in the corner. He didn't know who it was but he was dead, shot in the chest. He ran quickly back to Sharpe.

He tore his T-shirt off and wound it into a twine. He fixed it around the top of her thigh, above the wound, then tied it off, so tight he thought she would react. She didn't. She was feeling nothing.

'Stay with me, Karen,' he said. 'Stay with me. I can get you out of this. You can live.'

He took her under the arms and dragged her out of the flat.

Pamela was huddled against the corridor wall, still cradling the child. He took the mobile off her and called 999.

'I have three bodies,' he said. 'I need a lot of medics. I have Sophie Kenyon.' The operator asked him to repeat it. 'Sophie Kenyon,' he said. 'Please make it quick. Everyone is injured. People may die.'

He looked down at Karen. Her eyes were closed now, her breathing irregular. She was slipping fast. He looked back into the flat.

'There's a fire as well,' he said. 'You'll need the Fire Brigade.'

He got Pamela to walk down the stairwell. He went with her, carrying the child. Sophie felt slight, fragile. There was blood running away from her legs somewhere. Her skin was red hot, bone dry. He began to cry as he placed her in Pamela's arms, a little away from the block on a stretch of overgrown grass. Then he went back and heaved Sharpe down as well.

When they were all away from the place he went back up. Still he couldn't hear sirens.

It didn't take long to piece it together. There were two bodies in the first room, a third in a room further in. The place was a charnel house and only Sharpe could have done it. There were automatic weapons near to all the bodies.

He stepped through to the containers of petrol. They had planned for raids, planned escape routes, thought about it. Burn the evidence. That had been their last-ditch option. Sharpe would need that help now. He opened a container and sloshed the fluid around the walls. Then he stood back, took out a match book, struck one and tossed it. The walls leapt to life.

Outside Sharpe had come back to consciousness, but she wasn't responding to anything he said. He could finally hear a siren. From the corner of his eye he saw an ambulance turning into the estate just as a tongue of flame leapt out from between the metal plating they had fitted over the windows to the flat. Smoke started to pour from the open doorway.

As he stood up to meet the paramedics the tears were still running down his face.

SIXTY-TWO

She awoke into a hazy, drugged dream filled with drips and monitors, journeys on trolleys, harsh theatre lights, the faces of men she didn't know. Many faces all at once sometimes, sometimes just one. Never faces she recognized or knew.

They appeared briefly in the blurred circle of her vision, giving quick professional glances followed by reams of technical instructions she didn't understand, spoken to people she never saw. She watched as if from the bottom of a goldfish bowl. They moved her, inspected her, manipulated her, stuck needles into her arms and hands. The world floated away and returned.

The bullet had entered her leg almost five inches above the knee, about two inches from the midline, to the left. They explained it to her many times, explained how fortunate she was. She tried to stay conscious while they spoke to her, tried to take it in. They even showed her the X-rays. The trajectory was straight through, one side to the other and out again, just missing the bone and three major blood vessels. It looked bad, but it hadn't endangered her life.

The head injury had almost killed her. She had a clot on her brain and was deep in shock when she was admitted. They told her that if Pete Bains had not arrived when he had she would have been dead within the time it took them to get her to a hospital and operate. They told her blood loss and shock would have killed her within fifteen minutes of arrival, without treatement.

On the third day after surgery she started crying and couldn't stop. They gave her drugs for it, but they didn't work. A tall, lean African doctor with a public school accent told her it was normal after brain surgery. But she thought differently. She lay in the hospital bed with Bains beside her and tried to control it. Bains's face was etched with concern and frustration. He took hold of her hand and began to stroke it, saying nothing.

'I keep coming back to Dean Head Farm,' she told him, the words very unclear. She felt stupid, engulfed by emotions she could neither understand nor prevent. 'That's what I'm crying about,' she said. 'Of all the things I could be upset about, I'm upset because I forgot her. I completely forgot her.' He nodded, as if he understood – but how could he? 'You don't know what I'm talking about, do you?' she asked.

He looked up at her, face serious. 'You're talking about Mairead,' he said. 'I understand.'

She tried to speak to him, but the sobs got the better of her. She began to get angry with herself. 'I was meant to go to Nottingham,' she blubbered. 'They were waiting for me. If I had done that none of this would have happened. Instead I forgot she even existed. What is *wrong* with me?'

She was sobbing so hard she couldn't breathe properly.

'If you had gone to Nottingham, Sophie Kenyon would be dead,' he said. 'You saved the girl's life.'

Saved for what? she thought. Sophie Kenyon was still in a specialist hospital in London. She had been raped and injured, almost starved to death. She would be dealing with her problems for the rest of her life.

'Let me tell you about my daughter,' Bains said, speaking quietly.

She looked over at him. His daughter had died in an accident. His wife had committed suicide. She remembered that much.

'She was three years old and almost three and a half feet tall when she died,' he said. 'She was called Millie. Her hair was quite long and jet black...' He smiled slightly, eyes looking at her but far away.

'I think she was clever – cleverer than most kids. On the day she died I was looking after her. We were in our house...' He stopped suddenly, faltering.

She brushed the tears out of her eyes and turned her hand around in his, reversing the grip so that she was clutching his fingers. She squeezed them, tears still rolling out of her eyes.

'You've been there,' he said. 'You've been to my house. You've been where it happened. On that morning her mother was out shopping. I was looking after her. It was a warm enough day, but we were inside. I had the door closed – the door to the garden. She had never been able to open that door before, though she had tried. Usually we kept it locked.' He stopped again, forcing himself to take a breath. 'I sat down with her in the kitchen and we read a book I had bought her. *The Three Billy Goats Gruff*. She knew the story off by heart. There were pictures in it. One of them showed the river and the bridge beneath which the Troll lived. The artist had painted wild flowers by the banks of the river. They were quite good pictures, though very small. Three weeks before this day I had read the same story to Millie and I had showed her the wild flowers and told her the names of two of them. Foxgloves and Bulrushes.' He stopped and held his finger up in front of her. 'Once,' he said. 'I told her *once* only, three weeks before. Foxgloves and Bulrushes. On this day I pointed them out to her again and asked the names. She told me. Immediately, no hestitating. Foxgloves and Bulrushes.' He stopped and smiled. 'Like I said, she was clever.' He bit his lip. 'She drowned in our swimming pool,' he said. 'About ten minutes after she said, "Foxgloves and Bulrushes." She opened the door, walked down, fell in and drowned. I was on the phone. I didn't hear her shouting.'

Karen kept her eyes on him, her face quivering.

'You've stopped crying,' he said.

SEPTEMBER
1997

The clinic was set in what looked to Karen like the back garden of a stately home – landscaped over two hundred years before with lakes, summer houses, vast, spreading chestnuts and oaks. Sutherland had arranged it. At the time she had been so stuffed with drugs she hadn't even thought of resisting. For everything Sutherland gave her, she knew, he would eventually come to expect something in return. Aside from that, the only drawback was that the place was on the borders of the Peak District, a long way from home.

She could walk, unaided by anything other than a stout walking stick, as far as the perimeter wall and back, a distance of nearly four miles. She thought that was good enough to leave, but they wanted her to stay for another week.

The raw puckered mound of new skin at the back of her thigh still suppurated a weak green fluid on a daily basis. The centre was an angry red indentation, which looked gelatinous, big enough to rest the point of her finger in, if she could have borne it. For two weeks they had run a tube into it and drained off the pus. Before that they had kept the wound open for almost a week, to stop an infection building up. They had grafted skin from her back to fill the hole. The entry wound, at the front, was smaller, less gruesome.

Her head was a different matter. They had shaved her hair, opened her skull, drained the clot, put it all back together again. When she looked at herself in the mirror she saw an ugly, bony skull with a stiff mass of new hair just beginning to cover the thick metal staples they had used to join the bones. She was told she would recover fully from the head injury within two years. Meanwhile she could expect the intense headaches and dizziness she presently suffered nearly every day.

'At some point' she had also broken her nose. They had re-set it as best they could, but it wasn't straight. As they were keen to point out to her – it was harder to get things straight if the injury was a repeat, and it wasn't the first time her nose had been broken.

'At some point' was about as clear as most of it was for her. Her last memories of Saturday, 28 June were when she was leaving Dean Head Farm. The rest was gone.

It was 14 September – in the outside world a Sunday – a day she had been fearing for nearly three weeks.

After breakfast she walked down to the wood by the big lake, and wandered through the beech trees there, feeling the chill September weather on the bald patch at the back of her skull. She had agreed with Bains over three weeks ago that she would do this today, but she didn't want to. She checked her watch. Neil would be there within twenty minutes, with Mairead. She had to work herself up to it. It was only the first of many things she had agreed to change.

She sat down on an old stump and looked out across the flat, black surface of the water, remembering. Many things had happened in a short space of time. When violence arrived in her life it had always been like that.

It had been the end of July before she could begin to move around. By that time she was under arrest and being investigated, interviewed on an almost daily basis for an entire week. The physiotherapy started at the same time. They needed to get her on her own two feet again – in time to stand trial. There was a man called Farquar in charge of the enquiry. That was his joke about it.

But there wasn't going to be a trial. Farquar had finished now. He was waiting for the CPS to 'knock it', as he put it. There had been a fire at Helmsley House. No one knew who had set it, but it was assumed to have been started before Karen even entered the place. It had gutted number five and the flat above. Most of the fine detail forensics they might have got to reconstruct the mayhem inside went up in the flames. The only witness who might have been able to remember anything was Pamela Mathews, and she was refusing even to speak to them.

But worse than that, Mark Harrison – their own assistant chief constable – had vanished. To prosecute her for murder would mean having the truth told about Harrison. They wouldn't want that. The official story was that he had resigned.

They wouldn't want any own goals either. The chief constable had visited her here, awarded her some kind of gong. In the outside world she was a hero. She had saved lives, killed evil men. The tabloids didn't need anything more complicated than that.

Neil had cared for Mairead since it happened. He would bring her today and she would tell her what she should have told her over a year ago. That would be the start. After that – when she was back at home – she would steel herself to do something about Neil. Throughout the time she had been getting better he hadn't put a foot wrong. In their entire relationship he hadn't put a foot wrong. But all she had for him was gratitude.

She stood up and began the walk back, practising in her head what she would say to Mairead. In the blackest moments after the shootings – pumped full of painkillers, senses dulled – she had hoped that the day would never come, without properly knowing why. The therapist here had told her it was a problem with her self-esteem. What wasn't? But in the most secret part of her heart she had hoped that James Martin would be released before the decision arose.

That had been another of Sutherland's little gifts to her. The murder charges had been dropped against Martin, but Sutherland had made sure he was shipped back to Northern Ireland to serve a two-year explosives sentence, passed down in his absence over three years before. Sutherland had meant well, perhaps. But she felt more ambivalent about it than she could ever admit.

She was halfway across the long lawn when she heard the child's voice, shouting to her from the back porch of the building.

'*Aunty Karen! Aunty Karen!*'

The words filled her with dread.

They were early. She watched Mairead running across the immaculately kept lawn at full speed, fearing with every step that she would fly headlong, break something. But she didn't. As she got nearer Karen braced herself, tucking the walking stick under her arm. She could see Neil behind her, coming down towards them at a slower pace.

She stooped as Mairead reached her and they hugged for a long time. Long enough for Neil to catch up. Mairead was chatting, full of stories about a visit to a swimming pool the day before. As Neil reached her Karen smiled at him, pecked him lightly on the cheek.

'How are you today?' he asked.

'I'm good,' she said.

She took Mairead's hand. She could feel her heart speeding up, feel the adrenalin starting. She looked down at her daughter, then crouched down to her level.

'I've got something I need to tell you,' she said.